# Hide and Seek

Mary Lu Warstler

In Memory of

Friends who gave me courage to write

# Word from the Author

As I have said before, no book is ever written in a vacuum. God has blessed me with many abilities, but I need the help and insight of those who see what I don't see and know what I can never comprehend. A mother's greatest joy, I believe, is when her children are adults and she can ask them questions and seek their help (Payback time maybe?) My husband and my children have been invaluable in my writing. I love my computer, but I don't understand all the inner workings of it. I rely on my younger son to keep mine in shape for all the wonderful ideas God sprinkles my way. My older son drives a Taxi and understands people in a way I don't. He reads my manuscripts and gives me new insights into the working of the human mind. My librarian daughter has a completely different understanding of books and how to market them. She also reads with the eye of one seeking new books for her patrons. And my nurse daughter is full of information of the medical variety and she is willing to share that knowledge with me when my characters get into medical difficulties. My husband, nor really a fiction reader, is willing to go through the manuscripts and point out things that don't make sense to the average reader. And so many friends and acquaintances have been willing to help – my friends Don Shilling, Roberta Zagray (recently deceased) and Pam Ritchey. I want to extend my heart-felt thanks to all who have helped with this project.

Just a word about the story. It is fiction through and through. The setting is in the 1990s. I realize that some things such as cell phones were just beginning to become popular, but I have taken some liberty in assuming that the FBI would have access to the latest gadgets available. The Dodge Omni may not have been the greatest car on the market, but it almost became the first car I had in my own name. I settled for a Plymouth Horizon. I felt that Kendra Donovan would want something different from what most of her friends had. She is not a showy person out to impress, but she is smart, talented and devoted to her family.

When our children were small, we vacationed each year near Mio, Michigan. Vacation and Michigan were synonymous. Some of the scenery I've described came from those vacations. However, there is no Palisades Lodge – never was. That is strictly in Kendra Donovan's life.

The characters are all imaginary and any resemblance to anyone living or deceased is purely coincidental.

# Prologue

The Donovan family – all except Kendra – was on the way to one of Calvin's mystery vacations. Kendra would have been with them, but stayed behind to finish a report for her boss.

"We might want to stop for a break and maybe an early lunch." Sarah, always watching the health and wellbeing of her family, checked the map. "There's a rest area in a few miles."

"Mom's right," David said as he stretched his legs across the dividing hump in the back seat. "I could use a short walk." They drove in silence for a few minutes then he added, "Am I being paranoid, or are is that black car following us?"

Calvin checked the outside mirror then the rearview mirror. "Let's find out. I'll slow the car to just under the speed limit and see if he slows also or passes us."

The black car in question passed them and Calvin grinned at his son by way of the rear view mirror. "Can't be too careful. Good observation."

Minutes later, however, a black van overtook them, pulled even with the Donovan car and stayed in the passing lane. At the same time, another black vehicle moved to within inches of the back bumper. The car that had passed earlier now waited, blocking the road. With his blinker, the driver signaled for Calvin Donovan to follow him. He had no choice. Like a caravan of tourists, the three cars and van weaved their way to a hidden, abandoned farm road.

Further down the weed covered path sat what was left of a farm house and barn. Fields overgrown with trees, weeds and broken fences gave the place an eerie feeling. Even the low-hanging clouds turned dark and threatening.

"Calvin?" Sarah wasn't easily frightened, but her heart beat faster as she glanced at her son and daughter in the back seat.

"It's all right," said Calvin. At least he hoped so. "Stay calm. We'll see what they want." He laid his gun on the seat beside him.

David pulled his phone from his pocket, but before he could press even the nine, all four doors flew open. Michelle screamed.

"I'll take all your phones," said the man dressed in black with dark glasses hiding his eyes. Everyone stay calm. You, sir," he said jabbing a gun in Calvin's shoulder, "come with me."

Calvin raised his eyebrows at the formality. He recognized the man as a fellow agent. What was Severs up to? He nodded for his family to obey while he went with the man just out of hearing range.

"Sorry, sir," said the man. "I don't understand, but Severs said we're to treat you like a witness protection client. We'll transfer all your belongings to the van. Your car will be driven south of here and destroyed. It will be assumed you all died in the crash."

"What? Has that man lost his mind?"

"That I don't know, sir, but he says it's the only way to save your lives as well as that of the undercover agent."

"Give me my phone. I've got to talk to him."

"Sorry sir. He gave specific orders. No calls."

"Where are you taking us?"

"I have a map. It's some hunter's cabin where the undercover agent can contact you when it's safe."

"And then what? How is Severs going to resurrect us?"

"I don't know sir. I only know…"

"Never mind. I'll find a way to contact him later. You're only doing your job."

Minutes later Sarah joined David and Michelle in the back seat of the black car behind them. Calvin sat in the front passenger seat looking grim and angry with the driver. The four other men emptied the Donovan car into the van. Another Agent, who had been in the rear car, removed Calvin's car keys from the ring, handed the rest back to him. He then got in their car, turned it around in the field beside the road and drove back to the highway.

"Calvin?" Sarah leaned forward and laid a hand on her

husband's shoulder. Placing a hand on hers, he answered through clinched teeth. "It's all right, Sarah, I'll explain when we stop."

David looked from one parent to the other. This wasn't an ordinary kidnapping. The man in the driver's seat didn't seem intent on harming them – didn't even hold a gun. But the man had said something that made his father angrier than David had ever seen him.

***

The driver of the first car watched the Donovans leave with their escort then returned to his vehicle with his partner. He pulled out his phone and punched in the familiar number. "It's done," he said. "Hank took their car. He'll drive it south into the mountains and destroy it. All four Donovans are on their way. No witnesses...What do you mean? There were only four – Agent Donovan, his wife, son and daughter... She has brown hair, hazel eyes, about eighteen. Nothing we can do about it now. We did what you told us to do. You'll have to deal with it from here."

He closed the phone and slammed it down on the seat beside him.

"Trouble?" His partner knew without asking.

"There should've been five."

# One

The Big Ben chime of the front doorbell echoed through the nearly empty Donovan house – Angel and Kendra being the only occupants. Her parents, brother and sister had left for a mystery vacation earlier that morning. Her father, Calvin Donovan was to send a clue to help her find them.

"Maybe this is the clue, Angel," she said, setting the calico cat on the computer chair. She ran down the stairs, jumped over the last step and reached for the door.

She saw a man in a police uniform and a chill of apprehension slithered down her spine in spite of the mid May warmth. Some soundless voice warned – *this is not a message from Dad.* She knew most of the men and women in the Akron Police Department. The man facing her was a stranger.

"Kendra Donovan?"

"Yes." Kendra held the door open door, keeping the screen fastened. Not only was the man a stranger, she could tell his uniform was fake.

"I'm Officer Lewis of the APD. I have some bad news for you. May I come in?"

Raised in the home of an FBI agent, Kendra's consciousness of crimes outreached that of other young women her age, and so did her knowledge of self-protection. She knew most of the police officers in her home city of Akron, Ohio. This man she'd never seen. His Brooklyn accent told her he wasn't even from Akron and his fake uniform sent up red flags of warning.

"We'll talk through the screen for now," she said. "You must be the new man Sergeant Walker mentioned when I saw him the other day." She knew there was no new man and Sergeant Walker was a figment of her imagination.

The man removed his hat, swiped his hand across his sweating, balding head then played with his hat like a kid driving a make-believe steamboat. He nodded in answer to her question, cleared his throat and sounded as if he had swallowed a large frog.

"Miss Donovan..." His voice faltered. He cleared his throat again and tried once more. "Seymour Severs sent me..."

Caught in a lie, he turned a bright shade of red and hesitated then stuttered on, "... eh, that is...Mr. Severs sent word to Sergeant Walker...who, eh...asked me to...to inform you that the car your father was driving when he left this morning went over a cliff south of here...There were no survivors. Mr. Severs will contact you as soon as he has more information."

For possibly the first time in her life, Kendra was speechless. Had she spoken she probably would have said a good many things she would later regret. She stared at the man. The reddish color now included the man's neck and ears. He rushed on as if the words would stick in his throat if he didn't spit them out.

"I know this is hard for you, but...well...there's more." He hesitated, waiting for Kendra to respond. She stared motionless, soundless. *Whatever practical joke he is playing, I will not help him with it.*

His Adam's apple bobbed up and down as he swallowed again. As if he could stand the silence no longer, he continued, "It...it appears to have been...murder/suicide. The FBI will conduct an investigation."

Kendra could stomach his lies no longer. She wouldn't let that last remark pass without comment. "Excuse me?" She kept her voice low and controlled.

The man looked surprised as if he didn't think she could, or would, speak. She ignored him and continued, "This is either a very poor attempt at a practical joke, or you have the wrong Donovan."

"I assure you, it's not a joke and I do have the right Donovan." He couldn't look her in the eye, but continued as if reading from a script, "Someone saw Calvin Donovan driving erratically and with excessive speed up the mountain – possibly under the influence of alcohol. There was no attempt to make the curve. The car went through the guardrail and over the cliffs. It exploded upon impact. When the flames died away enough for firefighters to get near the site, there was nothing left but ashes and a few small pieces of metal from the car."

Kendra felt as if someone had simultaneously punched her in the stomach and poured a bucket of ice water over her head. Before she could catch her breath and ask questions, the man turned and ran for his car. She put her hand on the door, thinking to run after him, but his tires screamed as he sped away before she could even open the door.

Kendra stared after him until his car turned the corner and fled from sight. Closing the door, she backed into the living room and fell onto the nearest chair. Surely, a time warp had shot out of the universe and squeezed the last twenty-hours into impossibilities. Nothing had really happened. If she were to close her eyes, when she opened them, her family would still be there getting ready to leave for vacation.

Two or three minutes passed before she slowly opened her eyes. Not for a second did she believe the man's story, but *something* was wrong. Kendra knew with an uncanny sixth sense that her family was in trouble.

Angel, her sister Michelle's cat, suddenly plopped onto her lap. She patted Kendra's face as if trying to console her. Or maybe she was simply saying, "I'm here."

The feel of the soft fur under her hand helped calm Kendra enough to think – to try to understand what had happened and when. *Surely, it is all a mistake and Dad will call soon with his clue as to their destination. I'm a logical person and I'm good at finding clues and solving mysteries. There has to be a reason – even this strange development. Did I miss something? Everything was fine until Robert called late yesterday afternoon.*

Kendra closed her eyes and replayed that conversation.

***

She had just finished packing and was closing the last suitcase when the phone rang. She let her sister answer it. Shelly, finishing her junior year in high school, was sure every call was one of her boyfriends. Robert knew Kendra was leaving the following morning and they had said their goodbyes earlier that afternoon.

"Kendra," Shelly called from the foot of the stairs. "It's *Rob*ert." She sounded as if reporting a skunk was in the basement. Needless to say, Shelly didn't like Robert. "Probably wants to see you tonight. Doesn't he know we're leaving early in the morning?"

Kendra didn't bother to answer her sister's sarcastic remarks. She was probably right anyway. Robert was unpredictable. Kendra picked up the phone beside her bed while she closed the last suitcase and snapped the locks.

"Hello, Robert."

"Kendra, I know you're busy, but I seemed to have forgotten that the McDougal report is due Monday morning. Could you…?"

"Robert!" Kendra had become a master of hiding her feelings outwardly when she wanted to do so. Inside, she felt like a bubbling pot ready to boil over. "There's no way I can do a report before we leave in the morning. Besides, Monday is a holiday."

"All right, then, Tuesday."

"How about Susan? She could…"

"Susan isn't as thorough as you. This is too important for her to do."

"Then why wasn't it important enough to remember it before now?" Kendra tapped her foot in an effort to keep back the rush of anger. Robert Holderman – boss/boyfriend – had been pressuring her to spend weekends with him at his cabin. When she refused, he began pulling nasty little tricks like making her work late and doing extra busy-work jobs. But, this was going too far – even for him.

"Robert, our family has been planning this vacation for months. It's the first time in six years we can all be together."

"Kendra, if you want a job when you return you will do this

report and have it on my desk Tuesday morning."

Kendra held the phone away from her ear, expecting to see frost coat the phone from the chill of his voice. She could almost feel the sting of it. Taking several deep breaths, she tried to think reasonably. *I could always find another job, but…I suppose if I get to work on it right away…I could e-mail it to him in the morning. I would have to stay behind and drive to wherever the family is going later in the afternoon. I would miss looking for clues and solving Dad's puzzle together on his "secret mission" trip.*

"Kendra? Are you still there?" The voice still sounded cold and far away.

"Yes."

"I will have that report by Tuesday?"

Kendra sighed heavily and answered reluctantly. "Yes."

"I'm glad you see it my way." Suddenly his frostiness turned to warm syrup – sweet and sticky. "I'm sorry about messing up your vacation."

"Yeah, sure you are." She didn't bother to hide her anger or sarcasm.

"We'll go to my cabin for the rest of the week. We can…"

Kendra didn't wait for the rest of his preplanned speech. She let the phone drop into its cradle none too gently, hoping it would give him at least a little pain.

***

As irritating as that call from Robert had been, there was nothing in it to explain the weird visit from a fake cop. *I would have been with the family when they disappeared if I hadn't stayed home to do his stupid report. Did Robert know something was going to happen? Probably not. He doesn't even know what's going on in his office half the time.*

As if sensing Kendra's agitation, Angel snuggled closer and purred under her chin. Kendra stroked her calico fur.

"Angel, what is going on? Surely, that man was trying to play some kind of practical joke. But I haven't heard from Dad. He was supposed to send me a clue so I can follow them."

Angel purred louder and stared at her human with her round green eyes. Did she understand that if what the man said was true, Shelly would never return to pet her again?

# Two

Time has a way of speeding up when a person is lost in a fog of confusion. Thoughts circle the parameters of logical thinking so many times that the beginning is lost in the ending. So, Kendra was surprised when she realized that the sun had already dropped over the horizon and deep purple shadows of twilight spread across the room. Darkness was fast approaching. She had lost several hours and had nothing tangible to show for it. She was still confused and befuddled. *The fake police officer certainly gave me the mother of lies, but the fact remains that my family is in trouble somewhere. Dad has not sent me a definite clue, which means he was unable to either get to a phone, or use his cell.*

Angel, lovable cat that she was, probably didn't understand why Kendra sat so long stroking her fur. She certainly wasn't going to complain. While the unconscious pattern of stroking was relaxing, Kendra still struggled with endless questions. Angel's soft purr hummed in her ears. Somewhere down the street, a car horn shattered the otherwise silent night. A cool breeze shifted the curtains, carrying the fresh scent of lilacs into the room. True to spring evenings, the temperature was dropping – possibly even a light frost tonight. Kendra shivered, but couldn't make herself move to close the window – not yet anyway.

"Angel," she said, lifting the small animal to look into her eyes, "that whole story is a lie." She gazed into shiny green eyes that stared back as if understanding what Kendra was saying. "If only you could give me some insight. Dad might send a cryptic message to let me know where he is, but that wasn't cryptic. That was weird."

Kendra set Angel back on her lap, but Angel stood with her

paws on Kendra's shoulder and licked her chin, before settling on Kendra's lap.

Kendra fell back to her monologue to Angel. "That sounded more like something Seymour Severs would think up. But why? I know he doesn't like me, but he is Dad's boss. Why would he pull such a stupid stunt – unless Dad is in some kind of trouble, or danger? Then, he might fake an accident to get him to safety, but murder and suicide? Why would he make such a blatant untruthful statement unless...Does he want someone to believe Dad is dead?"

The new idea whirled around and around until it integrated itself with all the other questions circling her mind. "When we were kids, David and I often went to Dad's office with him. Mr. Severs never liked us – and especially me. The feeling was mutual. He reminded me of the rat in the Cinderella story. Most of the people didn't mind us being there, but I suppose it was unusual, considering the nature of their work. David and I knew every nook and cranny in the building as well as people in every office. We knew who would tolerate us, who would chase us away and who would treat us like adults. I wonder why Severs even allowed it when he obviously didn't want us there. It was as if Severs was boss, but..."

Angel raised her head and gave a soft mew as if to let Kendra know she understood. Kendra stroked her fur a few times then said, "Angel, Severs called Dad last night. I wonder if that had anything to do with what has happened."

***

Visions of the previous night came to mind as clearly, as if it had been only minutes ago. The phone was ringing as she entered the kitchen.

Her mother answered and turned to her. "Tell your father's he's wanted on the phone. He's in the garage packing the van."

Kendra opened the garage door and told him. When he came in and reached for the phone, Sarah said, "It's your boss."

"If he thinks he's going to ruin my vacation, he just better think again." He sat at the table. "Donovan here."

He listened, a frown crossing his brow. "I'll call you on my cell," he said and hung up the phone. He pulled out his cell phone and started for the garage. "Sorry," he said to Sarah. "Must be an emergency."

"Oh Calvin, don't let him…never mind," Sarah sighed. She'd been through this before. "Do what you need to do. We'll adjust."

He turned back, kissed her cheek and went to sit in the car to make his call. When he came back in the house, he looked worried.

"Calvin?"

"Nothing to worry about," he said. "One of our agents is in a spot of trouble. He just needed my input."

Calvin Donovan glanced at his Kendra. Sapphire blue eyes met. He might fool her mother, but Kendra knew there was more to that call than Mr. Severs seeking her father's input. Calvin Donovan was a man of integrity. He would never speak of any of his co-agents. His family never even knew any of their names, except the ones she and David met at the office. Whatever Severs had to say, it was important enough to call her father at home, the night before he left for a well-deserved vacation.

Nothing more was said and plans were adjusted because of Kendra's decision to stay and do Robert's report. David wanted to stay and ride with her. From the time they were children, they never knew where they were going on trips. Their father would give clues and they worked them out on the way using the road map, markers along the way and riddles he would make up. Kendra thought David needed to be a part of that. It had been six years since he'd been able to vacation with the family. He just finished law school and planned to take his bar exams when he returned from this vacation. It would be a long time before they could all go together again.

By morning, Severs' call forgotten, the rest of the family left after an early breakfast. Kendra went to her computer to finish the report hoping she could be on the way by noon.

***

"There had to have been something in that call, Angel – more than Dad could tell us. But how can I find out? I could call Severs, but he won't tell me anything."

Darkness filled the room. The breeze from the window was becoming colder, so Kendra set Angel on the chair and got up to close the window. She pulled the chain of the Tiffany lamp and returned to the overstuffed chair upholstered in blue velveteen. Rainbows of light filled the corners of the room where shadows once were. Under the lamp, a gold frame held a family picture, taken when David was home for the Christmas holidays. Kendra reached for the picture, grasping the metal frame with both hands as if she could shake the captives free from their flat existence within the frame. Angel poked her head between Kendra's chest and the picture as if wanting to see too.

Smiles spread across each face forever caught in a happier time. One by one, Kendra ran a finger over the images protected by the smooth glass covering.

The two men – David and Calvin – towered over the women seated on the couch. Calvin Donovan's blue eyes seemed to twinkle even from the confines of that frame – as if he had a secret and was dying to share it. She moved her finger to touch the photo of David.

Headlights from an approaching car flashed through the window. Kendra laid the picture down, eased Angel off her lap and went to the door, heart pounding, nerves jangled. *Maybe they came back for some reason or maybe someone is bringing a clue from Dad.* She reached for the doorknob, but the headlights turned slowly and started back down the street. Only red taillights reflected in the darkness.

Disappointment replaced the spark of hope. *I should have known. Many people use this cul-de-sac as a turn around.* Returning to her chair, she picked up the picture and continued her pondering.

*David, my twin and best friend.* People were often surprised to learn that Kendra and David were twins. Kendra looked more like her father with black silky tresses, iridescent blue eyes that changed with moods, and almost Polynesian colored skin. David, on the other hand, looked more like their mother with brown wavy hair, hazel eyes and fair skin.

David always wanted to be a lawyer. While the Donovans were not rich, they were frugal and felt they had provided for their children's education. They had been upset with Kendra when she dropped out of the university and took a job to help with David's school expenses. David was the only one who really understood that Kendra wanted to be a part of David's crusade against crime. He accepted her help as she had accepted his help in holding her music for hours while she memorized a piece.

Kendra's fingers moved to the three women seated on the couch. Michelle and Kendra sat like bookends on either side of their mother. Michelle, whom they called Shelly, was ten years younger than the twins. Like David, her hair was brown and eyes hazel. Sarah Donovan, even in her maturity, could easily match her daughters in beauty. They were all about five feet, six inches and so near the same size that they often interchanged clothes.

"Angel, this is ridiculous. I can't sit here and mourn a lie. I need to be doing something to find them."

Angel looked at her, jumped down and started for the stairs. "I'm sorry, sweetie. I'm not very good company tonight and Shelly isn't home."

Angel continued up the stairs. Kendra assumed she was going to hunt for Shelly. *I have to find a way to hunt for all of them. But where do I begin. I don't even know where they were going. Dad was going to leave a clue, but he probably didn't have time.* A thought suddenly squeezed between the worries. *The computer. Maybe...*

Having a sudden thoughtful insight, Kendra replaced the picture on the table and followed Angel up the stairs. Angel sat outside Shelly's closed door. "She's not there, Angel. Come on in the computer room with me."

Sea life in a myriad of colors drifted back and forth across the computer screen. A sound of underwater bubbles like an aquarium filled the small room. Downstairs the mantel clock chimed its hourly ritual, announcing nine o'clock. Where had the day gone?

The report for Robert had been finished and e-mailed. Kendra's suitcases were still packed and ready to go as soon as she knew where to go. "There has to be something here, Angel," she said as the cat joined her.

A tiny ding sounded and a message box popped up on the screen reminding her to check her appointment schedule. *That's it. The bell reminded me of an appointment just before the doorbell rang. I didn't check it yet.*

For the first time in hours, Kendra felt like smiling. She clicked on the message that was short and to the point. "Kendra. Sorry to leave you behind. Look for you to join our *VACATION* soon. Will contact you later. Love, Dad."

Calvin Donovan had taught all of his children to use their minds – to think and figure things out. He made up games to help look for clues. "Seldom is anything what it seems on the surface. From the time they were very young, he repeatedly told them to look beyond the obvious," he said. When Robert threw a roadblock in their plans, he repeated his adage and said, "I'll leave a clue then send a message. You'll find us."

They had all laughed, knowing stubbornness and persistence were Kendra's trademarks. She and David always figured out the answer before they even arrived at their destination. That was then. This is now. Except for this message on her computer, she'd heard nothing except for the visit from that bogus cop with a totally ridiculous lie.

The word vacation was always synonymous with Palisades in Michigan. Her father didn't have much time to put together clues, but he said he would send another message. The current one told her enough to know where they intended to go but not enough to be sure that he didn't change his mind – especially in light of the reports from Severs. *I could call Palisades, but they might not be there yet – and if there is some kind of danger there, I don't want to complicate their safety.*

Angel butted her head against Kendra's chin. "It's obvious that *cop* wasn't with the APD," she said, stroking the purring cat. "Severs must have sent him, but why?" A chill sent a shiver across her shoulders. "Because I was supposed to be with them and somebody goofed. Now Severs is trying to cover his backside. But why would he insinuate that Dad was drunk? He knows my father never touches alcohol in any form. And to say Calvin Donovan would kill himself and his family is the most preposterous lie imaginable."

Anger and frustration mounted. Kendra was not one to wait for things to happen. "I have to *do* something, Angel. Fretting and stewing never solved anything. If Severs is behind this – and I'm sure he is – then he's the one to have some answers for me."

Kendra grabbed the phone and dialed his home. No answer. "All right, I'll try Alice. She knows everything that goes on in Severs' office."

Alice answered on the first ring as if she'd been waiting for a call.

"Alice, this is Kendra. I had a strange visit from…"

Before she could explain, Alice interrupted, disappointment clearly marking her tone. "Kendra if this is about what happened to Agent Donovan and your family, you'll have to talk to Mr. Severs. I'm sure he will contact you when he gets back. He's gone to the site and will conduct the investigation personally."

"But, Alice…" Kendra couldn't believe she was brushing her off. "There must be a mistake. Dad's on vacation. What is going on and why is there a need for an investigation?"

"There is no mistake, Kendra. It's true that your family is dead and because your father was an FBI agent and seems to have gone off the deep end killing not only himself, but innocent family members with him, there has to be an internal investigation."

"Alice, you knew my father…"

"Sorry, Kendra, I know nothing more than I've told you. Mr. Severs will contact you when he returns." Her curt tone exceeded even Alice's usual abruptness. Kendra was left holding a buzzing phone.

"Angel, this whole charade is getting stranger by the minute.

Alice knows *everything* that goes on at that office. She sounded so angry that either she *doesn't* know what's going on – which would irk her – or she knows and has been told to keep her mouth shut – which would irk her more. Well, I simply won't accept their verdict. One way or another, I will find out what's going on."

"Meow?"

"You think so too, sweetie?"

One by one, Kendra checked off a mental list of questions that popped into her mind like popcorn in a kettle. "How long would a car have to burn and at what temperature in order to disintegrate even the metal of a car? I'm sure it would take longer than the nine hours they were gone before that fake police officer rang my doorbell. If they went over a mountain, that would indicate he went south through West Virginia, but they packed clothes for cooler weather to the north and the computer message would indicate Michigan. Was there some reason Severs didn't want him to go to Michigan, or are they simply trying to send me off on a wild goose chase? What kind of proof does Severs have of their death? What makes him think murder/suicide? Does he really expect me to sit back and accept this without a fight? He should know me better than that."

Angel squirmed. "Sorry, sweetie," she said. "I didn't realize I was holding you so tightly. I don't believe they are all dead in the first place and certainly not murder/suicide. Either Dad will call soon and straighten this mess out, or I will begin my own search for him – and it won't be south of here."

But, he didn't call. Kendra paced and prayed most of the night, but morning brought only the sunshine of another day. She checked the phone. *It works, so why hasn't someone called?*

After trying all day every half-hour to reach Severs, Kendra sat in her favorite blue chair and reached for the phone once more. It rang as the mantel clock struck ten. Surprised, she drew her hand back. It rang a second time. She lifted it and quickly said, "Dad?"

It wasn't her father. Seymour Severs' harsh, gravelly voice

grated on her already frayed nerves.

"Kendra, I'm so sorry about your family, honey. Do you know where they were heading? I'll…I'll call and cancel the reservations for you."

"No, I didn't know. It was one of Dad's mystery trips that we had to guess along the way." She tried to hide her disappointment.

"Well, apparently they were heading south somewhere. The car went off a mountain in West Virginia. I checked the site myself. Everything was burned to a powder."

"Mr. Severs, we both know that is impossible." She didn't bother to hide either her anger or scorn for the man who was supposed to be so bright.

"I'm sorry, Kendra," he said again, ignoring her observation, but with a little less camaraderie. "It's been a long twenty-four hours. I need some rest before work tomorrow. We sent some of the ashes to our forensic lab. As soon as we can identify enough for you to bury, I'll give you a call. It will probably be the end of the week because of the Memorial Day holiday."

"Mr. Severs, what am I supposed to do in the meantime?"

"Kendra, there's nothing you *can* do to bring them back. I suggest you begin making funeral arrangements and get some counseling if you need it. Then, get on with your life. In the meantime…"

She hung up on him.

"Angel, I can't believe even Seymour Severs is that cold hearted. He sounds as if he doesn't believe it either. Maybe he has reason not to believe."

# Three

As far as Robert was concerned, Kendra was on vacation, so she spent the holiday as well as the days following researching either on the computer or in the library. Between her many trips to the library, Kendra called Severs' office several times a day for an appointment. According to Alice, he was always either busy or gone, but Kendra knew him too well to believe that. She would bide her time. When she was ready, he *would* see her and answer her questions. In the meantime, she would continue to arm herself with facts. *If I keep calling for an appointment, he'll think I'm following the rules – his rules.*

Almost a week had passed while she waited – searching for clues, gathering data and information, looking for answers to impossible questions, or proof of the death of her father, mother, sister, and brother. She'd learned far more than she ever wanted to know about cars exploding, burning and leaving behind crumpled remains of iron, steel and plastic. She researched accidents in the surrounding states on the Saturday her family left. While she had no positive proof of what happened, neither did she have proof of *any* accident as described and reported to her.

The doorbell sounded throughout the house. Leaving her computer on, Kendra ran down the stairs – hoping it would be word from her father. She knew instinctively, however, that it was more bad news. Seeing the Fed Ex delivery truck in the driveway, she knew the last piece of the puzzle had arrived.

"Kendra Donovan?"

"Yes." The young man looked as if he should be in school, not delivering messages.

"Sign here, please."

She signed, thanked him and closed the door. Taking the package to the dining room where other papers and research spread across the table. She glanced at the return address – Foster's Forensic Lab. *Surely not...*

For a brief second Kendra stared at the square package in her hands then carefully set it down on the table. Tearing into the wrapping like an anxious child at Christmas, she ripped off the brown wrapping – hoping it wasn't what she thought it might be, but knowing it probably was.

She stared. Among the shredded paper was square cardboard box that contained a ten by ten inch metal box. Supposedly within its walls were all the FBI could retrieve from the death of four members of her family. The sight of it brought angry tears stinging her eyes, but she fought them back. She had shed no tears up to this point and she would not start now – or ever, until she had tangible proof.

"How dare they imply that my entire family can fit into such an obnoxious, common ugly box?"

Kendra paced across the already worn carpet. Angel, who followed her down the stairs, fell into step beside her. The movement calmed her somewhat until the phone interrupted the silence. Glancing at Angel who stopped and looked up at her, she asked, "Severs?"

"Meow?"

With that sixth sense of impending doom, she knew it was. "It's almost as if he's watching the house, or had the delivery boy call him so he would know when the package arrived."

The phone pealed a second and a third time. Taking a deep breath, she picked up the receiver.

"Kendra." Seymour Severs spoke with that chilling, grating, patronizing voice that always made her cringe. "Kendra, honey, did you receive the package from the forensic lab?"

She considered hanging up on him again. She hadn't heard from him since last Sunday night. He never returned her calls. She held the phone waiting for him to continue.

"Kendra? Are you there?"

"I'm here."

"I'm sorry it took so long to get the ashes to you, but we had to make sure they were human ashes."

"And are they?" She didn't try to hide her skepticism.

"Well…eh…of course they are."

She could almost see Severs perspiring and pulling at his suddenly too tight collar. That gave her comfort as she waited for him to continue. She wasn't about to help by prodding him.

He cleared his throat and said, "I'm sure you'll want to have a funeral now and move on with your life. Do you want me to help you with the arrangements?"

"No, Mr. Severs. I don't need your help and I don't want to have a funeral. I will buy an urn and keep the ashes on the mantel."

"I don't think that's a good idea, Kendra. You need to bury them. It's morbid to…" His voice lost its patronizing tone and became more authoritarian.

"Mr. Severs, are you *asking* me or *telling* me to bury them?"

There was a pause and when he spoke again, a hard, cold sound replaced the patronizing tone completely. "Kendra, the ashes *must* be buried and a funeral *must* be announced."

"Mr. Severs, since when does the FBI dictate how a person is to grieve?"

"Just do it Kendra Donovan. Don't be difficult." The buzzing phone indicated he had nothing more to say.

More questions pounded across her numbed brain. *Why should I bury the ashes rather than put them in an urn? Is he afraid I'll get them analyzed? Why make a big deal over a funeral? A lot of people don't have funerals. Does he want to make sure someone believes they – and especially my father – are truly dead?*

"All right," she said to Angel, who was becoming her sounding board, "I'll have a funeral, but not a big one in the church complete with flowers and eulogies from Severs and his FBI friends. We'll have a graveside service with just a few friends. No more."

"Meow."

"I'm glad you agree with me." Kendra picked Angel up and held her close for comfort.

"There must be more clues," she whispered to her. "When the graveside service is over, Severs will wash his hands of the matter then I can handle the mystery in my own way."

# Four

Monday – two weeks after Memorial Day – the buzzing alarm competed with the morning storm. Angel snuggled under the covers as if hiding from flashes of bright lightning, booming thunder and the pelting rain against the window. Reaching to turn off the alarm, Kendra stared at the rivulets cascading down the outside of the window. She sighed and sat on the side of the bed.

"Well, Angel," she said, helping the cat get untangled from the covers, "it looks like a perfect day for a graveside service. I hope it keeps up all day – or at least until after eleven o'clock."

"Meow?"

"It's all right, sweetie. You don't have to go out in it and I don't mind the rain. Now, let's get breakfast then I need to get dressed."

***

Kendra had arranged to meet Reverend Zeucher and Martin Cramer from Cramer, Cramer and Sons Funeral Home at the cemetery. Both, Reverend Zeucher and Mr. Cramer had wanted to have the service either at the church or at the funeral home. She refused. Mr. Cramer called to insist that he pick her up in the limo since it was raining so hard. Again, Kendra refused.

Kendra had talked to her pastor earlier about what she believed. He listened politely, but his non-committal answer said he didn't believe her. He thought she was in denial. She would not dignify Severs' plans by putting on a show of grief complete with a full funeral service and burial. She wanted to be alone, not surrounded with professionals whose job it was to make a memorial service meaningful.

Rain drummed on the car, giving the windshield wipers a good workout as she drove through the gates of Greenlawn Cemetery. A tent on top of a nearby hill covered the site where the graveside service would take place. Parking by the office, Kendra began to walk toward the tent. Mr. Cramer, Jr. from the funeral home ran down the hill with an umbrella.

"I have an umbrella," she said trying not to take out her frustration on someone who was trying to be helpful. "I appreciate your offer, but I prefer to walk in the rain. Please leave me alone."

The man looked shocked and started back up the hill, glancing over his shoulder occasionally in case she changed her mind. When Kendra arrived at the tent over the small twelve-inch square hole in the ground, she nodded to the few friends and ignored the professionals from her father's office. Rain continued to drum on the roof of the tent and umbrellas of those outside. Drops scattered over puddles, making tiny plopping volcanoes then sending circles connecting with circles across them.

Again, Kendra refused the funeral director's umbrella with the same stubbornness she had refused a full funeral. She preferred the feel of the rain running down her hair, washing over her face, cleansing the despair, renewing her spirit of determination.

Reverend Zeucher motioned for her to sit under the tent. She shook her head and mouthed the words, "I'm fine here. Start the service."

She had insisted on a private service at the graveside, but somehow even that made it to a small corner on the front page of the *Beacon Journal.* She called and complained, but it was already in print. Severs had paid to make sure the notice included the words murder/suicide. This hopeless charade was for the benefit of Seymour Severs, the FBI and whoever they intended to fool. Kendra was only there because it might be important to her family, wherever they were. One thing she knew for certain, they were not in that box in that twelve-inch square hole.

Staring at the mound of dirt, breathing in the pungent odor of fresh dug earth and rain-soaked roses, Kendra tried to listen to Reverend Thomas Zeucher, her long time pastor and friend. But she heard little of what he said. Words meant to heal and comfort were absorbed by the rain and carried away by the wind. Water dripped from her hair and washed down her face, but the only emotion she could summon was old-fashioned anger. Two weeks of tension, researching and grappling with lies, had left her agitated, uneasy and anxious to get started on her quest.

"Ashes to ashes and dust to dust...," Rev. Zeucher intoned the words and concluded the service. Friends would have packed the church, but she couldn't stomach the farce of a funeral for people who weren't dead.

One by one, close friends from church hugged her, squeezed her hand and murmured their condolences. The next person in line sent a surge of rage through her. Hiding her feelings, she looked into the phony contrite, falsely compassionate eyes of Seymour Severs.

"Kendra, I'm really sorry about this. I hope you can put it behind you and forget..."

She bristled. Long ago, she had learned to control her emotions, but as long as Severs had known her, he should've known by the tight jaws and narrowed eyes that she was beyond anger. She was livid.

"Mr. Severs," she interrupted keeping her words cold and clipped "I hope you are not seriously suggesting that I forget my family. I will not forget them, nor will I believe they are dead. They are alive somewhere and wherever they are, I will find them."

"Kendra, don't meddle in things that don't concern you."

"Things that don't concern me?"

Seymour Severs narrowed his eyes and through clenched teeth said, "Kendra Donovan, don't meddle." He turned and walked away leaving her more determined to find answers to puzzling questions.

"We'll talk again, Seymour Severs," she muttered under her breath. "You'll give me answers that only you have, or I'll know the reason why."

The gentle pressure of a hand on her arm reminded Kendra that Reverend Zeucher was ready to leave. His large green eyes almost hidden behind his thick lenses, still managed to convey their compassion. As much as she appreciated him and his professional skills, she didn't want, or need, his compassion. What she wanted, and desperately needed, were answers that made sense.

"Come with me, Kendra. Let me take you home."

"Thank you, Reverend Zeucher for your help and kind words. My car is parked down by the office."

"Let me take you to it."

"Thank you, again, but I really need to walk."

***

Rain continued throughout the day and into the night. Lying sleepless in bed, Kendra heard it splatter against the window as if even the clouds mourned in her place. The night finally ended. The rising sun pushed reluctant clouds aside and promised a new beginning. Robins, sparrows, cardinals and finches all sang with such freedom and happiness that she felt a sudden jab of envy as she stared out the window of the house that had been her home for almost twenty years.

"Meow." The tiny voice of Angel startled her. "Meow," she cried again, begging for attention.

"Poor Angel, you miss Shelly, don't you." Lifting the cat, Kendra held her close and stroked her soft fur. "I would've been with them if it wasn't for that stupid report Robert wanted. Speaking of Robert, he talks of marriage, but I haven't heard a word from him, not even a sympathy card. I even called to tell him what was happening. He didn't have time to talk to me. You know, Angel, it sounds like he's dumped me. Well, if he hasn't, I'm dumping him."

Angel bumped her head against Kendra's cheek and purred. "One way or another, Angel, I'll find the answers to all my questions. Now that all the pomp and circumstance is over and Severs is probably relaxed, believing he has taken care of the problem, I'm going to the Federal Building and get some answers. Then I'm going to get rid of Robert – figuratively, of course. After that, you and I are going to find our hidden loved ones."

# Five

Having made the decision to go to the Federal Building, Kendra picked up her jacket and purse and started for the garage. Hearing the metal snap of the mail shoot dropping into place, she switched directions and went to check the mail.

She glanced at Angel who sped to the living room ahead of her. "You think there might be something for you?" she said. "Maybe there's something from Dad."

Kendra let Angel bat the various envelopes across the entryway, then picked them up and shuffled them like a deck of cards. "Nothing here but bills and advertisements." She pulled one out and added the rest to the stack of mail on the hallway table. With trembling hands, she opened the isolated bill and smiled. It was Calvin Donovan's credit card bill. Running her finger down the list of items, she stopped near the end of the list. The last date and place of purchase for gasoline was Toledo, Ohio, May 26, 10:30 a.m.

"Bingo. I was right about the computer message. Vacation did mean Michigan. Now I know where to begin my search. But why did Severs insist that the accident occurred in West Virginia? Is the danger in Michigan and he wants to keep me away from there?"

She added the information to the mound of papers on the dining room table where she had been working while she waited for either the ashes or word from her father. Angel jumped to the table to explore. Kendra picked her up to keep the playful cat from scattering her efforts.

"If Severs thinks I've been wasting time, he's in for a rude awakening," she said. "My computer has hummed for hours at a time and the printer spit out volumes of researched items." Angel rubbed her head against Kendra's chin. Kendra smiled at how much she had discovered.

"Severs expected me to bury the ashes before I thought to have them analyzed," she said as she set Angel on the floor. "He thought my mind would be dulled by grief, not sharpened by anger. My friend in forensics agreed to check out the samples I sent him. He'll have results for me soon."

Angel followed Kendra back to the kitchen, jumped on a chair and fixed her green eyes on her human. "It's all right, sweetie," Kendra said, patting her furry head. "I'll only be gone a couple of hours then we'll get ready for our trip."

Angel jumped down and scampered back to a soft chair in the living room and Kendra, armed with all the knowledge she had gleaned from the internet and library research, left to face Seymour Severs.

Fastening the seatbelt with a click, she pushed the garage door opener. Mr. Severs would never willingly, or knowingly, tell her what she wanted to know. But Kendra was an expert at recognizing innuendoes and hidden agendas. She knew she was more than a match for Seymour Severs any day of the week!

***

Downtown Akron had changed over the years – adding new buildings, tearing down old ones. Cosmetically, the Federal Building was pretty much the same inside, but outside the front looked more professional, matching other Main Street buildings. Across the street, the new library drew many visitors each day. Parking had always been a problem, but with the addition of the new parking deck, the Federal Building was easier to access.

Kendra parked her red Dodge Omni, a gift from her father when she graduated from high school five years ago. He had wanted to give her a BMW, but she had wanted the Omni since she drove her friend's car once when she first go her license. Now it was 1990 and she just heard the Omni was history. The last ones would roll off the factory conveyor belt that year. She stepped out of the car, gave it a pat on the top realizing she would never have another. She must baby this one.

Shaking her head to remove the negative thoughts that were creeping in like a pack of wolves after their prey, she closed the door and steeled herself for the confrontation to come. The sound of the closing door echoed around the cavernous parking deck and bounced off hard walls, ceilings and floors. Smells of oil, gas fumes and rubber on asphalt collected like city smog in pockets of the cement building.

Walking briskly to the back entrance, her heels tapped the rhythm of her heart, sending more echoes into the nearly empty space. It was early – only 8:30. Not many workers, or visitors, came out that hour of the morning. Her shoulder length hair flew in the breeze like a flock of ravens.

A long passageway led into the spacious lobby at the front of the building where a man and two elderly women waited for an elevator to carry them to their intended destinations. The door slid open and the four passengers entered, making two stops before the door opened at the seventh floor. Confident she was on the right track, Kendra walked to the suite of offices marked Federal Bureau of Investigation.

Taking a deep breath, she opened the door and stood for a moment looking around the room she knew so well. Nothing had changed in the twenty years she had been in and out of this room. A number of stuffed chairs and straight-backed chairs – all of them empty – occupied one corner. Thick gray carpet flowed from wall to wall like murky waters overflowing a flooding river. Wall sized paintings of the four seasons of the year hung sporadically around the room, as if the hanger had been in a hurry to escape the watchful eye of the FBI. Along the back wall, a row of doors with names in gold lettering on frosted glass marked the office space of agents. At the left, behind Alice Markle's desk, was a highly polished walnut door with no name. It needed none. That was the office of Seymour Severs, Director.

"Kendra." Alice had been receptionist and secretary to Mr.

Severs for as long as Kendra could remember. Alice looked surprised, glanced at her appointment book and said, "Did you have an appointment, honey? I don't seem to see it." She smiled as if Kendra were still that small child visiting the office with her father.

*Is she going to offer me a piece of candy, too?*

Alice always looked like a professional model even though she must be pushing sixty. Her face – eyes, mouth and makeup – all looked as if she just finished a camera shot for *Glamour Magazine.* Her perfectly tailored suit must have cost a small fortune, adding to the illusion that she was only early forties. Kendra refused to glance down at her J. C. Penny's pink linen suit that must have seemed out of place. Her makeup consisted of a light layer of lipstick. But, instead of feeling intimidated, as Alice intended, she felt free – free from the cumbersome chore of applying all that makeup and caring for expensive clothes.

Alice continued to check her appointment book. *She intends to keep me from seeing Mr. Severs and unless I move quickly, she will warn him and he will conveniently disappear.* Alice finally looked up as if to punctuate the fact there was no appointment.

"No, Alice, I didn't have an appointment. I just thought I would take a chance on catching Mr. Severs before he got too busy for the day. Is he in?"

"Well…eh…yes, but…he's with someone."

"Someone I know?" Even though technically she shouldn't know any of the agents, she knew most of them at least by name.

"I don't think so. He's the new agent who's taking your father's place."

"I see." Kendra hoped her anger didn't show. She couldn't believe they had already replaced her father. *I suppose Severs must keep up the charade.* "Then I need to get my father's things from his office."

Kendra started toward the door where her father's office had been. Maintenance had already scraped his name from the door, a new name not yet painted in its place. Glancing back at Alice, she saw her reach for the intercom and changed directions. She reached

Severs' office and had her hand on the doorknob before Alice could stop her.

"Kendra, you can't go in there." Alice jumped up from her desk, but she was too late. The door opened.

Mr. Severs was talking to a tall, blond, young man, who immediately turned his back and moved into the adjoining office without looking at Kendra. However, she saw his profile before he entered the room next door. She was also aware of the two-way mirror hanging on the wall beside that door and the young man had left the door slightly ajar. She knew he was watching and listening. Mr. Severs, of course, had no idea that she knew about the mirror. Even her father wasn't aware of her knowledge.

"Kendra! What are you doing here? It's good to see you again, honey, but you'll have to wait until I'm finished here. Why don't you be a good girl and wait with Alice?"

"Aren't you going to add, 'she'll give you a lollipop,' Mr. Severs? In case you haven't noticed, I'm not a child any longer and I won't be treated like one. I want some answers and I won't leave until I have them. I'm not stupid and I know you too well."

"Kendra, I think…"

"No, Mr. Severs, I'll not wait. The minute I leave the room you and Mr. Whatever-his-name-is will take the back exit while I sit and wait for eternity." She nodded toward the adjoining room. "No thanks. Like I said, I want answers and the quicker you give them to me, the quicker you can get back to your important discussion."

"Kendra, dear, I don't know what kind of answers I can give you. Like I told you yesterday, I'm sorry about your family. You need to talk to your doctor or clergyman if you are having difficulty dealing with their death."

"I'm not having trouble dealing with their death. I'm having trouble dealing with your lies about a death that didn't happen."

"Kendra…"

"Only you can give me the answers I want. To begin with, where did the so-called accident occur? I won't accept some vague answer like out in the mountains. I want the exact location."

"Kendra, I can't…"

"And, murder/suicide? Come on, Mr. Severs, you knew my father better than that. Who are you trying to protect? What are you trying to cover up?"

"Kendra, you're beside yourself with grief. You don't know what you're saying."

"I know exactly what I'm saying. My father was set up by this office for some reason that you're not willing to share with me."

"Kendra, you're being childish."

Kendra stared at the man behind his desk. His gray hair, combed to one side, did little to hide the shine at the top. Behind the wire rimmed glasses dark eyes shifted from Kendra to the door of the next room to the main entry door.

She knew his mannerisms well and would not be distracted. "Am I being childish? Then, humor me. Tell me where this so-called murder/suicide occurred. I want to see the place for myself. I want to comb every inch of the ground for something – anything – I can have as a reminder. Given the period of time when they left and when I received word, it was impossible for an entire car with all its passengers and cargo to completely disintegrate unless a bomb was dropped on it. Where is this mysterious spot?"

"I can't tell you that, Kendra. It's classified information. I was afraid you would be difficult, so I prepared some pictures that should prove it happened. That's the best I can do." Severs straightened his conservative gray, silk tie and brushed at the lapel of his expensive black suit.

"It's a start. Maybe you can also show me four death certificates."

"Those would be with the funeral director."

"He said *you* have them in Dad's file whatever that might mean." She continued to stare at the man who refused to look her in the eye.

"Kendra…" Severs pulled a large handkerchief from his pocket and dabbed at his brow. He reached across his desk and pushed the intercom button. “Alice, bring me Donovan’s file. Kendra you’re making a mountain out of a molehill. You always did have a vivid imagination.”

“I always did have complete trust in people, too, Mr. Severs – especially people my dad worked with and for. Now, I’m finding even that was maybe a figment of my imagination.”

Alice brought a thick file folder into the room and laid it on Severs’ desk. “I’m sorry, sir, I tried to stop her.”

“It’s all right, Alice. I had to do this eventually. I should have known this nosey little miss wouldn’t believe me.” He glared at me then pulled three eight by ten photographs from the folder.

“These pictures should convince you. This first one we got as the car was heading up the mountain,” he said as he handed the picture to her.

“You just *happened* to be there to take a picture of an accident that you *didn’t know* was going to occur?” Kendra lifted her eyebrows in surprise and reached for the picture. She carried it to the window for better light and took her time perusing it.

“Well, eh…yes…eh…that is a photographer was there taking pictures in the area…and eh…by chance he saw this car driving erratically…eh…at an excessive speed…eh…he thought he might help the police…eh…in case there was an accident.”

“A photographer? *Sure* there was. And does this photographer have a name?” She didn’t bother to hide her disgust. Her extra sensitive ears heard a soft snicker from behind the mirror. She pretended not to hear and continued to look at the picture. However, her respect for the young agent moved up a notch. Although she knew that was her father’s car in the picture, complete with clear license plate view, she gave no hint of recognition.

From the corner of her eye, she saw Mr. Severs watching for something in her expression that would let him know he had fooled her. She let him see nothing. That car could have belonged to a total stranger, but they both knew it was Calvin Donovan’s car.

Getting no response from her, he held out the second picture.

"This second picture was taken by the same photographer…as the car exploded several minutes later." He wiped his brow again as she took the photograph. He still couldn't look her in the eye and Kendra kept her expression non-committal. Again, she took the picture to the window and studied it as if cramming for a final exam – life's final exam. Again, she said nothing.

Kendra took so long studying the pictures that Mr. Severs was getting edgy. He couldn't stand the silence any longer and handed her the third picture.

"This one is an aerial photo of the place where the car exploded."

Kendra let him hold the third photograph for what seemed like several minutes, but was only seconds. Then she took it and studied it with the same intensity as she did the other two. Examining the three photographs, she shuffled them like cards then pulled out the third photo.

"Was this one taken before or after the accident?" Kendra turned and stared at him. She had recognized things in all three photographs that immediately told her much more than she knew he wanted her to know. She kept the discovery to herself.

"I don't understand," he said, wiping his brow again.

"Of course you understand," She didn't even try to hide her disgust. "Was this photo – the third one of the aerial shot – was it taken before the accident, or was it taken afterward?"

"Well, afterward, of course, later that same day."

"How much later? Where are the flames? The smoke? The ashes? The blackened spot of earth? The mountains?" Kendra stared at him. She knew who took that photo and when. She had one like it in her room at home.

"Kendra, you're getting too nosy for your own good." He tried to return her stare but was unable to keep eye contact.

"Is that a threat, Mr. Severs?" She knew he was uncomfortable and intended to push him to the limit.

"I'm simply saying stay out of things that don't concern you."

"But, Mr. Severs, I would say this *does* concern me. I have lost my entire family. You only lost one employee, whom it seems was easily replaced." She nodded and glanced once again at the adjoining room.

"Kendra, I think you better leave before I have to call security." Fear and insecurity popped out as perspiration across his forehead and upper lip. His face became red and blotchy.

Accepting that she had reached the limit of what she would learn from Seymour Severs, Kendra smiled and even chuckled. "That's all right, Mr. Severs," she said. "You don't have to call security. I got most of the answers I came for and some I never would have thought to ask. Now if you don't mind, I'll clean out my father's desk and…"

"I'm sorry Kendra," he said. "His office has already been cleared. It's ready for a new agent."

Kendra had started for the door, but stopped and whirled around. "Then where are his pictures and other personal items?"

"They're all a part of his file." Severs replaced the pictures in the folder and closed the file. He kept his eyes averted, his hands flat on the file folder.

"And why do you need a file of his personal items?" Anger flared once again. Kendra was angrier than she'd ever been in her life, but refused to give him the benefit of making her lose control. Her voice was low and even, every word measured like pure gold.

"Maybe you would like to come to our house and strip it of anything that would remind you that Calvin Donovan ever lived. If you work at it *really* hard, you might even be able to destroy his birth certificate and say he never existed!"

Feeling her anger moving out of control, she paused, took a deep breath and continued. "Mr. Severs, my father trusted you. I know you never liked me, but I thought I could trust you. It looks like I can't. Nevertheless, you have given me all the information I need – much more than I had hoped for. You not only affirmed my belief that they are all alive, but you also reassured me that this office is responsible for their disappearance. That gives me comfort, knowing some unsavory cutthroat bandits didn't kidnap them. Hopefully *you* won't have them killed before I can get to them."

"Kendra, I don't know what you're talking about." Seymour Severs perspired heavily. With a wild, fearful gleam in his eyes, he grabbed the file folder and started leafing through it.

Kendra shook her head in disgust. "Mr. Severs, you aren't half the agent that my father is. I know my family is alive and I know where they are. I assume you're hiding them because of some threat of danger, so I'll be cautious. I won't do anything to cause them harm, but I *will* get to them, eventually. One way or another, I will contact them. Thank you for your help, Mr. Severs. Have a good day." She turned and resumed her exit.

"Kendra, wait. What are you talking about? I told you nothing. I showed you three pictures to prove their deaths. Beyond that I told you nothing."

Kendra smiled, enjoying the panic in his voice. He grabbed the pictures and poured over them once more.

Her smile broadened. "Mr. Severs, you not only told me they are alive, but where I can find them. One thing still puzzles me, however. Why did you come up with such a ridiculous story as murder/suicide?"

"I have a note that your father left." Seymour Severs sounded sulky and looked wary.

"Written on a typewriter or computer and unsigned, I presume. No fingerprints."

Seymour Severs glared.

He knew the note in Calvin Donovan's file was exactly as she said. It would be impossible to prove it actually came from his hand.

Still smiling Kendra shook her head, turned and walked out the door without glancing back.

***

Kendra had no more than left when the tall blond man emerged from the adjoining room. He laughed a soft chuckle until Severs glowered at him, which made him laugh louder.

"I think that young woman is pretty sharp," he said, getting his laughter under control.

"She's a troublesome child," said Severs. "She's been trouble ever since Calvin insisted on bringing her and her brother to work with him. I tried to tell him children didn't belong in the FBI offices, but he wouldn't listen. Said he wanted them to learn to look for the inconspicuous in an ordinary world, whatever that was supposed to mean."

"Sounds like she's learned her lessons well."

"You don't know Kendra Donovan like I do. I say she's trouble and she'll get herself involved in things that don't concern her and blow the whole project. I'll put a tail on her for now. As soon as we know where she's going and what she's up to, you'll take over."

"Me? I don't think..."

"That's an order. Don't let her get in our way and don't let her know you work for us. Whatever you do, don't feed her inquisitiveness. Tell her absolutely nothing." Severs reached for the phone and punched in a number while the young man waited. "This is Severs," he said to the voice at the other end. "The Donovan girl just left here. Put a tail on her. I want to know the minute she even looks like she's leaving town."

He turned back to the young man before him. "You'll take your turn watching her until we know what she's up to. Then you'll follow her any way you can. You're young and good-looking. She's a woman. I think you know how to handle that."

# Six

Kendra left Severs' office knowing he wondered what she was up to. He would find out soon enough, but she wouldn't make it easy for him. She heard laughter behind her as she pulled the door shut – not the harsh cackle of Seymour Severs, but a soft chuckle of a much younger man. Glancing at Alice's desk as she walked by one of the telephone lights was blinking. *Severs is calling someone to tail me.*

"Have a good day, Alice," she said and kept walking toward the door.

"You too, Kendra. I hope you get over your tragedy."

"Oh, I will – eventually," She said over her shoulder as she opened the door and stepped out into the hall. She was so anxious to get started on her search that she ran to the elevator. As if the gods of inanimate objects smiled on her, the elevator slid open. There was no wait.

Kendra stepped into the empty elevator and pushed the button for first floor. Knowing she'd made progress, she mulled over all that she had learned. *The photographs told me almost everything I need to know – my family is alive and safe and I know where they are. What they didn't tell me is why they are in hiding in the first place. The FBI is hiding them because their lives are in danger, but what kind of danger, from whom and why the entire family?*

Pieces of the puzzle were falling into place. Her father had taught her from the time she could talk how to solve puzzles – and to have patience in the process. All she had to do was follow the clues she already had – the type of clothes they took with them, the credit card information, the computer message, the clues Severs inadvertently provided and the pictures in the file. *They expect him to return to work. Otherwise, Mr. Severs wouldn't have kept his personal items.*

The elevator door slid open and Kendra stepped out into an empty lobby. She walked down the long passageway to the parking deck. Bill, the security guard – all these years and she had never learned his last name – had just made his rounds and stood near the door. He always treated her and David as adults, even when they were children.

"Good morning, Bill," she said. "It's going to be a beautiful day."

"Good morning, Miss Donovan. I sure was sorry to hear about your dad and the family. Mr. Donovan always respected me. The FBI and the city of Akron lost a good man and I don't care what anyone says, Calvin Donovan would never commit murder or suicide."

"Thank you, Bill. I appreciate your faith in him. I don't believe that either."

"You know what I think, Miss Donovan?" He didn't wait for an answer but continued to tell her. "I think the FBI is behind this. They either had him killed or sent him into danger so he would be killed or else they're hiding him someplace."

"Why would they do that, Bill?" Kendra hid her surprise.

"Because he was maybe getting too close to something that would upset the applecart for someone." He took off his hat and rubbed his shiny head.

"You might be right, Bill, but I'd be a little cautious about who I said that to."

"Oh, you don't need to worry none about me, Miss Donovan. Nobody but your dad and you and your brother ever stops to talk to me. And if I ever do hear anything that might help you in any way, I'll call you. I would never tell them." He nodded toward the building.

Kendra laughed. "Thanks Bill. I appreciate that. You have a good day now and stay out of trouble."

He laughed too and waved as she retrieved her car from the parking deck. They waved again to each other as she drove down the ramp. As she pulled into the traffic and turned left on West Market toward Fairlawn, she glanced in the rearview mirror and smiled. *That was quick.* A dark colored car pulled out of the lot, cut across in front of a car making a turn and fell in behind her.

***

Kendra glanced at the clock on her dash – 9:15. *Rush hour's over, traffic's light but steady.* Driving out West Market, she made a left turn onto Maple, wove in and around several streets then back to West Market. Half a block more and she turned into the parking lot connected with the office building that housed among other offices, the Fifth Avenue Employment Services. Keeping the car behind her in sight via the rearview mirror, she drove around the lot as if turning around, headed for the exit then suddenly pulled into the next to the last spot. The FBI tail had to exit the lot, drive down the street, turn around and hope that she was still there when he returned. Kendra laughed as she walked into the building and down the familiar hall to the elevator. Eight-foot plate glass windows lined the outside wall. While she waited for the elevator, she saw the dark car pull back into the lot and park where the driver could watch the door as well as her car.

Shiny stainless steel doors slid open and she stepped into the elevator. In less than a minute, the door opened at the fourth floor. Kendra walked down the corridor to the office where she had worked for the last five years. Feeling exhilarated because she had a direction in mind and knew there was a future, Kendra approached the office door. She would work out details with Robert to have an early vacation then go test her theories. In the meantime, she would continue her computer and library research. Knowing for sure that her family was safe, helped her bide her time.

She breezed through the door into the secretarial area. "Good morning, Margaret." She smiled at her friend.

Margaret, twenty years older than Kendra, was always fearful of losing her job. She tried a different diet each week to keep her weight down. Robert wouldn't tolerate obesity in his office – obesity meaning more than ten pounds over the national average. Margaret's hair was beginning to show gray, which also worried her.

Margaret's eyes widened as she looked up. "Kendra, we didn't expect you back…today. We thought you might take more time off." Margaret hadn't made it to the funeral, but Robert's policy for funerals or other emergencies was immediate family members only.

"I've been gone long enough, Margaret," she said. "I can't sit around and mope forever. I need to keep busy. I'll take an early vacation in a couple of weeks if Robert doesn't mind."

Margaret's gaze darted from Kendra to Robert's office and back to her friend. Her face blanched.

"Margaret, is there something I should know?"

"Kendra, I shouldn't be the one to tell you. I feel terrible." Margaret shook her head and wrung her hands.

"Come on, Margaret, out with it. Whatever it is, I'll have to know eventually and I'd rather hear it from a friend. I'm sure Robert is up to something," said Kendra, mentally bracing herself for more trouble.

"Mr. Holderman hired another girl. He said you quit."

Kendra stared at Margaret, anger rising from deep within her. She turned and with broad, staccato steps crossed the room to Robert's office and jerked open the door without bothering to knock. Robert was snuggled on the sofa with a pretty, red head. When Kendra left minutes later, Robert was furious and she was on her way to pick up a six months' severance pay check.

"You can pick up that check next Monday." He spit the words out as he called after her. He rammed his hands in his pockets and turned to retreat to his office.

"I'll pick it up today on my way out," said Kendra and waved farewell to her friends in the secretarial pool. When she reached the payroll office three doors down the hall, Nancy, the payroll clerk, was smiling.

"Kendra, I'm so sorry about your family and all the mess here, but I'm sure glad you were able to get something more than a pat on the back from Holderman." She laughed as she handed the check to Kendra. "What will you do? Do you have another job in mind?"

"No, I didn't know I would lose my family, my boyfriend and my job all in one fell swoop. I have very few bills, so this will be enough to live on for the next six months. I think I'm going to go to a little place I know in northern Michigan where I can think and try to get over it all."

"I think that's a wonderful idea, and if you need any recommendations for a new job when you return, I can do that for you even if Mr. Big Shot won't."

"Thanks, Nancy. I'll remember that. Have a good day, what's left of it."

***

Kendra left the agency, took a roundabout way home to give Severs' man another workout then drove into the cul-de-sac and into her garage. Angel met her at the door. The calico cat, small for a six-year-old feline, was hardly larger than a year old kitten. Kendra picked her up and held her close. "How would you like to spend some time in Michigan, Angel? I'm sure the folks are somewhere near Palisades' Lodge – or at least that's where Dad planned on going. As soon as we can get prepared, we're going to go search for our family."

She set Angel on the floor, picked up a catnip mouse and tossed it across the room. "Here you go, sweetie. You chase this mouse, while I call for reservations."

Reaching for the phone, she was startled by its shrill ring. She jerked her hand back as if the phone had been electric. *Severs? Robert?* Hesitantly, she lifted the receiver. "Hello."

"Kendra, this is Joe over at the Medical School forensic lab. Got your information, but for the life of me, I can't figure out why you would want a handful of burned pine needles and dirt analyzed. You taking up gardening?"

Kendra burst into laughter and it felt good to really laugh. "No Joe." She laughed again and gave him a short version of all that had happened. "…all off the record," she added.

"You sure you don't want me to send an anonymous report to Seymour Severs?"

"That sounds like a great idea, Joe, but I don't want him to know how much I know – not yet anyway. Thanks for your help. I'll keep you informed."

She replaced the phone and with a much lighter heart phoned Palisades' Lodge and Cabins, Inc. for reservations.

# Seven

"...Rain likely today...thunderstorms possible by mid-morning...high today in the low seventies ..." The nasal voice on the radio accompanied by low rumbles of thunder in the distance announced it was time to wake up. Kendra rolled over and reached for the button to stop the obnoxious voice, toppling Angel off the bed as she turned.

As if she had landed in a puddle, Angel shook herself and jumped back to the bed giving Kendra a cat's version of, "What'd you do that for?"

Kendra laughed and cupped the cat in her hands, pressing her nose against her soft fur. "Sorry, sweetie," she said, "I didn't mean to throw you off the bed." She put Angel back on the bed and stood. "It's going to be a beautiful day for traveling."

"Meow?"

"I know, the only traveling you've ever done is your yearly visit to the Vet. This travel will be different – much longer."

Filled with an excitement she hadn't felt since that fateful Saturday before Memorial Day, Kendra started for the stairs.

"Rain or shine, today we take our search further than paper work." Sweeping Angel into her arms, she carried the cat into the hall. Angel turned on her motor and purred until Kendra set her down at the top of the steps.

Kendra ran down the stairs, but Angel ran around her and sat beside her bowl waiting for breakfast when Kendra arrived in the kitchen. She filled Angel's dishes with food and water then started the coffee pot. While the coffee brewed, she showered and dressed in jeans and a white T-shirt with a picture of a lounging cat on the front. Slipping her bare feet into the waiting brown leather sandals, she sniffed the air for the aroma of coffee beckoning her. *Not much time for breakfast today but always time for coffee.*

The car packed with everything except Angel's carrier, Kendra checked and double-checked windows, doors and appliances. Assured that the house was as her father would have left it, she placed Angel in her plastic carrier, set it on the front passenger seat and fastened the seatbelt around it. Angel looked a little wary, but didn't complain.

Carefully Kendra backed out of the garage, going over the mental checklist once more – doors, windows, appliances, note on the kitchen table for Mrs. Knowles about the houseplants, stopped newspaper and mail service – again. "Well, Angel, I've done everything I know to do. We are on our way." She backed into the turnaround area then headed out to the street glancing at the sky.

Heavy dark clouds hung low, holding the sun prisoner in the sky. Instead of rays of warmth, a cool mist kept the windshield wipers moving intermittedly. From the looks of the dark sky, the mist would soon turn to a downpour – probably before they left Akron. Northern Ohio is usually warm and wet in early June, but northern Michigan can be rather chilly – sometimes even a thin coating of ice by morning. But, Kendra wasn't concerned about the weather. This wasn't a vacation trip – at least not until her family could join her.

"We'll stay at Palisades' Lodge and Cabins, Inc.," she said as they started down the street. She didn't know if Angel knew, or even cared what she said, but she needed to hear the sound of her own voice. Besides, Angel would probably travel better if she heard a familiar voice now and then.

Traffic was still light, but picked up, building steam for the rush hour. She hoped to be on the turnpike before then. She drove to West Market, headed for Montrose and was soon on Interstate 77. Another ten minutes or so and she would be on the turnpike heading for Toledo, then north into Michigan.

Glancing at the rearview mirror, she smiled at the black car that fell into traffic behind her. *I hope he has a full tank of gas if he intends to stay with me. Severs would never think of switching cars. He thinks I don't know he has a tail on me.* Kendra was ready to drive all day – or at least most of the day. She ignored the car following her and turned her attention back to Angel.

"We won't stay at the lodge. They rent cabins by the week or month. I asked for Wolverine Cabin for two months with an option of renting longer. It's the one our family always stayed in."

"Meow," answered Angel. Kendra smiled at her companion, not knowing if she agreed, disagreed or complained. Then her thoughts turned inward. She wouldn't dwell on what it would be like to be alone in the cabin – how difficult it would be to sleep, knowing her family wasn't in the next rooms. She would handle the difficulty. Her family wouldn't be at Palisades, but she knew they would be nearby.

"When I arrive, I'll have to pretend to believe they're dead while I search for clues – like who was Dad pursuing?"

Angel seemed to listen for a while, giving a tiny little meow now and then in response to her prattling. Soon, however, she curled into a sleeping ball, leaving Kendra talking to herself. She switched on the radio.

Miles slipped by under the rolling tires as if on a conveyor belt. Time fled with the same speed. Angel stirred, poked a paw through one of the holes in her carrier. Kendra touched her paw and glanced at the dash clock.

"Almost noon. Another three hours and we should be there, Angel. But I need a break and I expect you do too."

Glancing back at the gas gage, she remembered the tank wasn't full when they left. "Oops, I should have checked that sooner," she said. "Hope I have enough fumes to get me to that station ahead."

"Meow?"

Kendra turned into the gas station, pulled up beside the pump and reached to turn off the key. The car sputtered. "Just made it, Angel," she said.

Once the car had fuel, she realized it was lunchtime and breakfast had been rather sparse, so she moved the car to the parking area. Leaving Angel's carrier open and a litter box on the floor, along with a bowl of water and food, she went into the restaurant.

Refreshed, she returned to find Angel back in her carrier. "Do you like it in there, Sweetie, or does it just feel safer?"

Angel ignored her and snuggled into a ball.

Pulling back onto the highway, Kendra glanced back, as she had been doing off and on all morning. The dark colored car was still with her. *I wonder if I will meet him at Palisades.*

Michigan clouds always looked low enough to touch the treetops. Today they seemed even lower, spilling their cargo occasionally as they rumbled across the sky.

Kendra switched on the radio and scanned the stations for some music to pass the time and help calm the churning in her stomach. Music was her tranquilizer of choice – music of any kind. She liked all music. It calmed and helped her forget any unpleasantness. The closer she got to her destination, the more familiar landmarks brought unexpected stabs of nostalgia. After much searching, she found a station with good reception and music from a couple of decades ago.

Without thought, she began to tap the rhythm of the music on the steering wheel. She stopped then laughed. She was *signing* the words to the songs with a finger language she, David and Lenny made up as children. *Lenny Richardson, I wonder where he is and if he still remembers our secret language. We were so close until...*

***

Kendra hadn't thought about that last day at Palisades ten years ago for ages. Suddenly, she saw Lenny's sixteen-year old face as clear as the road ahead of her. Both of their families had spent the summers at Palisades since she and David were four and Lenny was six. The three always went to the island their last night together.

That night they reached the shore, gathered sticks and built a fire in the circle of stones prepared their first visit of the summer to the island. Smoke rose from burning marshmallows. They pressed the gooey marshmallows between graham crackers with slices of chocolate sending a mouth-watering aroma into the air before they even tasted the first bite. It had become almost a ritual of departing – sadness mingled with pleasure.

Sensing trouble with Lenny, Kendra had said, "All right, Leonard Richardson, what's wrong? You've been too quiet. I'm the one who mopes the night before we leave. So, out with it. What's wrong?"

"What do you mean?" He tried to avoid her eyes.

Lenny gazed into the fire, saying nothing.

"It can't even be Paul Brooks," Kendra continued trying to pull Lenny out of his funk. "He's a jerk, but we've put up with him for over ten years."

"No, not Paul – this time." Lenny continued to stare into the fire as if he expected some kind of oracle or genie to appear.

Suddenly, as if she were clairvoyant, Kendra knew. "You aren't coming back next year, are you?"

David punched her arm. "Don't be silly. Of course he's…" but he too saw the stricken look on Lenny's face.

"Lenny?" Kendra waited for an answer, tears from streaming down her face.

Lenny swiped at his own tears. Lenny never cried. "You're a mind reader. I shoulda known I couldn't fool you."

Kendra dropped to her knees, facing him. She reached for his hand and waited.

Lenny sighed. "My parents told me tonight they're separating. Dad's going to New York. Mom's taking a job in California."

"What about you?" David joined his sister on his knees.

"They want me to choose."

"What will you do?

"They don't care about me, why should I care what they want?"

"Come, live with us," David and Kendra said together.

"No, it's time to make it on my own.

"Lenny, you can't…"

"Why not? I'm sixteen, almost seventeen. I have a job waiting when I get home. I'll find a room for rent. One more year and I'll be off to college anyway."

"You'll write, won't you?"

"Sure," he said.

But Kendra knew he wouldn't.

***

And he didn't. Kendra blinked furiously and swiped the back of her hand across her face. Of course, he didn't write. She hadn't seen Lenny, or heard anything from him, since that night ten years ago. She didn't know where he was or if he was even alive. *Will this trip keep bringing back memories that will sidetrack me?*

Kendra blinked again and turned her attention to watching for familiar landmarks that would pull her closer to what she hoped would be truth.

The song on the radio ended and a news bulletin followed. She reached to change stations, but stopped when she heard the familiar name, Palisades. Instead, she increased the volume. The reporter was saying, "…still have not identified the body of a man found floating in the lake at Palisades' Lodge and Cabins, Inc. yesterday. The man had no identification and apparently had been in the water for several months. Sheriff Paul Brooks told reporters he was probably a visitor to the area who went fishing last winter and never returned. Sheriff Brooks didn't know who the man was, or where he was from – somewhere out west, he thought. We'll keep you posted as we get further details. And now back to the music you love to hear."

Kendra's churning stomach didn't feel a whole lot better after that announcement. "*Sheriff* Paul Brooks? Will wonders never cease?" She glanced at Angel who opened one green eye, stretched her paws out, tucked them back and covered them with her tail.

Kendra smiled at her then her disturbing thoughts brought back her frown. *A dead man in the lake? I wonder…* She shook her head. *Forget it, Kendra Donovan. You're going to find your family, not identify dead men floating in the lake.*

But, an eerie feeling surrounded her like a warning that the man's death *was* related to her family's disappearance in some way. She shivered and glanced out the window to replace the thoughts with the scenery. Field after field of green meadows and trees, dotted here and there with red barns and unpainted houses met her gaze.

The mileage gauge continued to accumulate numbers while she passed one familiar site after another, sending anxiety and hope swirling through her. Then there it was – a tiny dot growing as she drew nearer – the sign that read, Fairplain 35 miles. Her heart lurched. *Palisades is only ten miles this side of Fairplain.* Although she still had plenty of gas, she pulled into another station five miles from Palisades. The black car that had been with her since leaving Akron pulled into another station across the street. Tempted to go over and talk to him, she refrained and returned to her car.

# Eight

Back on the road, Kendra set her face toward the place that had always been a fun vacation for the family. This time she was alone. This time it was no vacation. This time she would engage in a most serious game of hide and seek – searching for clues, messages and her family.

Taking a deep breath, she made a right turn onto Palisades Lane to a fearful, but hopeful, unknown. The black car that had followed her since she left Akron that morning drove past the entrance. "Well, Angel," said Kendra, "that's interesting. He followed me all this way then drove off into the sunset without a backward look. That can only mean one thing – someone is already here to pick up the tail. But, how did Severs know where I was going? Did he have my phone tapped? Anything is possible, I guess."

"Meow." Angel stretched and came out of her carrier to look around. A sign painted in fresh, bright colors arched across the entrance of the vacation resort. It looked like a horseshoe offering good luck. In spite of her apprehension and uncertainty, Kendra had to smile at the words, PALISADES' LODGE and CABINS, INC. Life-sized facsimiles of birds and animals of various kinds that were attached to the sign looked so real she half expected a bird to fly away or a chipmunk to land on her car as she drove under the arch. But, each clung to its proper place waiting for the next visitor to enjoy.

"Looks like they've done a lot of sprucing up," Kendra said as she stopped just inside the entrance. "They never had a *Welcome Center* before."

A twelve by twelve foot gingerbread house located to the left as visitors entered had the word WELCOME, painted in a rainbow of colors hanging over the door. Kendra stared like a doe caught in headlights. She felt like Gretel standing before the witch's cottage. As she got out of her car, she looked all around, half expecting a hand to grab her as she approached the door. All was quiet, however, except for nature's serenade that surrounded her. Trying to expel the feeling that a witch must surely await her, she breathed in deeply enjoying the aroma of pine trees, wild flowers and even the smell of water from the lake. She opened the door.

There was no witch, but a stifling mixture of strong body odor, pine-scented air freshener and stale cigar smoke hit her with such force that had she not needed a key to Wolverine Cabin, she would have backed out. Coughing she approached the desk.

The man behind the desk didn't look like a witch, but he ignored her as if she were invisible.

"Good afternoon," said Kendra. The unfriendly man continued to read whatever he had been reading. She tried again. "I'm Kendra Donovan. I have reservations for Wolverine Cabin."

She gave him her best smile and waited for an answer from the somber face behind the desk. For a brief second she had the feeling he was a flat, cardboard poster picture propped in the chair. Then he moved, looked up from the magazine he was reading and suddenly slid it under a stack of papers on his desk.

"Thought you would be here earlier," he said. "Reservation deadline is noon." He glared. His voice was as flat as the cardboard figure she'd pictured earlier. A sudden sense of panic immediately gave way to anger. She would not let him intimidate her.

"I told them when I made the reservations that I wouldn't arrive until late afternoon. They assured me that would not be a problem."

"Gotta check it out. You shoulda called." He continued to glare as he picked up the phone and punched in a couple of numbers. Kendra bit her lip to keep an angry retort from escaping. Instead, she looked around the *office* – a one-room space with no pictures on the wall, two file cabinets in one corner and two doors on the back wall. Probably a closet and a rest room of sorts. The large executive-size desk was metal, not wood – if there *was* a desk under the clutter on top. There was nothing to identify the man in charge.

Finally, he hung up the phone and turned his back without a word. Kendra waited, giving him a count of twenty – in Spanish. At last, he reached a huge, pudgy hand to the hook on the wall and pulled down a small ring of keys, remaining seated. *Maybe has a disability of some kind, but I don't see a wheelchair. He is very obese. Maybe, he has a breathing problem.*

Engaged in her silent game of trivial pursuit, she barely kept her temper under control. After what seemed like hours, he turned around and threw the keys to Kendra. They landed on the edge of the desk and she caught them as they slid toward the floor taking a stack of papers with them. Kendra let the papers fall.

"I assume the rules and instructions are the same as they used to be," she said, placing the keys in her pocket. "I will be responsible for my own cleaning and cooking, unless I choose to go to the lodge for meals. Someone will bring fresh linens once a week and pick up used ones at that time."

"We made some changes. We do keep up with the world up here, you know." He spoke with almost a sneer as he handed her an eight and a half by eleven sheet of paper with the rules and regulations printed. "Read it and follow it or you'll be charged extra."

"Thank you." Kendra bit her tongue to keep from asking, "How did you ever end up in a job of greeting the public?" She took the paper and retreated to the car, gulping in the fresh air as she closed the door behind her.

Before starting the car, Kendra took a moment to glance over the list. As he said, there were a few changes. Linens were now stored in the closet at the cabin and she only needed to return used ones at the end of her stay – or before if she needed more. A bold yellow streak highlighted the rules about using the fireplace and stove. They added a note about making long distance calls. The cabins didn't use to have phones.

*Well, enough procrastination.* Kendra started the car and headed down the tree lined, dirt and gravel lane that snaked its way to the lodge and beyond to the cabins. She paused at the main lodge – a two-story brick and stone building – long enough to breathe in the beauty and let memories wash over her. Heaving a deep sigh, she continued down the half-mile lane to Wolverine Cabin, crossing the bridge over the tributary stream that ran to the lake. She could almost feel the water lapping around her feet and see the minnows racing downstream toward the lake.

The last three hundred yards to the front of the cabin seemed like three hundred miles. It was a good thing she was driving, not walking. Her heart began pounding as if she were meeting an old acquaintance who might have forgotten her.

"Angel, what was I thinking anyway? I'm not sure I can walk into that empty cabin alone."

She sat for a minute or two, observing her surroundings, giving her nerves a chance to settle. Wolverine Cabin hadn't changed in outward appearance over the years. Gray cement still oozed between the spaces holding large, brownish gray logs together. A split log swing, which used to make evenings so enjoyable, still tightly gripped the ceiling of the front porch, begging someone to come and sit awhile.

Kendra couldn't see the back porch, but in her memory, she knew it would have a glider and a wooden table and chairs made from split logs. She smiled remembering the meals and nighttime snacks, the sound of the frogs in the lake, and fishy odor of the water.

Neither could she see inside the cabin from the car, but knew exactly what it would be like. The front porch opened into the large living/family area complete with fireplace, couches, chairs, lamps and a small butcher-block table that held a game board. She and David spent hours playing chess on it. When Lenny joined them, they played other board games. Shelly was just a baby.

Beyond the family room was a long hall with two bedrooms on each side and the bathroom at the end. The dining area was sandwiched between the family area and the kitchen, which folded back creating a U shaped building with a space between the bedrooms and the kitchen. The back porch off the kitchen faced the woods and a smaller lake.

Kendra could see it all – every piece of furniture, every scratch on the walls, every pot and pan in the cupboards. She could almost hear her mother preparing meals, her father walking down the path with a stringer of fish, she and David fighting over who would build the fire and Shelly crying because she forgot her favorite doll. It was all so clear. But this time would be different. There would be no family.

"Angel, can I bear the loneliness? Maybe I should turn around and leave." Angel bristled. Before Kendra could touch her, someone tapped on the window. She glanced up into the smiling green eyes of a young priest beside her car – at least, she assumed he was a priest from his clerical collar. She rolled down the window.

He smiled. "Are you all right, Miss?"

"Yes, I…I'm tired, I guess. I just drove nine hours and…"

"I understand." His voice was low and soothing. "Would you like some help? I was just walking in the woods and saw you pull up here. When you didn't get out right away, I was afraid you might be ill."

For a priest the man was very young and not bad looking either. Although Kendra was still in her car, she could tell he wasn't much taller than her own five feet six inches.

"Thank you, Father," she said as she gained better control of her vocal chords. "I'm fine now. I just needed to sit for a minute – to stop the motion."

The young priest glanced in the hatchback. "Let me help you unpack the car. It looks like you plan to stay awhile."

"Yes, my doctor recommended a long vacation. I guess this is it." It was time for her to begin her role-play – even with a priest.

"Oh, you've been ill?"

She pushed the button to open the hatchback, swung her legs out and stood beside the car. "I lost my family in a terrible accident almost three weeks ago and I'm having a hard time accepting it. I needed time to think."

"I'm sorry. Grief is my specialty. If you ever need to talk, I'm available. Mark Phillips, Episcopal Priest at your service, but please call me Mark. I'm on vacation." He extended his hand with a firm handshake.

"I'm Kendra Donovan, but if you're on vacation, you don't want to be bothered by a blubbering female who can't get over her grief." She smiled at him.

*Episcopal priests can marry, but is this one married? He isn't hiding his appreciation of me as a woman.* She could feel him looking her over from head to toe and wondered if that glint in his eyes was appreciation or lust. David always warned her that her smile, which he said sent a sparkle to her eyes, would get her in trouble someday. She certainly hoped she wasn't sending a wrong message to this helpful young priest – although he *was* nice looking with red hair, green eyes, freckles across his nose and a smile like an Irish leprechaun. But, developing any kind of relationship with anyone was not on her agenda.

"Grief never takes a vacation, Kendra." Mark was saying as he walked to the back of the car, pulled some of the parcels from the car and moved toward the cabin. Kendra picked up Angel's carrier and followed.

"Thank you, Mark."

She opened the cabin door and set the carrier on the floor of the main room. "I'll let you out when we're all through, Angel. I don't want you sneaking out and getting lost." Angel hissed, spat and stuck her paw out the holes to swipe at everything nearby.

"Angel, what is your problem? You were such a good kitty all the way up here." Kendra turned to Mark. "She must be tired of being in the carrier."

Mark cringed and kept his eye on the carrier as he carried the last box of miscellaneous items to the kitchen. "If you don't mind, I'll wait on the porch when you let the cat out," he said, closing the screen-door behind him. "Cats and I don't get along. They don't like me for some reason."

"Angel is usually quite gentle, but it's been a long drive for her." Kendra opened the carrier and Angel, fur standing on end, rushed at the screen, scratched at it and hissed at Father Phillips.

"Angel! Stop that, or I'll put you back in the carrier." She picked the cat up and tried to stroke her into calmness, but Angel emitted growls rather than her usual purrs. Baffled, she set her down and stepped outside to the porch, closing the main door so Angel couldn't see them.

"I'm sorry, Mark. I've never seen her act that way before. She's my sister's cat and I guess she's had too many upsets in her life. She'll calm down, I hope." Kendra frowned. She could still hear Angel complaining. "She was never like this before. I hope she's not getting sick."

Mark laughed a nervous kind of laugh, "Don't worry about it, Kendra. As I said, cats don't like me for some reason. I guess they know I prefer dogs."

"She's pretty smart. I imagine you're right. I really appreciate your help. My family always used this cabin when we came here for vacations. That's the real reason I was sitting there. I couldn't face coming into it alone. I'm glad you came along."

"So am I. Are you coming to the lodge for dinner?"

"I think I'll just fix some soup here. I don't think I can face a lot of people yet – maybe tomorrow."

"The quicker you get into the social fellowship, the easier it will be. If you put it off, you might find yourself alone down here in the woods." Mark smiled showing a row of dazzling white teeth. His green eyes should have been sparkling, so why did Kendra feel them boring through her like a laser gun? Leer? Lust? Something more diabolical?

Giving herself a mental shake to clear away the fanciful thoughts, she said, "I know you're right, but…well, I'll have to think about it. Depends on how tired I am after I get settled."

"Cocktails are at six and dinner at seven. I'll be watching for you." He smiled and started up the road.

Kendra went back inside and shook her head at Angel's behavior. Angel was standing on the back of a chair, front paws against the window. The farther Mark moved up the lane away from the cabin, the calmer she became. When he was finally out of sight, Angel shook her whole body like a dog emerging from the lake, sat on the chair and washed her ears and face.

"Angel, what was that all about? Mark was just trying to be helpful."

# Nine

For a few brief moments, Kendra held Angel and breathed in the essence of years past. If she closed her eyes, she could hear her mother in the kitchen humming as she fixed meals. She could feel the heat as she and David started a fire in the fireplace.

"Meow?"

Kendra opened her eyes. Angel wanted down. "Angel, keep me in the present, sweetie. Don't let me fall into yesterday."

"Meow." She jumped from Kendra's arms to the couch and Kendra headed for the bedrooms. Choosing the one that was always hers – the first on the left – she took her time unpacking then went to the kitchen to put away what few items she brought with her.

That done, Kendra headed for a long hot shower to relax tense muscles. The water felt wonderful cascading down her body, but all too soon, it began to cool. *I must have drained the hot water tank.* Reluctantly, she turned off the flow, stepped out on the white shag rug and reached for her extra-large, fluffy blue towel.

"Time for a nap," she said to herself. Angel was still in the living room curled up on the couch. Wrapping in her terry robe, Kendra fell across the bed. She was just closing her eyes when Angel pounced in the middle of her back. She turned over, scooped the cat into her arms and forgot the world until Angel stood to stretch, waking Kendra who sat up and glanced at the clock.

"Supper time, sweetie?" she asked. Angel jumped down and trotted toward the kitchen. Kendra followed and opened cupboard doors. The meager supplies she brought along dotted the long, mostly empty shelves. "I guess I wasn't very hungry when I put this trip together," she said.

"Meow?" Angel answered as if asking if she forgot her food too.

Kendra laughed. "Angel, I'm so glad I brought you along. I have plenty of food for you, sweetie." She opened the cupboard where she had put the cat's supplies. Retrieving a can of Angel's favorite kitty food, she opened it and put some in her dish. Then she put fresh water in her water dish and went back to perusing the store of staples.

The thought of sipping tomato soup alone just didn't feel right. She felt a pang of longing to be where people were. The mantel clock in the living area sounded six chimes. Angel continued eating, paying no attention to her human. *Maybe I should go to the lodge.* Kendra closed the cabinet and hurried to change into something more presentable. *Will Mark really be waiting for me?* It wasn't that she was anxious to see him again, but she really hated to eat alone.

Searching through her clothes, she chose black slacks and a light blue summer-weight shell with a matching sweater. Even though her hair hid them, she inserted a pair of Sarah's tiny pearl earrings. Wearing them made her feel closer to her mother.

"Angel, I'm just going to the lodge for dinner. I'll be home early. You take care of things and be a good kitty while I'm gone."

Angel sat cleaning her face and whiskers. Kendra smiled and left, wondering what people would think if they heard her talking to Angel as if she were a person – not that she really cared what they thought. She needed to hear her own voice occasionally and Angel needed the comfort of a human voice.

The earlier rain clouds had moved eastward leaving a clear sky that promised a comfortable evening and a star filled night. Kendra enjoyed the leisurely stroll up the lane to the lodge. Birds sang from branches high above as if welcoming her back to what she used to think of as a second home. A chipmunk scurried across the road, stopped beside the thicket and chattered. She stopped and waited for a blacksnake to slither across the road, flicking his tongue at her. Hearing a sudden splash in the stream, she turned in time to see a kingfisher fly off with a small fish in its beak. The mixture of pines, spring blossoms of so many different kinds and the clean freshness after the rain sent an overwhelming moment of nostalgia through her. She, David and Lenny used to count the number of different smells as they walked.

Kendra arrived at the steps of the veranda a few minutes before seven. Piano music drifted in waves from open doors and windows. She felt that twinge of pain, remembering Lenny as a young boy with brown hair and eyes, fingers flying over the keyboard. Slim and gangly, black hair in a ponytail, blue eyes smiling at him, she stood with her violin. Her fingers moved across the neck of the instrument, bow sliding up and down across the strings. *I wonder if he still plays.*

Mingled laughter and boisterous chatter competed with the music. While not interested in the drinks, she ambled into the large room where three fireplaces blazed away as if winter snow was falling. Large pictures of mountains and fishing streams dominated the space above each hearth. She had enjoyed those same pictures when she was a child. They'd lost none of their charm over the years. At the corner bar, the waiter began to close for the evening. Closer to the center of the room nearer the floor to ceiling windows, a young man at the Steinway Grand piano seemed lost in his music.

Kendra glanced away from the piano, afraid she would see Lenny when he wasn't there. She looked for others that she might know from former years. Seeing no one familiar, she started toward the dining area. A very tall, broad-shouldered, man weaved his way toward her as if he knew her – or wanted to know her. His thin, mouse-brown, hair made him look older than he probably was. He seemed to be with a group of men gathered in the corner. They watched him snickering as he weaved his way across the room. *They're up to something.* Kendra ignored them, but kept them in sight as she continued toward the dining room.

"Well, hello there." The man reached her before she had taken two more steps. "When did the angel express land?"

Kendra tried to ignore him and continue moving away, but he stepped in front of her. "My name is Vincent. What can I get this lovely angel to drink?"

Vincent lost his balance and fell toward Kendra, but she stepped aside and he caught himself before he fell.

"Thank you Vincent, but I don't care for anything." She smiled and took another step toward the dining area.

He stepped in front of her again. "I never saw a beautiful lady without a drink in her hand before. You must be joshing me." He leaned forward until his nose came within inches of her cheek. The smell of alcohol was so strong she had to turn away to breathe.

"Excuse me," Kendra said and stepped around him. She had learned long ago that it doesn't pay to argue with an inebriated person. Unwilling to be ignored, however, Vincent grabbed her arm and pulled her back against him.

Kendra had had enough. She pushed her hands against his chest removing his alcohol breath from her face. "Mr. Whatever-your-name-is, if you don't unhand me this instant, you will be picking yourself up from the floor." She deliberately made her words slow and measured. She was not afraid of him, but anger flared. The men with him began circling them. The pianist continued to play as if he hadn't noticed anything unusual, but Kendra's keen musical ear knew he missed notes and slowed the tempo.

"What are you going to do about it, angel? Zap me away in your chariot?" Vincent laughed a harsh cackle, blowing his alcohol breath in her face again. He gripped her arm tighter. From the corner of her eye, she saw movement from a different direction. *Help for me, or more of Vincent's friends?* It didn't matter. Before any of them could reach the swaying man, he was on the floor holding his leg and his stomach, bellowing like a wounded bull. One of his friends grabbed Kendra from behind, but found himself on the floor beside Vincent.

"Anyone else want to join them?" She said. The rest of the group began to back away.

"Hey, what'd you do that for? We didn't mean no harm." Vincent still clutched his stomach and glared at her.

"Could have fooled me." Kendra smiled and sauntered away leaving Vincent's cronies clamoring around him. She started again for the dining room, but before she reached the door, the piano player began to play the Miss America theme song. *He's laughing at me through his music.* Kendra whirled around to face the bearded man who stood and continued to play. A broad smile twitched at the corners of his mouth. Kendra stopped, stared then ran to him with open arms, a smile spreading across her face.

"Lenny?"

Lenny stepped away from the piano, caught her in a bear hug, lifted her off her feet and swung her around. He had grown since she last saw him. He was now three or four inches taller than she was. His brown hair matched the beard, brown eyes smiled at her. His arms, well developed by years of working out, wrapped tightly around her, pulling her to his medium framed body as he kissed her.

"Lenny? Is that really you?" Kendra leaned back and stroked his beard laughing. "What is all this?"

"I'm not sixteen anymore, Kendra, my love. And obviously you aren't fourteen anymore either." He held her away from him and eyed her from head to toe. "Don't sock me for saying so, but you've become a beautiful young woman."

"From you, Lenny, I'll accept that as a compliment, considering you used to tell me I would always be a skinny, scrawny old maid. You were only half right."

"And why are you an old maid? Surely, not because you haven't had enough men falling at your doorstep. Let me guess. You were waiting for me." He hugged her to him again then released her except for his arm that he kept around her shoulders.

Kendra laughed again. "What are you doing here? And you really learned to play the piano!"

"Of course sweetheart, remember we used to play together. Well, we had fun together anyway. You were always much better on your fiddle than I was on the keyboard. I've improved somewhat. How about you? Still playing? Let me guess. You're getting ready for Carnegie Hall."

Kendra laughed. "Not quite. I solo sometimes for the Akron

Symphony."

"Do you have your fiddle with you?"

"Wouldn't be without my *violin*." She emphasized the word violin.

"Where is it? In your room? Go get it and we'll play like old times."

"I'm not in a room. I'm in our old family cabin."

"What are you doing in that big cabin all by yourself?" Kendra bit her lip and blinked back the sudden stinging in her eyes. "I'm sorry, Kendra," he said. "That was very insensitive of me. I heard about the accident."

"Thanks for calling it an accident and not murder/suicide. If one more person says my father killed himself and the rest of the family, I'll deck them good."

"I'm sure you will." Lenny smiled and glanced over at Vincent who glared at them.

Suddenly Kendra felt such a strong sense of longing and homesickness that she could have thrown her arms around Lenny's neck and stayed in his arms the rest of the evening. She felt safe, like old times.

Hearing someone move up beside them, Kendra turned and looked into Father Phillips' smiling face. She tried to keep her disappointment from showing, but Lenny could always read her like a musician reads his composition. He smiled and winked as he removed his arm from her shoulder.

"Kendra! I knew you would come. You will dine with me, won't you?" Mark wasn't as successful as Kendra was in hiding his emotions. A flicker of something like jealously crossed his face.

Kendra shrugged it aside as her imagination. "Lenny, do you know Father Mark Phillips? Mark this is Lenny Richardson an old friend from childhood. We used to play together."

"Music?" Mark gave Lenny an odd look, which definitely had the shading of jealousy.

Lenny chuckled. He was sure to have seen it and unless he had changed in the last ten years, he would have a response. He answered, "Music and anything else we could get away with." He winked at Kendra and smiled. She felt her cheeks turn pink.

Mark frowned, but before he could say anything, Lenny added, "Hey, I have a break in a couple of minutes. Why don't you give me your key and I'll get your fiddle. We can play after dinner."

"Do you think that's a good idea, Kendra, letting strangers in your house?" Mark looked concerned.

"Lenny's not a stranger," she said taking the key from her pocket and handing it to Lenny. "Just watch out for Angel. She's usually gentle, but she tried to attack Mark this afternoon. She'll probably hide and you won't even see her, but I thought I should warn you, just in case she tries to get out."

"Angel?" Lenny lifted his eyebrows and cocked his head.

Kendra laughed at his expression. "Shelly's calico cat. I inherited her." She didn't try to explain further. There wasn't time to get into a discussion. Maybe later.

# Ten

The dining room was set up with a variety of tables for parties of two to parties of eight or more. A white lace cloth covered each table. A bowl containing a floating candle and an open rose adorned the center of each. One side of the room, like the adjoining lounge, was entirely glass – floor to ceiling windows and French double doors.

"Please forgive me if I use you as a shield," Mark said as two very large women, obviously mother and daughter approached them. He didn't exactly hide behind Kendra, but he took her arm as if he would have if she'd allow it.

"Father Phillips, where have you been keeping yourself? We looked all over for you today." The older woman spoke to Mark, but stared at Kendra as if she were an alien from another planet.

"Mrs. Moore, Lillian, I want you to meet Kendra Donovan. She just arrived today and I was going to have dinner with her so she wouldn't be alone on her first night here. Where is Mr. Moore tonight?"

"He'll be along shortly. I'm sure we can find a table for five. Miss Donovan is welcome to join us, isn't she Lillian, dear." The words said Kendra was welcome, but the hard, cold eyes and stiff smile said the opposite.

"Yes, Mama." The younger girl blushed and dropped her gaze to her feet. Was she embarrassed by her mother's obvious snub, overly conscious of meeting new people or just aware of Mark's presence?

"Thank you very much, Mrs. Moore," Kendra answered, "but Father Phillips and I have some things to talk about. I'm recovering from the loss of my family and he's offered his services. I wouldn't want to cry all over your table. Maybe another time."

Not waiting for the woman to answer or for Mark to comment, Kendra turned toward a table for two by a window. She heard Mark snickering to himself as he followed her.

"Thank you, Kendra. My church sent me here to find a bride – which I might add I don't want. I'm happy with my singleness. The Moores found out about it and want to make sure their daughter is the one."

"You're kidding me!"

"Not at all." Mark seemed serious.

Kendra laughed then made a show of placing her napkin in her lap as the waiter approached the table. It was a pleasant meal and she enjoyed hearing about Mark's church. He shared some of the lighter moments of serving a small town congregation. The waiter cleared the table and brought coffee.

"Now, how can I help you?" Mark asked when they were alone again.

"You already did, remember? But, you can tell me who some of these people are. Some look familiar. I'm sure I knew them from earlier years when our family came here. It's been over ten years since I've seen them."

"Well, I'll do the best I can. Some I don't know."

"How about the two matronly ladies over there? They are the Franklin sisters, aren't they?" She nodded toward the table at the end of the row near the front window.

"Yes, they've been coming here for years they told me. Elizabeth and Dorothy Franklin – they're from down around Detroit."

"I remember them. They were always nice, but a little strange." She smiled at the memory of the way they used to be and the way she used to be as a child.

"Strange? In what way?" Mark looked as if it were really important.

"I don't know." Kendra frowned then smiled at him. "Don't

children always think older people are strange? I thought they were old then, they must be near seventy now."

He laughed and answered, "You're probably right. I guess I had forgotten what it was like to be young and looking at my elders."

His words sounded like bait for a compliment, but Kendra ignored them and continued scanning the room. She nodded toward Vincent and the group of loud, boisterous young men surrounding him. "I met Vincent, who are the fellows with him?"

Mark laughed again. "Yes, you certainly did meet Vincent. The younger look-alike beside him is his brother, Thomas. Beside him, the blond-haired person is Donald Shoemaker. They're all single men looking for women to pick-up. Over there by the wall is another rich playboy looking for who knows what. He's been here about a week. He's picky about his women but doesn't seem to go for the boys – although one never knows. It's hard to tell what he's looking for."

"He looks familiar. What's his name?" Kendra recognized the young man immediately as the one she saw in Severs' office the day she dropped in. They were never introduced, since she wasn't supposed to even know he was there. *Now I know why the tail didn't follow me into the resort. But, how did they know I was coming here?*

"Brian McNeil. I think he said he's from somewhere out west. The piano player seems to know McNeil better than most of us – at least he talks to him more. Richardson is also a photographer – not very good at either photography or music from what I hear. Well, you've heard his piano. He's not bad, but I've heard better."

*Lenny and Brian McNeil? That's interesting. Is Lenny with the FBI? That would explain how they knew where I was going, but why is Lenny here in the first place? Maybe that's the reason they had to keep Dad from coming here. He and Lenny would certainly recognize each other.*

Kendra ignored the remarks about Lenny's abilities. Mark seemed like he wanted to pull her into an argument of some kind or discredit Lenny, but she had no idea of why he would want to do that. She glanced away from them and focused on other diners.

"Anyone else here you know?"

"Well, let's see," he turned to look around the room. "Oh, there's our illustrious sheriff, Paul Brooks. He's a local boy who used to own a restaurant over by Fairplain. Went out of business, so he ran for sheriff."

"I remember Paul. He was a little older than my brother and I, but I'm surprised he's a sheriff."

"Just goes to show people can change," said Mark.

Having enough of Mark and his innuendoes and snide remarks, Kendra finished her coffee and rose to leave. Mark also stood.

"Shall I walk you back to your cabin? It's a long way in the dark."

"Thanks, Mark, but I think I'll see if Lenny got my violin. Music helps to calm me when I'm upset. The last few weeks have been terribly upsetting for me."

"Do you mind if I stay and listen?"

"Of course not," She flashed him a smile that she hoped didn't say more than she intended.

Lenny was just returning from a brief supper break. He smiled when he saw Kendra enter the lounge. "Kendra baby, I've got it. Come on let's give these folks a real live show."

*Kendra baby!* Lenny used to call her that all the time. He'd heard her father use the term once. Her face lit up. Lenny could always put her in a better frame of mind if she was feeling out of sorts. She never considered him as a boyfriend, although her first real kiss was from him. He would probably have taught her more about life if David hadn't interfered.

Kendra took her violin out of the case and tuned it with the piano. For the next two hours, she and Lenny played everything from Bach to Beethoven to Rogers and Hammerstein to country-western hoedowns. Mark stayed for a while, but left after twenty minutes or so.

Finally, Lenny said, "Kendra baby, I think you could play

forever, but this boy's about had it. You ready to call it a night?"

She chuckled. "It has been a long day. Thanks, Lenny. I really needed that time to unwind. It's the first time I've been able to forget for more than a few minutes."

"We'll do it again. Soon – like maybe tomorrow?"

"We'll see," she answered. As she moved to put her violin back in its case, she noticed Brian McNeil leaning against one of the fireplaces. Had he been there all this time? Then there was Vincent and his gang still milling around. She placed the violin in the case and snapped it shut. Before she could pick it up, Vincent grabbed her arm. She tried to pull away, but he held tightly to her wrist, keeping her at a distance so she couldn't touch him.

"Come on beautiful, let's go to my room and make some real music." His words were slurred and he couldn't stand without swaying.

"Let me go, or you'll pick yourself up off the floor again," she warned.

"Not this time, beautiful. I think it's your turn." He suddenly jerked her toward him then gave her a quick shove backward. "Your turn to see what it's like looking up." He laughed and turned to walk away as Kendra stumbled backward trying to regain her balance. She was falling toward the hard, unforgiving floor.

# Eleven

Kendra struggled to find her balance. Instead of feeling the smack of a hard floor, strong arms caught her and pulled her against a man's muscular chest. *Lenny?* She couldn't help but feel the gun in the shoulder holster. She struggled to free herself, intending to take on Vincent and his entire gang.

"Cool it. You'll only make things worse. He's drunk." Not Lenny. Brian McNeil's smooth chin brushed against her cheek as he whispered in her ear. Kendra knew he was right, but she was angry. He held her tighter. Taking a deep breath, she relaxed and stopped struggling.

"Are you all right?" Brian asked, loosening his grip.

"I think so. I guess I shouldn't have been so rough on him earlier." Kendra turned to him with a smile as he released her. "Thanks for keeping me from making a greater fool of myself than I already have." She extended her hand. "We haven't met. I'm Kendra Donovan. Mark told me you're Brian McNeil."

Brian smiled as he held her hand, not shaking it – just holding it. She couldn't read his eyes, but she knew he had to have recognized her from Severs' office. She returned his smile.

"I think I'd better go back to my cabin. I seem to be getting into too much trouble up here." Reluctantly she withdrew her hand. Somehow, she had a hard time associating Brian McNeil with Seymour Severs.

"Maybe you better let your friend walk with you until that nut cools off." Brian nodded toward Lenny.

"My friend? Oh, you mean Lenny. Well, thanks for your concern, but I'm perfectly capable of walking by myself." He arched his eyebrows in question. Kendra grinned and added, "Except when someone pushes me. I'll be fine. They've all gone now anyway."

"Uh-huh, to waylay you on the lane, I expect. Vincent is mean and when he's drunk, he's even meaner. His friends aren't any better. If Lenny's busy, I'll walk you home."

Kendra set her jaw in preparation for a fight until Lenny's sudden laughter caused her to turn sharply to look at him.

"You still do that?" Lenny asked. "David and I always knew just how far we could push you before you got really mad. We just had to watch your eyes and jaw. When you clenched your teeth and your eyes turned sapphire, we knew we were in trouble."

Kendra had to laugh with him. "Am I that transparent?"

"Sometimes you are and Brian's right. I would feel better if one of us walked you back to your cabin. Actually, I have some things I have to clear up here, but you can trust Brian. If he gets out of line, let me know. I'll take care of him." Lenny chuckled and started gathering his music.

"Shall I carry your violin for you?" Brian asked flashing a broad, toothy smile. "Or do you only trust friends with it?"

"I only trust people who will respect it," she said. "Obviously you know the difference between a *fiddle* and a *violin*, so I guess you'll do." She glanced back at Lenny who blew her a kiss.

Brian laughed and picked up the instrument in one hand and took her hand with the other. "Do you mind? I like to hold a pretty hand."

"That's a line I've never heard before," Kendra said. "Just don't get fresh or you'll find yourself on the ground, like Vincent."

"I'll remember that, but how fresh could I get with a violin in one hand and your hand in the other?" His eyebrows arched in question.

They walked down the lane talking about the evening, the music, the dinner – small talk to pass the time until they arrived at her cabin.

"This is a long way back here. Are you sure you want to stay out here all alone?"

"Is that a request to share it?" Kendra asked not bothering to hide her anger.

Brian laughed. "No. I never move in, or kiss on the first date, and since this isn't even a date, that would be premature. I was just concerned about the distance you are from help if… well, if anything comes up."

"I'm sorry, Brian. I'm still edgy. Thanks for your concern. I guess I really didn't think it through when I made the reservation. I just wanted to be where my family had stayed when we came up here. I thought it would be comforting, and it is…but it's lonelier than I ever thought it could be, but I'll be all right."

"I heard about your family. It must be very difficult to lose a whole family at once."

"It wouldn't be so bad if…"

"If what, Kendra?"

The moonlight gave a ghostly appearance to the trees and shrubs. She felt herself becoming far too comfortable with someone she hardly knew. And what she did know, she wasn't sure she liked. After all, he took her father's place.

"Never mind," she said. "You didn't walk me home to listen to my tale of woe." Kendra forced a smile and reach for the screen door. She stopped sure she had heard something on the porch. She waited with her hand on the door, listening.

"Kendra? What is it?"

"I heard something on the porch."

Brian set the violin case against the house, pulled a small flashlight from his pocket and sent its beam around the floor of the porch. Although, she'd left a lamp burning inside the cabin, the area directly in front of the door was lost in its shadows. She listened and again heard the sound – a soft rattle, different from leaves in the trees.

"There," she said. "Shine your light below the door on the rug.

A coiled rattlesnake shook its rattles as the light fell upon it. Startled, Kendra jumped back. She would have stepped on it when she opened the cabin door. Brian reached for his gun.

"Wait," she said, laying her hand on his arm. Her mind began to focus logically again. "What is the possibility of this happening? Something isn't right."

"What do you mean? Certainly a rattler on your porch ready to strike isn't right."

"But, if it were going to strike, it would have done so already. It's still in the exact same position. I don't know how much you know about snakes, but I never saw a rattler up here in all the summers we spent at Palisades. And the snakes we did see preferred the warmth of the afternoon sun to cool nights. And how did it get on my porch? And why is it right in front of my door and not moving while we stand here and talk about it?"

"Kendra, do you always ask so many questions?" Brian gave her a curious look. "But, you're right." He looked around for a long branch off a tree. "Here hold my flashlight while I check it out."

Kendra held the light while Brian poked at the snake, which still didn't move an inch, except to shake its rattles as she opened the screen door. She reached around him and pulled on a piece of fine fishing line tied to the door. The other end was on the tail of the fake rattler.

"Why would anyone want to do something so stupid?" Brian asked in disgust. "You could have been scared out of your wits if you'd been alone."

Kendra arched her eyebrows and cocked her head at him. Brian stared at her in the moonlight then suddenly laughed that soft chuckle she'd heard from Severs' office. "All right," he said, "maybe *you* wouldn't have been scared out of your wits, but it certainly would have startled you. Probably Vincent and his juvenile gang trying to pay you back."

"Maybe. I hope that's all it was."

"What else could it be? Are you running from the Mafia or something?" Brian tried to sound teasing, but she heard concern in his voice.

Kendra laughed and unlocked the cabin door. "Not that I know of," she said, "but, then these days, who knows? What about you? Maybe it was a trap for you?"

"Me? Why would anyone try to trap me?" Brian looked startled as if that possibility hadn't occurred to him.

"It all depends," she said as casually as possible, "on how many people know you carry a gun." Brian stared at her in amazed silence and she continued. "If you're trying to keep it hidden, firing at a rattler would certainly give you away."

"How did you know I had a gun?"

"You just reached for it as if it was an automatic reaction. Besides that, I felt it when you caught me tonight after Vincent pushed me."

"I can explain," Brian started, but Kendra knew he really couldn't explain without giving himself away, so he would probably lie to her.

"I don't need an explanation," she said. "We both know to be more careful. If it was for my benefit, someone is out to scare me away. If it was for yours, someone is interested in who you are. We both have our reasons for being here and need to keep our eyes and ears open."

"How did you know it was there – the snake, that is?" Brian changed the subject.

"I have sensitive ears. It's a blessing when you play the violin and hear rattlesnakes on your porch." Kendra tried to laugh, but it sounded more like a cough, or half-sob. Brian picked up the violin case and set it on a wicker chair by the door.

She didn't dare look at his face, but realized she was more shook up than she cared to acknowledge – not because she thought the snake was real, but because someone was trying to scare her away. She was sure it was a warning for her, not Brian. The FBI? Or the people her father had pursued? The tensions of the last few weeks and the day's travel were closing in. Tears were too close to the surface – tears of loneliness and frustration. If she ended up crying the night away, she didn't want to start while Brian McNeil was here.

“Thanks for your company, Brian. I would invite you in for coffee, but…”

“But you’re afraid I’ll take advantage of you?” He leaned one hand against the doorframe and smiled down at her.

“No, that’s not what…”

“Kendra, you’re right to be wary. You don’t know me and who knows, I just might take advantage.” He slipped his arms around her. “But then, I might anyway.” Before she could answer, he pulled her close to him and pressed his lips against hers. She pulled back and looked up at him – surprise and anger rising from deep within, along with another feeling she refused to recognize.

“Do you have a good cell phone?” Brian brought his arm back, reached into his pocket and changed the subject as if he hadn’t kissed her at all.

Confused, Kendra answered in the same tone. “Yes. My dad got us all one when he got his from the bureau. It’s as good as the agents have.”

Brian didn’t look surprised. “Use it if you have any problems. Don’t use the phone in the cabin.” He pulled a small notebook and pen from his pocket, scribbled some numbers, tore the page out, and handed it to her. “These are Lenny’s and my cell numbers. Call either, or both of us, if you feel the need. I promise I won’t take advantage.”

Brian pushed the door open and waited for Kendra to enter the cabin and close the door behind her before he left. She leaned against the door, still shook up – not only because of the fake snake, but also because of Brian’s kiss. Did Severs instruct him to make me forget my mission? She sighed and glanced at Angel on the table beside the lamp batting at something on the shade.

“What have you got there, Angel? You find a butterfly? Good girl, Angel, but it’s part of the decorations. You can’t play with that. Come on, I’ll find you a nice treat, but you’ll have to leave the butterflies alone.”

Angel followed her to the kitchen for a treat. While she ate,

Kendra returned to examine the butterfly stuck on the lampshade. Several similar ones were on various objects around the room – the curtain, the fireplace, a picture frame and this one on the side of the lampshade. She checked all the other monarchs. None had the tiny little transistor dot except the one on the lamp.

*It's a bug all right, but not the kind that flies. Who put it there? Mark and Lenny were the only ones in the cabin as far as I know. Maybe I can set a little trap and find out.*

Angel returned and leaped to the table. Kendra picked her up and held her, listening to her purr. "You finished with your treat already? Good girl. Let's go to bed then."

Kendra paused then smiled as a thought struck her. *Lenny used to love to come to our cabin when her mother made spaghetti.* She turned toward the *bug* and spoke as if talking to Angel.

"It's been a long day, Angel. It was nice eating at the lodge tonight, but I think I'll stay in tomorrow night and make some spaghetti like Mom used to make." Angel cocked her head as if to say, "What about me?"

Kendra laughed at her. "I know you don't like pasta, sweetie, but I do. I'll open a can of tuna for you. Anyway, that's tomorrow. I think it's bedtime now."

Setting Angel on the floor, she checked the locks on the windows and doors then turned off the lights. Angel ran ahead and leaped to the bed. Kendra closed the bedroom door, checked her small stash of inexpensive jewelry and found a small box with cotton in it.

"Tomorrow I'll place the butterfly in this. With the lid off, the *bug* will pick up everything. With the lid closed, I can talk softly in the kitchen without anyone hearing. It's a trick David and I learned snooping around the FBI building."

"Meow," said Angel who didn't wait for Kendra to settle. She purred contentedly and by the time Kendra turned off the lamp to enjoy the moonlight streaming through the window, Angel was curled up asleep.

Too much had happened. Kendra was tired, but thought she probably wouldn't sleep. She was wrong. Sleep came peacefully and quickly.

# Twelve

Angel stirred. Sunrays filtering though tree leaves fell across Kendra's face. She sat up, feeling alive and refreshed for the first time in weeks. Outside treetops sounded alive with various birds singing their special morning songs. Under the window, chipmunks and squirrels chattered as if arguing over a hidden morsel of hickory nut. The mournful cry of a loon floated across the lake. Beautiful wake-up sounds of nature that soothed rather than grated nerves like the radio voice that was her usual fare. These sounds of nature were much more welcome.

Wolverine Cabin, surrounded by trees, held the coolness of the night, the scent of pines and the freshness of morning. Visions of her and David shivering in the predawn cold, waiting for the fire in the fireplace to leap into flames flashed through her mind. While the others slept, they had giggled and fixed *smores* using only the fireplace for light.

A wave of self-pity threatened to overcome her. Brushing aside the memory, Kendra grabbed her robe and slipped into waiting slippers. She would not give in to self-pity. There was too much at stake. *David isn't here to help build a fire and I don't want smores – not without him.*

"Come on, Angel. Let's get some breakfast," she called and started to the kitchen, stopping only long enough to place the butterfly *bug* in the box she'd prepared for it. Instead of the chocolate, marshmallow and graham cracker treats, she now preferred a cup of steaming coffee first thing in the morning – although she would eat all the *smores* David could fix if only…

Again, she shook the intruding memory from her mind. Soon

the aroma of morning coffee permeated the cabin. The sound of Angel munching her favorite food mingled with the sounds of the woodland creatures outside the cabin. All played a discordant tune to her internal struggles. All Kendra wanted was to bring her life back into harmony.

She glanced at the clock as she poured her coffee. "It's already eight-thirty," she said.

Angel paused long enough to look up at Kendra as if to say, "You talking to me?"

Kendra smiled and sipped her coffee. "Just thinking out loud, sweetie," she said. "Maybe I'll skip breakfast and join the Franklin sisters for an early lunch. For now, I think I'll take my coffee to the back porch, sit on the glider, enjoy Little Lake and meditate."

Kendra sat in silence until Angel joined her and made herself comfortable on Kendra's lap. Stroking the cat, she mused. "If the folks are where I think they are, they're safe and nearby. I don't dare go to them as long as someone is following me – and they *are* following me. I probably could lose the tail, but I can't take that chance. I don't know who all the players are in this little game of hide and seek, so I'll have to be cautious and play the game by their rules until I'm sure who I can trust."

"Meow." Angel wrapped her paws around Kendra's free hand.

"Lenny used to be my best friend, but people change, and I haven't seen him for over ten years. He might be with the FBI or..." She continued to stroke Angel and speak in a soft voice that wouldn't scare away the wildlife. "I'm glad Lenny's here, whatever his reason. I can't believe he's on the wrong side. I hope we can soon sit down and talk like we used to do."

Kendra sipped the hot coffee, enjoying both the taste of the brew and the peace and solitude that went with it. Remembering the fake snake, she knew the peace was only temporary. Someone was trying to scare her away. But who? Severs? Brian would have known about the snake if the FBI put it there. More than likely it was the person, or persons who were a danger to her father.

A splash in Little Lake brought Angel's head up. She perked her ears.

"Did you see that frog jump from the rock and grab a bug? It was history in half a second," said Kendra. "Wish I could get rid of my problems as easily."

Angel responded by purring louder and batting at an imaginary bug. Kendra laughed at her, thinking what a joy it was to have the cat with her.

"Speaking of bugs, I wonder who put that one on my lamp. It matches the other butterfly decorations around the room, so whoever put it there knew something about this cabin. I never would have noticed it if you hadn't shown it to me, Angel." She sipped her coffee, stroked Angel and watched the ducks on Little Lake.

"Whoever put it there only needed a few seconds. We'll see if either Mark or Lenny mentions anything about pasta or anything else I've said."

Kendra took another sip of coffee and made a face. "It's lukewarm, Angel. I need to refill my cup with hot coffee."

Setting Angel aside on the glider, she went to the kitchen, refilled her cup then returned to the glider and her speculations. Angel pounced on her, grabbed her free hand and wrapped her paws around it again while Kendra's thoughts drifted back to that confrontation with Seymour Severs. "The young agent listening in the adjoining room had to be Brian."

The thought of Brian sent a wave of warmth to her cheeks. "He's a tall, good looking man, Angel," she said, "thick, blond, wavy hair, and hazel eyes that are almost gray-green. Maybe under different circumstances I could find myself attracted to him. But for now, I can only concentrate on one thing – finding our family. Severs probably sent him to keep an eye on me and stop me from searching further."

Kendra eased her hand away from Angel and rubbed her temples and forehead. She could feel a headache coming on. Stroking Angel again, she continued her pondering. "What do any of them – Vincent, Mark, Lenny, or Brian – have to do with our family's disappearance – if anything? Brian has to know where Dad is. So is he watching me or just taking Dad's position on the case or both? And what about Lenny? He's no more of a photographer than he is a pianist, but he probably took the pictures Severs showed me – but not on the day the folks disappeared. I know the aerial shot is his. Why those particular shots? Did Lenny expect me to see more than Severs would? Does Severs know Lenny and I were friends? And what about Mark? Whose side is he on? Or is he simply a priest like he says he is?"

Kendra could feel her frown deepen. "Well, Angel, all this brainwork is giving me a major headache. I think I'll shower and dress, then see what's going on at the lodge. You can sleep and guard the cabin. Does that sound like a plan to you?"

Angel sashayed to a cushioned chair, jumped on it and settled down for her morning nap.

While the mornings were often cool enough for a fire in the fireplace, the afternoon could become very warm – especially away from the shaded cabin. This day would be hot and shorts and sleeveless blouse would be comfortable by afternoon. Maybe even a swim later in the afternoon would help drive away the nagging gloom.

Leaving the *bug* open and Angel sleeping, Kendra strolled up the path watching for more wild life. Nature was far from silent. Birds sang, bees hummed and buzzed, small animals scurried and scratched under the low-lying brush. Nature was calm and relaxing. City life was good, but never had the smells and sounds of the wilderness. It felt wonderful just to walk and take it all in.

***

Reaching the lodge, Kendra chose the door to the lounge where she'd gone the night before hoping to meet someone she knew – maybe Lenny. He wasn't there, but the buzzing sweeper and the smell of lemon polish said someone was doing morning cleaning. Jonathan Cox, owner of the resort, pushed the vacuum cleaner around the room like a small lawn mower while his wife, Myrtle, dusted the piano. Although they seemed slower than she remembered, they still had a lot of energy for folks in their early sixties

"Good morning." Kendra raised her voice to be heard over the sweeper.

"Kendra!" Myrtle dropped her dust cloth and hurried to embrace her like a long lost child. Jonathan turned off the sweeper and followed his wife.

"Kendra just look at you!" Myrtle gushed. "I always knew you would be a beautiful young woman. We were busy in the kitchen last night and couldn't get out here to greet you, but we heard you playing your violin with Lenny. It was beautiful. Maybe we can hire you for the summer?"

Kendra laughed and returned the embrace of this tall, wiry woman. Myrtle was thin and strong – a hard worker.

"I don't think so, Mrs. Cox. I need a rest."

The woman's face sobered. Her husband gave Kendra a peck on the cheek. "We were so sorry to hear about your folks. It's hard for us to believe, so we know it must be very difficult for you. Are you sure you're all right in that cabin alone? We can move you to a room upstairs anytime you say the word."

"Thank you, Mr. Cox," she said looking into his dark eyes, which now sported trifocals. He was at least six feet, six inches tall and his once brown hair had turned to snow white, but was just as bushy. "So far I've had nothing but good memories that help keep the hounds of grief away. I really slept last night for the first time in weeks. Thank you for making it available for me."

"Kendra, you're welcome to stay for as long as you want. Actually, your father had rented the cabin for two weeks beginning with Memorial Day weekend. I was concerned when he didn't show up or call. Figured he had a last minute change of plans – with his work – until I saw a small article in *The Fairplain News.* We thought you were with them. It was quite a shock when you called for a reservation. We're glad you're safe, but it must be difficult for you. The cabin is yours for as long as you want it. If you need anything, let us know." He smiled much the way he used to when he offered her a ride on the tractor hauling a trailer of wood to the cabins when she was a child.

"Thanks again," Kendra said forcing a smile. "It just feels good to be among friends. I didn't realize how few of them I had until all this hit. Speaking of friends, are the Franklin sisters here for lunch? They used to eat early. I thought I would join them."

"I saw them go into the dining room about five minutes ago," said Myrtle. "I'm sure they'll be delighted to have you join them. By the way, the Palisades Princess will be going out at one o'clock. You and the boys loved going on the boat and swimming at the island. Maybe a trip around the lake will be relaxing."

"Sounds like fun. I'll try to make it." Kendra started toward the dining room. Jonathan and Myrtle returned to their cleaning. Kendra paused and looked around the large dining area. Tables, which had been formal the night before, now were set with placemats over the wood. They looked like tiny islands in a sea of red carpet. To transform the area into a ballroom it would be easy to move the tables. Diamond teardrops hanging from the chandeliers reflected the red plush carpet at one end of the room. Smooth shining hardwood floors at the other end displayed its own myriad of colors from the sun's reflection through the windows and French doors that led out to the flagstone veranda. White painted iron tables with glass tops and umbrellas were set up for those who wanted to eat outside. The sisters were at one of the patio tables.

Kendra couldn't remember a time when the Franklin sisters weren't at the resort. Elizabeth, the older of the two always either contradicted, or explained, her sister's words. Both women, well into their sixties, maybe even seventy, were slim to the point of being too thin. Gray hair pulled to a knot at the nape of their necks gave them an old-fashioned look that even their expensive, modern pantsuits couldn't dissipate. Neither had ever married.

Putting on her best smile, Kendra approached their table. Dorothy, whom she remembered as being overly fussy about tiny details, was straightening her silverware and napkin.

"Good morning Miss Elizabeth, Miss Dorothy." Kendra greeted them the way she had done as a child. "Do you mind if I join you for lunch?" Not waiting for an answer, she pulled a chair from an adjoining table and seated herself at the round table large enough for four people. The waiter who had just brought an order to a table nearby took her order for soup and salad.

"Kendra Donovan! How good to see you, dear. Of course, you may join us. I was just telling Dorothy that I hoped we would see you. We knew you were here, of course. You know how the gossip mills run." Elizabeth Franklin laughed, a soft cackling sound, as she reached to pat Kendra's hand.

"Yes, my dear," echoed Dorothy, "we're honored that you would search us out and dine with us. It has been a long time since we've seen you."

"What Dorothy means is we've been here every year, but you haven't been here for a while." Elizabeth smiled.

"I know. It's been ten years or more since I've been able to come with my family, and now they…" Kendra bit her lip, pretending to hold back the tears that she knew they expected.

"We were so sorry to hear about the accident that took your family." Elizabeth once again patted her hand. "If we can be of any help, you just let us know."

"Thank you. You already have, just allowing me to join you like old times."

"Had your father been depressed?" Dorothy asked.

"Dorothy, dear, maybe Kendra would rather not talk about that." Elizabeth continued to smile even though her words sounded like a reprimand.

Caught off guard, Kendra was surprised, then angry. The waiter chose that moment to bring her lunch, giving her time to bite back her anger.

"I'm sorry." she said, when the waiter left, "I don't believe my father took his own life, if that's what you mean. I know that was the report, but reports have been wrong before. Whatever happened, I'm sure he did his best to prevent it."

"I'm glad to hear that, Kendra. I never believed your father capable of murder or suicide. He was always too kind and gentle." Elizabeth once again patted her hand as if she were an obedient puppy.

"Thank you Miss Elizabeth. You don't know how much that helps to hear someone else say what I believe." Kendra smiled and looked into the steel gray eyes of the older woman, feeling confused by Elizabeth's lack of compassion. Somehow, that cold look in her eyes didn't match the words she spoke – or the thin smile on her lips. Before she could consider this further, however, Dorothy spoke once again.

"Maybe he was working on a case and got too close to someone dangerous." Dorothy continued eating her salad without looking up.

Elizabeth keeping the smile in place and the strange, cold eyes on Kendra interpreted. "What my sister means is since he was an FBI Agent, maybe the case he was on was more dangerous than he suspected and they blew up the car or something."

Kendra felt Miss Elizabeth's eyes boring into her, watching for something. But what? The whole conversation felt weird. "I wouldn't know about that," she said. "Dad never talked about his work. David and I used to tease him to tell us stories. He always said, 'If you want stories about the FBI, buy a book.' I suppose anything is possible, but I have no clue."

"That's too bad," said Elizabeth. "Surely it would help you understand their deaths if you knew why."

"Maybe, but they would still be just as dead." Her voice sounded as dead and lifeless as her family was supposed to be – even to her own ears.

"Of course, you're right, dear. Forgive us for being nosy." Elizabeth patted her hand once again. She had forgotten the woman's irritating habit of doing that. It used to irk her as a child and it was getting to her again as an adult. Maybe this lunch wasn't such a good idea after all.

"Why did you come up here all by yourself?" Dorothy asked. "I would think it would increase your grief to be in the place your family enjoyed for so many years. Did the accident occur up here someplace?"

"What my sister means is it seems odd that you would come here alone. One would think you would want to visit the scene of the accident – to mourn and maybe learn more about it."

Kendra leaned forward and took a sip of the hot tomato bisque. She could feel Elizabeth watching for some kind of reaction. She took time to swallowing her growing anger with the hot soup. Then She laid the spoon on the table, patted her lips with the napkin then answered in a controlled, even manner.

"The FBI told me there was nothing left of my family, that the explosion totally disintegrated everything, including the car – somewhere in some mountains."

"Is that possible?" Elizabeth gave her a shrewd look as if expecting her to deny the report.

"That's what they told me and beyond that I know nothing. You know how government offices can be possessive of information. I needed to touch something, or someone, who knew my family. This place used to be a time of fun for us. We met a lot of folks whom I considered to be friends. I guess I wanted to be with others who knew and remembered them the way they were. I suppose it might seem odd to some that I would run off on a vacation when I should be mourning, but this is my way of mourning."

"Kendra, dear, we didn't mean to offend you. Dorothy can be quite nosy sometimes. Please forgive her." Elizabeth picked at her salad.

Kendra forced a smile and reached over to pat Elizabeth's hand. "I know you mean well and certainly I'm not offended, but I hope you will excuse me if I leave now. The Palisades Princess is going out at one for a trip around the lake. I want to change my clothes before I go."

"Thank you for lunching with us, Kendra. You will join us again soon?" Elizabeth tried to look concerned and compassionate. She looked more as if she had a secret that she thought Kendra would love to know, but she would never tell. Dorothy continued to eat her lunch without raising her eyes at all.

Kendra repressed a shudder and hoped her smile did not look as plastic as Elizabeth's. "Of course, why don't you come take a trip around the lake with us?"

Elizabeth and Dorothy both laughed – a cackling duet. "No, thank you, dear," answered Elizabeth. "We're getting too old for those kinds of excursions. We'll watch the water from here. It's much safer."

Kendra bade them goodbye and hastened back to the cabin to change clothes. Someone followed her – Lenny or Brian? Vincent? She didn't see anyone, nor hear anything. It was just that gut feeling that someone was watching. Her lunch with the Franklin sisters left her confused. *Maybe I am being unjustifiably paranoid, but I don't think so.*

# Thirteen

A chipmunk scurried across the path and into the brush beside the porch. Kendra opened the screen door slowly, scanning the porch for more practical jokes. Nothing out of the ordinary there, but as she stepped into the living area, something sharp grabbed her ankle. Remembering the fake reptile from the night before, Kendra yelped and jumped aside pulling a little ball of fur off the floor.

"Angel! You startled me."

Angel let go of her ankle and scampered behind the couch, tentatively poking her head around the corner.

"All right, sweetie." Kendra laughed and moved toward her. "We'll play a little." She grabbed a toy on a string and played keep away with Angel for a few minutes ending in the bedroom where Angel leaped to the bed while Kendra changed clothes.

"I'll wear my swimsuit under my clothes in case the Palisades Princess docks at the island to give us time for a swim." She put away the kitty toy and slipped into her one piece, aqua swimsuit, then donned navy shorts and a light blue T-shirt over it.

The summer Kendra learned to swim – with the help of David and Lenny. – flooded her memory. She was only five and they repeatedly threw her in the lake until she had to either sink or swim – at least that's what she thought then. The water wasn't that deep and they both stayed near enough to help if she got in trouble. She did learn to swim, but when they returned to Akron that fall, her father enrolled her and David in a Red Cross Swimming Class at the YMCA to learn better techniques. Later they both passed their lifeguard tests.

Leaving Angel curled on the bed, Kendra started back to the

lake trying to put aside her worries and concerns. Answers would come when she had the necessary facts. Until then it would only increase the anxiety to fret about them.

Before she reached the dock, she could see shimmering ripples of waves from small motor boats crisscrossing over the lake. She heard waves lapping at the shore. As she got closer, she could see them run upon the shore and scurry back to the lake. Terns padded across the wet sand leaving footprints for the next wave to wash away.

The Palisade Princess waited at the dock with it's gangplank down for boarding passengers. Memories of all the fun she, David and Lenny had as kids washed away some of the fear and anxiety – at least for a few minutes. But, like the tide that ebbs and flows, worries returned.

Everyone seemed interested in her, which was probably normal. What didn't make sense was their interest in her father's activities. Even the Franklin sisters had spent more time quizzing her about his activities, than they did talking about themselves, or even about Kendra. *Why would they be interested in Dad's activities before his disappearance? Idle curiosity? Maybe.*

Lost in impossible questions and even more unmanageable answers, Kendra walked into Mark Phillips. "Mark!" She stumbled and grabbed his arm to keep from falling. "I'm sorry. I guess I wasn't paying attention to where I was going. My mind was going one direction and my feet another." She tried the hide her embarrassment by laughing as she released his arm.

"Kendra, it's good to see you out this morning – or is it afternoon already." He laughed also, ignoring her embarrassment. "Are you going on the cruise around the lake?"

"Yes, I thought it would bring back good memories. Are you going?"

Something splashed behind her and Kendra turned to see ripples where someone had dropped something in the lake. No one was near. *A kid throwing pebbles? Probably*. Mark answered, apparently not hearing the splash, or indifferent to it, if he did.

"It seems like a good way to relax in God's natural sanctuary," he said, then added, "Oh, by the way, do you like Italian cuisine?"

Mark was sure to have noticed her surprise had she been looking at him. *Is he referring to my comment into the bug last night? If so, he must have put it there. But, why? I thought sure it was Lenny playing some kind of joke. Things are getting curiouser and curiouser as Lewis Carroll's Alice would say.*

Kendra watched the rippling surface of the deep blue lake where clouds looked like they were bobbing under the surface of the water until she was sure her thoughts were under control. Mark laid a hand on her shoulder.

"Kendra? Are you all right?" *He probably thinks I'm ignoring him.*

Kendra turned around and forced a smile. Her tone gave no indication of her internal struggles. "I'm sorry, Mark. I got lost in the beauty of the lake for a minute. You must be a mind reader. I love Italian food. As a matter of fact, I intend to make spaghetti for supper tonight. Maybe you would like to join me."

Mark smiled like a man with a secret. "I don't think your cat likes me, but I have a better idea. I know a new place called the Italian Café – just opened a couple of months back about ten, maybe fifteen, miles north of Fairplain. Would you like to go tonight?"

"I would love to. It sounds great. We should be back from the cruise about five. I could be ready by six. Does that sound all right?"

"Six it is. That will give us plenty of time to talk, hopefully without the Moores." He grimaced and shuddered.

Kendra laughed with him at the thought of Mrs. Moore and her daughter, Lillian, who hoped to be the future Mrs. Mark Phillips. Mark held her elbow as they walked together up the gangplank of the Palisades Princess.

Not a cruise ship by any stretch of the imagination, the Palisades Princess was a large paddleboat that seated twenty-five or thirty people, although Captain Marshal hardly ever took that many out at one time. The double-decker had seats on the top deck for those who wanted more sun.

The lower deck also had rows of bench seats protected by windows for those who wanted to see the lake without the weather. In the corner near the stairs to the top deck, was a mini bar. Small round tables dotted the area for those who preferred to drink and view the lake. The same bartender from the night before took care of the bar.

Kendra stopped to look out across the lake once more before they reached the stairs. She loved the water and the memories it released. Children playing at the beach sent little ripples across the surface like tiny fractures on a mirror. She hugged herself, wishing she could jump in and swim until she could forget all her cares.

"Do you see something I don't see?" She'd almost forgotten Mark was beside her. The amusement in his voice took some of the pleasure from the scene, so she sighed and turned to move through the lounge to the stairs.

"No, just memories," she answered.

"Kendra, it's been almost two months since their death. You need to let it go. Let the 'dead bury the dead' as our Scripture tells us."

"I wish I could, but it's only been three weeks, not two months." Kendra began weaving her way through the dozen or so passengers who waited for a chance to get drinks. She needed to reach the stairs and move to the upper deck before she said more than was wise to say. Mark seemed to be losing some of the compassion she'd first seen in him.

Ignoring the boisterous gathering at the bar, Kendra reached the steps and had one foot on the bottom one. From the sound of Vincent and his friends, their drinking had started much earlier. Vincent's loud, grating voice brought conversation to a halt.

"Well, look who's going on our little boat ride fellows. Little miss cutie pie." His friends laughed as if he had told a joke.

Kendra refused to respond and took another step up. Vincent's hand suddenly grabbed her wrist and pulled her off the step to him. "Come on, pretty girl, have a little drink with me."

"Vincent, I told you last night, I don't drink. Please let go of me." Kendra struggled to pull herself away from him, but he held her wrist in a vise-like grip. Her hand began to throb from the pressure.

"I'm ready for you this time, missy. You ain't going to knock *me* down again." Vincent sneered and jerked her closer. Anger boiled over. She was determined his lips would never touch hers. She struggled harder. He laughed.

"You heard the lady. Let her go."

Vincent whirled around to see who challenged him. Brian stood with hands on hips waiting for him to comply. Vincent laughed like a maniac and jerked her arm up behind her. Kendra bit her lip to keep from crying out. Taking the opportunity of Vincent focusing on Brian, she forced her body to relax and slid like a jellyfish to the floor. Vincent had to either, let go or fall with her. He let go and Brian's fist made contact with his jaw. Vincent fell backward into the arms of his friends who cursed and glared at Kendra and Brian.

Brian reached out his hands and pulled her to her feet. "Are you all right?" He grinned and added, "It seems we've been down this road before."

"Thanks for being here – again." Kendra gave him a smile of thanks and rubbed her wrist. Then glancing at the men who gathered around Vincent, she spoke to his brother. "You know, young man, if I were you I'd get a leash for him." She nodded toward Vincent. "He's going to get himself hurt if he keeps going the way he's headed."

They scowled. Kendra turned to look for Mark. He always seemed to disappear when there was trouble.

"If you're looking for Mark, he went upstairs." Brian spoke without a hint of a smile, but she knew he was laughing at her.

"Not everyone is handy with their fists," she answered and turned so abruptly that her hair flew around her face. She pushed it back and started up the stairs without a backward glance. Brian chuckled behind her and she couldn't keep from smiling.

At the top of the stairs, Kendra stopped and looked around for

Mark. He seemed to be in a private discussion of some kind with Lenny at the rail, so she stood trying to decide whether to interrupt them or just find a place to sit. After all, she didn't come with Mark. They just showed up at the same time.

"Are you going to stand there all day, or do you need help moving?" Brian asked from behind her. His hands went around her waist and he lifted her aside so he could step up.

"Sorry about that. Just trying to decide where to go."

"Looks like there are plenty of choices. How about over here?" He continued to keep an arm around her and led her to a couple of lounge chairs in the corner opposite the end from where Lenny and Mark were talking. Kendra went with him because she could do nothing else without creating another scene. And it wasn't worth it. At least Brian wasn't drunk.

With a blast on his tugboat-sounding horn, Captain Marshall's voice crackled over the intercom.

"Ladies and gentlemen, welcome to the Palisades Princess. This is Captain Rolland Marshall speaking. The Princess and I have traveled the waters of Palisades Lake for twenty-five years.

"Palisades Lake is six miles long and three miles wide at its widest point. The water is always clear and cold because it is fed by underground springs as well as tributary streams. Several islands dot the lake. Most are just trees and shrubbery for wild life habitat. Only one is large enough to visit. We sometimes stop there for a brief swim for those who care to cool off.

"From time to time I will point out attractions, but in the meantime, sit back, relax and enjoy a smooth ride."

Kendra leaned back in the lounge chair and closed her eyes. A warm breeze created by the movement of the boat blew through her hair and around her face. At the same time, the sun warmed the rest of her. She sensed, rather than saw, Brian leave. Her mind continued to whirl with the questions until she felt a shadow block the sun. She opened her eyes in time to see Vincent swinging his leg over to straddle her lounge chair.

"Vincent, what do you think you're doing? Haven't you had

enough? Get away from me before I pitch you overboard." The chaise lounge had been comfortable for resting, but it became an obstacle when she needed to get up in a hurry.

Vincent laughed a harsh, unnatural laugh that sent a chill up her spine. Not only was he drunk, he sounded as if he was on something stronger. Kendra looked around for help and saw Brian, Lenny and Mark some distance away. She tried to get up, but Vincent leaned forward and clamped his hands on her shoulders, pinning her down.

He leered and laughed. "Let's see, what shall I do first? Kish you? Feel your…"

His words ended in "oomph" as Kendra pulled her feet up to her chest and kicked him in the stomach. He fell backward and by the time he regained his breath and righted himself, she was on her feet. His cheering section arrived to watch the show. From her peripheral vision, she saw Brian and Lenny approaching.

"Don't let her do that to you Vince," shouted his brother. The others joined in the taunts. Vincent gave a scream like a wounded animal, lowered his head and charged like a raging bull. Kendra moved so she had her back to the rail. He was almost to her when she stooped for better advantage, caught his shoulders with her hands and raised her body up. His momentum kept him going as she flipped him up and over the rail. He screamed. A loud splash followed.

"What are you doing you dumb broad?" His brother screamed. "Vince can't swim. Help! Someone help. She's trying to kill him."

"Oh, shut up," Kendra said, stripping off her shirt and shorts. She kicked her sandals to the side and before the brother could yell again, she was over the rail, hearing the air whistle around her. The cold water rushed up to meet her, almost taking her breath away.

Vincent was in trouble and she had to help him before getting concerned about her own discomfort. Kendra heard another splash behind her as she swam toward Vincent. He struggled and fought when she tried to help him. She knew he could pull her under if she didn't knock him out first, but the way he was flailing, she couldn't get close enough.

"Get his arms out of the way," Brian called as he swam to them.

Kendra reached for Vincent's arms, which he immediately wrapped around her and pulled her under the water. She struggled to free herself, but he had a death grip on her. *Where is Brian? Has he led me to my death? Was I mistaken about him?*

Kendra had read of a person's entire life rushing before them when death was imminent, but she didn't have time for such frivolous thoughts. Her lungs felt as if they were going to burst if she didn't make it to the surface soon. Forcing herself not to panic, she began to slowly exhale bubbles that gently rose to the top of the lake. With one last kick, she pushed upward sending Vincent and herself toward the surface. She only hoped Brian was there to help her, not push her back under.

# Fourteen

Water churned around them and Vincent's arms suddenly fell limp. Kendra kicked harder. Her head cleared the water and she gasped in the precious air. Brian had hold of Vincent's hair helping to pull them upward. He took the unconscious Vincent and swam for the life preserver. Kendra swam ahead and held it while Brian got Vincent tied in with the rope the skipper dropped to them. They tied more ropes to the preserver so Captain Marshall could haul Vincent up to the deck.

"Thanks – again." Kendra pushed her wet hair from her face while treading water. They waited for Captain Marshall to lower a rope ladder for them. Having become acclimated to the temperature, Kendra loved the feel of the water around her. She watched the skipper lower the ladder with a touch of regret. She didn't want to go back yet. With a half-turn, she saw their special island in the distance. A smile spread across her face. "Tell Captain Marshall to pick me up on the way back," she called over her shoulder and settled in for the long leisurely swim to the island.

"Kendra, come back. That island is a half mile away."

"I know." she called back. Already the distance between them was broadening. Kendra was in no hurry and enjoyed the freedom of the water all around her. The sound of water splitting nearby told her Brian was following.

***

"Keep an eye on her," Severs had said. Surely, nothing could happen on that island. The water was very cold as Brian watched the captain haul Vincent up to the deck. He turned to see Kendra putting more distance between her and the boat.

He signaled Lenny on the boat and turned to swim after that beautiful, elusive, Kendra Donovan. He'd had some tough assignments in his work and he'd had pretty girls to keep track of, but this time it was a challenge to keep a step ahead of Kendra. He had the feeling she knew more than she was saying, and that she would find what she wanted no matter what he did to stop her.

***

All too soon, the swim was over and Kendra felt the added weight of her body as she half walked, half staggered through the shallow water to the shore. She dropped to the ground, stretched out with her back on the warm sand and felt the sun warming the rest of her. For the briefest of moments, she felt completely alone with God in His universe. Then she heard the splash and felt cold drops of water as Brian collapsed beside her.

Getting his breathing back to normal, he laughed. "You're nuts," he said.

With the coolness of Brian's shadow shielding her face, Kendra opened her eyes a narrow slit and smiled at him. She felt like a child who just received the most treasured gift in the world.

"But, wasn't it wonderful?" she said. "The water all around, like being held in the palm of God's hand, then to feel the warm sand. I wish all life could be this peaceful and…"

Kendra stopped, appalled that tears should find their way to freedom. Brian watched the sudden crack in her stoic façade. She wanted to run.

"Kendra, it's all right." Brian had his arms around her before either of them knew what was happening. "It's all right to cry, you know. You've not only had a horrible experience at home, but that clown keeps harassing you up here."

He held her for a minute or two, as if reluctant to let her go. She tensed. Brian changed the subject, as if wanting to make her forget. "How did you manage to throw him overboard anyway?"

Kendra leaned back and looked into his eyes. Not prepared for a swim, he still had on khaki shorts. He'd left his shoes, green polo shirt and jacket, which probably held his gun, on the boat. He was laughing, but she knew it wasn't at her. He was amused that she could handle someone as tall and heavy as Vincent.

Kendra grinned, chasing away the last of the tears. "David, my brother, taught me. It's come in handy a number of times. Would you like for me to demonstrate on you?"

"You know, you have the most beautiful eyes I've ever seen?" He still held her.

She laughed. "How many women have you said that to in the last month?" She wondered if she should say something about what she knew, or wait for him to make the first move. While she was deciding what to say or do, he slipped his arms around her, pulled her closer to him and kissed her much more passionately than he had the night before.

Kendra thought she should be incensed, but when she recovered her breath, she said, "I thought you said you never kiss a girl on the first date."

"I don't, but we haven't had a date yet." He grinned and let her go – although he seemed reluctant to do so. Kendra knew she would have to be careful. She didn't have enough energy to search for her family and fight the emotions Brian was stirring within her.

"We better walk around to the other side of the island," she said. "There's a dock where the Palisades Princess can pick us up. We probably have a half hour before they get around the lake and back to the island. Would you like a tour?" Kendra jumped up and started across the grassy path without waiting for his answer.

She turned to see if he were following. Brian jumped up, brushed sand from his body as he ran. Kendra waited for him to catch up with her. He took her hand and they walked along an overgrown path through the tall grass. When they came to a hill, she pulled him up the grassy slope. From the crest of the hill, they could see across the lake on three sides of the island. The Palisades Princess was making its way leisurely around the lake in the distance. On the fourth side was a larger hill with a large outcropping of rocks showing through the trees here and there.

"David, Lenny, and I used to spend hours on this island. Once or twice, we even slept over. We were grounded for a day or two for that." Kendra laughed and Brian smiled.

"How did you get here? Did you have a boat?"

"It's only a mile or so from the lodge. We usually swam. This was our favorite place to watch for spies."

"Spies?" Brian sat down on the hill and pulled her down beside him.

"Yes. Our favorite game was spying. We were FBI agents looking for crooks."

"FBI agents? How come none of you ended up as agents?" Brian focused on the sky.

Kendra gazed into the distance seeking to recapture the past. "Maybe we had enough as kids," she said. "Maybe I saw the loneliness and anxiety of the family of an agent. David preferred to get a law degree and work to put the criminals away when he saw how often Dad risked his life to capture a crook, only to have him released on a technicality. And Lenny? After his parent's divorce, we lost track of him. He never came back to Palisades and then we stopped coming when David and I were out of school and working."

"Kendra, your dad must have been a very good agent." Brian still held her hand and squeezed it.

"He was the best. He could outwit and out-maneuver Seymour Severs any day of the week." Her voice cracked and tears begged release again. She pulled her hand away and brushed at the stray tear that slipped out unbidden.

"Who is this Seymour Severs?" Brian wouldn't look into her eyes as he asked.

Kendra noticed his discomfort, but knew he had to ask even though he already knew. She smiled. *I'll play the game his way, at least for now.* "He's the head man at the Bureau in Akron where my dad worked. But…enough of that before I cry all over you again. Come on, you've got to see the spring before we go meet the boat."

Kendra jumped up, excitement spilling over to Brian as she grabbed his hand and pulled him to his feet. He laughed and ran to keep up with her. “Kendra, don’t you ever run down?”

She grinned. “Sometimes – when I don’t have to worry about saying, or doing something that’s going to cause me more pain.” Before he could say anything, she pointed to a narrow path. “It’s back there – not far.”

Brian followed to the clearing where a boulder about the size of a Volkswagen stood guard over a spring of clear water, bubbling up from the ground. “It’s the coldest, cleanest, best tasting water anywhere. Try it.” She fell to her knees, cupped her hands, filled them with the water and drank thirstily.

Brian followed her example. “Wow! It sure is the coldest water I’ve felt for a long time, even colder than the lake. And it is good.”

Kendra scrambled up to the top of the rock and sat on a ledge over the spring. “Come up here and you can dangle your feet in the spring.”

“And get frost bite on my toes?” Brian cocked his head and looked at her as if he thought she was kidding.

“It’s not *that* bad,” she said demonstrating for him.

“Oh well, why not?” Brian shrugged, climbed up beside her, and let his feet dangle in the spring. “Kendra, you’re completely nuts. Swim half way across a freezing lake, then dangle your feet in a spring of water even colder.” He had to laugh again.

“It’s not someplace I want to stay long,” she said, “Lenny, David, and I used to have a contest to see who could keep their feet in it the longest.”

“You don’t need to tell me who won hands down every time.” Brian laughed as he drew his feet out of the cold water and jumped off the boulder, lifting his arms to catch her as she jumped down beside him. “Any other interesting places we should see?” Brian took her hand again as they started down the path.

“Just one – for now anyway. There are caves to explore and cliffs to climb on the hill at the other end of the island, but not today. You have to see this, though. I think we might be just about on time.” Kendra glanced at the sky and started pulling him along the path.

"Why so mysterious?" Brian smiled but looked puzzled. She led him along the path from the boulder to another little hill.

"Another hill?" He smiled.

"Hurry," she said. "We don't want to miss it."

"Miss what?"

"You'll see. Over there." she pointed where they had just been. "You can see the spring from here."

"Kendra we were just there and…"

Brian stopped. The scene always took Kendra's breath away and she heard him gasp behind her. The sun was in the perfect position to strike the mist from the spring sending a rainbow of colors cascading around the boulder until they arranged themselves into a perfect arc.

"Isn't it beautiful?" she whispered.

Brian glanced at her. She couldn't stop the tears of joy from tumbling down her face.

"The reflections of the rainbow sparkle in each little stream," he said caressing her face. "I'm not sure which is more beautiful, the vision before me, or the one beside me."

The rainbow faded and Kendra brushed the tears away again feeling embarrassed. "Brian McNeil, have you been to Ireland, kissing the Blarney Stone, lately?"

Brian laughed. The moment had been shattered. Kendra was sure he would have taken her in his arms again and who knows what would have happened. He kissed the tip of her nose and said, "No, it was pure inspiration. We better go before I get more ideas."

She stopped and cocked her head to one side. "I hear the boat and unless we want to swim back to the lodge, we better be at the dock. Skipper doesn't wait for anyone."

Glad the boat was on its way Kendra took his hand and started toward the dock. Brian looked as if he was ready to declare more than she was ready to hear. And yet she felt herself longing to be in his arms, feeling his lips on hers. *Kendra Donovan, get a grip. Send that imagination back where it belongs and get on with your quest.*

The Palisades Princess moved toward the dock as they ran onto the beach. Leaving the grassy, wooded area of the central island, the sand felt hot on bare feet. "I have to walk across the boulders once," she said and ran for the boulders off to the right of the dock. They caught the white foam of the waves sending mists billowing around them.

"You might end up swimming back." Brian sat down on the sand to watch her climb the stones.

"Maybe, but it will be worth…" Kendra saw something that she didn't want to see. "Brian…"

He leaped to his feet and ran to her, knowing something was wrong.

"Kendra? What is it?"

"There." She pointed toward a pool of water between two boulders. "There's a man floating in the water."

# Fifteen

Kendra watched Brian move across the boulders much more quickly than was probably safe on the slippery rocks. In the pool of clear water, fed by the waves jumping the surrounding boulders, a man's body floated face down. Although, she couldn't see his face, she could see enough to know he'd been in the lake for some time – maybe even several months. Fish had nibbled at fingers and other body parts, giving the man a gruesome appearance. Even his clothes, dark colored sweats, had holes as if giant sea moths had been at work.

Brian glanced at Kendra. "Are you all right?" he asked.

"I'm fine," she answered. "I'll stay here while you get the skipper to call the authorities. I don't think *he's* going anyplace." Kendra glanced down at the man. "And I would guess he's been in the water some time."

Brian arched his eyebrows as if to ask, "How would you know that?" But he didn't say anything. Kendra settled down on a boulder to wait for him to fulfill his obligation. He had to catch the skipper before the Palisades Princess left. Running and waving his arms to make sure they saw him, he arrived at the dock as Captain Marshall put the engine to idle. He lowered the gangplank and Brian trotted aboard.

From the boulders surrounded by waves beating the rocks, Kendra couldn't hear what they were saying, but the captain glanced in her direction. Brian and Captain Marshall moved toward the captain's cabin and Lenny stood at the top of the gangplank as if guarding it. She knew they had to call the sheriff and didn't want anyone going ashore and messing up any evidence that might be there.

***

"She planning on staying here?" The captain glanced back at Kendra still sitting on the boulder.

"Not exactly," said Brian. "We got trouble. Better call the sheriff and keep folks on board – except Lenny. He can help until the sheriff comes."

"Something in the water over there?"

Brian nodded and Captain Marshall started walking to the cabin. He called over his shoulder, "Hey, Richardson, keep folks on the boat."

Lenny moved to the top of the gangplank and stood feet apart, arms crossed. Brian followed the captain.

"Another body?" Captain Marshall asked as he punched in his phone to call shore.

Brian nodded. "'Fraid so."

Captain Marshall gave the message into the phone and turned back to Brian. "He'll be along soon as he gathers Doc and his gear. You better stay – maybe Richardson too. The Donovan girl is level headed, but her and the sheriff are like oil and water."

"We'll watch her," said Brian, glad the skipper had been the one to tell him to stay. He intended to anyway, but less chance of blowing his cover this way.

"Come on Lenny," he said when he got back to the gangplank. "Skipper suggests we stay with Kendra until the sheriff arrives."

"As soon as you're down, I'll take the boat out for another round. Keep inquisitive eyes from getting in the way."

"Good idea, Captain," said Brian.

He and Lenny started back to the boulders. Kendra was still sitting where he had left her. *Calm as can be. She must have nerves of steel.*

Brian had met many women in the government, some who could be just as calm under pressure. He had only known Kendra Donovan since yesterday – except for what Severs had told him. Somehow, the picture of a hysterical, nosey, child didn't fit. He'd seen her in Severs' office and he'd seen her with Vincent. She could be hard as iron, but he had seen a softer, gentler side that he never saw in any of his women colleagues. *Severs is dead wrong about this girl.*

***

Kendra waited watching a school of perch swim by and a gull perched on another boulder, ready to dive for a treat. Slithering across the wet sand, a water snake made its way to a sunny rock. The smell of dead fish, which often scented the shores of small lakes, was missing. This lake was spring fed and clear. Pollution hadn't found its way to this utopia – at least some pollution. She glanced back at the body lying in the shallow pool.

The paddleboat's motor revved. Brian and Lenny ran down the gangplank. Captain Marshall pulled it aboard and turned back to the lake. Brian and Lenny started for the boulders.

"Maybe we better get him out of the water," said Lenny. "I don't think there's much chance of messing up any evidence."

"Probably right," said Brian and they started toward the body.

Kendra joined them and watched as they pulled the man ashore. Brian glanced at her as if he thought she might faint, or get sick. She ignored his look. She was more interested in the dead man. Although he was badly decomposed she had a feeling, she had known him from somewhere.

"Someone you know?" Brian must have seen the hint of recognition in her eyes.

"What?" She pretended not to hear then shook her head. "Sorry. I was thinking he looked familiar, but it's a little hard to tell."

"Possibly someone from your past," said Brian.

"Probably someone who resembled someone I once knew," she said.

"It might take the sheriff a while. We may as well sit on one of those boulders in the shade." Lenny was already moving toward the stones.

***

They waited, each lost in thought for what seemed hours,

although it was probably only about twenty minutes. Then a buzz – like a giant bumblebee from the direction of the lodge drifted across the lake. As the sound grew louder, Kendra shaded her eyes and saw movement.

"See him coming?" Lenny asked.

"A dot on the horizon speeding closer."

Within a minute or so, the police marine vehicle skipped across the water as if it were a speedboat. Sheriff Paul Brooks zipped into the docking area so close that he added a streak of blue paint to the dock. He killed the motor mere seconds before running the boat aground. Doc Jones, the resident doctor for Palisades wasn't a coroner, but the sheriff often called him for cases at the lake. He scowled and muttered something under his breath. Paul laughed like a kid who had just pulled a practical joke.

"He hasn't changed much, has he?" Kendra commented.

Lenny laughed. "Did you really think he would?"

"No, but surely…oh, never mind. Hopefully he has sense enough to conduct an investigation on a body that looks like murder."

"What makes you say think it was murder?" asked Brian, turning abruptly to face her. "The poor man could have fallen overboard from his fishing boat."

She glanced at Lenny, then back at Brian. "I saw the hole in the back of his head. I'm not blind."

"You're probably right, Kendra," said Lenny, "but…maybe you better not point it out to Paul. He hasn't changed that much and you know how he hates to be shown up." Lenny glanced at her with a troubled look.

"But…" She wanted to ask what was going on. Lenny combed his fingers through his hair and Kendra realized he was using their finger language to tell her they would talk later. "I guess you're right," she said. "It will all work out eventually."

Lenny winked at her and Kendra was glad he still remembered their secret language. Brian looked at them as if they were children playing a game he didn't understand. And maybe they were.

Sheriff Brooks swaggered over to the boulders with one hand resting on the butt of his gun and the thumb of the other hand hooked through a belt loop. He was still tall and slim almost to the point of being emaciated. His dark hair had receded leaving a higher forehead than Kendra remembered from childhood. The hooknose and sneer were still prominent and steel gray eyes glared at the three of them. *He looks much older than he is and acts as juvenile as he did when we were children.*

"Well, well, well. Kendra Donovan," Paul gloated. "I might have known *you* would be here. Always could depend on you being wherever there's trouble. I suppose you know what this is all about."

"Why would I know anything about it? I was just walking across the boulders and saw the body in the water." Kendra forced herself to look more relaxed than she felt. With Paul Brooks, one never knew what direction his diabolical mind would take. Truth had nothing to do with it. Paul created his own version of truth.

"Sure you did." His caustic tone said he didn't believe her. "Probably pushed him in, or pitched him over your shoulder like you did Vincent."

*How does he know about Vincent since the Palisades Princess hasn't docked yet? Captain Marshall wouldn't have told him.* Kendra decided it wasn't worth pursuing at this point. He was practically accusing her of murder and that she would address. Because the sun was behind him, she had to squint, but it also prevented him from seeing the anger in her eyes, not that it would have stopped her.

"Paul Brooks, you are even crazier than you were when we were kids. You might want to examine the body before you start hurling accusations, considering I just got here yesterday and that man has obviously been in the water much longer than that."

Paul continued to sneer and threw a warning glance at Lenny who ducked his head onto his folded arms and snickered. "And of course Leonard Richardson would be here." He glanced around as if looking for someone else. "Where's the brother? The three of you were always in trouble of some kind. Oh, yes, now I remember." Paul tapped his finger against his temple as if trying to remember something important. "The brother was murdered by his father."

Kendra snapped. She leaped from the boulder and started for Paul. Brian was on his feet and had his arms around her, but she flipped him over her shoulder before she even thought about it. He landed on his back in the sand. Paul giggled and laughed like a maniac.

Lenny took a try. "Kendra baby," he said wrapping his arms around her. "Don't let him bait you like that. You're stronger than he is." Kendra relaxed and Lenny turned his dark look on the sheriff.

"That was the most despicable, low down trick I have ever heard from you, Paul Brooks."

Paul curled his lips and spat on the ground. "Everyone knows about the murder/suicide and Kendra's problem with denial. Obviously she belongs in an institution somewhere to learn to accept the inevitable truth."

"One more word, Brooks and I'll not only turn her loose on you, but I'll help her in the process. Now you better do what you came to do and leave her alone, or you'll answer to a judge on false accusations." Lenny glared at Paul while he held tightly to Kendra. She struggled, wanting to get to Paul and give him the beating of his life.

Paul stuck out his lower lip like a pouting three year old. "You always did stand up for her, but then, why not? Everyone knew you two were making out behind the cabins."

It was Lenny's turn to feel the hot flow of anger. He let go of Kendra and started after Paul. She had recovered enough to see what Paul was doing and stuck her foot out in Lenny's path. He went sprawling on his stomach in the sand.

"Paul Brooks, you haven't changed one bit," Kendra said. "How you ever became a sheriff, I'll never know. You always did goad us into doing something stupid to make you look good and make us look like delinquents. You almost did it again, but Lenny's right.

We're stronger and smarter than that. It won't work anymore. You're a jerk and always will be. If you don't need me anymore, I'm leaving."

"Where do you think you're going? I've got the only boat and if you're thinking of stealing it, I have a cell waiting for you." Paul gave her a leering look that clearly had nothing to do with the boat.

Kendra laughed and reached out a hand to Lenny then stepped over to Brian who was still lying on the ground. "Are you all right, Brian? I'm sorry."

"Remind me never to get her really angry," Brian said to Lenny. He grinned and turned back to Kendra as she helped him up. "I'm all right, but now I know how you did it." He laughed then became more serious. "The sheriff's right, however. He has the only boat, unless you plan to swim."

"I've done it before."

"Not alone. I'll swim with you. Meet you back at the lodge, Lenny."

Brian and Kendra walked into the cold water. Without a backward glance, they slowly immersed themselves in the water until their bodies adjusted to the coldness. As if they were simply out for a leisurely afternoon swim, they started toward the distant shore. They were about half way across when the Palisades Princess as if watching for them, appeared and dropped a rope ladder.

"I thought you might try something like that Kendra Donovan," said the skipper. "You always were like a fish in water and like a cat and dog with Paul Brooks. Figured you'd rather swim than ride with him. I watched for you." He chuckled as he helped them aboard.

"Thanks for the lift," grinned Brian. "I don't mind a swim, but I prefer the water to be a little warmer."

Mark met them as they boarded with no reference to the excursion. He nodded toward Vincent, who was asleep on one of the chase lounges. "Maybe he'll leave you alone now," he said.

"Maybe, but I doubt it. Why in the world wasn't he wearing a life jacket if he can't swim? He's not only drunk, he's stupid to boot." Kendra glared at the sleeping man and his friends who surrounded him ready to protect him from the vicious female.

Mark didn't bother to explain why he didn't try to help her, nor did he mention the body that they'd found. *Probably has something to do with being a minister and not wanting to get involved with violence.*

"Do you still feel up to dinner at the *Italian Café* tonight?"

"I'm fine, Mark. The swim, or maybe I should say swims, were just what I needed to get rid of some of the cobwebs in my mind. Better make it seven, though. Finding that body put us a little behind schedule," Kendra said as she slipped into her shorts, T-shirt and sandals.

"*Italian Café*?" Brian asked as he put on his shirt and shoes.

"Mark invited me to an Italian restaurant north of Fairplain. Must be something new. There never was anything like that around before." Kendra combed her fingers through her still wet hair.

"Seems like Lenny said something about Paul starting a Country Western theme restaurant near Fairplain," said Brian.

"That's the one," said Mark. "It went belly up about three years ago. Paul ran for sheriff and a couple of brothers from down south somewhere bought it."

"It's been a while since I had Italian food," said Brian. "Maybe Lenny and I will try out this new place."

Kendra turned, hands on hips, jaw tight and stared at him. "Are you guys following me for some reason?"

"No, we're following you for no reason. There always seem to be fireworks when you're around." Brian laughed again as she turned and stalked to the opposite end of the boat where she sat alone watching the scenery until the boat docked at the lodge. Her mind was still whirling – trying to process the events of the last couple of days.

# Sixteen

Not waiting for either Brian or Mark to offer to walk her home, Kendra was one of the first passengers to disembark.

"Thanks, Captain Marshall," she called as she headed for the gangplank.

"Thank you, Miss Donovan. It's been about ten years since I've had so much excitement on a simple cruise around the lake." His laughter followed her as she stepped onto the dock.

She turned around, shielded her eyes with her hand and called up to him, "Maybe we'll try again."

He laughed again. "Give me a few days to recover," he said.

Kendra smiled and started toward the cabin, wondering if they would have a few days left before disaster struck.

A few small animals and birds greeted her as she hurried down the lane. *I don't hear anyone following me, but then I left everyone on the boat that usually does the following – except Lenny.*

Angel met her at the door with a catnip mouse in her mouth. She dropped it at Kendra's feet and turned her green eyes on her expectantly.

"You want to play, sweetie? All right," Kendra said stooping to pick up the toy. "Just for a few minutes then I'll feed you and get dressed."

She threw the toy across the floor. Angel scampered after it, pounced on it then batted it back and forth until it came back to Kendra, who threw it again and started toward the kitchen. Angel abandoned the toy and trotted after her.

Kendra fed the cat then headed for the shower. By the time she was back in the bedroom, Angel was sitting on her bed washing her face, ears and whiskers. While Kendra pulled on white slacks and a yellow button-up blouse, Angel moved to the corner of the dresser watching Kendra brush her long black hair until the shine reflected in the mirror. When she inserted tiny, gold butterfly earrings, Angel put a paw in the jewelry box to push small, shiny objects around. Kendra picked her up and placed her on the bed.

"Sorry Angel," she said, "you can't play with those things."

Angel glared, swished her tail and jumped from the bed. She swaggered into the front room, where she leaped to a favorite corner of the couch. Kendra closed the door to the bedroom and removed the lid from the *bug* box. When she saw Mark's car coming down the lane, she said goodbye to Angel and went to the porch to wait for him.

Mark wore dark slacks and a gray polo shirt. Kendra was surprised that he wasn't *in uniform* – clerical collar. He made a big deal of hurrying around to open the door and taking her hand as she stepped off the porch.

"You look refreshed and beautiful tonight," he said as he helped her into the car.

"Thank you, Mark." Kendra gave him a non-committal smile as she let him help her into his black Lincoln Continental. "This is quite a car for a poor preacher," she said when he slid into the driver's seat.

Mark looked defensive then laughed. "It's part of the package deal from the church," he said. "They thought it would help me snag a quality wife – whatever that might mean."

Kendra had to laugh with him. She couldn't imagine a church like that. Certainly, her church in Akron would never presume to run the pastor's life in that way, but, each to his own. "Well, it's certainly impressive."

They passed under the arch and turned north onto the highway toward Fairplain. Kendra leaned back and relaxed in the super-size, black leather seat. Glancing out the window at the twilight's clear sky and gentle breeze, she wondered if her family was enjoying the evening and if they worried about her. Feeling Mark's eyes on her, she remarked, "This is a beautiful night to end a beautiful day."

"Yes, it is," Mark agreed. "It certainly was a busy day for you." His tone of voice was indecipherable, angry more than pleasant.

Kendra glanced sideways at him, but Mark was looking straight ahead and she couldn't see his eyes. *What is he getting at?* She decided to ignore his innuendoes and take the words at face value. "It was a good day, except for the encounter with Vincent and finding a body. What's his problem anyway?"

"He seems to think you owe him something."

"Why would he think that? I don't even know him. I wouldn't even know his name is Vincent, except he told me."

"You didn't know him from when you and your family vacationed here before?" Mark sounded like he didn't believe her. "He told me he used to come here every summer."

"If he was here, I don't remember him. Lenny is the only one I remember from childhood, but then he, my brother and I spent a lot of time together. Since we all came for the entire summer, we didn't really get to know many of the other kids who only came for a week or two at the most. I remember Paul Brooks because he lived around here. Anyway, maybe Vincent will cool off by tomorrow." Kendra smiled to herself remembering flipping him over the side of the boat.

"Did you enjoy your excursion with Brian McNeil?"

Surprised at his tone of voice as well as subject of conversation, Kendra turned abruptly to stare at him. He sounded petulant and jealous. "What is that supposed to mean? I enjoyed my swim to the island. I didn't know Brian would follow me. But, yes, we had a nice chat and walk to the other side of the island. He didn't think it was safe for me to swim that far alone. He came along in case I got in trouble."

"You don't need to explain to me, Kendra. It's your own business if you want to…"

"Mark! You sound like a jealous boyfriend. You're a minister so I can't believe you're jealous and you certainly aren't my boyfriend." Kendra didn't bother trying to keep the annoyance out of her voice.

Mark scowled emitting a sound that was supposed to be a laugh, but it was more cynical than joyful and left Kendra with the feeling that he didn't believe her. She stared at him.

Mark glanced sideways at her and said, "Sorry Kendra. You're right. I have no reason to be jealous, but ministers are human too, you know. We have the same feelings that everyone else has. Maybe I'm letting the church's edict to find a wife, control my actions more than I thought."

They drove through Fairplain, a little town of about 2500 people. Familiar buildings in which she and David had spent many happy hours rummaging still stood waiting for customers – the general store, ice cream parlor, even the hardware store. Some needed a coat of paint, but were pretty much the same as the last time she was there. At one time, a miniature golf course was on the edge of town. Like so many memories, it was gone now.

"Good memories?" Mark asked.

"Yes." She saw no reason to elaborate.

The remaining miles slipped by in silence. Thoughts whirled like an out of control carrousel. Kendra didn't dare chance speaking. One of the flying horses of memory was bound to escape and get away from her. Thankfully, Mark respected her reverie and didn't press the issue of her afternoon's activities further.

"There it is," he said, not needing to point it out. The large green neon sign could be seen for several miles away – *Italian Café.*

Mark maneuvered the car into a spot at the edge of the parking lot. "Looks like it's a busy place," Kendra commented glancing at the number of cars that already dotted the lot. The flashing neon sign looked even larger and more overpowering close up that it did at a distance. They certainly knew they were at the *Italian Café.* The plate glass window identified it further offering *The best pasta in Michigan.*

"I've been here a number of times," Mark said. "They have a good variety of Italian pastas as well as good entertainment. I think the brothers will make a go of it." He got out and walked around the car to give Kendra a hand. She was glad for his arm since he had parked off the paved lot. The ground was uneven in that unlit corner.

As they walked through the entrance, Kendra took in the size and shape of the room, a habit developed in earlier years when she, David and Lenny looked for a way out as if they were chasing spies, no matter where they went. The room was larger than it looked from the outside. The eating area extended toward the back and off to one side, giving the building more of a square look with a wing to the right. Tables and booths filled the area. Mark led the way to the extension where more booths lined the wall, allowing more privacy.

Kendra scanned the restaurant to acquaint herself with her surroundings look for familiar faces. Seeing no one she recognized, a feeling of unexplained disappointment settled over her. Did she really expect to see someone? Although Brian teased earlier on the boat, she felt comfortable and safe with him around. Maybe he would show up later.

Mark took her arm and led to a booth at the back corner of the room. Hurricane lanterns hung over each booth and covered candles stood on each of the tables, providing a soft romantic atmosphere. Red and white checkered cloths covered each table and booth with large red linen napkins wrapped around the silverware at each place.

Most booths in that section were empty, but Mark wanted the one in the farthest corner. Two elderly men occupied the booth connected to it. He mumbled something under his breath that sounded a lot like profanity. Kendra raised her eyebrows in question. Mark's forehead furrowed into a frown. "Why do those old men have to sit there?"

"We can sit somewhere else if they bother you," she said with a touch of sarcasm.

"But I want the end one. It's more private," he said sounding more like an unreasonable child than a minister. "Maybe I can ask them to move to another booth."

"Mark, it isn't that important. We aren't going to talk about anything that a couple of older men enjoying the night out can't hear. They probably have hearing problems anyway."

"I suppose you're right, Kendra. I just wanted you alone." Kendra ignored his attempt at being caring and followed him to the booth at the end. *If he really wanted to be alone with me, he could have come to my cabin.*

She smiled at the old men as she walked by their booth then turned quickly back to Mark, who was chattering on about something. *I would know Lenny's eyes anywhere and Brian's gray-green eyes aren't very easily disguised either. What are they up to? Are their disguises for my benefit or someone else's? Whatever, I'll play along with them until I can ask.*

Kendra slid into the seat with the back adjacent to the booth the men occupied. She knew Brian was right behind her and for some reason that gave her a sense of wellbeing. Mark stood for a minute staring at her. She knew he wanted her to slide over so he could sit next to her, but Kendra ignored him and pretended to examine the menu on the table. Mark glared then slid into the opposite side without saying a word.

"Bring us a bottle of white wine," he said as the waiter stopped at their table.

Kendra smiled at the waiter and said, "Make mine iced tea please – unsweetened."

Mark glowered. "Kendra that wasn't very considerate of you. You must learn to accept a gift. A glass of wine with your meal isn't really the same as drinking cocktails."

Kendra laughed. "Mark, lighten up. You aren't my father, my brother or my keeper. I don't care for alcohol in any form. That is simply my preference. You're the one who was discourteous when you ordered it for me when you should have known I didn't want it."

Mark stared at her then laughed – at least he made an effort. His eyes were hard and cold. "You're right – again, Kendra. Sorry. I'm just not getting off to a very good start tonight, am I?"

Kendra smiled not bothering to affirm or deny the obvious.

The waiter returned with their drinks and took the order. "So,

Kendra, are you making any progress in your search for truth?" Mark asked.

"Mark the truth is always with us, but you know that. If you mean am I coming to terms with my problems, I don't know. I'm still struggling."

"I thought you were searching for your family."

"Mark, whatever gave you that idea? I told you they were all killed in an accident. I'll never accept that my father took his own life and that of my mother, brother and sister. That's the only truth I'm looking for – a way to clear my father's name. I came here hoping I would find…I don't know… memories to chase away the feeling of loneliness? Friends to reassure me? Maybe I'll go away relieved, maybe I won't. I had to try."

"Kendra, your father was in the FBI. Surely, he made some enemies in his lifetime. Did you ever think that someone set him up and the rest of the family just happened to be in the wrong place at the wrong time?"

Kendra stared at him. *Why is everyone so interested in my father's activities?* "I suppose anything is possible," she answered, picking up her glass for a sip of tea.

"Didn't he ever say anything about any of his cases? Maybe that would give you an idea that you could take to the FBI and…I don't know…maybe get them to investigate."

Kendra felt more and more confused, but sipped her tea until she could respond without anger. "Mark, you're not the first to suggest that I should know something about my father's work. My father was *always* a professional. His business was decisively confidential. Never once did he even accidentally slip and say something that might compromise an assignment. He was on vacation and business should not have interfered. Whatever happened to my family, I know he did everything in his power to prevent it and protect them as well as he would have done any case he was working on. I may never know the complete truth, but I will always believe that in life, or in death, my father and integrity were synonymous."

The waiter brought the food, interrupting their conversation. When he left, Mark apparently decided to abandon that topic. "Didn't I tell you this is the best pasta around?"

Kendra sampled a bite and smiled. "It's marvelous. Thank you for thinking about me. I haven't tasted spaghetti sauce like this in years."

"Oh, you would consider this on par with other pastas you've eaten?" Mark smiled as he sipped his wine.

"Only one. A friend in college took me home with him several times. His mother made a sauce that was so close it would be difficult to tell the difference.

"You can remember tastes that well?" Mark raised his eyebrows and looked at her as if he thought she was kidding.

"Some things you never forget. I guess it's associated with pleasure in general." She refused to accept his bait for an argument.

"Oh? This college friend, you liked him a lot?"

"Mark, don't let that green-eyed monster raise his ugly head again. Next you'll be asking me if I was ever involved with Lenny."

"That's a good question. Were you?"

"Mark!"

"Kendra, I don't want to sound jealous. Maybe I am, but I don't think you know Lenny any more. He's changed since you were children." Mark sipped his wine and watched her over the rim of his glass.

"Really? And how would you know that?" Had Mark known Kendra very well, he would have known she was on the edge of exploding anger.

"Don't get all huffy," Mark laughed. "We all change. I'm just saying you have to be careful. You're vulnerable in your grief. Some of these guys will take advantage of that."

"Like Brian McNeil?" Kendra raised one eyebrow and glanced at Mark, a fork of food halfway to her mouth.

"You don't know him at all, do you? Personally, I think he puts on a good act. He's no more a rich playboy looking for a good time than I am, at least not with a pretty girl."

"Mark, what are you trying to say? Spit it out and get it out of your system." Kendra laid her fork down, picked up her napkin, dabbed at her mouth and stared across the table at him.

"Only that I've heard rumors that he's gay. I would hate for you fall for him and then get hurt."

"Brian McNeil? Gay? Mark, you're out of your mind."

"Am I? Have you ever noticed the way he hangs around Lenny?"

"Lenny?" Kendra shook her head, a frown furrowing her brow. Surely, she wasn't hearing what she thought she was.

"Sure. It's pretty well known that musicians are that way."

Kendra stared at him, her mouth open in disbelief. Then she laughed until tears ran down her face. "Mark, I think that wine you're drinking has gone to your head. I'm sure Lenny has changed in the years since I knew him as a child, but not that much. He's as straight as…as…my brother David. I trust him like I would my brother and if he says Brian McNeil is all right, which he hasn't, because I haven't asked, I would believe him implicitly."

"Kendra," Mark sounded injured and close to anger, "you said yourself Lenny and your brother spent a lot of time together. Maybe…"

Kendra threw her napkin down on the table and slid out of the booth. "Good night, Mark. I'll see myself home." She started to walk away.

# Seventeen

Mark jumped to his feet and grabbed Kendra's arm as she started away from the booth. "Kendra, I'm sorry," he said. "That was totally out of line. As you said, it must be the wine. Come on finish your dinner. No more of that kind of talk. Let me tell you about my church."

Kendra stared at him. Feeling others watching, she decided it wasn't worth a scene. They had been standing beside Lenny and Brian's booth. Lenny was drumming on the table – or so it seemed. He was swearing in their finger language. Both men had moved as if to get up and follow her if she left.

"Sorry," she murmured to the *two old men,* then shrugged and ran her fingers through her hair. With that same finger language, she told Lenny to watch his language and turned to go back to finish dinner. Suddenly Lenny began coughing and choking.

"You all right, Bart?" His friend looked concerned. Kendra turned around to see if he needed help.

"I be fine," he wheezed. "I be fine."

Kendra returned to their booth and sat down. Mark, true to his word, talked about his church, ad nauseam, until the waiter took away the empty plates. Before she could ask to go, she heard violins playing. Knowing that style, she glanced up at Mark. "Music?"

"That's the owners, Tony Estrada and his brother Giorgio. They serenade the guests for an hour or so each night when most of the rush is over. You want them to play for you? Name it, they'll play it."

"Blue Spanish Eyes," she said without hesitation.

Mark looked surprised, but hailed the waiter and told him to tell

Tony what Kendra wanted. She slid over and looked around the corner of the booth, watching the waiter take the message to the brothers, who were moving toward that section as they played. Waiting until the brothers finished the number they were playing, the waiter gave them the request. Tony said something to him. The waiter pointed toward their booth.

Tony grinned broadly and spoke to his brother, who also grinned. They began to play *Blue Spanish Eyes* and strolled toward the booth. There they concluded the number, adding a little run of arpeggios with a different twist. Kendra clapped her hands and laughed like a child who had just received a long coveted gift.

"Kendra Donovan!" Tony handed his violin to his brother, slid in beside her, threw his arms around her and planted a kiss on her lips. "Padre, why didn't you tell me you knew the love of my life?"

Mark looked as if he would explode. Kendra laughed again. Letting Tony hold her hand, she looked up at his brother. "Giorgio, how are you? How did you ever let your brother talk you into a venture like this?"

"Kendra, sweetheart, you know how he is. Besides, it's a good living."

"Is Mamma Estrada with you? That's her sauce."

"You remembered! No, Mamma passed on a few years ago, but she gave me the recipe and my Maria makes it almost as good. You still play?"

"Yes. I didn't finish school, but I keep up my music."

"Giorgio, give the lady your fiddle. We make music together."

"Tony, not here! Not now."

"Why not?" Tony grinned, slid out of the booth pulling Kendra with him. He handed her his brother's violin. "Here we go, follow me if you can."

"Tony Estrada, I can play anything you can play – and better." Kendra said as she stood beside him. Rapidly his fingers ran across the strings in a melody. Kendra's fingers found the same notes and her bow flew back and forth as she repeated it. Tony repeated the melody and Kendra went into a countermelody, as if they had played together for years. They laughed with joy making their violins sing together. Mark glared. Almost twenty minutes later, Kendra noticed the scowl on Mark's face, laughed and signaled Tony to wrap it up. They finished with the little arpeggio flourish that he had used before.

Applause erupted from the other customers, calling for more. Kendra had been too involved in the music to notice that they were the center of attention. She blushed with pleasure. She could have gone on for hours, but she and Tony bowed to the applause.

"Thank you," Kendra said then handed the violin back to Giorgio. "Thank you, Giorgio. That was fun, Tony. Thank you for asking me."

"Kendra, you can come and play anytime you want. I'll even give you dinner on the house."

Before Kendra could respond to Tony's invitation, another familiar shadow towered over her and an even more familiar voice boomed, "Well, if it ain't little Miss Wonder Woman."

Kendra whirled around and saw Vincent swaying over to her. She turned to Mark, picked up her purse and said, "I think we better leave. I don't want any more trouble."

Mark got up, but didn't move quickly enough. Vincent loomed over her, blowing his alcohol breath in her face. "You and me have some unfinished business." He laughed a harsh horselaugh as he reached for her.

"Vincent, please leave me alone. I have nothing against you, so why do you insist on harassing me?"

"Because you're beautiful and you think you are somebody and because your father was a big shot FBI Agent. Well he got what was coming to him and so will you. I'm somebody too and when I want something, I get what I want."

"Then apparently you want some more of what I gave you before, because that's all you'll get if you don't leave me alone."

"Not this time girlie. I have some back up."

Vincent grabbed both of her arms and started to pull her closer to him. The rest of the boys surrounded them on three sides, pushing her against the table where Lenny and Brian sat. She couldn't run and they couldn't get out of the booth to help her.

"You touch me and my brother will take you down in a hurry," said Vincent and tried to pull her into an embrace. He didn't seem to notice how unsteady he was on his feet.

"Vincent, you'll never learn, will you?" Kendra dropped to the floor. Surprised and slow to react, Vincent let go and started to sway. Kendra rolled into his legs like a bowling ball after the spare. He toppled into his circle of friends. Kendra jumped to her feet and ran for the door, hoping Mark would have the car waiting. He did. She was in the car and they were on their way back to the cabin before Vincent hardly knew she was gone. From the side mirror, Kendra saw another car leave the lot. *Vincent? Lenny and Brian?* Whoever it was passed Mark's car as soon as they were on the main highway.

They arrived back at the cabin and Mark walked to the door with her. He waited for Kendra to open it.

"Kendra, I don't want to butt in where it's none of my business, but you seem to be running into trouble at every turn with Vincent. Don't you think you ought to maybe…?"

"Go home? Sorry Mark, but I've never let people like Vincent prevent me from doing what I have to do. I came for a relaxing vacation to relive good memories and I refuse to leave until I'm ready to go."

"Kendra, he can be pretty nasty."

"I've noticed," she said, "but I can be nastier if need be. I have nothing against Vincent. I don't even know him. I don't understand why he has latched on to me, but I hope he gets over it soon. If he would sober up, I think he would be a different person."

"Kendra, I'm not a violent man. I can't stand violence of any kind. Please don't expect me to back you up when you get in too deep."

"Mark, I didn't ask for trouble from Vincent, from the FBI or from anyone else and I haven't asked for help in dealing with them. When I can no longer handle the Vincent's of this world, I will seek help from those who are trained for that kind of trouble. You offered kindness when I was hurting. That's your profession. That's all I ask of you."

"Kendra, I hope we can move beyond that point before your vacation is over."

"Mark, please don't say anymore. I'm not interested in anything beyond getting my life back together and understanding what happened to my family."

"You'll want more before you leave, Kendra. I'll give you time. Can I come in for a cup of coffee?"

"I think I've had enough conversation for one day," Kendra said. "I'm really tired."

"I understand. Goodnight, Kendra." Mark leaned over to kiss her, but Kendra backed away, offering her cheek instead of her lips. Mark left and she entered the cabin to find Angel with her fur standing on edge and her back arched. She hissed and spat at the door but began to relax when Kendra picked her up and stroked her fur.

"It's all right, Angel. Did you have a bad time while I was gone? Come on, I'll get you a snack and we'll call it a night. Tomorrow has to be better. Hopefully Vincent will get the message and leave me alone."

# Eighteen

The car plunged over the cliff. It tumbled, rolled and bounced until nothing but the cloud of dust and smoke drifted from the valley. Faces of David and Shelly rose above the canyon like wisps of fog then broke apart as if the morning sun had risen. Forms like Calvin and Sarah Donovan followed. Calvin tried to send Kendra a message by blowing on a tree as he passed, sending tiny branches tapping at her window in a weird sort of Morse code combined with her secret finger language.

Kendra's eyes flew open. She sat upright in the bed and pushed her sweat-soaked hair out of her face with trembling hands. Taking several deep breaths to clear her mind of the nightmare's residue, Kendra waited for reality. But the vision stuck tenaciously like tiny little spiders clinging to a web blown about in the wind. Feeling her heart rate slow and the silvery threads of the vision depart, she reached for Angel and clutched her for comfort.

"It had to be a dream," she whispered. "Dad doesn't know our secret language. But, I still hear the tapping branch on the window. Maybe a new storm is blowing in."

Kendra shook her head and listened to the light tap, tap, tap. That wasn't coming from a tree branch against the window. Someone was at her window. She reached for the phone and remembered Brian's warning not to use the phones. He never said why, but… Still damp and shivering from the nightmare, Kendra set Angel back on the bed and shoved aside the blanket.

Moon and stars were visible through the window. No storm clouds in sight. The digital clock beside the bed said one o'clock. The tapping became more urgent and persistent. It definitely wasn't a part of the nightmare.

Angel stretched then jumped to the floor. Kendra grabbed her robe and moved toward the window as she tied the sash. Shadows fell across her room as the moonlight silhouetted the form of a man outside. She knew that build and hair even without seeing the face.

Kendra slid the window open and Brian put a finger to his lips to keep her from crying out. "What are you doing out there?" Common sense told her she should be shouting for help, but she wasn't frightened, only surprised.

"Let me in and I'll explain," he said just above a whisper.

Kendra hesitated, wondering what to do. *After all, it is the middle of the night. And what do I really know about Brian McNeil? Not much. I should call security for help.*

Brian must have sensed her indecision. "Kendra, it's very important. Please believe me, I wouldn't think of doing this if there were any other way."

*Any other way for what? Brian is with the FBI. Does he have some information about my family? Maybe he...* Kendra abandoned the questions, came to grips with her indecision and whispered back, "Come to the back door and be quiet."

Brian didn't wait for her to explain, but started around the corner of the house to the back door. Kendra hurried through the cabin, switching on a lamp in the living area and the light over the sink in the kitchen. She was already unlocking the door when he reached for it. He started in and she motioned with a finger to her lips for him not to say anything.

He gave her a curious look and followed her back to the main room. Kendra walked over to the lamp by the front door and spoke as if someone stood next to it.

"Angel," she said, trying to sound full of worry and sympathy. "What's the matter, sweetie? Did you eat something that didn't agree with you? Come on, Sweetie," she continued, "I'll fix something for you. Poor baby, you'll be all right. Come on, sweetie."

Having given this long speech to someone or some *thing* that wasn't anywhere near, Kendra placed a lid on the little white box on the table. Brian continued to stare with a curious smile on his face. Silently he followed her back to the kitchen.

"Are you going to explain what was that all about?" he asked in a voice just above a whisper.

"No. Are you going to tell me why you're here in the middle of the night?" She spoke just as softly.

"No. I'm feeling a little wobbly on my legs," he said slurring his words as if he had suddenly become drunk.

"Brian, what…?"

"Shhh," he put his finger to his lips. "I was out there…shomewhere…drank too much." He swung his arm around to indicate somewhere outside and lost his balance in the process, falling against Kendra's shoulder. She reached to steady him.

"Brian you were as sober as I am two minutes ago." The old feeling of confusion surrounded her.

Brian tried to straighten up and pulled away from her. "That's the problem," he said. "It hits me shud…shuddenly. I knew you would let me stay here."

"Brian you can't stay here. I'll call Mark." Kendra was horrified at the thought of him spending the night in her house, not that she was afraid of him or necessarily concerned about what people would say. She just needed to understand.

"No!" He was suddenly very sober and very much against calling Mark. But just as quickly, he slipped back into his apparent drunken state. "Mark don't like me."

"Then I'll call Lenny."

"No, not in his room…please, Kendra. Let me sleep it off. I promise I won't even try to…to…kish you." He gave her a crooked grin.

"Brian, I don't understand."

"Please, Kendra." He turned his gray-green eyes on her pleading like a ten year old asking to stay up late and watch a special movie.

Kendra took a deep breath, ran her fingers through her hair to comb out doubts and confusion. Finally she said, "Wait here a minute." She went back to the closet at the end of the sleeping area. She took sheets and made up the bed in the room across the hall from her room then returned to the kitchen with Angel at her heels. The cat strolled over to Brian and began rubbing against his ankles, purring loudly.

"She likes me." He grinned and picked Angel up, stroking her soft fur.

Kendra smiled. "Brian, meet Angel. Angel, meet Brian."

"Angel?" Brian laughed as if he suddenly understood what she had done earlier. "She was the diversion?"

"Uh-huh. Brian, I don't understand what you're doing here, but I won't ask you to explain. I believe you would tell me if you could and I know why you can't. Don't ask me how I know. And don't ask me why I trust you, but drunk or sober, I do." She flashed him her best *I like you* smile.

"Come on," she said. "I've fixed a bed in one of the other rooms for you and unless you want someone to know you're here, refrain from talking or moving about too much."

"*Bug*?" he asked nodding toward the front room?

"Yes." Kendra wasn't surprised that he knew. If anything, she felt pleased that he was professional enough to know and respect it.

They started toward the hall and Kendra stopped to open the box on the table and click the lamp off. "Feel better now, Angel?" I said. "Come on then sweetie. Let's go back to bed. If you aren't better in the morning, I'll find a vet for you. That's my girl."

Angel jumped to the table and purred near the box. Kendra smiled at her, picked her up and started back to bed, nodding toward the room across the hall for Brian.

He grinned and kissed her on the forehead. "You said you wouldn't do that," Kendra whispered.

"I'm drunk. I don't know what I'm saying, or doing," he answered.

Kendra put her hand over her mouth to smother the sudden laugh that bubbled up. Pushing him into the room, she closed the door behind him then returned to her own room, closing the door quietly so the *bug* would only pick up the sound of one door closing. She would find out eventually what Brian was up to – probably sooner than she wanted to know. Angel curled up beside her and they were both soon asleep.

# Nineteen

Something brushed against Kendra's cheek then landed with a light thump on her chest. Startled, her eyes flew open. A cry of alarm was working its way to her lips, when she saw two round green eyes staring at her. Angel tapped a soft paw against her cheek again and butted her head against Kendra's chin. Relieved, she wrapped her hands around the cat and held Angel against her face, smiling with contentment. For a brief moment, she'd forgotten her grief and frustration.

Outside birds sang their morning song around their breakfast table. A squirrel in the tree chattered as if scolding Kendra for sleeping so late. She set Angel down and followed the cat's example, stretching first one arm and then the other, then standing to stretch her arms toward the ceiling.

She was rested and ready to face another day, hopefully one without a sight of Vincent Whoever. Maybe she would find some answers today. Kendra stopped mid-stretch. Someone was in the cabin. She heard movement. A tingle of panic shot through her. She reached for the phone then remembered her late night visitor – Brian.

"Oh no, I hope he remembers the *bug*," she said to Angel, who jumped off the bed, trotted to the door and waited for it to open. Kendra grabbed her robe, slipped into her slippers beside the bed and hurried after Angel.

She opened the door just as Brian called from the living area where he was sure to be heard by the little butterfly *bug*. "Kendra, sweetheart, where do you keep the coffee filters?"

He moved down the hall and she ran straight into his open arms. "Brian, are you out of your mind?" Kendra was so confused she forgot to keep her own voice down.

He laughed as her hand flew to cover her mouth. "Just wanted some coffee and maybe a bite to eat," he said louder than was necessary. "All that bedtime activity made me hungry." He laughed again at the look of horror that crossed her face. She felt the color rise to her cheeks as the intent of his words registered.

"Brian…" Kendra wasn't sure what to say. The damage had been done. If anyone was listening to the *bug* they already knew Brian was there and had been there all night. The assumption would be clear. Before she could remind him of all this, he pulled her closer to him and pressed his lips firmly against hers.

While Kendra caught her breath, Brian whispered close to her ear, "Sorry, but this is the way it has to be for now." He kissed her again, giving her time to absorb his words.

*He wants whoever is listening to know he is here. Why?*

"Okay?" He whispered, still holding her close. Kendra nodded, so he released her.

She stared at him for a moment, trying to understand her emotions. She should be incensed, but she wasn't. She should be embarrassed, but it all felt so…comfortable…and normal. She shook her head, took a deep breath and pushed past him. Two could play his little game.

"Why didn't you wake me sooner?" she said moving toward the kitchen. "The least I can do is make a good breakfast in exchange for a most enjoyable night."

Kendra didn't wait for his answer, but heard him gasp and then burst into laughter as he followed her to the kitchen. She put on the coffee and fed Angel then began frying bacon and preparing scrambled eggs. She could feel Brian watching her as she worked, but didn't trust herself to look at him.

She heard him move toward her then felt his presence before he placed his hands on her shoulders, the warmth of his breath near her ear as he spoke. "Kendra, I'm sorry if I've caused you any embarrassment or pain. I don't want to hurt you."

"I'm all right," she said, "just confused."

"I hope nothing comes of this," he said, "but I needed to be prepared just in case. Someday I hope we can really be honest with each other." His breath caressed her hair sending more confusion surging through her.

"I would like that," she whispered. "It's hard not being able to talk to anyone, not even Angel, without worrying about someone listening."

"How long have you known about the *bug*?" He still kept his hands on her shoulders.

Kendra turned around and grinned up at him, glad to move the conversation in a less emotional direction. "Since my first night here."

He looked surprised. "Do you know who put it there?"

"Uh-huh."

"Do you want to tell me?" He looked hopeful.

"Not unless you're ready to share information with me."

Brian looked deep into her eyes. She could almost feel his eyes boring into her soul. She saw indecision and knew he must be struggling with how much he could share. Severs would have given him orders not to tell her anything. She couldn't put him in the position of choosing to follow orders or give her what she wanted.

Kendra sighed. "If it's important for you to know, I'll tell you. I shouldn't ask you for information because I know you can't tell me what I want to know and I know why you can't tell me. I won't press or haggle for it again. I guess I thought the *bug* was someone playing a joke at first – like Lenny. Now, I'm not so sure why it's there."

A look of relief spread across his face. "I don't need to know about it, at least not right now. However, it's good to know I can have the information when, and if, I need it." He squeezed her shoulders and looked as if he were about to kiss her again, but thought better of it. He quickly released her and moved toward the cabinet. "Where are the plates? I'll set the table."

Breakfast finished, Brian went back to the lodge to shower and change for the day. Kendra showered and dressed in tan shorts and light teal T-shirt. It was going to be another beautiful day. *Maybe I'll find someone who will unknowingly give me a clue.*

"Maybe I'll go for an early lunch with the Franklin sisters again," Kendra said to Angel. "Although I'm not sure I'm ready to be grilled further about Dad's business. But, I'll decide that closer to lunchtime. Right now, I'm going for a walk. Be back in a little bit, sweetie."

Kendra latched the screen door so Angel could stay on the porch and sleep, then went back through the house and out the front door, locking it behind her. For a moment, she stood breathing in the fresh Michigan air – the trees, the lake, the air itself. Everything smelled fresh and clean compared to the city.

Behind the cabin, an old deer trail meandered through the woods. Kendra, David and Lenny had spent many happy times on all the paths – and even some unofficial paths that only they knew about. This one was well worn and still as she remembered it, except for possibly more undergrowth and taller trees. Animals that played in and around them were still evident. She hoped the walk would clear the cobwebs and help her think.

A squirrel grabbed something from the ground and scurried up a tree. Kendra stopped to watch. He made it to a high limb and sat holding his treasured morsel in hand-like paws, tail flipping behind him. Before Kendra could move again, a chipmunk skittered across the path, its thin little tail held high like a flag in a parade. She came to the feeder creek that fed minnows and smaller fish from Little Lake into the larger Palisades Lake. A kingfisher grabbed a small fish and flew away. Beavers had chewed on a tree to add to their home that must be nearby.

Kendra could almost hear David and Lenny laughing at her childish delight over the simple pleasures. Suddenly she stopped, hardly breathing as orange and black wings slowly emerge from a brown cocoon on a low branch. She swiped at her eyes as the beautiful butterfly, flapped its wings a few times to dry them, then lifted off and made its maiden flight.

The boys used to laugh at her sentimental tears over anything so beautiful. They said she would never play beautiful music because her tears wouldn't let her see the music. They were partly right. Tears often got in the way of her music, but she had an exceptional gift of playing – or hearing – a piece of music once and remembering it. She didn't need the music in front of her.

Reluctantly, Kendra started back to the cabin. Although the time with nature was refreshing, she didn't dare forget her reason for being at Palisades. With new resolve and determination, she strolled back to the cabin. *Maybe I can talk to Lenny today. Surely, he can enlighten me about some things.*

Kendra emerged from the woods swinging a small branch she had picked up – partly to chase away the gnats and mosquitoes, but partly just for the freedom of doing so. She started around the cabin and stopped. Paul Brooks was leaning against his cupped hands against the living area window, trying to see inside. *Why is he there and what is he looking for?*

Kendra dropped the branch and walked up behind him. "Are you looking for something, Paul?" She didn't bother to hide her irritation.

"Just looking for you, *Miss* Donovan," he said jerking around as if startled. "And the name is *Sheriff* Brooks. We ain't kids no more."

"Well, here I am *Sheriff* Brooks. What do you want?" Kendra stood with hands on hips as if expecting trouble. Paul Brooks' name was always synonymous with trouble.

"Answers." Paul didn't bother to hide his animosity.

"Do you have specific questions?"

"Not here – in my office."

A shiver of warning flickered through her. *Paul Brooks is up to something guaranteed to be no good. I'll not get any information from him, so I'll have to play along until I learn what he wants. I've had enough trouble with Vincent. I don't need more from Paul.*

She answered in what she hoped was an amiable tone of voice. "Let me get my purse and car keys and I'll follow you to Fairplain."

"Get in the squad car. I'll drive." Paul's left hand shot out and gripped her wrist in a tight grasp – his right hand reaching for the cuffs on his belt. He pulled her toward the car.

"And how am I supposed to get back?" Kendra had no reason for fear or guilt, but anger flared like a barn fire in a windstorm. The Paul Brooks she knew as a child didn't need a reason for anything he did. He would harass her just for the fun of it.

Paul snorted an evil sort of cackle. "You can either walk, or wait 'til six o'clock. I know a private little place we can go. Have to admit, I'm surprised that you entertain men over night. But, people do change, don't they?"

"What's this all about? I thought you were required to have a reason for arresting people." Kendra tried to pull away from him. Fear began to join her anger. Even Paul Brooks had never been this crazy. And how did he know about Brian?

"We'll talk at the office where I can record everything – and put you in a cell if necessary." Paul jerked her arms behind her back and clipped the handcuffs on much tighter than needed to be. When he pushed her into the back seat of the car, she fell then struggled to pull herself to a sitting position. The cuffs cut into her wrists, but Kendra ignored the pain. She wouldn't give him the satisfaction of knowing how much it hurt.

"Paul Brooks, you were crazy when we were kids. Now you're over the edge. You can't treat me like this without reading my rights or allowing me to call my lawyer."

"Shut up," He said and walked around to the driver's side. "*I'm* running this show," he said and started the car.

# Twenty

Neither of them spoke the rest of the trip to Fairplain. Kendra had a feeling he knew something she should know, but didn't. *He's trying to trick me into getting myself in trouble the way he used to do. I won't say anything – let him make the first move.*

The road to Fairplain contained few curves, but many small hills. Oncoming traffic was light, for which Kendra was thankful. Paul drove faster than the legal limit and didn't mind passing other cars – even across double lines, on curves or the crest of hills. They flew into Fairplain, causing a few pedestrians to jump to sidewalks, shaking fists at Paul. He laughed maniacally and gave the car horn a blast as he passed an older vehicle driven by a senior citizen, forcing the older driver to the curb.

He slammed on the brakes and made a sharp U-turn in front of his office. Kendra fell to her side, striking her head against the door. Paul ran around the car and pulled her from it before she could sit up. She stumbled to her knees. Paul laughed again, a manic sort of giggle, as he jerked her up and pushed her into his office.

A plate glass window with the words Sheriff's Office in bold, black print made up one side of the office. Paul's desk took up most of the space opposite the door, where he could see out the window. Behind the desk was a door with a barred square in place of a window. Kendra assumed the door led to the cell area, which looked about the same size as the office. She had no idea how many cells were there, nor did she want to find out. The other side of the room contained filing cabinets, four straight-backed chairs and a square card table as if playing was a daily affair. Kendra cringed against the smell that hung in the air – stale smoke, spilled beer and an unflushed toilet somewhere.

Paul pulled one of the chairs to the side of the desk and shoved her onto it so that she faced his desk. Sitting in his well-worn swivel chair, he reached to the corner of the desk and pushed the button to activate a tape recorder.

"Now, Kendra Donovan," he said, leaning back until the chair came dangerously close to tipping over, "let me hear the *right* answers and we'll see where we go from here. If you're *really* nice to me we can go play at my place later." He laughed again.

*Is this one of Paul's infamous practical jokes?* Kendra ignored his innuendoes. "Are you going to take these cuffs off? My hands are hurting."

"Too bad, I ain't giving you a chance for your fancy karate stuff. (He pronounced it ka-*rah*-tay.) Now just answer my questions."

"Why am I here? You have no right to haul me away without any explanation." Kendra tried to keep her voice even. She wouldn't let him know how scared she was.

"I ask the questions. You just answer. Where were you last night?" He glared and waited for an answer.

Kendra stared at the wall beyond him ignoring him as completely as possible. Ignoring the pain in her arms was more difficult.

"I asked you a question." His voice rose with each syllable. "Where were you last night?" Paul pounded his fist on the desk sending a cup of pencils scattering across the desk and rolling onto the floor.

Remembering Paul's violence when he was crossed, Kendra decided she'd better say something since she didn't have David or Lenny there to help her this time. With her hands cuffed behind her back, she couldn't do much to protect herself. "What time last night?"

"It doesn't matter what time. Where were you?"

"*Sheriff* Brooks," Kendra's anger was becoming greater than her fear, "I have no idea why you brought me here, but I have a feeling that you're setting me up for something that isn't good. You won't get another word from me until I have my attorney present."

"Don't get high and mighty with me, Kendra Donovan. I'm the law in this area. I don't let no high falutin' lawyers come in here and tell me what I can do and can't do. Now answer my question." Paul raised his voice another decibel or two.

Kendra turned in her chair and stared at the wall. *He's trying to pin something on me, but what? And why?*

Fists clenched, Paul Brooks stood and strutted closer to her. Kendra braced herself for the blow he was sure to give. Instead, he took her face in his hand and squeezed like a vise. "Answer my questions if you expect to walk out of here on your own."

Kendra closed her eyes, still refusing to speak to him. She would ignore him – pretend he didn't exist.

"Answer me." Paul jerked her head upward. She said nothing. He released his grip on her face and drew back his hand. The slap across her face knocked the chair over. Pain shot from her wrists up her arm. She bit her lip to keep from screaming. Anger-driven, Paul raised his foot to kick her. Caught in his anger and *interrogation,* Paul was oblivious to anything else – in his office or outside if it.

Suddenly, the door flew open and banged against the wall, followed by footsteps moving toward the stalemate questioning.

"I wouldn't do that if you want to be live to see another day, Brooks. There are laws against police brutality even in Fairplain, Michigan." Brian moved closer.

"Stay out of it, McNeil. This is none of your business. I'm interrogating a suspect."

"That kind of interrogation went out with the Mafia. Now unfasten those cuffs and be quick about it." Brian, eyes flashing, fists clenched, spoke through teeth clamped tightly together.

"You can't do nothing to me," said Paul. "I'm the sheriff. You just get out of here or I'll lock you up for impeding justice and interfering with police work."

Paul glared at Brian, forgetting his prisoner for the moment.

Ignoring her pain, Kendra swung her legs around and clipped Paul's ankles with her feet. Before he could right himself, he was on the floor beside her. Brian leaned over him, removed the gun from his holster and the keys from his belt loop.

"You won't get away with this McNeil. I'll have you arrested for assault."

"I didn't touch you, *Sheriff.* I believe the little lady whom you have in handcuffs and were prepared to kick senseless knocked you to the floor. Do you want to take that to the DA? Now, what's this all about, anyway?" Brian picked Kendra up as he spoke and unlocked the cuffs. He released the cuffs and gently caressed the angry red welts around her wrists.

Lenny used to say Kendra could shoot daggers from her eyes, but Brian looked as if a fire-breathing dragon lived beneath his skin. He released her hands, muscles tensed, fists clenched. Kendra knew he would regret whatever he had in mind to do to Paul Brooks. And as much as she wanted him to do it, she laid a hand on his arm, letting her eyes plead with him not to make matters worse. He relaxed the tight fists to a loose ball.

"All I want is answers. Shoulda remembered how stubborn she is." Paul picked himself up from the floor sounding like a petulant kid.

"Kendra, what does he want to know?" Brian asked, keeping his eyes on Paul.

"I don't know," she said rubbing her wrists. "He wanted to know where I was last night. He's trying to set me up for something, but I don't know what. I told him I won't answer any question without my attorney present. He didn't read me my rights. He kept me in cuffs and made insinuating remarks about what he would do later tonight."

"I don't know what you're trying to pull, Brooks, but you heard her. She'll answer any questions you have for her as soon as her attorney can be present. Until then, I suggest you either book her, or release her. And if you book her, you better have a case strong enough to go to the DA, or you'll have trouble getting a position pushing a broom around the dog pound."

"Get out." Paul dropped onto his chair with such force it started to spin. He grabbed the desk to stop the twirling. "Don't try to run away. I'll get the proof I need and have you back here. And you better tell your lawyer to fly 'cause I want you here by nine-thirty in the morning. Now get out of here." Paul gripped the desk with white knuckles, an angry sneer on his face. Kendra laughed at him, which made him even angrier. Then she remembered the tape.

Nodding at the still running recorder, she said, "Brian, I want a souvenir."

Brian followed her glance to the corner of the desk and smiled. Before Paul realized what he was going to do, he had the tape out of the machine.

"Hey, you can't have that. It's evidence." Paul jumped to his feet and grabbed at the tape. He missed as Brian pulled his arm away.

"I know," said Brian, dropping the tape in his shirt pocket. "Come on Kendra, it's getting hard to breathe in here. Someone must have locked a skunk in one of those cells."

# Twenty-one

Back on the street, Kendra and Brian walked until they were out of view. Kendra felt her bravado ebbing like a slow leak in an inflatable toy. Her knees felt shaky. Her arm and wrists hurt, but the confusion was even greater.

Brian stopped and turned her toward him. With a gentle touch, he laid his hand on the side of her face where a dark bruise already covered her eye.

"Kendra, I'm sorry. I got here as quickly as I could."

"I'm glad you've been following me." She grinned then winced.

"You knew? How long?" He was surprised. "I thought I did a good job of covering my tracks."

"Since the beginning. I wasn't sure who but I knew someone was following me and you always appeared when I was in trouble. I'm sure Lenny followed me part of the time and possibly Mark or Paul."

Brian lifted his eyebrows, a habit she noticed he did when he was surprised about something. "How did you know? Never mind. I'm not sure I want to know – not yet." He shook his head, but smiled at her. "I have a couple of things to do in Fairplain then I'll take you back to your cabin, unless you want to wait for the sheriff to do it?" He grinned as she grimaced.

"I'll wait for you. I would rather walk than let him take me, thank you very much." She glanced up at the sky, "Especially on a beautiful day like this."

"That's a ten mile hike back to the lodge, Kendra."

"David and I used to walk it just for the fun of coming over here for an ice cream cone." Suddenly that seemed so long ago. Kendra sighed then smiled. "But, I don't think I'm up to it today. The way my luck is going, Paul would come along and arrest me for vagrancy, or something."

Brian didn't laugh as she thought he would. He looked more serious as he answered, "You might be more right than you think. Did he ever tell you why he brought you in?"

"No. He was only interested in where I was last night. Brian, what happened last night? Why did you really come to my cabin?"

Brian hesitated. Finally, he slipped his hand around hers and answered as they started walking down the street toward the *Town Café*. "I can't tell you everything, Kendra, but you deserve something. Someone murdered Vincent Burke last night and dumped his body in the lake. I was afraid *they*, whoever *they* are, might try to pin it on you. They knew you would be in your cabin alone with no one to verify your alibi."

"So you staged that little scene last night and this morning in case I needed an alibi?"

"I didn't know your cabin was bugged, but it worked to our advantage." He grinned. "Now they know, but can't let on that they know."

"Except Paul did." Kendra glanced up at Brian. "He made some remark about me spending the night with a man in my cabin."

"That's interesting. Paul put the *bug* there?"

"No. He hasn't been in the cabin, at least not that I know of. Mark put it there."

"Mark? Are you sure?" He stopped walking and turned to face her.

"I'm positive." Kendra explained how Angel reacted to Mark and how the cat found the butterfly-shaped *bug*. She told him about putting it in the box and setting a trap – making a comment about being hungry for Italian food.

"It wasn't much of a trap," she said, "but I knew it had to be either Mark or Lenny. I really thought Lenny was playing some kind of trick on me, so I was surprised when Mark asked me to go to the

*Italian Café*." She laughed at Brian's expression.

He shook his head and grinned. "Kendra, where did you learn so much about *bugs* and how to deal with them?"

"You wouldn't believe me." They started walking again.

"Try me. I've seen you in action enough in the last couple of days to believe almost anything." Kendra heard the admiration in his voice, which sent warm pleasure through her.

"David and I used to go to the Federal Building with Dad when we were kids. We knew every office and most of the personnel in them. We picked up a lot of helpful information on those visits." She looked up at him and grinned.

Brian threw back his head and laughed. "You learned all that from the FBI while you were just a kid? Kendra, that's wonderful, in more ways than you can imagine. I would love to see the expression on a certain person's face if he knew that."

Kendra knew, of course, that he was speaking of Seymour Severs, but she only grinned and nodded in agreement.

"Pretty lady want to buy a paper?" They hadn't noticed the barefoot boy approaching them until he spoke. His unruly red hair waved in the breeze. Freckles danced across his nose and cheeks when he smiled. Green eyes sparkled with the joy of childhood. He held out a homemade paper for Kendra to see.

"What kind of paper do you have?" She stooped and reached for it, but the boy pulled back.

"You want to read, you gotta pay first," he said narrowing his eyes and trying to glare, but the sparkle never left his eyes and a grin twitched at the corners of his mouth.

"How do I know if I want the paper if I don't know what kind of news is on it?" She smiled at the boy.

"Moppet says it's good news and pretty lady would want it."

Kendra was glad she was kneeling with her back to Brian and he couldn't see her face. He wouldn't have missed the momentary blink of her eyes and her slight intake of air. She recovered quickly from surprise, but Brian saved her from making a fatal comment.

"Moppet? Who is Moppet?" Brian looked at the boy quizzically.

"Moppet is little sister," he said and glanced toward the alley where a little girl of about five stood shyly watching them. "She wants to be writer." He gave them a toothless grin.

"How much does Moppet want for her paper?" Kendra asked the little boy. She knew Moppet wasn't *his* sister, but *hers.* It took her only seconds to get her emotions under control. She didn't know how Michelle got the message to this child, but she knew there was more to it than a child making a few pennies.

The boy gave his toothless grin again and held the paper for her to see. "Only a quarter for an ice cream cone."

"Only one ice cream cone?" Kendra asked glancing at the little girl.

"We share." He giggled.

Kendra stood and reached into her pocket then remembered she didn't have any money with her. Paul didn't let her stop to get her purse. Disappointed, she bit her lip and shrugged.

"I'm sorry. I left all my money at home," she said then added, "Would you trust me to bring it tomorrow?"

Before the boy could answer, Brian chuckled and reached into his pocket. "Are you sure you can get an ice cream cone for a quarter?"

"Sure. Pop Allen is a nice man."

"Here's two dollars in case his price went up. Now give the lady her paper and take Moppet for her ice cream."

"Thank you, sir. Maybe Moppet will make another paper some day, when we need more ice cream." The boy giggled and skipped over to the little girl, who like the boy sported red hair and was shoeless. He took her by the hand and they ran to Pop Allen's Ice Cream Parlor.

"Do you always buy papers from unknown kids?" Brian smiled as she read the one page hand printed story with stick people pictures.

"Thank you, Brian. I do what I can for kids. It's not a bad paper – for a child."

Brian took it and looked it over. "I thought it would be one of those Doom's Day messages. All they have is a Scripture reference and some pictures– Old Testament at that. I don't remember any end of time prophecies from Genesis."

Kendra laughed and reached for the paper. "At least you know enough about the Bible to know Genesis is in the Old Testament and isn't one of the prophets. This is the story of Joseph and his coat of many colors, a favorite of many kids. Joseph was sold into slavery and became the Pharaoh's right hand man during the famine."

"Ah, yes, I remember the story, but why would those kids sell a paper with that story on it?" He looked at Kendra as if he thought there was more to it than she was telling him – and of course, there was.

Kendra laughed and said, "Why do kids do anything, except for fun?" She folded the paper and slipped it into her pocket. She knew he suspected the paper was more than a child's drawing, but apparently, he didn't know what. Kendra couldn't tell him it was a message from her sister Michelle that told her, like Joseph, everyone thought her family was dead, but in reality, they were alive and well. *They have to be where I thought they were in order for Shelly to get that message to me. But, how did she manage to get it to Fairplain? Maybe I could get an answer back to her.*

They continued walking toward the café. A blind man wearing dark glasses slowly approached them tapping his cane on the sidewalk ahead of him. They stopped and moved to one side so the man wouldn't run into them.

"Morning, folks," said the man in a high pitched, scratchy voice.

"How did you know we were here?" asked Brian, frowning.

"Hee, hee, hee," The old man snickered. "Young man is skeptical. Wait 'til you get my age. Hee, hee, hee," he snickered again. "When a person is blind, other senses become stronger," he said. "I heard you walking then you stopped. There are two of you. The other one is a pretty lady."

"Now, how can you know she's a pretty lady?" Brian asked, obviously skeptical. Kendra hadn't said anything – couldn't have if she'd tried. Her heart skipped a beat and she put her trembling hands in her pockets. She would know that disguise anywhere. *Now I know how the message got into the hands of the boy.*

"Well, son, anyone as careful as you are would want to walk with the prettiest lady around."

By the time Brian and the blind man finished their exchange, Kendra once again had her emotions under control. Brian laughed and took her arm to move on, but she held back, reluctant to leave her brother.

Combing her fingers through her hair, she spoke to him in their secret language, while saying aloud. "Do you live around here, or are you just panhandling in this town?"

Brian again looked as if he thought she was up to something. Had he only known! Her fingers flew through their finger language asking him, *Why are you in hiding?*

"Does it matter?" asked the old man pulling at his beard. While he answered the spoken question, his fingers also answered her silent one – *too much to tell. Lay low. Go back home. We're fine.*

"No, just curious. Do you have a name?" Once again, she pushed her hair from her face answering him with her fingers, *not a chance. I'll be careful, but I'll not leave until we all leave together.*

"Hee, hee, hee." The old man snickered again. On the head of his cane he drummed, *Then trust Brian and Lenny. Be careful.* Aloud, he continued their normal conversation. "Little missy, smart. To know a man's name gives her power over him. Melvin McElroy at your service, missy."

"Well, Melvin McElroy, may God bless you. My name's Kendra, so we're even." She laughed.

The man snickered again and started to move on. Brian had watched the exchange with curiosity. "Kendra, why don't you go in and order a burger for us. I'll give the man a couple of dollars for you." He grinned as she smiled at him.

"Thanks again, Brian. I owe you big time after today."

"Somehow, I think it will all work out. Burger with the works."

***

Brian turned and ran after the old man who moved with surprising speed for his age and blindness. Brian caught up with the blind beggar, whom Brian knew was David Donovan, as he turned the corner.

"What was that all about?" Brian's tone was angry, almost panicky. "You trying to blow the whole project? You know you were told not to contact her."

"Sorry, Pal. I don't work for Severs. Dad has to follow his orders. I don't. She's my twin sister. I had to see her for myself. What happened to her face?"

"Brooks – he's trying to pin Burke's murder on her."

"I suppose she has no alibi. I wish she hadn't…" David gripped the cane so tightly that he felt the knob cut into his hand.

"She's covered. I'm her alibi."

David's beggar eyebrows lifted. He wanted to hear more, but Brian said, "I've got to go. She'll wonder why it took so long to catch you and give you a couple of bucks. Tell your father we're on it and I'll call later. We'll need a lawyer tomorrow morning."

"Brian…"

"Yeah?"

"Don't underestimate that girl. She's sharp. She knows far more than you think."

Brian said nothing. He turned and ran back to the café. He heard the old man's cane tapping down the alley.

***

While Brian ran after the blind beggar that Kendra was sure he knew was David, she found a booth and placed their order. How could she feel so happy and so sad at the same time? She had Shelly's message in her pocket and David told her with their finger language to trust Brian and Lenny. But, she still didn't know why they were in hiding and why Severs put out that lie that they were all dead. She understood why Brian wanted to see David. If only they could stop the game playing and she could work with Brian and get this mess – whatever it was – cleared up. Then they could all go home.

# Twenty-two

In spite of the harrowing morning, Kendra smiled as they drove under the arch at the resort. Brian smiled too. "Those birds and animals look so real, I sometimes think they'll fly away or leap on the car," he said.

"You noticed that too." She grinned. "Someone did a super job of carving and painting, not only the birds and animals, but also the rainbow arch."

"I'm not sure, but I think I heard Jonathan say the area high schools worked together on the project all last winter in their art classes. They put them up here early in May."

Brian drove down the lane and stopped in front of Wolverine Cabin. "You have your key?"

"Yes, I had it in my pocket when Paul picked me up. It's all I had." Kendra reached in her pocket, pulled out the key and held it up for him to see.

Brian held her hand and looked into her eyes as if trying to read her thoughts. He blinked, looked very serious and asked, "Do you think you can stay out of trouble for a couple of hours?" He grinned then added, "I need to make arrangements to get a lawyer out here first thing in the morning."

Kendra tried to frown at him, but grinned instead. "I'll try, but trouble seems to find me no matter where I am. I can call Dad's attorney in Akron, but I doubt he could be here by tomorrow morning. Do you think it would be safe to go for a swim?" She wasn't really asking his opinion as much as she was letting him know what her plans were.

"I would go to the pool. Stay away from the lake. You probably shouldn't talk about the murder with anyone, either."

"Brian, I have no way of knowing anything about a murder at the lake," she said. "Paul never told me why he hauled me off to jail. If no one else tells me what's been going on, I don't know anything. And…" She studied his face, trying to decide whether to say more.

"And…?" he prompted.

"If you were with me all night, you don't know anything about it either."

Brian looked chagrined then laughed. "You're right. I probably would've blown it by making some stupid remark. Thanks for reminding me we're in this together. And Kendra," he paused once again looking deep into her eyes, "thanks for trusting me. For all you know, I could have killed him myself and I'm using you for my alibi."

"You had the opportunity, but you didn't do it," she said.

"What makes you so sure?"

"If you did, you went back to the lodge, took a shower and changed clothes before you came to my cabin. You didn't do that because your hair wasn't wet and you didn't smell as if you came fresh from a shower. You weren't wet at all and didn't smell like the lake, so you didn't come from down there either. And for a drunk, you hadn't been anywhere near alcohol."

Brian shook his head, let go of her hand and got out of the car. He walked around to give her a hand, noticing wrists that were turning blue and purple. She winced as he touched her swollen left elbow.

"Maybe you better put some ice on that elbow then go see the doctor at the lodge. That arm looks pretty swollen."

"It'll be all right. It's probably just a little sprain. Cold water and exercise will be good for it." Kendra tried to smile through the pain.

"It's your arm, but I would see the doc if it were me. See you later. Call me if you have any more trouble."

*Why call, you're following me wherever I go.* She ignored the temptation to express her thoughts and went into the cabin. Meows, purrs and general "I want some attention" noises from Angel met her before she hardly opened the door.

"Do you need some attention, sweetie?" Kendra took time to caress the soft fur and play *chase the mouse* with Angel before she went to the bedroom to put on her swimsuit. She found it difficult to change clothes without pain in her arm.

Picking up the paperback she'd been trying to read for weeks, she gave Angel another pat and stepped out to the porch, making sure the door closed behind her. She took her time walking up the lane to the pool at the lodge. Most of the other guests were already lounging in the sun, drinking everything from alcoholic beverages to soft drinks.

Matthew Zachary, one of the many college youth the Cox's hired for the summer, rushed over to her as she found an empty lounge and settled herself in it. "Hi, Miss Donovan. We were all wondering where you were. What happened to your face? Run into a door?"

"Something like that," she answered.

"Did you hear about Vincent Burke?" His eyes widened and he leaned closer to speak in a stage whisper.

"What about Vincent? I was in Fairplain all morning." Kendra held her book to shield the sun from her eyes as she looked up into the face of the young waiter. He was tall and sported a dark tan. His brown wavy hair and brown eyes gave him a melancholy look that drove the girls wild. He loved it.

"He was found in the lake this morning – dead."

"Really? What happened? Did he fall in? His brother said yesterday that he couldn't swim." Kendra was glad the sun made it easy to squint.

"No, actually, they say he was shot and then thrown in. It was pretty hectic around here for a while this morning."

"I would imagine it was. I'm not sorry I missed that kind of excitement. How about a glass of iced tea – with a sprig of mint?"

"Sure thing, Miss Donovan." Matthew left to take care of her order and Kendra leaned back in the chaise lounge, wincing as she bumped her elbow on the cold metal arm.

The pool was smooth as glass waiting for someone to dive into it, but Kendra opened her book and ignored all the chatter around her. She became so lost in the pages of the book that she didn't hear Lenny approach.

"Well, there she is," he said. "Finally decided to show up, did you? I thought you were going to sleep all day." Lenny grinned when she dropped the book in her lap.

"Lenny. I wasn't asleep. I was in Fairplain." She shielded her eyes and squinted at him.

"Shopping so early in the morning?" He gave her a quizzical look.

"Our friend, *Sheriff* Brooks, decided I knew something he didn't and was determined I would tell him."

Lenny frowned. "From the look of your face, I take it he didn't get what he wanted from you. Mind if I ask what he was looking for?"

"You can ask all you want to, but your guess is as good as mine. He never did tell me why he took me in, just wanted to know where I was all night."

Lenny took a closer look at her and noticed not only the dark coloring on the side of her face, but also the red welts surrounded by purple on her wrists. He muttered something under his breath and Kendra laughed.

"That's not very nice language for a musician."

"It's not half as bad as I would like to say, but can't with a lady present." He smiled. "Come on, I'll race you to the end of the pool." He grabbed her arm, pulled her to her feet, and started toward the end of the pool without looking back. Thankfully, he didn't see the tears form unbidden in her eyes or hear the gasp of pain as she dropped the book on the lounge and followed him.

Diving into the pool behind him, she started for the other end. She could always easily catch up with Lenny and pass him if she wanted to. But, she wasn't even half-way when she realized she couldn't keep up with him. Her arm hurt too much to force the speed. Lenny stopped.

"Hey, are you cheating to let me win?" He swam back to her. "Kendra? Did he hurt you more than what I saw? You would've passed me and been half way back to the other end by the time I reached the first one. What's wrong?"

"My arm. I fell on it in Paul's office. Must have sprained it or twisted my elbow. Sorry Lenny, I can't race you. It hurts too much."

"Can you make it back to the ladder? Or do you want me to call for the lifeguard?"

"I'll make it. I've caused enough commotion around here. I promised Brian I would stay out of trouble this afternoon." Turning to use a sidestroke, pulling with her right arm, she made it to the ladder. Lenny helped her out of the pool and took a look at the arm."

"Why didn't you tell me you were hurt? I wouldn't have pulled you up…" Lenny stopped and looked stricken. "Kendra, baby, I'm sorry. I must have hurt you more. Did you see the doctor?"

"No. I thought the sunshine and cold water would make it feel better."

"Oh? You're adding medicine to your fields of expertise?" He arched his eyebrows and pulled at his beard.

Kendra laughed at him. "No, I just didn't think it was that bad."

"Kendra, that's your fiddle arm. You've got to take care of it. If it's broken and doesn't get set, you may never play again." Lenny was alarmed.

Horrified at the thought, Kendra replied, "Lenny, I never thought of that. I thought…"

"You're right. You couldn't think. You're just surviving, not thinking. Come on, let Papa Lenny take care of you. We'll go see the doctor and I promise I won't let him hurt you any more." Lenny took her right hand and began pulling her toward the infirmary.

"Lenny." Kendra laughed at him. "You're nuts, but thanks. Wait a minute. I need to get my sandals and book. I'm halfway through it, so I don't want someone to walk off with it."

"I'll get it, but don't you try a disappearing act." His wagging finger in her face accompanied Lenny's stern warning.

Kendra laughed and promised to wait for him. "I'll be glad for your company," she replied when he returned with the book. "Remember when David and I brought you to Doc when you got a fish hook in the back of your head?"

"Ouch. Don't remind me," he said.

They continued to reminisce until they came to the infirmary, which was located in the basement of the lodge. They approached from the outside – a curved driveway under the patio. Doc Jones had been with the Cox's for as long as the lodge had been open. He smiled up at Kendra and Lenny when they walked into his waiting area. Doc was a short man – only about five foot – so he looked up to just about everyone. He was passing the slow afternoon by reading magazines.

"Leonard Richardson and Kendra Donovan. Someone have a fishhook in their scalp again?" He laid the magazine aside and rose to greet them.

"Not this time, Doc. Kendra fell on her elbow and it looks pretty swollen to me. She can't even beat me in a swim across the pool, so I know it hurts. Thought you ought to take a look."

"Come here, child, and let me see." Doc Jones took Kendra to one of the examining areas, which was only a stainless steel topped table and curtains hanging from a circular rod around a table that moved up and down like a dentist's chair. The florescent light directly over the table made it easier for him to see his patient. He prodded, poked and looked sympathetic when she winced and involuntary tears slipped down her face. He examined the bruised face and looked at the wrists. "Hmm. Looks like you did more than fall. Did that young man do this?" He nodded toward Lenny, who leaned against the wall, arms crossed, concern on his face.

"No, Doc. Lenny wouldn't dare. He knows what I'd do to him." Kendra smiled at him.

"Someone hurt you and I'd give a farm in Georgia to know who.

I'd slip him something and do some surgery on his fingers and toes and…"

Doc!" Kendra tried to look horrified, but found it difficult with the laughter that slipped out. "I won't tell you who did it, because I don't want you to get in trouble with the law over my problems."

"Hmm. All right. Over here. I want to X-ray it. Then we'll see what we need to do." She followed him to the corner where he had a small X-ray machine. "I was so sorry to hear about the accident that took the lives of your family. We all thought you were with them. Must have been a shock for you."

"It was. I was supposed to be with them, but I had to stay behind to finish a report for my boss. I was to join them the next day."

"I knew your father too well to believe it was other than an accident," Doc said. "Did your doctor send you here to get away for awhile?"

"He suggested a vacation. I chose this place because of all the happy memories. And Doc, thanks for believing in my father."

"It must be hard knowing you would have been here with them."

"I didn't know where they were going. My father liked to play guessing games with our vacation. We had to look for clues and figure it out. He was supposed to call me later with more clues so I could find them. I thought they might have gone south because the accident occurred in the mountains."

"Cox told us he made reservations here. We were looking forward to seeing all of you again."

"I was surprised when he told me about the reservations. I guess Dad changed his mind after he left, or decided to take a little detour through the mountains. I don't suppose I'll ever know." *I wish I could take a chance and tell Doc and Lenny the truth, but with all the weird things happening, I'd better wait. I'm not even sure of Lenny and Brian.*

Doc Jones shuffled over to the developing machine and pulled the X-ray film from it, holding it up to the special lighted viewing screen. "Hmmm," he muttered. "You're lucky. It's not broken, but you got a nasty sprain. You're going to have to refrain from using it for awhile." He wrapped the elbow in an ace bandage then got a sling from one of his cabinets.

"Wear this all the time for the next two or three days, then during the day for a couple of weeks. After the first couple of nights, you can judge if it feels better to keep it elevated. Use a pillow, if you can, when you sit or lie down. Put ice on it for swelling. I'll give you some pills for pain. I know you'll use them sparingly, so I'll only give you a half dozen. If you need more, come see me."

"Thanks Doc." Kendra took the pills from him.

He squinted at her and said, "If I know our despicable sheriff like I think I do, he's the one that did this to you. He's been a bully from the time he learned to crawl."

"Doc..."

"Don't worry. I won't say anything, but some day that joker will get what's coming to him."

His concern touched her, but Kendra wasn't surprised at his attitude. Doc never liked Paul, even when they were kids.

***

"Well, so much for swimming," Kendra grumbled as she and Lenny left the infirmary. "I'm really beginning to feel weary, Lenny. If you don't mind, I'll go back to the cabin and think about a nap. My mind's in a whirl and now my body isn't feeling too perky either. At least God hasn't let me down – yet. I think I need to have a long talk with Him."

"I think you're right, sweetie. Can I walk you home, today?" Lenny asked with the feigned shyness and excitement of a junior high school boy. "I'll even carry your book."

Kendra laughed and handed him her book and took his hand as they walked down the lane to Wolverine Cabin. Lenny kept up a flow of non-stop chatter about nothing in particular, either to keep her mind off her troubles, or to deter anyone who would be waiting for her along the way. Either way, Kendra was glad not to have to think or talk. When they got to the door, Lenny helped her unfasten the chain around her neck with the key on it. He opened the door and Angel greeted her with all the enthusiasm of a small cat lonely for company.

"See you later, sweetie," said Lenny as she started inside. "If you need any help getting dressed or anything, give me a call."

"Lenny!"

Lenny went into a fit of giggles. Very few things ever surprised, or rattled Kendra Donovan, and he always enjoyed it when he was able to render her speechless. He continued to chuckle as he started up the lane to the lodge. Kendra went inside, locked the door then shuffled to the kitchen to take one of the pills Doc gave her.

"Come on Angel," she said and moved to the bedroom where she slipped into a pair of shorts and a button up shirt.

Angel purred and jumped to the bed where Kendra propped a pillow under her arm. The cat waited for Kendra to settle then curled up on her stomach. They were both soon deep in contented sleep until a persistent pounding on the front door forced Kendra awake. She glanced at the clock then at Angel who bristled, arched her back and hissed.

*Mark.*

# Twenty-three

Pulled from a deep, pain-drugged sleep, Kendra dislodged the hissing Angel and sat up. Remembering her injured arm when the pillow slipped, she clenched her teeth and drew in a couple of deep breaths. She sat on the side of the bed for a minute to get her bearings. The rapping at the front screen door continued with more urgency adding rattling with each rap. Angel, fur standing on end, hissed and growled.

"Just a minute," Kendra called, shaking away the last of her drowsiness. The mantel clock gave six chimes as she stumbled from the bedroom, closing the door behind her to keep Angel in the room. She knew from Angel's reaction that it was Mark.

*I suppose he wants to go to dinner.* Opening the cabin door, Kendra stepped out to the porch to unlatch the screen.

"Mark, I'm sorry if you had to wait long. I was asleep." She combed her fingers through her hair trying to untangle thoughts more than hair.

"I didn't wait *that* long," he said. "I haven't seen you all day and thought I should check on you. What happened to your arm? And your face?" His words said he was concerned, but his expression said *you asked for it.*

Kendra decided she didn't need to go into detail. "I fell. Just a bad sprain. No broken bones, but I won't be playing my violin for a while."

"How awful! Where did you fall? In the cabin?" Mark stood with his hands in his pocket rocking back and forth from toe to heel as if he were in a hurry to dispense with the unimportant trivia and get on to his agenda.

Nodding toward the hall where Angel pawed at the bedroom door with as much noise as her larger, wilder, relatives would have done, he said, "You probably tripped over that dumb cat. Honestly, Kendra, I don't understand why you brought an animal with you on vacation." Kendra frowned and he hurriedly added, "Especially when you're trying to overcome your grief."

"She's a lot of company." Kendra refused to let him pull any information from her about the *accident* or get her riled up about bringing Angel.

"Do you feel like going out tonight? Maybe we ought to just go to the lodge for dinner. I'll go get my car and drive you up."

"I'm not lame, Mark. I hurt my elbow not my leg." Kendra sounded irritated, but really didn't care. She was tired, in pain and still felt groggy. She just wanted him to go away. "I really don't feel like getting dressed to go anywhere tonight. It's been a rather long and tiring day."

"And I hear the night was a little short as well." Mark clipped his words with more than a hint of angry jealousy. "Honestly, Kendra, I thought you had more moral sense than to let a man like Brian McNeil spend the night with you. You didn't really sleep with him did you?"

Caught off guard, Kendra stared for a minute, her mouth open. Finally, not bothering to hide her surprise or anger, she said as sharply as possible. "Mark, I can't imagine where you get your information, but I'm old enough to take care of myself. It's no one's business if I choose to sleep with anyone – or not. If you're going to make insinuations and snide remarks, maybe you better leave."

"I'm sorry, Kendra. You're right of course. It is none of my business, but I guess I'm beginning to believe my church folks were right. I do need a wife and I've found the perfect woman for me. Kendra, I know we've only known each other for a couple of days, but I'm falling head over heels in love with you. I can't help it if that flares jealously in me, but I can't stand the thought of McNeil's hands on you."

Mark grabbed her arms, held them tightly as he pulled her close to him and pressed his lips hard against hers. Kendra had difficulty getting her breath. Pain shot up her arm from the pressure of his hand. Anger shot through the rest of her body with just as much intensity. Before she could stop herself, she was into her protective training mode. Her knee caught him in the groin and he let go, bent double with pain. Backing up, he sat in the swing behind him, breathing hard and cursing under his breath, until he could stand.

"You didn't need to do that, Kendra," he said through clenched teeth. "A simple no would have been sufficient." Mark was still bent over and groaning.

"I'm sorry, Mark, but you were hurting me and you didn't give me much opportunity to say anything. I panicked. You had better go while we are both still in control of what emotions we have left. I told you before I'm not interested in long-term relationships with anyone. I have a lot of sorting out of my own problems and troubles before I take on any more. Thank you for being concerned about me, but I'm doing fine. Good night."

Kendra stepped back into the cabin, closed the door and leaned against it until she heard the screen door slam shut, bouncing from the force of Mark's hand. She returned to the bedroom to let Angel out. She was still a frizzled ball of fur, so Kendra picked her up and held her close to her face to help calm them both. They watched through the window as Mark stomped his way up the lane. She was sorry she hurt him – but not very much.

"Well, Angel, let's go see about some supper. Maybe some tuna. You can have yours plain and I'll put mine in a macaroni salad and make some toast." They went to the kitchen, where Brian was leaning against the door chuckling. He'd heard – and probably seen – everything.

"Don't you believe in knocking?" Kendra asked, holding her arm that was still throbbing from Mark's grip. "And how did you get in?"

"You had two keys on your key chain. I took one."

Too angry and confused for the words to register, she turned and opened several cabinets, slamming each shut, until she found the tuna. She got the can-opener from the drawer, but when she tried to open the can, she couldn't turn it with one hand. All the anger, confusion, pain and grief suddenly rolled together in one giant lump and tumbled out before she could stop it. She threw the can and the opener down on the counter and burst into tears, burying her face in her one good hand. Angel rubbed her ankles meowing. Brian took Kendra in his arms and turned her around so she could bury her head in his shoulder. Careful not to hurt her any more, he kept his arms around her until the tears stopped flowing.

"I'm sorry, Kendra. I don't mean to add to your frustration. Will you let me help you with whatever you were going to do?"

Feeling like a fool, she nodded, pulled away from him and grabbed a tissue from the counter top. "I'm sorry, Brian. I don't know what hit me – everything all at once, I guess. If you will open that can of tuna, I would appreciate it. I promised Angel some for supper." Kendra grinned through the remaining tears at his questioning look.

"How does Angel rate?"

"She's my closest friend, right now. I have to take good care of her, because she takes good care of me." She got a pan down from the cabinet over the stove and put water on to boil for the macaroni. "Do you like macaroni salad with tuna? You're welcome to join me for supper if you do. That's what I'm fixing."

"I don't know as I ever ate it, but if you cook it and invite me to join you, I'll eat it. Do you share the can of tuna with Angel?"

"Yes, but maybe you better open two cans."

"Shall I put this in her dish, or do you let her eat at the table with you?" He cocked his head and grinned.

"Put it in her dish – about half a can," Kendra answered ignoring his sarcasm.

Soon the macaroni was ready. Brian chopped the onion and celery. The salad made, garlic toast in the oven and fresh coffee in the pot, Kendra felt a little more human. She hadn't realized how difficult it would be to do things with one arm. Remembering

Lenny's words, she started laughing. Brian arched his eyebrows, glanced at her and waited for her to explain. His expression brought more laughter. She told him what Lenny said about coming back to help her dress.

"I didn't know how helpless I would be," she said.

"Oh? Well, I plan to stay here again tonight, so if you really need help..."

"Brian! Am I going crazy? As far back as I can remember I've been able to keep the men in my life in line. Now, all of a sudden, men who want to get their hands on my body are popping up everywhere. You would think it was made of solid gold or something. Well, I can still take care of myself if I have to, thank you very much. When it comes to getting dressed and undressed, I don't need any help."

Brian was laughing so hard he couldn't respond right away. "I'm sure you can take care of yourself. I've seen you do it too many times to believe otherwise. As far as your body being gold, it's much softer and more alluring than gold. If I ever wanted to really get serious…" He cleared his throat and continued, "Well, enough said, before I get myself in more trouble. I am staying here, however. That part is no joke. You've been through enough today without having someone try to break in tonight. And, like you said, there are enough men out there who want you, they just might try it."

"Do you really think it's wise? I mean…I don't know what I mean." Kendra shrugged, feeling helpless.

"I know what you mean, even if you don't. Don't worry. We'll get it all straightened out when we need to. Trust me."

"Do I have a choice?" Kendra grinned, remembering her brother's words. *If only I could talk to Brian, or even Lenny, about my family's disappearance.*

"Not much at this point." He returned her grin.

"I think I'll take another of the pills Doc gave me and call it a night – early. I don't want to be rude, but…"

"You didn't invite me, I invited myself." He smiled. "We'll give the *bug* just enough to let whoever is listening know that I'm here and intend to be here all night, then you can go to bed and I'll catch up on my reading. You can even lock your door if you're afraid of me," he teased.

"Brian, I'm not afraid of you. You wouldn't be in my house, if I thought there was any danger. Come on let's give our little performance. I'm tired."

As they approached the hall, Brian began, "Kendra, darling. I'm sorry you hurt your arm. I'll be very gentle with you. Maybe we better just…"

Before he could finish his sentence, Kendra interrupted. "It doesn't hurt that much, Brian. Doc said prop it up, I'll use you for a pillow." She smiled at his expression.

"Kendra, you *are* full of surprises," he said with feeling. "Come on, let's call it a night."

***

They went down the hall and made a point of opening and closing one bedroom door. Kendra went into her room to a good night's sleep. Brian waited until he was sure Kendra was asleep, then went to the back porch and pulled out his cell phone. He punched in the number.

"She's down for the night. I'll be here to watch."

He closed the phone, then as an afterthought opened it again and punched in another number. He repeated the message. Then he called Severs to give his report.

"I told you she would be trouble. Make her go home."

Brian knew, as well as Severs, that wasn't going to happen.

"Sure," he said.

"Maybe that sheriff can put her in jail for a few days."

"Maybe." Brian knew it would do no good to explain the explosive feelings between Kendra and Paul Brooks. Or remind him of the sheriff's involvement in the drug operation.

"Whatever you do, don't blow this case. We're getting closer to the truth."

"We'll be careful."

Brian cut the connection knowing he had withheld information from Severs and knowing what his orders would have been had he told him about the lawyer he had engaged for Kendra. He went back to his room and left his door open enough to hear her if she called out. Then he had a good night's sleep.

# Twenty-four

"Come on sleepyhead. Breakfast is getting cold. Do you need some help getting dressed?" Brian called loud enough that whoever was listening to the *bug* would hear him.

Kendra opened her bedroom door, grinned and said, "You can fasten me in the back if you would be so kind."

Brian shook his head and laughed. She was already dressed in jeans and a western style plaid shirt. "Come here," he said and made a point of sounding like he was having trouble getting hooks hooked. "Maybe we ought to just go back to the bedroom and forget about getting dressed."

"Later," she said not missing a beat. "You said breakfast was getting cold and I hate cold eggs." Kendra put the lid over the *bug* box while Brian went to the kitchen chuckling.

After a leisurely breakfast without much conversation, Brian took his last swallow of coffee, picked up the dishes and carried them to the sink.

"I'll do up these dishes then go back to the lodge to shower and dress. Do you want to go with me and wait there? Or do you want to wait here? We'll meet Attorney Ira Thoburg in Fairplain at the sheriff's office about nine-thirty. And don't look so worried. He's the best lawyer in these parts."

"I guess I am worried – and scared. I don't understand why Paul is trying to pin a murder on me when he obviously knows better. And why did he treat me the way he did? We never got along as kids, but that was a long time ago. I can't believe he would carry a grudge that long."

"Kendra, I'm sure there's more to it than kid stuff. I don't know what, but hang in there and we'll find out. In the meantime, Ira will get him off your back…that is…I…"

Kendra laughed at his awkwardness as she grabbed a dishtowel to dry. "I know what you mean," she said then changed the subject. "Has Mr. Thoburg been your attorney long? How did you get him here on such short notice? Does he have a good track record? Can I afford him? Has he handled many cases similar…?" She stopped and laughed at Brian's expression. He stared with his hands in the dishpan.

"You do ask a lot of questions, don't you? Maybe you would like a complete bio on him. Don't worry about the cost. I've got more money than I know what to do with and…"

"Ah, yes. Mark said you were a rich playboy. Well, I'll have you know there are some things and some people you can't buy." Kendra was surprised at her anger. She knew who Brian was and where the money came from. She just hated the games.

"I'm sorry if my money bothers you," said Brian. "It bothers me, too."

Did he understand the real reason for her anger? Was he saying he hated games, too? She took a deep breath. "I'm sorry. I don't mean to sound ungrateful. I guess I'm more worried than I thought."

Brian grinned and finished his task-at-hand. "Believe me, Mr. Thoburg knows what he's doing and you'll be out of there in ten minutes, or less, without a scratch on your record." Brian frowned. "I just wish I could have had him there yesterday before that jerk hurt you. I'm sure Ira will want to take that to the highest court he can." He laid a warm hand against the side of her face where Paul hit her.

"I don't want any more trouble with Paul," she said gazing into Brian's eyes. "Just get him off my back, as you so aptly put it and I will be relatively happy." Kendra blinked then dried the last dish and put it in the cupboard. Even though her arm still hurt, she could use it some as long as she kept it in a sling.

"Only relatively," he teased.

"For now, anyway," she answered. "I guess only time will heal the other hurts."

"I'm sorry. That was insensitive of me."

"It's all right. I can't get upset every time someone says something that I can interpret in a different way. I would always be looking for intended barbs. I know you didn't mean that. Back to your original question." She flashed a smile at him. "I think I'll go to the lodge and wait in the lounge for you. Or," she paused then reconsidered. "On second thought, maybe I'll drive on over and meet you there."

"Do you think that would be wise with your sore arm?"

"I drive with my right hand and I don't have to shift gears. I think I can handle that. Besides I would like to do some shopping later." Or maybe some snooping. Brian didn't say anything, but his frown said he didn't approve of that solution.

"I'm not a child. I can even meet with that lawyer friend of yours alone. I'm sure you have other, more pressing things to do. You don't even have to go to Fairplain."

"Kendra, don't push your luck."

"Meaning?" She glared at him feeling the old stubbornness returning.

"Meaning, I'm going to Fairplain, anyway, with or without you. If you want to drive, I can't stop you, but neither can you stop me from dropping in. Just promise me you won't go in there without Ira. He's to meet us outside the sheriff's office. If he's not there, wait in the car until he arrives. Please?" Brian's eyes locked with Kendra's, his pleaded, hers glared, but not for long. She couldn't stare into that pool of concern and not feel the effects.

She lowered her gaze and sighed loudly. "All right, I'll wait for Mr. Thoburg, or you, or whoever shows up first." She raised her head and grinned. "Shall I give you time to shower and change before taking off?"

Brian laughed with relief. "That would be nice. Why don't you give me twenty minutes before you leave, just in case there's any trouble?"

"What kind of trouble could I get into on a ten mile drive to Fairplain?" Kendra gave Brian a surprised look then added, "Never mind. Don't answer that. I seem to be attracting trouble the way a honey pot attracts bees. Your twenty minutes started one minute ago. You better leave."

"Yes, ma'am," he said and started out the door. He stopped and turned back with a more serious expression. "Please be careful. Don't take any chances."

"Go," she said waving her hand in a shooing motion. "I'll be careful."

Kendra decided to straighten up the cabin before leaving. She found making beds and sweeping floors with one hand more difficult and time consuming than she thought it would be. It was actually twenty-five minutes later when she finally got in the car and started the engine. *Maybe I was a little hasty with my decision. My arm aches and anxiety is churning in the pit of my stomach. Maybe I should call Brian and go with him after all.* She glanced at her watch. It was too late. Indecision led to following her plan by default. Brian had probably already left.

***

Kendra turned the car around and headed up the lane to the highway, glad she was in Michigan, not in West Virginia where Severs tried to make her believe the accident occurred. She couldn't take those winding, mountainous roads with her arm in a sling. At least the lane to the highway was mostly straight and she knew the highway would be.

Turning onto the highway, Kendra breathed a sigh of relief. She always loved the way the trees lined the road on either side. It made her feel like she was driving through a tunnel of evergreens. Even the blue sky above, dotted with white fluffy clouds looked like a painted ceiling of the tunnel. Michigan clouds always looked like they hung low enough to reach up and touch them. It was like having balls of cotton ready to drop on her if she stopped moving through the tunnel.

Memories of years gone by pricked her consciousness: herds of deer crossing this road in front of the car; she and David walking the ten miles to get an ice cream cone and waiting for their father to pick them up; memory upon memory brought stinging tears, seeking release. Kendra fought them back and tried to focus on the present. Her mission in Fairplain wasn't that pleasant, so she tried to think of other enjoyable times. Nothing seemed to work. She was slowly sinking into a funky despair. Before she could think of anything pleasant to chase away the gloom, she heard what sounded like a gun shot.

Another shot followed the first making a ping on the hood of the car. A third followed close on the heels of the second, shattering the passenger side window. Kendra felt the air stir as the bullet whizzed close to her forehead and out the window next to her that was already down.

*Someone is shooting at me!*

Another tiny missile shattered the back window on the passenger side.

*If I could speed up a little, maybe I could outrun them and...* Two more shots in rapid succession hit both tires on the passenger side. The car flew off the side of the road. There was nothing Kendra could do except ride out the storm and pray that someone came along before the killer finished the job – if the crash didn't do it first.

She had hit the gas pedal in an effort to outrun the sniper, so the car sailed over the ditch and found the nearest tree. The jolt felt as if she had gone off a cliff. Kendra fell forward. The seatbelt jerked her back. Her head hit the steering wheel.

Before the pain hardly registered, the sound of crunching metal faded into soundlessness. Darkness engulfed her as the car slid down the tree and settled with one last groan – hers and the car's. She floated in and out of that timeless, pain-induced night that could have lasted hours or minutes. She wasn't sure when the murkiness began to lift and tiny sparks of light teased her brain with urgent signals from beyond the shadows. Pictures, ideas, words, – she couldn't explain or describe them. She only knew it was imperative that she get back to the waking world – something about an attorney and a dead man in the lake.

# Twenty-five

Muted voices drifted over the airwaves – familiar but not yet recognizable. The would-be killer coming to finish the botched job? Someone trying to help? Either way, she was helpless and could only wait immobilized between the steering wheel and the seat.

Without opening her eyes or giving any indication she was conscious, Kendra mentally took inventory of her body parts and decided they were all intact. Except for the closeness of the steering wheel to her chest, she was breathing without much difficulty. Her head hurt so badly she knew it had to be still connected to her body. She could move arms and legs – no broken bones.

Finally, voices began to clear. Brian and Lenny were on either side of her. Doors squawked and groaned as they opened. Brian's fingers checked her pulse. The seatbelt gave way and she would have fallen onto the steering wheel if Brian hadn't been holding her. *Lenny must have cut it loose on the other side*. Her eyelids felt glued shut. A small groan was the only sound she could push from her throat.

"She's alive," Lenny said. His fingers carefully probed her neck and shoulders. "She doesn't seem to have any bones out of place. Can we lift her out, or should we wait for an ambulance."

"No ambulance," Kendra whispered with difficulty. Her eyes still wouldn't open – not that she wanted them to. She dared not risk a peek at what she would, or would not see. *I probably don't look much better than the pile of metal that used to be my car. How did Brian and Lenny get here so quickly? Are they responsible for my predicament? Was David wrong about them? Or is Severs behind my troubles?*

Lenny chuckled as he pulled the seat belt away. "Sounds like she's coming around enough to give us orders. I guess she's going to be all right."

"I hope you're right," said Brian from the other side. "You ease her from that side and I'll take this side. Let's see if we can slide her out from under that steering wheel. It doesn't seem to be resting against her, just close. The seat belt held her back."

Kendra couldn't keep back another groan as they pushed and pulled her free and eased her down on the ground beside the car.

"Where are you hurt?" Brian's fingers explored for obvious punctures and protruding bones.

"My arm…you pulled too hard," she managed. "Head hurts…better shape than…car."

Brian checked the lump rising on her head. "Open your eyes and let me see if you can focus," he said holding up two fingers for me. "You need to see a doctor."

"I did…yesterday."

Lenny, knowing her longer, accepted that as an attempt at joking and gave a nervous laugh. Brian didn't think it was funny at all and ignored Lenny's fit of giggles. "The nearest hospital is about thirty miles," he said. "I'll take you there."

"No. I'll see Doc Jones when I get back." Her cognizance was quickly returning. Once she was out of the car and away from the immediate danger, the reason for urgency became more acute. She struggled to sit, supported by Brian's arm around her. Lenny knelt before her on one knee looking anxious and concerned despite his previous fit of giggles.

"I have a date with a lawyer," Kendra said, rubbing her temples. "I don't intend to let Paul Brooks send out a team of thugs to arrest me on contempt charges, or whatever he decides to trump up because I didn't show."

"You think this was an attempt to keep you away from his office?" Brian looked at her with concern as well as admiration.

"Don't you?" Kendra asked trying to stare at him. The pain

made it impossible to keep her gaze without blinking.

"Probably," he answered. "We can call him and tell him there's been an accident and you'll be in tomorrow."

"I think he already knows there was an *incident.* I refuse to dignify it with the word *accident*. Help me up. We'll go now." She leaned forward and tried to sit up, but fell back against Brian.

"Kendra, you need to…"

"Brian, my head hurts and I feel thoroughly shook up, but I think I can function, at least long enough to take care of Paul Brooks. I just tried to get up too quickly." She lifted her head and tried to smile. "But, I'll postpone my shopping for another time."

Brian shook his head in disbelief and turned to Lenny. "I'll take her from here, Lenny. You get out of here before anyone sees you. Call the *authorities* and let them know what happened. See if you can get someone out here to remove the car before the wrong people see it."

Lenny nodded, patted her cheek and left. Lenny was gone by the time Brian picked her up and carried her to his car. Placing her on the passenger seat and closing the door, Brian went to retrieve her purse. When he got in the driver's side, Kendra glanced at him, but said nothing.

In her state of physical pain and emotional upheaval, she had nearly missed Lenny's words in their finger language, *Hang in there, baby. We'll talk soon.*

Brian started the car, but paused before pulling onto the highway. He didn't look at her but had such a serious look on his face that she knew something was on his mind. She watched him, her own mind whirling with questions. Finally, Kendra broke the silence.

"I know," she said with sigh, repressing a shiver. "You told me to stay out of trouble, but how was I to know someone would use me for target practice? I guess I should have known. If I didn't show up, or if I ended up dead, Vincent's murder would be solved and I would be out of their way."

Brian glanced at her, but avoided her eyes. "How did you get so smart about the law if your dad never talked to you about his work?"

"Brian, I told you before, Dad never once spoke of a case. David and I learned to listen and observe by simply being at the Federal Building so often. We were just kids so they figured we wouldn't know what they were talking about. By the time, we were old enough for anyone to worry about us, we'd learned enough to become invisible when it was necessary. I could tell you more than you would ever want to know about almost any person in that building, but the greatest lesson I learned from my dad, was integrity. Just because *I* know something, doesn't mean *everyone* should know it."

"Kendra, you are truly one of a kind," he smiled at her.

"Aren't you glad of that?" Kendra grinned then winced.

"Now, that you mention it," he answered, "I don't think I could cope with more than one of you."

They both laughed.

# Twenty-six

Silence hung heavily in the air for a minute or two. Kendra didn't want to believe Lenny and Brian had anything to do with the accident – especially after Lenny reassured her with his finger language – but she had to ease her doubts and fears.

"Brian, how did you and Lenny just happen to be there when I needed you? I left later than I thought – not intentionally. I just couldn't move as quickly as I wanted to."

Brian spoke without hesitation, not taking time to form a lie. "I got a phone call about the time I should have left. By the time I got off the phone, I was running late. I ran into Lenny in the lobby. He came to get me, hoping you were with me. He overheard a conversation that made him think you were in trouble. We both realized the phone call was a ruse and you *were* in some kind of trouble, so we took off. We saw your car go off the road. A black sedan left rubber on the road heading for Fairplain. I hope no one saw Lenny's car behind me. He could be in real danger."

"What kind of danger? Can't you tell me what's going on?" Kendra pleaded but knew the answer even before Brian turned to face her as he pulled to the curb in Fairplain.

"Kendra, I wish I could, but it's so complicated."

"And you think I'm *only* a woman and can't understand?" Anger flared then fell into her pool of pain. "I'm sorry, I know better than that, but I can't stand the thought of Lenny being in trouble because of me."

"Lenny would give his life for you. I think you know that. He's an intelligent young man. I'm sure he can take care of himself. There's Ira Thoburg with Sheriff Brooks. He doesn't look too happy.

Wonder what's going on?" Brian nodded at the two men across the street as he eased his car down the street opposite the sheriff's office.

The tall, gray haired man with a white mustache and Paul Brooks stood outside the police station. Neither of them seemed to notice Brian's car and like Brian said, Mr. Thoburg didn't look very happy. Paul, on the other hand, looked as if he had just solved the murder of Vincent Burke. He turned, strutted into his office and closed the door behind him. Ira Thoburg stood on the walk pounding one fist repeatedly into the other open hand, staring at the closed door.

Brian opened the car door. Ira looked across the street to the car and began taking long, striding steps that closed the distance between them. He was still glowering, his mouth moving with silent mutterings until Kendra got out of the car on the other side. Then a broad grin replaced his angry glower. He ran the last few steps with his arms extended. Brian grabbed Ira's hand and shook it as if he were a long, lost friend, preventing the man from catching Kendra in a bear hug.

"Brian," Ira said with obvious relief, "Sheriff Brooks said I was too late – that my client was killed in an automobile accident and the case is closed. Kendra Donovan killed Vincent Burke."

"He was a little premature in his predictions," said Brian. "Ira, I want you to meet your new client, Kendra Donovan. Kendra, Attorney Ira Thoburg."

Ira looked at Kendra with a more professional expression, but she hadn't missed his earlier expression and, like Brian, believed he had intended to hug her. She was glad for the exchange between the two men that gave her time to force her feelings back under control. She wanted to run into her brother's arms. Why did he have to keep his identity secret? When could they stop all the game playing? She forced a smile and turned her attention to Ira Thoburg, Attorney at Law.

"Believe me, Miss Donovan," he said, "I can't say how relieved I am to see you alive and... but, you don't look so well. What happened?"

"Someone used me for target practice. If the sheriff knew about it, why didn't he come to my aid? Unless of course he was the one who took the pot shots, or hired someone to do it. At any rate, Mr. Thoburg, I'm glad to meet you. I hope you can get me out of this mess." Kendra smiled again and extended her hand to shake his. He took it and held a little longer than would have been considered a normal handshake, releasing her only when she gently tugged her hand back.

Once again, with their finger language her brother expressed his concern. She told him she would be all right. Brian frowned, but said nothing. He started for the sheriff's door.

"Shall we burst his little bubble?"

"With pleasure," Ira Thoburg said. "I'm looking forward to wiping the smug grin off his face."

Paul sat at his desk in his swivel chair with his back to the door. He held the phone to his ear as he rocked from side to side in his chair. He didn't bother to turn around when he heard the door open. "Come back later," he said over his shoulder. "I've got things to do this morning. Don't have time for petty gripes."

"Oh, but we have an appointment with you *Sheriff* Brooks." Kendra didn't bother to hide her sarcasm or disgust.

Paul whirled around in his chair so fast he turned a complete circle, pulling the phone cord around him. The handset fell to the floor as he continued to twirl. Paul's head jerked up and his jaw dropped when he saw Kendra, Brian and the attorney he had just met standing in front of his desk. He managed to untangle the cord and retrieved the phone from the floor while his three visitors watched with exaggerated smiles.

"I'll call you back," Paul said once he had retrieved the handset. "The Donovan girl just walked in here with her lawyer." He didn't sound at all happy. He didn't bother to say goodbye to the person on the phone. He slammed the phone back onto its cradle.

"Well, Kendra Donovan. Didn't expect you to show up." There was that sneer again.

"I'm sure you didn't, Paul." She purposely used his first name. "Your aim was a little off."

"You accusing me of something? You better be careful or I'll arrest you for…"

"For what, Sheriff?" Ira Thoburg asked.

"Who are you? I never saw you around here before."

"We just met outside. You were all excited that your murder case was solved because your primary suspect was just killed in an accident. Looks like you were wrong. I'm Ira D. Thoburg, Attorney at Law, graduate of Harvard Law School. I practice in Grand Rapids and I'm here to represent Miss Donovan."

"Let's get this over with. I got more important things to do."

"Ask away, Sheriff. Miss Donovan will only answer what I tell her she can answer. Then we'll deal with her treatment while in your custody yesterday – and do you suppose you could offer the lady a chair?"

Paul glared. He nodded to the chairs around the card table. "Help yourself," he said then made a point of searching his desk for his list of questions. He cleared his throat, picked up a freshly sharpened pencil and began. "Where were you night before last?"

Brian pulled a chair over for Kendra and stood behind her with his hands on her shoulders.

"That depends on the time." Kendra answered as calmly as she could.

"You know what time I mean," he bellowed.

Kendra held her head between her hands and squeezed her eyes shut to ease the throbbing pain. "I'm sorry," she spoke in a low, even, controlled voice, "I'm not a mind reader, nor am I deaf. I have a splitting headache, so please do not raise your voice to me again, or you will ask these questions another time – in court."

Attorney Ira Thoburg chuckled and Paul gripped his pencil so hard it broke in two. He threw it in the wastebasket, grabbed another one, and tried a different approach. "Did you see Vincent Burke night before last?"

Ira nodded to Kendra and she answered, "Yes."

"Where?" The sheriff didn't raise his head but continued to look at his paper searching for something on which to hang this interrogation.

"At the *Italian Café*."

"You were with him?"

"No."

"You talked to him?"

"Yes."

The affirmative answer brought his head up. He looked as if he hoped she would say something to trip herself. "What did you say to him?"

"I don't remember the exact words," she answered. "He made some comment about wanting time alone with me and I told him he would get more of the same that he got before if he didn't leave me alone. He and his thugs surrounded me and I said, 'Vincent, you'll never learn, will you?' I maneuvered away from him and left him picking himself up off the floor – again."

"You don't deny you threatened him?" Paul sounded pleased that he had her on this one.

"I didn't *threaten* him, Sheriff. I *clobbered* him." Kendra returned his glare.

Ira chuckled. "Miss Donovan, please don't offer more information than the sheriff is asking for."

Brian watched the proceedings with interest.

Paul glared at Mr. Thoburg and then at Kendra. He looked back at his list of questions. "Did you see him later that night?"

"No."

"What time did you get home?"

"About ten."

"Did you go out again?"

"No."

"Were you alone all night?"

"No."

Paul raised his head again and sneered at her then glanced at

Brian. "Who was with you?"

"You don't need to answer that question at this time," said Ira.

"I need to verify her story," said Paul turning his glare at the attorney.

"It's all right, Ira," said Brian. "I was with her all night. I will verify the fact that she didn't leave the cabin from ten o'clock until after we had breakfast the next morning."

Paul didn't look surprised, nor did he look pleased. He looked back at his list. "Did you sleep together?" he asked without looking up.

"You don't need to answer that question, Miss Donovan. It's irrelevant to the issue." Ira Thoburg clenched his fists and glowered at the sheriff.

"If he wasn't in bed with her, how could he know whether she was in the cabin all night?" Sheriff Brooks raised his head and glared first at the attorney, then at Brian. Anger replaced the sullenness as he realized he had just trapped himself. Three grinning faces met his sullen look.

"Like I said, Sheriff, she didn't leave the cabin," said Brian. "You can draw your own conclusions."

"Sheriff, in light of the way my client was treated yesterday – I heard the tape – I think you owe her an apology for the treatment as well as an explanation of why you even brought her in for questioning in the first place. And believe me, if she doesn't receive both within the next two and a half minutes, you can expect to receive a summons to court for harassment and whatever else I can fit into the space provided for complaints." Attorney Ira Thoburg stared at Paul.

Paul Brooks fixed his gaze on Kendra with such hatred that she could almost feel the intensity of it. "Vincent Burke was murdered sometime between midnight and three a.m. We have a witness who said he saw you with him about midnight. Considering how you *clobbered* Vincent several times, I wasn't going to take any chances with you when I brought you in yesterday. I'm sorry if you misinterpreted that as harassment."

"I don't suppose you can tell us who saw my client with Burke?"

"That's confidential information."

"Then your confidential informant was mistaken this time. And that, in my book, is not an apology."

Kendra watched the perspiration begin to dot Paul's brow. "Forget it, Mr. Thoburg," she said. "I wouldn't want the sheriff to choke on his words. I might have to do mouth to mouth resuscitation and I would be too tempted to let him suffocate. If you're through with me, *Sheriff* Brooks, I need to see a doctor – again."

"Don't leave town, Kendra Donovan. This case ain't closed yet."

"Is that a threat, Sheriff?" Attorney Thoburg looked intently in the eyes of his opponent and made a big deal of removing the micro tape recorder from his shirt pocket.

"Get out." Paul snapped another pencil in two and threw it in the wastebasket. Before they even closed the door behind them, Paul grabbed the phone. They knew he was getting back to whomever he had been talking with when they entered the office.

"Thank you, Mr. Thoburg," Kendra once again extended her hand to the lawyer, who took it in his hand. With the finger language she said, *David, please tell me what, or who, I'm looking for.*

He answered, *I wish I knew. Please go home.*

She said, *I can't. No car.* This time David gently withdrew his hand.

"Send me a bill," Kendra said and handed him a small business card with her name and address on it, "unless you want cash."

"It's all taken care of Miss Donovan. I'm glad I was able to help. If you ever need my services again, just tell Brian. He has my number. I'm semi-retired and don't take a lot of cases anymore."

"I see. In other words, don't call me, I'll call you." Kendra tried to laugh, but it sounded more like a half sob.

Ira said, "You might say that. I guess I don't want a lot of people knowing where I am. I would be inundated with calls."

"I'm glad you were willing to come out of hibernation to help me," Kendra said. She felt so close to tears that she turned toward the car. She knew her brother. Another second or two and he would have had her in his arms.

"I think Kendra has had more than enough shock for one day," said Brian. "She needs to get back and see Doc Jones. I wanted to take her to the hospital, but she refused."

The attorney nodded and began walking in the opposite direction. His car was at the other end of town where no one would notice it. Brian took Kendra's arm and started across the street.

It took all her will power not to look back at the fake attorney. The pain in her heart was so much greater than the pain in her head. *Will we ever be able to stop playing this game of hide and seek?*

# Twenty-seven

Storm clouds gathered forces for another march across northern Michigan as Kendra and Brian left Fairplain. Except for the rain on the trip up from Akron three days ago, the weather had been sunny and pleasant. *Has it been only three days?* Another enjoyable memory from childhood crowded in between the pounding of headache and the prospects of spending the day in bed. *David and I loved to sit in the dark on the porch, watch the storms and listen to the drumming of the rain on the roof. Maybe that sound will help me sleep and soothe my aching head.*

Brian was as engrossed in his own thoughts, so silence prevailed. They met no more trouble on the return trip. Kendra hoped they'd left all the trouble in Fairplain, but she knew better. At least she had the satisfaction of knowing she was right in her assumption that whatever put her father in danger was in the lodge area.

She winced as they passed where she had left her wrecked car. It was gone.

"It's taken care of," Brian said noticing her glance. "You need to see the doctor and rest."

"It was totaled, wasn't it?"

"Yes, but it's only a car. You are safe and that's more important."

"But my Dad gave it to me and now they don't make them anymore and Dad is…"Kendra wanted to argue the point more, but felt too close to tears and she could hardly keep her eyes open. "I should have taken care of it myself," she said, "but you're right. I don't feel up to doing much of anything right now, except sleeping.

That's the only thing that will get rid of this headache."

Brian let out a sigh of relief.

*Did he think he would have to fight with me to see the doctor? I'm not stupid. I know when I need help – well, sometimes.*

"What are friends for," he said, "if not to help out in an emergency?"

"Brian, I haven't known you long enough for you to be that good a friend. There are folks I've known for years I wouldn't let take care of me the way you're doing." Kendra frowned, trying to make sense of what she'd just said. The throbbing in her head made it difficult to think. "I'm not sure I meant that the way it sounds. Please don't pay any attention to me. I think my brain got a little scrambled." She tried to smile but the effort was too great, so she turned to look out the window.

Brian said nothing as he drove around the curved driveway to the main entrance of the infirmary. Large drops of rain began to splatter the windshield. At least there was a roof over the entrance.

Doc Jones met them in the waiting room where she'd been the day before. He still wore the same spot-marked professional coat that should have been white, but years of wear left the sleeves frayed and the color a dull gray. Once again, Doc laid aside his magazine and stood to greet them.

"Kendra Donovan. I might've known you'd be back. You always did have a knack for keeping me busy. What happened this time? Looks like quite a bump on your head." Doc Jones approached them. "Sit down here child where I can reach you."

"Sorry, Doc," she said trying to smile. "Someone has to keep you busy. Don't want you to sleep the day away, after you read all the magazines in the waiting room."

Doc Jones laughed and said, "Let's get a closer look. Someone hit you with a ball bat or something?"

"No, someone used her for target practice and sent her car off the road into a tree," said Brian. "She was lucky he wasn't a very good shot, or you would be doing an autopsy instead of patching up a bump on the head."

Doc turned and looked up at Brian. "You must be Brian McNeil. Someone told me you'd taken a liking to our little girl." He turned back to Kendra, smiled and patted her shoulder condescendingly. A rush of anger sent a warm feeling to her cheeks.

"Well, you're right on one count," Brian said. "I am Brian McNeil, but I hardly think Kendra is anyone's little girl. She's a quite capable young woman. What can you do for her headache?"

Kendra flashed a grateful glance at Brian. He saw it and winked at her. She managed a small smile. Doc Jones hadn't missed any of it, but wisely said nothing. "Come back to the examination room and let's take a closer look," he said.

She sat on the edge of his special examination table. He made a big production of checking her eyes and feeling for other bumps on her head. "Do you have any other pain – arms, legs, internal?"

"No, just my arm from yesterday. The wreck didn't help that any. I think all I really need is a good long nap and I'll be fine. Maybe something a little stronger than aspirin for the pain and I'll go to the cabin to sleep it off."

"Hmm. Didn't know you had a medical degree. You might be right, but I think it would be better if you slept it off here, where I can keep an eye on you. Could have a concussion. You can stretch out on a cot back there and sleep the rest of the day then we'll see about going back to the cabin tonight. I don't think you should be alone." He purposely glanced at Brian as he stressed the word *alone*.

"Oh, I'm not alone, Doc. I have Angel with me and Brian has spent the last couple of nights. I'm sure he won't mind another." Kendra flashed a confident smile at the doctor, but averted her eyes from Brian.

"She's right, Doc," said Brian. "She won't be alone, but how about a compromise. You keep her here for the afternoon and I'll pick her up around five, or before, and take her back to the cabin for the night. That should give you enough time to make sure she's all right."

"Do I have any say in this?" She felt a surge of anger akin to the times she was a child. She felt as if she wanted to stomp her foot and scream at them.

"Of course, you do," answered Doc Jones winking at Brian. "You can either sleep on the cot back there or in a chair right here. I think the cot would be more comfortable. I'll give you something for the pain and you can forget all your worries."

"I'll be back as soon as I can," said Brian. He kissed Kendra and left her in Doc's care.

***

Brian breathed a sigh of relief. He had to check on some other matters and make some calls. Kendra would be safe in Doc's care.

Back in his room, he gathered a few clothes and toiletries. *Whether Kendra likes it or not, I'm moving into Wolverine Cabin until this mess is over, or until Kendra goes home. Somehow, I don't think that she will do that.*

He made his calls and checked the grocery supply, then made a quick trip to the store. It was close to two when he stopped by the infirmary.

"Isn't she with you?" Doc looked perturbed.

"No, I've been out. I said I would pick her up about five, but have all my errands run, so came early."

"She's not here. I went to the bathroom about an hour ago. When I checked on her a little later, she was gone. I assumed you..."

"She's gone? Doc, she's in no condition to..."

"I know, but you know Kendra Donovan. She makes up her mind and no one can stop her. She's probably at the cabin sleeping."

"She better be. Just wait 'til I..." Brian stomped out of the office and drove down to the cabin muttering to himself. "What a bull-headed, stubborn...just wait..."

Brian parked behind the cabin and hurried inside with the grocery sacks. He only took time to set them on the table then stomped down the hall, not caring if he woke her.

"Kendra, what do you think...?"

Her room was empty – hadn't been touched since she left that morning. He went from room to room. Kendra was not in the cabin. He grabbed the phone and called Doc's office.

"She's not here," he said.

"Well, don't get too concerned. Except for the headache, she was well enough to go wandering. You stay there. I'll send someone out to look around for her."

Brian replaced the phone and put away the groceries. He fed Angel and grumbled about stubborn women. *Just what does she think she's doing and where is she? Maybe I should call Lenny. She might be with him.*

He closed his phone more concerned. Lenny hadn't seen her.

***

Kendra watched Brian leave, feeling abandoned and close to tears. She knew it was residue feelings from the accident and possibly shock, but she wished she could have gone with him. *I really do need to lie down, though, and Brian will be back in a couple of hours. Maybe I'll feel better after a nap.*

Doc Jones handed her three tablets and a glass of water. Kendra looked at the tablets then back to Doc. "I never take more than one tablet for anything. Isn't three a little overkill for a headache?" she asked.

"Kendra Donovan, like I said before, do you have a medical degree?"

"No, but…"

"No buts about it. If I say you need three, you take three. They're mild pain pills and one or two won't do much good. Now be a good little girl. Take your medicine and lie down. I have work to do. I'll check on you periodically and give you more pills if you need them."

"All right," she sighed. But she still felt uneasy – that unfamiliar paranoia she'd been feeling a lot lately. She popped the pills in her mouth, lifted the glass of water to her lips, drank about half of it then handed it back to Doc Jones. As, she turned toward the cot, she grabbed a handful of tissues from a box on his desk and sneezed, spitting the pills into the tissue.

"Are you coming down with a cold on top of it?" he asked. "Maybe I better give you something for that."

"Not a cold," she said, "just allergy, or something. I sneeze sometimes when a storm is moving in. The wind must blow in some pollen. I'm fine." Kendra took some more tissues and went to the cot at the far end of the infirmary. She was asleep before Doc Jones hardly got back to the front of the room.

It seemed only minutes later when he woke her to give her more pills. Groggily she took them without protest, but promptly sneezed them into the tissue as he walked away."

"Are you sure you aren't coming down with a cold?" Doc turned back to stare at her.

Kendra felt groggy, even though she hadn't actually taken any of the pills. She thought it must be the stress and the bump on the head, but she managed to answer his question. "Maybe it's the pills," she said. "I only seem to sneeze when you give them to me, and only once, so I suppose it's all right."

"You might be right. If you start sneezing, or coughing, more I'll give you something else." He left and she promptly fell back into a fitful sleep until Doc woke her again to give her more pills.

Each dose prompted a sneeze, until he began to laugh. "I never knew them to do that before, but they don't seem to affect you any other way. How's the headache?"

"Still there, but getting better, I think."

The next time Kendra woke, it was to the sound of voices in the infirmary. It was so dark outside that she wasn't sure of the time. There were other people in the office, so Doc had drawn a curtain around her cot.

"Remember I have a patient asleep on the cot back there," Doc said, "so keep your voices down."

*Must be someone else with a medical need.* Kendra closed her eyes and started to drift again. Paul Brooks' voice brought her eyes wide open. She forced herself to stay awake and listen.

# Twenty-eight

*It has to be later than five o'clock. Where is Brian and why is Paul Brooks here after hours? He doesn't sound like he's in need of medical attention. Doc sounded angry when he told him to keep his voice down.*

"How long is she going to sleep?" Paul asked.

*Why does he sound so chummy with Doc Jones? Are they talking about me? They must be unless Doc brought someone else in after me.* Kendra tried to lie as quietly as possible so they wouldn't know she was awake.

"Long enough," said Doc. "I've given her enough stuff she'll sleep forever." He laughed as if he had told a terrific joke.

A sudden chill caused Kendra to clamp her teeth tightly together and grip the side of the cot to keep from shaking violently and crying out in protest. *All those pills he gave me were supposed to kill me. But why?*

As hard as she tried, it was impossible to keep from shivering as if a cold wind had suddenly blown over her. She closed her eyes, trying to make the voices go away. They didn't even fade, but continued to give her more reason for fear.

"What'd you want to do that for?" Paul sounded petulant. "You knew I wanted to have some fun with her. If McNeil can sleep with her, I don't know why I can't have a turn."

"Shut up, Paul. You're disgusting."

*Miss Elizabeth?* Kendra was glad she was facing the wall. Her eyes flew open again. Even though she knew the curtain was drawn, she didn't dare roll over for fear of making a sound that would bring Doc back to give her more pills – or worse. She closed a hand over her mouth to keep a gasp from escaping. It was all too real to be a dream.

"You always did ogle the poor child. You're just jealous because she always preferred Lenny to you and now it looks like McNeil even took her away from him."

*Miss Dorothy? I have to be hallucinating. Why would the Franklin sisters be here? Surely, they can't be in a secret partnership of some kind with Paul Brooks.*

"Well, I'm with Paul," said Mark. "I almost had her convinced to marry me until he came along. Must be his money."

*Marry Mark? Not in this lifetime. Is this what my father discovered? Is this why he's in hiding? Because these folks – except possibly Mark – know him? But, what are they doing that would cause him danger?*

"You're all wasting your time," Jonathan Cox said. "Kendra Donovan is only interested in finding out the truth about her father. You don't seriously believe she accepts that murder/suicide story. The head office knew if he came up here even for a vacation, he would smell a rat. They have *someone* working here already."

"Burke?"

"Possibly. I don't think Kendra knew him, but he's out of the picture now."

Kendra was close to tears. Jonathan Cox. *Is his wife here too? They were always so nice to me and seemed so concerned when I arrived.* Then Myrtle's soft chuckle filled the room.

"That little girl always was too smart for her own good. We can't assume she doesn't know anything. She's too perceptive not to have picked up some inklings of what we're doing. I'm sure those pictures told her something. I don't know what possessed Severs to ask for snapshots in the first place."

"Where did they come from anyway?" Doc asked.

"I'm not sure – some struggling photographer one of the agents met somewhere."

"Richardson? He a sort of photographer."

"Don't be stupid," said Paul. "Lenny doesn't know which end of the camera to point and which button to click."

"What could she possibly see in unrelated photographs anyway?"

"How would I know? I just know she told Severs she saw something and the next thing we knew she was here."

"Shut up, Myrtle. She might be listening," said Paul. "I'll go check and make sure…"

Paul started toward the cot. Kendra squeezed her eyes shut and held her breath, but Doc stopped him before he got near her.

"Leave her alone, Paul. She's asleep. I guarantee it. She'll stay out and will never know what hit her when we dump her in the lake. We have to wait until it gets dark and with that storm out there, we'll have plenty of cover. We've got to get her out of here before that next shipment arrives early tomorrow morning."

"Say, what about Lenny? We going to let him in on any of this?" Paul still sounded petulant, but then he always did.

"You don't seriously believe his story about drifting from bar to bar playing the piano since his parents' separated do you?" Miss Elizabeth asked.

"I only know his parents waited until the night they left to give him a choice of going to California or New York. He chose to make it on his own. The piano was about all he knew and he has improved." Myrtle Cox always seemed to like Lenny.

"That may be true, but that doesn't mean he's been on the streets since then. Has he said anything about drugs to any of you?" Doc asked and waited for an answer.

"No, but he said he was involved in a few scrapes and spent some time in prison for being at the wrong place at the wrong time."

"Personally, I don't trust him," said Paul. "He's too sneaky and too chummy with McNeil."

"What do we know about McNeil? Is he the playboy he claims to be?"

"Seems to be. But again, he's too chummy with Lenny and the Donovan girl."

"Well, we need to take care of this shipment then we'll decide about Lenny. I think we can ignore McNeil for now. If he starts getting nosy, we'll take care of him."

Kendra's mind was whirling. *So that's it! They're running a drug ring under the cover of a respectable vacation resort! Lenny is involved? And Brian?*

"Lenny's playing the piano upstairs. We might need someone to help with the shipment. Once he's in, we will be able to keep him with threats of becoming fish bate. He doesn't need to know everything. We better get upstairs and act normal for dinner." Jonathan Cox sounded irritated. He never even pretended to like Paul Brooks.

"What about McNeil? Did he believe you when you said Kendra left and you don't know where she went?"

*Brian was here?* Kendra felt a sudden tingling of panic. *Will he come back for me?*

"Yeah," answered Doc, "he said she would probably show up at the cabin. Listen, sounds like he's in the cabin now."

The crackling noise from the corner of the infirmary sounded like a static radio. Kendra had heard it off and on while she dozed. Brian talking to Angel, telling her he didn't know where Kendra was, but was sure she would show up soon. Laughter floated across the infirmary.

"He's as bad as she is. Talking to a stupid cat." Mark sounded disgusted.

"Well, we better get upstairs," said Myrtle. "People are going to wonder where we all are. Jonathan and I will leave now. Mark, you follow in a few minutes."

"Paul, you better check the boat and get it ready to take it out later," said Doc.

"Dorothy and I better go with Jonathan and Myrtle," said Elizabeth. "We usually dine early. Doc, give us five minutes then you follow."

"What if she's faking and tries to get out?" Paul was still

peevish.

"I'll know it if she does." Doc sounded exasperated with Paul. "If the door opens a silent alarm is connected to my beeper."

"What about the window?"

"She's not going to climb out the window in the shape she's in. And if she should try, it's a sheer drop down to the rain-swollen stream. She would be in the lake in no time. Besides, the window screen is also connected to the alarm. She can open the window but as soon as she slides the screen aside it will set off the alarm. Now, come on let's get out of here."

With the click of a switch, the room lost its light. The door closed, a lock fell in place and Kendra was alone in the dark infirmary. It must be near dinnertime, almost seven. Normally it was still daylight at that hour but the storm brought an early twilight effect that would last until the storm was over. By then it would be dark.

Flashes of lightening gave short spurts of brilliance to the room. Kendra moved the curtain from around her cot to get her bearings. Her eyes adjusted to the darkness but she could only see shapes, not specifics. *I have to get out of here before they return. I don't dare use the phone to call Brian, but at this point, I'm not even sure I can trust him. He's spent a lot of time with Lenny. Everyone I've known, loved and trusted seems to be in this mysterious drug ring.*

Kendra sat on the side of the cot, feeling lightheaded. She stood, eased over to the window and slid it to one side to let in some fresh air to clear her head. *I have to get out of here, but how? And where will I go? O God, I need Your help. Please, show me the way.*

# Twenty-nine

There were only two windows in the room. The other one had a heavy drape pulled over it. No light came around the solid door. All Kendra had was the twilight inside and the flash of lightning outside that gave brief blinding light to the room. She glanced around furtively for something, anything, to help her escape. The cool, moist air blowing in the window began to clear her head. It still throbbed, but at least she could think. She wasn't too concerned about getting wet. She just wanted to get out – alive if possible.

The pills that Doc had given her were in her pocket. *If I had swallowed them, I would either be dead, or nearly so by now*. Had someone asked, she couldn't have said what prompted her to pretend to sneeze and deposit the pills in a tissue each time he gave them to her. Something hadn't felt right. Her mother, who was a nurse, constantly preached about the danger of taking too many painkillers, so Kendra wasn't used to taking much medication and thought three of anything was too much.

When lightning flashed again, the equipment and supplies cart caught her attention. She looked closer and pulled a rubber surgical glove from a box, placing the pills in a finger of a glove. She rolled the glove into a small ball and stuffed it in her pocket. *That will protect the pills if I get soaked. If I get out of this alive, I want to know what's in those pills.*

Lightning flashed again, reflecting something metal – surgical instruments. Kendra picked up a scalpel, tested it against her finger. Perfect. *Hopefully I can cut out the screen without setting off the alarm.* She pulled a chair closer to the window, so she wouldn't have to stretch and accidently set of the alarm. Carefully, Kendra worked the blade around the perimeter of the screen, keeping it an inch away from the frame. Luckily, it was the newer soft mesh-type screen, not the old wire ones. As she finished the perimeter, the screen fell from the window, leaving the entire area open and the alarm still intact – hopefully.

Standing on the chair, Kendra looked down. It wasn't such a long drop to the ground, but the terrain slanted in such a way she was sure to slide down the hill toward the stream even if it had been dry. The rain-soaked ground would be even more slippery. With the storm, the water in the stream was flowing faster than usual on its trek to the lake.

Kendra studied the situation. *Not much time. Someone will return soon.* She looked out again and noticed a small ledge that ran along the side of the building about three feet below the window. *Maybe I can stand on that ledge and ease around to the end of the building where the slant isn't so sharp and trees and undergrowth are thicker. It won't be the first time I climbed out a window and I hope it won't be the last.*

Ignoring the pain, Kendra pulled herself to the windowsill, being careful not to move the frame in case it was super sensitive to the alarm system. She turned and backed out the window. She landed on the ledge, glad for tennis shoes instead of leather-soled sandals. Clutching the window ledge, she began inching her way across the side of the building. Digging her fingers into the tiny crevices between the bricks and keeping her feet on the ledge, she made it to the end of the building, lost in the darkness of shadows. She rounded the corner of the building and paused to catch her breath. Before she could let go, voices came from the open window. They were back and had discovered her escape.

Mark stuck his head out the window. "She went out the window. I thought you said she couldn't do that."

"I don't know how she could," answered Doc. He stood on the chair to see out the window. "She was so heavily sedated she couldn't possible walk very far and with her injuries there's no way she could survive the fall. She must have slid down the bank to the stream. Call Paul and tell him to get down there and find her. There's no place else for her to be."

Kendra froze against the wall, feeling like a lump of cement plastered to the side of the building. She didn't think anyone could see her, but she held her breath and closed her eyes – as if that would hide her more. Ignoring the pain in her arm and her throbbing head, she clung tightly to the bricks with her fingertips, keeping her toes on the ledge.

*Please, God, help me. I don't understand any of this. Help me get to my family. Maybe they can make sense of it all.*

Hardly breathing, Kendra had no idea how long she clung to the side of the building. Her fingers were so numb she could no longer feel the bricks. Had it not been for the pain in her arm and head, she would have thought she'd turned to a cement statue. The throbbing headache dulled her thinking. She would have to survive on instinct alone, ignoring the inconveniences of pain, cold and discomfort. For now, she had to hold on until it was safe to let go. Down by the stream, Paul and Mark searched downstream toward the lake. Their voices carried above the storm.

"She must have stayed in the water, if she survived the fall," said Mark, yelling above the roll of thunder and the pounding wind and rain. "Probably in the lake by now."

"You don't know Kendra Donovan very well," returned Paul. Another flash of lightning and loud boom of thunder distorted and lost some of his next words. "…knows the stream…deep…"

"Yeah, but… hurt…drowned," Mark called back.

"I tell you she's smart… think of something." Paul's voice carried his anger and petulance.

"Well, if you know so much about her, you look for her. I'm going in out of this cold rain. I'm soaked."

"You ain't going nowhere until we find her." Paul screamed.

"Yeah, well, let's go see what Doc says. She's not here."

Their voices faded, became louder as they moved up the lane then faded again as they went to the front of the building. Kendra waited for what seemed like hours until she could hold on no longer. Her fingers slipped away from the small crevice between bricks. Her stiff, cold body couldn't obey her command to run, so she fell, tumbling, sliding with the mud toward the fast moving stream. Small plants uprooted and slid with her until finally her numb fingers grabbed at them. A small, but stable sapling stopped her fall and Kendra forced her arms to pull the rest of her body across the wet terrain. She found a minimum of cover under the leaves of a small bush. Gasping for breath, she wondered if anyone had heard her fall? *Will they find me?* She buried her face in the wet leaves to muffle the sound of breathing.

The throbbing in her head, the pain in her arm and the ache in her heart at the shock of learning her friends weren't friends after all, sent her mind whirling as violently as the storm around her. Time no longer had meaning. She could have been there ten minutes or two hours. She only knew she was soaked to the skin and chilled to the bone.

*If I don't get warm and dry soon, I will go into shock and all the running will have been for nothing. But where can I go? What can I do? I can't stay hidden under this bush forever. By morning, I will be right where they want me – dead.*

Suddenly, she held her breath. Voices coming down the lane. They were faint but she recognized the manic giggle that Paul Brooks had when he was excited about something. The other voice was deeper and less excitable – Doc.

As they came closer she could make out words – "not in the stream – got away somehow – impossible in her condition.

"She had to have fell down to the stream," said Doc, his voice becoming more clear. *They must be on the path to the cabin.*

"Doc, you know Kendra Donovan as well as I do. She will always do what you don't expect her to do."

"If she's on the grounds, we find her. We'll see want McNeil has to say."

"Do you think he would tell us if she is there? We need to go in and search the cabin."

The sound of the rain through the trees and the wind above them began to drown out the voices as they moved down the lane. Kendra cautiously crawled from under the brush. With difficulty, she pulled herself up and leaned against a tree to get her bearings and make her legs feel alive. She heard a sound of something or someone crashing through the brush and froze, willing herself to melt into the tree. Fear coursed through her. She dropped back to the ground and flattened herself like a frozen log. The rain drenched dirt and rotting leaves pressed against her, making it impossible to breathe without a pungent odor assailing her sensitive nose. She held her breath to keep from sneezing. She felt as if her heart missed a beat – or several beats. *Doc and Paul went down the lane in front of me. Who is behind me?*

Hardly breathing, Kendra waited, watching from the corner of her eye. Another flash of lightning revealed the largest buck she'd ever seen. It leaped the bush under which she had taken refuge then continued across the lane where her pursuers turned and let out surprised yelps. The buck stopped in the lane long enough for them to register its size then it loped into the woods on the other side of the lane. Another crash of hooves meeting brittle twigs and he was gone. Thunder and lightning joined forces in applauding its disappearing act.

Paul broke the silence that followed. "Did you see that, Doc? Had to be a fourteen pointer." He giggled in his nervous, manic way. "Shoulda taken a shot at him."

"Never mind, Paul," said Doc, his voice quivering. He was obviously shaken as well, "we aren't here to go deer hunting. If the Donovan girl's in there, we would've heard her yell. Come on let's go down to the cabin and see if McNeil's heard from her."

Kendra had been too surprised and scared to even try to make her frozen vocal chords cry out. She waited flat on her stomach until the sound of their feet crunching on the wet sand and gravel faded or was swept away by the wind and rain. Lifting herself again from the ground, she held the little sapling for support. Her knees wanted to buckle like a rubber hose. Her hands and fingers were still numb. She stood for another second or two and took a few deep breaths without the smell of the dirt and rotting leaves.

Although her brain felt as foggy as the air around her was becoming, somewhere in the deep recesses of her mind she decided the first place they would have looked for her would have been her cabin. Maybe they would move on and not return. *But, Doc and Paul are on their way back there now. And Brian is there. Is he part of the drug ring? Was David wrong about him? Did Brian know about Doc and the rest? Is that why he left me with Doc?*

Kendra squeezed her eyes shut to block out distractions while she tried to think it through, but she became more confused and unable to think at all. Trembling and shaking like a young sapling in a winter storm, she wasn't sure she could move at all. It was well past the dinner hour, but could just as well have been past midnight.

*When we were kids, I knew those woods like the back of my hand. Can I still find my way? I will have to go through the woods.*

Instinct and the need to survive took over. With the next flash of lightning, Kendra saw no one near and heard no sound other than the storm, so she forced her legs to move. With a jerky motion, she crossed the lane. Once on the other side, her legs began to respond to her prodding and she plunged deeper into the woods where the deer had gone.

Even in her state of pain, exhaustion and fear, the terrain felt familiar, But Lenny and Paul also knew the area – Lenny better than Paul. *If anyone can find me, Lenny will be the one.* That brought stinging tears to her eyes. Except for David, Lenny had been her best friend. Even though she hadn't seen him for several years, she couldn't imagine him turning against her.

Step by careful step, she worked her way toward her cabin. *I will have to wait until it's safe enough to enter, but when? How will I know?*

Another uncontrollable tremble shook her body as the cold rain continued to wash over her, penetrating deep within each tiny little pore of her skin. She tried to think what to do next, but thoughts wouldn't focus. A sound behind her sent another shot of fear through her like an electric current. Instinctively she knew it was one of her pursuers.

A hand covered her mouth and strong arms pulled her against a man's body. His other hand went around her waist pinning her arms next to her side. He held her so close to him that she was sufficiently pinned and could neither move, nor scream – had she been inclined to do so. *Does he feel my heart pounding against his arm?*

Exhausted, Kendra leaned against him and felt the soft bristle of a beard against her neck. *Don't move and don't make a sound,* Lenny said with their finger language against her arm. Then he eased his hand from her mouth, but continued to hold her close to him.

Doc and Paul were on the lane moving toward them. Lenny shouted to them, "Another false alarm. It was just a skunk digging for grubs. I'll be back as soon as it moves on, unless you want me to come back smelling to high heaven." Laughter from the path mingled with the thunder rolling overhead.

Lenny continued to hold Kendra for a minute or two then whispered next to her ear, "Stay put until I can get them away." He dropped his hold and disappeared. Kendra felt as if she had turned to marble statue. She stayed where he left her, afraid to move, afraid to breathe if it hadn't been automatic. From a distance, Lenny called, "Some kids said they saw her up by the main highway, hitch-hiking. Maybe we need to check the motels at Fairplain or Wintersville. Did she have any money with her?"

"Probably not. McNeil took her purse with him when he left her this morning. She'll probably call him. Where's his car?" Doc responded.

"Behind the cabin. You want me to stake it out in case he goes looking for her?" Lenny asked.

"No, you go to Fairplain. We'll know if he gets a call from her. Mark, you watch the drive from the end of the lane. He might see you down there. I'll call the hospitals and see if she managed to get to one of them. Paul, you keep checking the stream and lake, but first let's check the cabin again."

More gravel crunched followed by someone pounding on the door. From her hidden spot behind the trees, Kendra could see a beam of light spread across the porch and spill into the lane as the cabin door opened.

"You heard from her?" Doc was addressing Brian who stood in the doorway.

"No. Are you sure she didn't say why she was leaving?"

"You ought to know Kendra Donovan better than that. She don't tell anyone anything if she don't want to. Like I told you, I thought she was asleep and stepped out of the office to the bathroom. When I came back, she was gone. I assumed you came for her until you came by later. Let me know if you hear anything. She's pretty unstable to be out in this weather."

"Sure thing, Doc, but maybe I ought to help you look?" Brian sounded genuinely worried and concerned.

"No, someone needs to be here in case she calls or shows up. You better stay close to the phone."

Brian closed the door and Paul and Doc trudged up the lane splattering mud and water everywhere. Kendra stood where she was, feeling as if her feet had grown roots and her body was turning into a tree. It wouldn't respond to her mind's instructions to move. She was scared, cold and soaked.

*How can I get in the cabin without Brian knowing? I can't just walk in the front door. What if he's really in alliance with the rest of them?*

Her throbbing head and aching arm reminded Kendra how vulnerable she was. Without permission, tears began to flow, followed by sobs, followed by more trembling throughout her body. *If I don't move, I feel like I'll die. But I might die if I do move. Oh, God, what should I do?*

Something brushed against her leg. Kendra jerked and glanced down at the opossum mamma carrying her little ones on their trek to wherever they were going. She wasn't afraid of the animal but it gave her incentive to move.

She found the two-plank footbridge across the stream and ran across it to the cover of the cabin. Slowly she crept behind the building to the window of her bedroom. She was glad she never locked the screen as it slid easily to one side. Carefully she lifted the window. A lot weaker than she realized, it took several tries before she could hoist herself up and through the open window.

As Kendra flung herself over the windowsill, the bedroom door flew open. Brian stood in the doorway casting a shadow across the room. Whatever his intentions, Kendra knew she was caught – half in and half out of the window.

# Thirty

Brian had paced from fireplace to kitchen, from front door to back door, pausing now and again to look out the window, but seeing only darkness and rain splashing against the pane. Angel trotted beside him until she suddenly stopped, looked toward Kendra's room and ran to paw at the door. Brian heard it too, a sound from her room, but what? He followed Angel and flung the door open. Kendra was half in and half out the window.

"Kendra! What are you doing?" Brian was at the window in two long strides. He caught her under the arms and pulled as she tried to push herself back out. Careful of her injuries, he kept a firm grasp on her so she wouldn't slip away. Once he had her in, he closed the window. Kendra backed away from him.

"Kendra?"

He reached a hand to push back the hair that hung in long, wet strings, covering most of her face. She drew back further, more like a scared, wounded animal than the girl he knew.

Brian frowned as Paul's angry voice accompanied the pounding on the front door. "Open up in there McNeil. This is the law." Brian uttered some words under his breath he hardly ever used. He saw the terror in Kendra's eyes and pushed down the urge to give the sheriff the beating of his life.

"Stay put," he said to Kendra, hoping she could comprehend a simple order.

***

Had Kendra been more alert, she would have caught the anxiety in his voice, but at that moment, all she could hear was the thumping of her own heart. When the door closed, she felt frozen to the spot.

Angel moved closer, sniffed, shook her paw when it touched the water on Kendra's leg. She sat back on her haunches to watch. Kendra's foggy mind hardly registered the fact that Angel was there. She wanted to run, but her muscles felt like a machine deprived of electricity. She backed into the corner behind the door and slid to the floor like a crumpled rag doll. She tried to make sense of what Paul and Brian were saying on the porch.

"What do you want Brooks? Doc Jones was just here and I told him I hadn't seen Kendra, if that's what you're here for."

"Yeah, well, let's just say I don't believe you. I want to look around for myself. I think she's been here all along. We've been searching these grounds for hours in this blasted rain. There's no way she could keep evading us unless she's hiding in here."

"Then maybe you better call in the State Police if you can't find her, because she hasn't been here all day and if you don't find her soon, *I'm* going to call them myself."

"Just open this door and step aside, McNeil. Let me have a look. I'm sure I'll find her in bed where you left her."

"*Sheriff* Brooks," said Brian his voice sounding strained and controlled. "I'm not accustomed to people calling me a liar. Nor am I accustomed to letting people into someone else's residence. Let me see your search warrant."

"I don't need no search warrant. I'm the law around here." Paul banged against the screen door again.

"Sorry, Brooks, but even *you* have to abide by the law of the land. Come back when you have that warrant. Until then, find Kendra Donovan."

The door closed hard, as if Brian had slammed it. Paul pounded the door again. Then all was quiet. But Brian didn't return. *Did he go with Paul or is he waiting for Paul to leave?* Then the bedroom door opened again.

Brian stared at the window. Feeling like a half-drowned animal, Kendra couldn't keep back a whimper. Brian whirled around and saw her huddled in the corner.

"Kendra, what's going on?" He reached to help her up, but Kendra was too scared to respond. She pressed back further into the corner – hoping if she pressed hard enough she would melt into the wall. Kneeling before her on one knee, Brian reached a hand to her in the same way he would to a terror-stricken animal. He stroked the hair from her face with the tips of his fingers.

"Sweetheart, you're soaked and covered with mud. Why don't you get out of those wet clothes and into something warm and dry? Let me help you. I won't hurt you. I never have, I never will. Please, Kendra, what happened to the trust you had in me?"

Kendra closed her eyes. Her voice was frozen like the rest of her. Brian gently lifted her to her feet. She didn't have the strength to fight him. Neither did she have control over the internal nerves that set her body shaking as if an earthquake had trembled across the terrain. Keeping one arm around her, Brian once again caressed the hair from her face. She cringed and tears began to flow from beneath her closed lids.

"Sweetheart, your skin is like ice. Come on, you need to get out of those wet clothes and into a hot shower."

Kendra felt like a store manikin, unable to move on her own. Brian carried her to the bathroom and stood her beside the sink. Finally, she opened her eyes, feeling less wary, but still unable to respond. Keeping an eye on her, Brian turned on the shower and adjusted the hot water. He pulled the shower curtain across the tub. *What is he going to do?* Panic began to rise again.

"I'll get you some dry clothes. Do you think you can get undressed and get into the shower?" He started backing to the door.

Kendra stared at him, feeling like a child who didn't know what was expected of her.

"You're going to get pneumonia if you don't get warm. Do you need some help?"

Kendra watched as he put his hands on her shoulders. They moved to the buttons on her shirt and began undoing them – one by one. Kendra frowned, but didn't seem to understand what he was doing, or why. Finally, he had the last button undone and started to slip the blouse off her shoulder.

Kendra blinked. *He shouldn't be doing that, but...*She finally found a tiny whisper of a voice. "What are you doing?"

He looked relieved. "I'm trying to get your wet clothes off so you can get in that hot shower before you freeze to death." His voice trembled almost as much as hers. *Is he scared too*?

Kendra frowned and glanced down at the unbuttoned shirt. "I can do that," she said, then added, "I think."

"I'll give you about two minutes while I put on some water for hot chocolate. If you aren't in the shower when I come back, I'll finish the job I started."

"Okay." Kendra's answer sounded vacant and far away even to her. It was as if someone else were talking through her vocal cords.

***

Brian closed the door behind him and stood outside the door listening until he heard movement in the bathroom. He heaved a deep sigh of relief and went to the kitchen where he put water on for hot chocolate.

*What is going on? Doc said she left early this afternoon. Has she been out in the storm all day? Why is she so afraid of me all of a sudden? And why did she climb in the window when she was obviously in pain? She could have used the door – at least the back door if she didn't want to anyone to see her. Something isn't making sense, but I'll wait and see what she has to say before I call anyone.*

While the water heated, Brian went back to check on Kendra. He didn't want her sneaking out again. She needed to get warm. He opened the bathroom door enough to see her clothes on the floor and her shadow behind the shower curtain. He closed the door and went to make the hot chocolate, adding extra sugar and cream. She would need it.

***

The steam from the running shower looked so inviting and the warmth of it in the room felt so wonderful that she undressed and stepped into the tub under the spraying hot water. It felt so good she didn't want to move. The hot liquid flowed over her body, warming the chills away. The trembling had almost stopped, when she heard the door open. She tensed, knowing how vulnerable she was. The door closed.

Kendra stood under the flow until the water began to cool. She managed to turn the cold water off and let only hot water flow. Even that soon began to cool, but she couldn't make herself move again. Once more, the door opened.

"Kendra, sweetheart, you've drained the hot water tank. You're going to get cold again if you don't get out." Brian reached behind the curtain and turned off the water. "Can you make it, or do you want me to wrap you in a towel and put you to bed?"

Kendra reached one arm around the curtain and he placed her giant towel on it. Pulling her arm back, she started drying herself.

"Here's a cup of hot chocolate and some dry clothes. Two minutes and I'll be back to help you." He closed the door and Kendra pulled the shower curtain aside and stepped out of the tub. The blue sweat suit he brought felt soft and warm against her skin. Kendra hugged herself as a tap sounded at the door. She stiffened. The knob turned.

"Are you dressed?" Brian asked opening the door only a small crack.

"I think so," she said.

He opened the door wider, reached for the cup of hot chocolate on the counter and pressed it into her hands. "You need to get some hot liquids inside you."

He almost dropped the cup as Kendra backed away from him. *It's a trick to get more drugs in me.*

"It's just hot chocolate. I put a little extra sugar and cream in it, because you need it. Would it help if I take a drink first?"

Kendra nodded, keeping her eyes on his. He lifted the cup and took two big swallows. "Now, I'll have to make you some more, since I drank half of yours." He smiled as he again placed the cup in her hands. It smelled wonderful as she lifted it to her lips and sipped, keeping her eyes on Brian. *The drink didn't seem to affect him, so maybe it's all right.* She drained the cup and handed it back to him.

"Feel better?" he asked. "Are you hungry? Doc Jones said you left sometime this afternoon so you probably…"

Just the mention of Doc's name sent panic surging through her. She shook her head.

"Kendra? Maybe I'd better hear your side of the story before I yell at you for running away. Did you have supper?"

She shook her head.

"Lunch?"

Again, she shook her head. Brian muttered something under his breath. *Is he mad at me? What did I do?*

"Come on, let's get you comfy then I'll get you something to eat." Kendra let him take her hand and lead her like a small child down the hall. "In here," he opened the door to the room he had been using, "in case someone comes snooping around your window."

Kendra was too tired to argue or try to run, so she got in the bed and Brian pulled the covers up to her chin, tucking them around her. Angel flew into the room and leaped to the bed. With a loud purr, she curled up beside Kendra, who managed a small smile.

"I'll fix you something and be right back. Please don't go out the window again. It's still raining and Doc and Brooks are still looking for you. I want to know what's going on before anyone knows you're here. All right?" Brian hung a heavy blanket over the window to keep light in and peering eyes out.

Kendra nodded. She wanted to trust him. *David asked me to trust him, but in the infirmary, they mentioned his name along with all the other folks that I thought were my friends. He seems to be pals with Lenny, and Lenny saved my life, didn't he?* Confused, Kendra wasn't sure if she could trust anyone. At least for the present, Brian seemed to be hiding her from the others.

Too tired to think any more, Kendra snuggled down in the bed, letting the warmth of the blanket, the soft drumming of the rain on the roof and the quiet purring of Angel soothe and comfort her. It felt so good to be warm, if only for a short time.

She would have to run again. But where would she go? And what would she do with Angel? She could never desert the kitty. Thoughts like bees buzzed around in her head. Like Scarlet, she decided she would think about it later. Her eyes were too heavy. She had to close them for a few minutes.

***

Closing the door softly behind him, Brian went to the kitchen, where he opened a can of soup, made some sandwiches and put on a pot of coffee. He took his time. She needed sleep almost as much as she needed food. She'd had some kind of shock. She could sleep more after she ate.

As he fixed her tray, he suddenly realized how hungry he was. He'd paced and worried all evening and forgotten to eat. He would join her in their late night snack. The tray ready, he returned to Kendra hoping she was still sleeping and hadn't tried to run again.

***

The door clicked as it opened. Kendra threw the covers back, toppled Angel in the process and prepared to run. Angel righted herself and glared as only a cat can glare and then forgiving as only a cat can forgive, she purred and kneaded the blanket near Kendra's feet.

Brian stood in the doorway with a tray in his hands. He waited for her fear to subside. She eased back on the pillow and he brought the tray into the room and set it across her lap. Kendra looked over the tray – two ham sandwiches, a bowl of chicken noodle soup and two cups of coffee. She was hungry, but… She glanced up at Brian.

"Do you mind if I join you?" he asked. "I was so busy walking the floor and worrying about you I forgot to eat." He picked up one of the sandwiches and a cup of coffee and sat on the foot of the bed, leaning against the wall. "If you're still hungry, I'll make more."

Tears suddenly spilled over and started down her cheeks. Kendra couldn't stop them, any more than she could understand why they were there. "I'm sorry. I don't know why I'm so weepy. I must have gotten too much rain in me." She tried to smile at her feeble attempt at joking.

"You need food in you. I don't know what happened, but I'm sure you've experienced some kind of trauma. Eat, then we'll talk."

"Thank you," She whispered and ate in silence avoiding Brian's eyes. She finished her soup and sandwich then drained her cup. She tipped it over and stared into the bottom hoping it contained a few drops.

"Would you like another sandwich? More coffee? Something else?" Brian stood and reached for the tray.

"I'm not an invalid," Kendra tried to glare. With the warmth of food and dry clothes, she was beginning to feel human again. "I'm sorry. I would like more coffee, please. No sugar this time."

Brian laughed. "All right. I think you're recovered enough that you don't need the sugar."

He returned with cups refilled and sat back on the end of the bed. "Now, tell me what happened, why you ran away and why you're so afraid of me all of a sudden."

Kendra leaned back against the pillow and closed her eyes.

Brian waited then said, "Why don't you start with why you left without telling Doc you were going and why you didn't show up here until almost ten hours after you left?" His voice carried a tinge of anger.

"I didn't leave the infirmary until after they all went to dinner."

"They? I stopped by about two. Doc said he went to the bathroom and when he returned you were gone."

Kendra couldn't speak. All she could do was shake her head. Tears started again and angrily she brushed at them with the back of her hand. Her head was throbbing again, but she tried to ignore it. "The pills…in my pocket." She had to start some place. Maybe that would be a good place.

"Pills? Did Doc give you some to take with you? Does your head still hurt?"

"Yes, it hurts, but…my pocket." Panic began to overtake her again and she was afraid she would run if he continued to press for information.

Brian left the room and returned with the surgical glove in his hand. He opened it and spilled the pills on the bed. He counted them and looked at her with his eyebrows raised in question. "Where did you get these and why are they in a surgical glove? What are they?"

"I don't know what they are. I sensed they were something I shouldn't take. That's what Doc gave me for pain – three at a time about every two hours."

"Kendra, there are a dozen of them. What do you mean he gave them to you every two hours? How…?"

Kendra closed her eyes as if trying to close off the memory. She sighed and tried to explain. "He gave me the pills and a glass of water. I slipped them under my tongue then sneezed them into a tissue when he turned away. They must be pretty powerful, because just the tiny bit I got each time combined with the bump on the head, kept me drowsy and sleeping most of the time." She opened her eyes and stared into Brian's.

Brian sat down suddenly on the end of the bed, the color draining from his face. "Kendra if you had taken all these you would…"

"I know." Her voice was soft and flat. "I would be floating in the middle of the lake about now. That was the intention."

"Maybe you better explain. I don't know how it can get any worse, but I have a feeling it will, or you wouldn't have come in here looking like a wild animal running from its predators."

Kendra took a deep breath then told him everything she heard in the infirmary and how she escaped after they all went to dinner. She told him she was afraid he was a part of the gang because they mentioned his name.

"I can see why you were afraid of me. No wonder you were near shock. Everyone you knew and considered a friend was trying to kill you. Why should you believe me, when you couldn't believe them?"

Kendra nodded, brushing at the tears again. "Brian, I'm so scared. Now they know how much I know they won't stop until they kill me. That's what put my father in danger, isn't it?"

Brian caught his breath and almost answered her, but he was

under orders. "Why are you asking me?"

"Brian, when can we stop playing games and be honest with one another? I can't handle much more of this hide and seek stuff without truth. Please help me."

Kendra could see him struggling internally with his conscience. *If he tells me, he'll lose his job. If he doesn't tell me, I'll suffer more.* Finally, he said, "I can't give you what you want, not yet. I'm under orders. I'm sure you understand that, but I can promise you this much, we'll have an honest talk, very soon, with or without orders. I don't want to hurt you any more, but please, hang in there with me just a little longer."

Kendra fell back against the pillow and squeezed her eyes shut. Tears flowed down her face unhindered. She understood. She nodded, slid under the covers and turned her face the wall too tired and emotionally spent to even be angry.

"Kendra, everyone has their limits and tonight you reached yours – physically and emotionally. You'll bounce back, but for now, at least I can give you what little comfort I can."

Brian stretched out on the bed beside her and took her in his arms. "Kendra, sweetheart, I'm sorry."

Kendra turned toward him and wept against his shoulder while he held her close. It felt good to be held, if only for a while. Soon she was asleep.

***

Brian eased her down on the bed, pulled the cover up over her shoulders, and left the room muttering under his breath.

He had closed the *bug* box earlier after Paul left. He couldn't go to the porch. Someone might be outside waiting and listening. He went to the bathroom, closed the door and turned on the water to further mask any sound. Then he pulled his cell phone from his pocket and punched in the code that took him directly to Severs.

"We have to tell her what's going on," he said. "She needs to know. Her life is in danger."

"No. She'll only get in the way."

"You've severely underestimated her. She knows far more than you think and has stumbled onto almost the complete circle."

"Then send her back to them and see what else she can find out."

"They'll kill her if they see her. They know she knows them."

"Then get your men in place to round them up as they take a shot at her. She's only a girl, not one of ours at that. I warned her to keep out of it. If she gets herself killed, it's her own fault, not ours. Now do what you have to do and don't bother me again until this mess is cleaned up."

Brian folded the phone and replaced it in his pocket, then angrily kicked the tub. If he went against orders, he could lose his job. If he didn't, Kendra could lose her life. As much as he regretted it, he would do what he had to do.

# Thirty-one

For the second time since she had been at Palisades, a tapping outside the window startled Kendra out of a deep sleep. That all too familiar feeling of panic sent her upright in bed, head cocked to determine where the sound was coming from. Was it inside, or outside? Placing a hand over her rapidly beating heart in an effort to slow its pace, Kendra forced her breathing to slow. She listened more closely. Angel jumped off the bed and slithered toward the outside wall where she crouched and waited to pounce on whatever was there. *I wasn't just dreaming. She heard it, too.*

The earlier thunder and lightning had moved on, but rain steadily drummed on the roof. There it was again – a tapping or scratching outside the window, not on the window itself, but rather on the outside wall. Angel touched a paw to the wall. Bare feet silent against the cold, tile floor, Kendra moved to the wall beside Angel and placed her ear against the wall. *It's not a mouse or bat inside the wall. Someone, or some thing, is scraping a stone on the mortar between the logs.*

With all she'd been through the last two days, Kendra knew better than to check it out alone. She was wide-awake and full of curiosity. The throbbing in her head wasn't as severe as earlier and although her mind seemed to be working better after a few hours sleep, the pain still slowed her thinking. *Brian used this room. Whoever is out there, probably wants his attention. Doc? One of the others? Can I really trust Brian?* The tap came once more, sounding weaker. *I need to do something – now.*

Kendra hurried across the hall and pushed open Brian's door, which he had left ajar. She tiptoed toward the side of the bed.

"Brian," she whispered not wanting the *bug* to pick up her voice, or for anyone who might be outside to hear. Afraid Brian wouldn't hear either, she reached out to touch him. He slipped out of bed fully dressed, gun in hand and stood beside her before she could open her mouth to call his name again. Startled, she took a step back.

"Kendra? What's wrong?" He caught her with one hand and held her at arm's length so he could see her face by the nightlight in the hallway.

"There's someone outside the window. They must want you, since that was the room you used." She glanced at the gun in his hand.

"What did they say? Could you see anyone?"

"All I heard was a soft tapping, or scratching on the wall. It might even be an animal of some kind, but I don't think so."

"Do you know how to use a gun?" It was an odd question, but Kendra understood.

"Yes."

He held out his gun for her. "Take this. If I don't come back and someone else tries to get in, use it."

"You might need it," she answered. "I have my own." Kendra opened a dresser drawer and retrieved her own gun.

Brian looked surprised, but said nothing. He started toward the back door. Kendra followed him to the kitchen and waited while Brian slipped around the corner of the porch toward the bedrooms. Less than a minute later, he approached the door with a man's body slung over his shoulder. Kendra rushed out to open the screen door for him. They hadn't turned on any lights, not wanting to alert anyone who might be watching. The little nightlights in the kitchen and hallway gave enough light to move without stumbling.

"Lenny?" Kendra knew instinctively who it was.

"He's been shot." Brian answered as he carried Lenny into the cabin.

Kendra moved to the sink and began running water. "Take him to your former room. Get some clean towels from the bathroom. I'll bring hot water." When the water was hot, she filled a large pan and carried it to the bedroom.

The blanket Brian had placed over the window earlier once again gave them privacy. He stripped the shirt away from Lenny's shoulder. The wound bled steadily. Lenny stirred and groaned as Kendra took a clean cloth and began washing around the area. He opened his eyes and tried to grin. "Am I in heaven? There seems to be an angel hovering over me."

"Shut up," she hissed. "Save your breath for staying alive." Then Kendra smiled at him and continued to work with the wound. She felt around the entrance of the bullet. Lenny winced. She looked up at Brian and said, "The bullet is still in there. He needs a doctor and we have to stop the bleeding."

Brian frowned. Kendra knew his dilemma. He couldn't leave her there and he couldn't take her with him.

"Get a clean sheet from the hall closet and tear it in strips. Hand me a couple of those clean wash cloths. They aren't sterile, but they're clean and will have to do. There's some alcohol in the bathroom cabinet."

Brian gathered the items Kendra instructed him to assemble. He could have done what she was doing, but he sensed she needed to do it. He returned with the items.

Kendra leaned close to Lenny's face and said, "I'm sorry, Lenny, this is going to hurt so much you'll think you went the other way." She folded one of the cloths and placed it in his mouth so he would have something to bite down on and avoid screaming. She took the alcohol, poured it into the wound and surrounding flesh, then placed another folded cloth over the wound and pressed firmly. Turning to Brian, who was holding the strips of sheet, she said, "Hold him up so I can tie these strips tightly around his shoulder and chest. That should stop the bleeding."

Lenny had gone pale and sweat popped out on his brow as he bit into the cloth and groaned. Brian held him while Kendra wrapped and tied the strips of sheet tightly around him. By the time she finished, Lenny had passed out.

Brian held her and brushed the tears from her face. "You did a great job, Nurse Donovan, but you have to learn to be a little more impervious to your patient's pain."

"Brian, what are we going to do? He has to see a doctor. He's already feeling feverish. You have to take him somewhere. I'll be all right."

"Do you have a license for that gun?" He was stalling while he considered the options.

"Yes. Dad taught David, Lenny and me how to use a gun when we were kids, then bought one for each of us one summer. He gave us the licenses at the same time. I keep it hidden for safety reasons. But, you're avoiding the problem. Brian, you have no choice. You have to take him."

"I do have a choice," he answered with a determined expression. "I'll take him to the hospital, but you're coming with us. I won't leave you here alone, gun or no gun. Besides, I'll need your help. You can stay with him while I return to the cabin. They'll be watching for me."

"If you leave, they'll think you're going to get me and will follow."

"Maybe not," he said as he quietly moved to the butterfly *bug* box. Kendra watched him pull one of her tricks. He removed the lid and said, as if talking to the cat, "Angel, I can't sleep. All I can think about is Kendra out there wandering around in the rain. She must be hurt, or scared, or both. I can't believe they've searched everywhere. Maybe I'm wasting time, but I have to go look for her. She'll call my cell phone if she calls, so I'll take it with me. You be a good kitty and watch for her here. I'll be back in a couple of hours, unless I find her. Then I'll be back sooner."

Angel seemed to love the attention when someone spoke her name. She stood by the lamp and purred loudly beside the *bug*. "Meow," she added as he closed the *bug* box.

Brian winked at Kendra as she watched from the hall entrance. "I'll get the car ready," he whispered. "Maybe you better get dressed."

Kendra wanted to argue with him and make him let her stay, but that would only waste valuable time. Lenny had to have medical attention. She wasn't a nurse. All she knew was what she learned in a college First Aid course and what little she picked up from her mother.

By the time Brian had Lenny lying in the back seat, Kendra was dressed in jeans, T-shirt and sneakers. She grabbed her windbreaker and purse and followed Brian out the door, glancing back at Angel, who stood in the kitchen watching them leave. A twinge of guilt and regret washed over her. There was a good possibility she wouldn't return.

Without waiting for Brian's instruction, Kendra slid into the back with Lenny, but flattened herself on the floor as best she could. Silently she prayed as Brian drove up the lane.

She felt the change as the tires rolled from rough gravel to smooth blacktop, but remained motionless until Brian spoke.

"We're nearing the hospital in Wintersville," he said.

Kendra eased herself to the seat and raised Lenny's head onto her lap.

He blinked. "There's that angel again," he said. Kendra stroked his face but he was already unconsciousness again.

# Thirty-two

Brian pulled into the emergency drive of the Wintersville Community Hospital with as little show as possible.

"Stay with him. I'll get a gurney and some help," he said. Not waiting for her to answer, he jumped from the car and ran for the entrance. In mere seconds, he was back with a couple of orderlies and a gurney. They took Lenny inside and Kendra followed while Brian moved the car away from the entrance. He returned to stand beside her as she gave information to the nurse.

"His name is Melvin McElroy. Age twenty-eight. Birthday 9/26/65. I'm his wife, Marie. He rescued me from a man who tried to abduct me and the man shot him. My brother-in-law and I cleaned his wound as best we could, then we transported him here. Please, can I stay with him? I'm so scared he'll die…" Her tears were real, even if the rest of her story wasn't.

Brian hid his surprise well as Kendra turned to indicate him as the brother-in-law who brought them in. "Please help us," she continued to the sympatric nurse taking the information. "The man was following and might come in here pretending to be a doctor. If he does, please don't let him near us. He'll kill Melvin." Again, her tears emphasized the point.

"Excuse me a minute," said the nurse and left to talk to the doctor in charge. She returned with the doctor who wore his stethoscope around his neck. Black rimmed glasses perched on his nose.

"This is Dr. McMichaels," said the nurse. "He's in charge of emergency tonight." She went back to her desk and Dr. McMichaels motioned for Brian and Kendra to follow him to a small examination room. He closed the door.

"Miss Porter says you're afraid that the man who shot your husband might still be after you. Want to give me a few details?"

He glanced at all Kendra's bruises – wrists and head and could see that she still favored her left arm. "Did that man do this?"

She nodded and told him what she had told the registering nurse.

"Mrs. McElroy, we'll have to take your husband to surgery to remove the bullet. You can't go in there with us, but you can wait in the room where we'll take him when we're done. He should stay for a few days, but we'll do what we can to protect you. Did you notify the sheriff?"

"I can't do that. The sheriff is a close friend of the man who shot my husband. He would just say I was a hysterical female and Melvin got hurt cleaning his gun, or something." Kendra let all the anger and bitterness of the last several weeks color her words. Brian listened, saying nothing.

"Come this way, Mrs. McElroy and Mr.…McElroy?" He raised his eyebrows and looked toward Brian for confirmation.

"Yes," he answered without a hint of a smile as he reached to shake the doctor's hand. "Brian McElroy."

The doctor led them to a room near the operating room where they could wait. Then he left to take care of Lenny.

"Do you think he'll call the sheriff?" Kendra turned to Brian when we were alone.

"Are you sure you aren't an actress?"

"Part of what I said was true. I didn't think we wanted his real name on the record if they come looking for him." Suddenly Kendra felt anxious. "I didn't make it worse, did I?"

"You did a far better job than I would've done. Now you have a reason to stay with him as well as to check him out of here if you need to. Kendra, I have to go back. I'm sure they'll be watching for my return. Do you have cash?"

"Some."

"Here," he opened his wallet and handed her a fist full of bills. "If I don't make it back in a couple of hours, get him out of here if you can. If they show up, don't worry about Lenny. Get yourself away. You're resourceful. You'll think of something."

"You mean, run away and leave Lenny for them to..." She couldn't even finish such a thought. "Never! He saved my life earlier tonight. He's been my friend for years. I won't bail out without him."

"He wouldn't want you to risk your life for him."

"Brian McNeil, you're wasting time. Go. I will do what I have to do to get both of us out of here and hopefully connect with you somewhere. Don't worry. Lenny and I have been through a lot of scrapes together. We'll make it. But, Brian, please be careful. Don't take any chances trying to be a hero for us."

Brian grinned. "You're my brother's wife," he said. "I don't want to lose either of you. Be careful." He kissed her bruised forehead and left.

Kendra felt the familiar churning in her stomach. Throbbing once again replaced the dull ache in her head. *I would have given anything to keep Brian here, although I know he's in as much danger as I am – maybe more. But, I felt safe and secure while he was here. Now I'm alone and Lenny is in the hands of a doctor who can easily keep him sedated and out of my reach until he gets Paul Brooks and Doc Jones here. The law requires that he report gunshot wounds.*

Kendra paced the small room from door to window and back again. She glanced at the bed with tight cornered sheets – top sheet turned back in preparation for her *husband* after his surgery. She looked out the window. The room was on the third floor overlooking a parking lot. *I hope it's the only parking lot, so I can see anyone familiar.*

The closet-like room with a toilet and sink took up the space of one corner of the room. A slim floor to ceiling locker waited for clothes and personal items to be stored. Creamy paint was only a shade better than stark white but flowered curtains gave a splattering of color – pinks, whites, and greens.

Constant chattering and movement outside the room brought both comfort and irritation. It was a comfort to know help was nearby if needed, but the constant paging of doctors by a nasal, twangy voice began to grate on her nerves.

Finally, Dr. McMichaels breezed into the room, his mouth cover dangling, green surgery cap still on his head. His eyes were red and bleary. He must be nearing the end of a very long shift.

"Mrs. McElroy?" Even his voice sounded tired and gravely.

"Yes." Kendra stood biting her lip, waiting, afraid of what he might have to say. Finally, she asked, "Is Melvin…?"

"Your husband is going to be fine." He laid a fatherly hand on her arm. "The bullet was imbedded in the collar bone. He will have to use a sling on that arm for few weeks, but he's going to be just fine. As I said earlier, we should keep him for a few days. I understand your anxiety, but surely you can't take him home like this if you live near the man who shot him."

"Oh, no, Dr. McMichaels," Kendra said, relief giving strength to her voice. "We have relatives north of here – up near Mackinac. My brother-in-law just stepped out for a cup of coffee. He'll drive us up there as soon as you can release Melvin."

"Someone did an excellent job of patching him up. Was that you?"

"Yes, my husband insisted that I take a course at the university. I didn't want to, but I'm glad now that I did."

"That probably will help him get out of here sooner – maybe even saved his life. They'll be bringing him in soon. When he's awake and the IV bag is empty, we'll reluctantly let him go with you. I'm sure you can take care of changing his bandages and keeping him quiet for a few days. Here are some antibiotics and pain medication for him to take for the next five days. I don't think you'll find a pharmacy open this time of night – or maybe I should say morning? It's four o'clock."

"Oh, thank you so much, doctor. I was so scared." The tears

spilled over again and Kendra threw her arms around the doctor, embarrassing him.

"Yes, well… eh…"

She grinned and stepped back. "I'm sorry," she said. "I get a little carried away sometimes – especially when you bring me good news about my Melvin."

"I'm sure you understand that I have to report this to the police," Dr. McMichaels said, "but we're so busy here tonight it might be tomorrow afternoon before I can get all the paper work done." He smiled and winked at Kendra, who returned his smile.

"Thank you, doctor," she whispered.

A few minutes later, the orderlies rolled the gurney into the room and transferred Lenny, who was still sleeping, to the bed. He groaned a little, but continued to sleep while Kendra paced the room. *Brian should be back by now.*

The nurse, a very pretty redhead with green eyes that sparkled, came in to check his IV. "It's just about empty," she said. "I'll get my cart and remove it. He really ought to stay at least twenty-four hours, you know."

"I know, Betsy," Kendra said, reading the girls nametag. "I wish I felt safe enough for him to do that."

Lenny heard the voices and half opened his eyes and groaned. Kendra leaned over the bed so he could see her. "Melvin darling, I was so worried."

Lenny's eyes popped open wide and stared at her then grinned as the name registered. "My angel is here again. Come on, baby, don't cry. I'm going to be fine."

Betsy smiled at them and opened the door to leave. Quickly she closed it and turned to face Kendra and Lenny. "There's a man out there who calls himself Doc Jones. He was asking about a gunshot victim named Lenny Richardson. Is that the man who's stalking you?"

Kendra felt the blood drain from her face. She nodded.

"It looks like he's checking all the rooms in case he was mistaken about the name," said Betsy.

“Where are Melvin’s clothes?” Kendra asked as Lenny sat up and dangled his legs over the side of the bed.

“Let me remove that IV. His clothes are in that bag by the chair. I’ll get a wheelchair while you help him get dressed. Maybe we can sneak him out before the man gets this far. He’s at the other end of the west wing right now.” Betsy removed the IV and left to get the wheelchair.

Kendra helped Lenny dress and get into the chair beside the bed to wait for Betsy. She opened the door a crack and saw Betsy get off the elevator, press the hold button and say something to a nurse standing near the elevator door. The nurse nodded and began to turn people away from that elevator, pointing to the other one. Before Betsy could get back to their room, however, Doc Jones emerged from the room across the hall, walked slowly in their direction, one hand in his pocket. *Does he have a gun?*

Kendra eased the door shut fighting the panic that welled up within her. There was no time to think. She grabbed her purse from the bed. Wishing she had had time to duck into the bathroom, she pressed herself against the wall beside the door as the doorknob turned. *If he leaves the door open, it will hide me behind it. If he closes it, I’ll be like a shadow on an iceberg.*

Kendra glanced at Lenny. He sat in the chair too weak to fight. He smiled, blew her a kiss, and hunched his shoulders as if to say, “Oh, well, that’s life.”

The door slowly opened and Kendra closed her eyes as if not seeing what was about to happen would make it go away. *Oh God, help me save my friend?*

# Thirty-three

The door opened just far enough for the portly body of Doc Jones to slide in and close it behind him. He didn't bother to turn around, but pushed the door shut with his free hand behind him keeping the other in his pocket. Kendra held her breath and took a step back pressing against the wall as the door closed, hoping the shadows would conceal her. Doc seemed interested only in Lenny.

"Well, Leonard Richardson," he said, "you gave us quiet a chase. I don't know how you managed to make it all the way out here without help, but I'll just give you a little shot of something for your pain and then leave you alone." He laughed a harsh sounding chuckle as he pulled a syringe from his pocket.

Lenny returned his smile as if he didn't have a care in the world. He raised his hand and pushed his hair back, speaking to Kendra in their finger language. *He doesn't know you're here.* Doc Jones was so absorbed in his self-satisfaction of finding Lenny, that he had no idea anyone else was in the room.

Glad for the cloth purse with a silent zipper, Kendra carefully pulled her gun from it and turned it in her hand to use the butt as a club. She was glad, also, that Doc was a man of smaller stature. She would be able to reach his head without finding something to stand on.

"I'm glad to see you're going to cooperate and not make this too difficult for me, Lenny. By the way, you haven't seen the Donovan girl lately, have you? I'm assuming she's in the lake by now, but you never know with her. Well my friend, any last words?" Doc laughed again as he held the syringe up to examine it. Almost in a reverent ritual, he gripped the cap on the needle. "This will only sting for a minute or two." He laughed again and took a step toward Lenny.

"Since you ask for my last words, Doc," said Lenny still smiling, "you might want to watch that needle doesn't prick your finger on the way to the floor."

Doc Jones laughed again. "Always joking, eh Lenny? Why would I fall to the floor? You're the one who's going to fall – very quickly."

"And one more thing, Doc," said Lenny, "you're right about Kendra Donovan. She's quite a gal. You never really know where she might turn up."

"That's right, Doc, you never know about me," Kendra said as she brought the gun down over Doc's head. He slumped to the floor and Kendra opened the door a crack to see where Betsy was. She was on her way. Kendra motioned for her to hurry.

Betsy wheeled the chair into the room, gaped at the man on the floor then shut the door quickly. Kendra grabbed a surgical glove and took the still capped syringe from Doc's hand. "Maybe I should use it on him," she mused aloud as she examined it closely.

Lenny's eyes widened, "Kendra, baby…"

Kendra sighed and shrugged her shoulders. "I know. It would be murder, even if he is responsible for who knows what. That doesn't give me a reason to do likewise."

Lenny let out the breath he'd been holding. "The Kendra I knew from childhood could never kill a man in cold blood – not even one like Doc Jones, but I understand how you feel."

Wrapping the syringe in the glove, Kendra placed it in her purse. "Someone will want this for evidence. It has his fingerprints all over it and I'm sure they'll be interested in whatever is in it."

"Good thinking," said Lenny as he lifted himself out of the chair and into the wheelchair with Betsy's help. Even that little bit of exertion left the sweat dripping from his brow and his breath coming in gasps.

Betsy checked Doc. "Hard to tell how long he'll be out, so we'll have to hurry." Kendra grasped the back of the chair ready to push it.

"I'll do that," said Betsy. "You walk beside me and don't look hurried. My friend is holding one of the elevators for me. I'm sure that man will be out at least five or ten minutes. That's enough time to get out of here."

There was no time for argument. They would have to trust Betsy. Kendra slipped the gun back in her purse and walked beside the wheelchair with her hand on Lenny's shoulder. Betsy pushed the chair into the elevator and said something to her friend who immediately called for the other elevator.

"She'll take it up another floor and hold it for five minutes. We'll put a hold on this one on the ground. No one will be able to use either for at least five minutes. I called my boyfriend when I went down for the chair. He'll be outside the door to pick us up."

"Us? Betsy, you can't…" Lenny and Kendra started to speak at once.

"I have to. I signed out before I got the chair. If anyone asks me anything, I was gone before you left. Besides, how did you plan to get him out of here? Call a cab?"

Kendra and Lenny exchanged glances. She hadn't thought that far. "I guess I hoped my brother-in-law would be back," Kendra answered.

"Well, he isn't and this one isn't going to walk very far." Betsy nodded her head toward Lenny. "You need help and Robbie and I are here for you."

Betsy took them directly to the exit where a late model, four-door Ford waited, engine idling. A tall young man leaned casually against it, the bill of his baseball cap pulled over his forehead, covering his eyes. He looked as if he were napping, but instantly jumped to attention when he heard Betsy's voice. He opened both doors on the passenger side and with a nod of his head indicated that Kendra should get in the other side while he helped Lenny into the car. She ran around to the other side and slid in beside Lenny. The young man pushed the wheelchair aside. Betsy was already in the front seat when he returned to the driver's seat, turned his cap with the bill behind him, and eased out into traffic. Hopefully they would be long gone by the time anyone discovered Doc.

"Betsy, why are you doing this?" Kendra gave the girl a skeptical look. Had she gone from the frying pan into the fire? Afraid to look at Lenny, she knew he must be thinking the same thing.

The nurse turned so she could face Kendra, her expression conveying both pain and seriousness. "I'm sure you don't remember me. Neither does that man who calls himself a doctor. My name is Betsy Williams and this is my fiancé Robbie Carlson. My parents and I were at Palisades for a week when I was twelve. I used to love to listen to you two playing the violin and piano. My dad got sick and your mother came to our Cabin. Doc Jones came too. He acted as if Mrs. Donovan didn't know anything. She said Dad was having an allergic reaction to a bee sting and needed a shot of antihistamine. Doc smiled at her, patted her on the shoulder, and said *he* was the doctor and *he* would take care of the patient. He checked my father, who was having difficulty breathing, and said he was having a heart attack. He sent me up to the lodge to call for an ambulance. In the meantime, he said he would give my father a shot of digitalis for his heart. Mrs. Donovan protested and he told her to leave or he would have her arrested for impeding medical assistance. My father was dead when I returned. Doc wrote the death certificate as heart failure, but Mom insisted on an autopsy when we returned home. It was heart failure due to an allergic reaction. We reported the events, but nothing was ever done about it."

"Betsy we appreciate your help but…"

"I don't know why you're pretending to be someone else and it doesn't matter. I know who you are. I became a nurse because of your mother. She tried to save my father's life, but that man who calls himself a doctor…" Betsy's voice choked and she swiped at the tear that trickled down her cheek.

"I want to help you so you can put him behind bars. Whatever you're doing, Mrs. McElroy, your secret is safe with us."

"I remember that incident," Kendra said. "My mother, who

hardly ever cries, wept for days. She was so mad and frustrated because she could do nothing to help. Although she never forbade us to go to the clinic, we knew she didn't trust Doc. But, Betsy, although we appreciate your help, we can't put you in danger. If you will just drop us off someplace and pretend you never saw us, you'll be much safer." Kendra tried to sound normal, but her voice had a ring of panic in it.

"How far do you think he would get?" Betsy nodded toward Lenny. "You need to find a place where he can rest. We can help. If we can help keep you alive long enough to put that man behind bars, then my father's death will be avenged."

"There are a number of thugs looking for us," Kendra said. "My brother-in-law…" she hesitated and decided to stay with her lie. "My brother-in-law should have been back to get us by now. I'm afraid to think what might be keeping him. But you're right. Melvin can't go far. He has to rest long enough to get some of the anesthetic out of his system and some strength back. Maybe a big motel where the office manager wouldn't remember me."

Lenny leaned against the seat, looking pale. "You should have left me there. You can still get away if you…"

"Shut up and save your breath. You might need it later." Kendra didn't sound too sympathetic. Betsy giggled nervously.

"She's right, you know," she said to Lenny. "Hey, I have an idea. The Red Roof Inn close to the Mall. Sometimes it's easier to hide in the open. Robbie and I can go in and register. If anyone is looking for you, the manager can honestly say that he never saw you."

"Betsy, it could be dangerous. I don't know." Kendra bit her lip trying to decide.

"There it is up ahead," said Robbie. "What do you want to do?"

# Thirty-four

They were approaching a small strip mall – K Mart, Hobby shop, liquor store, a couple of other unfamiliar businesses. Even a small local restaurant nestled in between the liquor store and the electronics' store. At the far end with parking lots connecting, was a two story Red Roof Inn. The motel was one long unit with the office at the end nearest the mall. A tall picket fence, a few trees and small brush separated the motel from the highway.

"Betsy's right," said Robbie, as he pulled into the strip mall. We can register under your name or ours – whatever is best. I'll drive down to the end of the building. We can see if the room on the end is available."

"Robbie, I don't want you and Betsy to get mixed up in this, but I don't know what else to do. I don't know how we can ever thank you." Kendra glanced at Lenny who had fallen asleep either from the medication or from the pain. Whatever the cause, he was so pale she was concerned. He needed to get in a bed somewhere and rest.

"Just get that nut behind bars," Robbie said. He drove to the end of the building and parked in the farthest spot from the office. "We'll walk back to the office. You can stay in the car where you'll be able to see anyone who approaches."

"Wait, Betsy," Kendra said. "Let's go behind the building and change tops. You don't want to go in there looking like a nurse getting off duty. We're about the same size."

Kendra and Betsy ran around the corner of the building where a short walkway between a six-foot high fence that kept out the highway traffic noise was on one side and shrubs against the building were on the other leading to the end door. They exchanged shirts and returned to the car. She gave Robbie a hand full of bills.

"Pay up front so we can leave without going to the office. Use the name Mr. & Mrs. Melvin McElroy," she said. "And if you see anyone who looks suspicious, or if the desk clerk looks like he's stalling for any reason, get out of there as fast as you can."

"Yes, ma'am," Robbie replied. "I'll leave the keys in the car. If you see anyone who looks familiar moving your way, take off. We'll manage – report our car as stolen or something."

He and Betsy strolled hand in hand back to the office. Kendra got in the driver's seat, where she could watch for any cars coming into the motel lot, as well watch the office door. Lenny roused and tried to help watch, but he still had too much medication in him and kept dozing. Kendra bit her lip and prayed silently for help and safety for the young couple who were so willing to help them.

Robbie and Betsy were gone about ten minutes, but it felt like hours. They returned with smiles that said they were pleased with themselves. Robbie opened the trunk, pulled out a big poster sign and took it to the door of the last room on the ground level. Betsy pulled out a roll of duct tape and together they fastened the poster to the door. Kendra laughed as she read the sign. Lenny rolled his eyes and groaned. In large bold letters were the words: JUST MARRIED! DO NOT DISTURB!

Betsy giggled as she opened the door to the room. They checked all the windows to make sure no one was watching then looked up and down the lot. It was late enough in the morning that most travelers were already on their way and newer ones wouldn't be arriving for several hours.

"This room hasn't been used for a couple of days," said Robbie, "so there's no need for housekeeping to check the room." He helped Lenny out of the car and into the room. Kendra, the last one in, looked all around outside and inside to be sure no one was following then she closed the door. Lenny collapsed in the soft chair.

Kendra was worried. "People will wonder where the car is when you leave," she said. "Betsy…"

"Don't worry, Mrs. McElroy," said Robbie. "We took care of

everything. We paid cash for the room for three days with orders not to disturb even to clean. We told the manager we were married last night and traveled all night."

"We said we had to get away from my father who didn't want us to get married," said Betsy. "We told him not to let anyone know we are here if they should come looking for us, except for a tall blond who is my brother-in-law. He's supposed to bring our passports, which we forgot. He should call first and let me – you – talk to him before sending him to the room."

"We told him we're going to park the car over at the mall," said Robbie, "and walk back, so no one would see it and know where we are."

"I'm sorry they don't have room service," said Betsy, "but Robbie and I can bring you something if you want. This room has a door to the outside and one to the hallway inside. Just to the left of the inside door, on the other side of the glass doors, are vending machines. Some have sandwiches." Betsy paused and looked up at Robbie who smiled at her. "Did we forget anything?"

"I don't know what it would be. Are you folks comfortable with all that?"

"Just one question," Kendra said. "Where did you get the sign?"

Betsy giggled and Robbie laughed. "We had it made a couple of weeks ago when we were going to play a practical joke on some friends. We've been carrying it around with us waiting for the right time to use it. This seems like a better time." Betsy giggled again.

Kendra glanced at Lenny who winked at her. "Sounds like our kind of gal," he said. "We should be all right. Brian will be back soon. I'm sure he'll find us and we'll get out of here."

"If you need anything else, just call me. Here's my number." Betsy hastily wrote the number on a piece of notepaper at the desk and handed it to Kendra. "Do you want us to come back and check on you, call you or anything?"

"You've done more than enough, Betsy. It's probably better if you stay away. The less we hear from you the less chance they'll have of connecting you to anything. Don't call, unless you get in trouble for helping us, or if you know something that will be vital to saving our lives. If you have to call us, use my cell phone number." Kendra wrote her number on a piece of paper from the desk and handed it to Betsy.

Betsy and Robbie left, not worried about anyone seeing them leave. Kendra locked both the doors and turned to Lenny. "Let's get your shoes off and get you in bed. Better stay dressed in case we have to leave in a hurry." She reached to help him up, but he sat still and stared at her with as serious an expression as she'd ever seen on him.

"Kendra, do you know how much danger we're in and I'm too weak to defend myself, much less you."

"Since when do I need you to defend me, Lenny Richardson?" She took his good arm and pulled. He let her help him to the bed where he leaned against the pillows. Kendra sat beside him and took his hand in hers.

"Lenny…thanks for saving my life the other night. I was so scared and after what they said in Doc's office, I didn't know whose side you were on. How could you be so dumb as to play both ends against the middle? I thought you were smarter than that."

Lenny tried to grin, but grimaced as a pain shot through him when he tried to change positions. Kendra put another pillow behind his back. "Is that better?"

It was his turn to be serious. "Why did you tell them I was your husband? You don't…?"

Kendra burst into laughter. Lenny's expression changed from concern to confusion.

"Lenny," she said patting the side of his face, "I have no designs on you, if that's what you're thinking. You're like a brother to me, always have been. It was purely Machiavellian. Someone had to sign you out if we had to leave in a hurry. The doctor would talk to your wife, when he probably wouldn't have talked to your friend."

"When did you get so smart?" He relaxed as he leaned back into the pillows.

"I had the best teachers," she said. "Now, you stop talking and go to sleep. I've got my gun and I won't leave the room unless you want something to eat."

"Now that you mention it, I am a little empty. But I think I'm more sleepy than hungry. Maybe Brian will be here by the time I catch a little nap."

"I'll try his cell phone and let him know where we are. He should have been back by now." Kendra took her phone from her purse and punched in Brian's number. She received a message that the phone was either, out of the area, or not turned on. "That's odd," she said, turning back to Lenny. He was sound asleep. She tried once more in case she had punched in a wrong number, but she got the same response. "I know he's not out of the area, so why does he have the phone off? Maybe he's somewhere where it would be dangerous for it to ring. I'll try later."

Weariness of the past two days made it difficult to stay awake. Kendra pulled a chair between the double beds and lifted her feet so she could watch Lenny without disturbing him. She didn't dare lie down, or even sit on the bed with pillows behind her. Even though she'd had little sleep in the last thirty-six hours, she had to stay awake for Lenny's sake. He had to recoup some of his energy. They weren't out of the woods yet, by any means, and wouldn't be until the *Palisades Gang,* as she had begun to think of them, were under lock and key.

Kendra glanced around the room – typical motel fare. On the outside wall was a door and a large plate glass window with the heater/air conditioner under it. Beige sheers were drawn across the window and brown drapes covered them, keeping out both light and most sounds.

Two double beds lined the wall to the left of the door. A night table with double lamps sat between them. The opposite wall had a long luggage table and the TV stand. The bathroom snuggled in between the TV stand and the door on the inside wall.

Not a bad place…

A knock at the door and voices on the outside of it jerked Kendra violently from a near sound sleep. Her heart pounded as she realized she had fallen asleep in the chair. She jumped to her feet then crawled over the bed closer to the door, standing by it, gun drawn. Another knock brought Lenny upright in bed. Kendra motioned for him to keep silent. She looked through the peephole and saw Jonathan Cox lift his hand to knock again.

*How did he find us? Will he go away?*

# Thirty-five

Before Jonathan could knock again, someone shouted at him from across the parking lot. The manager barreled down on him. Kendra moved to the window and eased the curtain aside a crack so she could better see what was happening.

"What do you think you're doing?" The manager yelled as he came along side Jonathan.

"I'm looking for a girl – black hair, blue eyes. The fellow she's with has a beard and brown hair and eyes. She's about five feet six and he's almost six feet. Her mother died and I'm trying to locate her for the family."

"Well, they aren't in that room. That's a couple of young honeymooners. Can't you read their sign? She has red hair and green eyes and he's dark-haired with hazel eyes. They were on the road all night and need their rest. You just get away and leave them alone, or I'll call the State Troopers to come and throw you off this property."

"All right. All right. Don't get so excited." Jonathan threw up his hands as if warding off physical blows. "It was an honest mistake. Just thought they might have gotten married and I'm checking all the motels around here. Did you rent a room to the couple I just described?"

"Nope. Been kind of slow the last few days. Would of remembered black hair and blue eyes. Remind me of my poor departed wife." The manager had his back against the door as if daring Cox to try to enter.

"Well if they do show up, will you call me? Here's my number." Jonathan handed the man his business card. "Like I said it's imperative that I get in touch with her."

"Yeah, I'll do that," said the manager. He crumpled the paper, stuffed it in his pocket and watched Cox walk back to his car, waiting for him to drive out of the parking lot. As the car drove away, the manager rammed his hands in his pocket and walked back to the office shaking his head.

"It was Cox, but he's gone," Kendra said, exhaling audibly. She dropped back into the chair. "Lenny, I've got to find us something to eat. I'm starving and I know you must be too. You don't have your gun, do you?"

"No. I'm not sure where it got to. I had it when I got to the cabin. After that I'm not sure what happened."

"Brian probably took it so the hospital personnel wouldn't find it. Here, take mine. I'll slip around to the vending machine and see what I can find. But, first I need to change my appearance."

"What are you going to do?"

Kendra laughed. "Don't worry. I know what I'm doing." she went into the bathroom and returned wearing a white terry robe provided by the motel over her shirt and jeans. She had wrapped a large white towel around her head turban style. Reaching into her purse, she pulled out her sunglasses. "That should hide my black hair and blue eyes if I meet anyone. Be back in a couple of minutes."

"Can't you wait a little longer? I don't want you to take any more chances." Lenny tried to get up, but fell back to his pillow.

"I don't want me to take any more chances, either, but I'll do what I have to do. Now please, be good." Kendra patted his cheek and went to the inside door, opened it, glanced up the hallway, then slipped out. She glanced around the snack room looking for the vending machines with sandwiches. They were all to the left of her. She stood staring at them dumbfounded. All they had were chips, candy bars and soft drinks. The sandwich machine was empty.

Kendra groaned. One after another, she fed the greedy monsters with silver coins. In return, they spit out a couple bags of chips and colas.

"That's not a very nutritious diet," said a matronly woman from behind her. She had been so intent on the machines that she hadn't heard the door open. She almost dropped the coveted snacks. *I'll have to be more careful.* "I'm sorry, child. I didn't mean to startle you," the woman said. "You don't look too well. Are you ill?"

"No, ma'am," Kendra drawled in her best southern imitation. "That is, not exactly. My husband and I – we were just married – well, we aren't having very good luck. He fell and cracked his collarbone and I came down with this dreadful eye infection. Our car broke down and we're waiting for it to be fixed. Well, this is all I could think of to keep the hounds of hunger away. I thought they had sandwiches, but that machine is empty. Hopefully by tomorrow, we'll feel like going somewhere for some real food." Kendra smiled at the woman who patted her arm.

"You poor thing! How awful. My name's Linda. My husband, Jim, and I are going out in a little while for dinner. Can we bring you something back?"

"Oh, would you?" Kendra paused then smiled again. "I'm Mrs. Melvin McElroy," she said with as much pride as if it were true. We would be ever so grateful. Some burgers and fries would be just wonderful. Let me get you some money. I didn't bring much out here with me."

The woman gave her a patronizing smile and moved to the ice machine, filling her plastic container from the room. "Never mind, dear. You can pay me later, when I bring the food. You sure burgers and fries are enough?"

"Oh, yes, ma'am. We ain't feeling much like eating a lot of food anyway." They walked through the double doors into the hallway. Kendra stopped by her door. "We're in here. Just knock when you get back. I don't know how I can ever thank you. You're certainly an angel of mercy."

The woman laughed. "I've never been called an angel before. Can I get you some medicine for your eyes? Or anything else?"

"Thank you ma'am, but I have stuff like that. Thanks a bunch, anyway. You and Jim enjoy your dinner and don't hurry none. These snacks will hold us. We're fine. Bye now." Kendra opened the door and slipped inside sliding the locks in place. She looked out the peephole to be sure the woman had moved on down the hall. When she heard a door close, she relaxed.

"What was that all about?" Lenny grinned. "I'm sure you were up to something with your southern drawl."

Kendra told him what had happened and he laughed until the pain made him stop.

"Baby, you always were innovative. I'm sure glad you're on my side."

"Lenny, you can't know how glad I am you're on my side. Did you know about Doc and all the others?"

"Actually, no, I just learned that last night – when they shot me. Do you think I would have taken you to Doc Jones if I'd known he was in on the drug gang?"

"He's not only in on it, but he and the others tried to kill me."

"The others? Who…?"

"You really don't know?"

Lenny shook his head and she told him all that had happened after Brian left her at the infirmary until they found him outside the cabin. He had the same reaction that Brian did. Color drained from his face. She handed him a glass of water.

"I'm all right," he said. "Kendra, I've been working both ends against the middle, as you call it, for almost six months. I knew there was a drug ring, but they were just beginning to believe my story about drifting from bar to bar after my parents' divorce. I told them I made what little I could by playing the piano. By snooping and observing, I was just beginning to find out some who were involved. I was sure Paul was in it. I thought possibly, Jonathan Cox and Mark were involved. I knew there were others, but…the Franklin sisters? How could you come in here and in two or three days, upset the apple cart and drive all the big wigs out? Severs wasn't too smart to brush you off. Whoops! You didn't hear me say that."

Kendra laughed. "It's all right, Lenny. I know you and Brian are both with the FBI."

Lenny sat up, eyes wide. "Kendra, how…?"

"Don't worry. Neither of you slipped. I learned through other means that I won't get into now. We have other things to worry about. We're still in a heap of trouble. I seemed to have stirred up a real rattlesnake's nest. We should've heard from Brian by now. I've tried all afternoon to call and can't get through."

"What do you mean you can't get through?" Lenny's look of alarm confirmed her suspicions. Brian was in trouble.

"He either has his phone turned off – which means he's someplace where the ring would mean trouble for him, or he skipped out on us – which I would never believe. When it gets dark, I'm going back to find him."

"Kendra Marie Donovan, you will do nothing of the kind. In the first place, you have no wheels. In the second place, it's too dangerous. In the third place, if you go, I go." Lenny tried to sit up and look like he was in charge of the situation. Pain made it difficult and weakness crumpled him onto the pillow.

"Eat," she said. "We'll figure it out later." They ate their chips and drank their colas in silence.

"You need to rest some more," Kendra said throwing the refuse in the wastebasket by the table.

"Sure, so you can sneak off and get yourself killed."

"I would never leave you alone if you're sleeping. It's too dangerous. You need to be awake to at least defend yourself."

Lenny glared then fell back into an exhausted sleep while Kendra paced until she was ready to drop with weariness. It was still only about eight o'clock. A soft tap at the inside door startled her.

"It must be Linda," she said, but grabbed the robe and towel and slipped the gun in her pocket. She looked out the peephole to make sure it was Linda, then slipped on her sunglasses and called out, "Just a minute."

Grabbing a twenty-dollar bill, Kendra opened the door wide enough to slip out, closing it behind her. "Poor Melvin is just dozing off again or I would invite you in. I do so much appreciate this." She took the bag of burgers and fries and handed the woman the money.

"Oh, no, I wouldn't dream of taking your money. Consider this as a wedding gift from Jim and me. You just enjoy. We're leaving very early in the morning, or I would offer to get you some breakfast. They do have rolls and coffee down by the office after six, however."

"Thank you, ma'am, these will be wonderful and I'm sure we'll feel up to getting something tomorrow. Ya'll have a safe trip."

Kendra returned to the room, opened the bag and let the aroma of the greasy fries and onions from the burgers with the works fill the air. Suddenly she felt ravenous and Lenny licked his lips in anticipation.

They enjoyed the quick meal and Kendra tried to call Brian again. "Still the same messages. Lenny, there's something wrong. I've got to go back."

"You can't. I won't let you."

"And how do you expect to stop me?"

"Kendra, please. Think." Lenny pounded his fist on the bed. "Darn it. If I had a car I could get us out of here."

"And where would you take us? Brian has orders to keep me away from my family and I'm sure you do too. I know where they are and would give anything to go there, but I won't leave until I know what's happened to Brian."

Kendra pulled the paper Betsy had given her from her pocket and dialed the number.

"What are you doing? Don't get those kids mixed up in this any more than they already are."

She ignored him and spoke to the girl who answered the phone. "Betsy? I need your help again. I hate to ask, but can I borrow your car for a couple of hours? Thanks." She replaced the phone and said, "She'll be here in a few minutes."

About ten minutes later a small tap at the outside door sent Kendra upright in her chair. Although she expected Betsy, the sudden sound sent a tingling sensation through her as fear and anticipation collided. She jumped up and checked the peephole. Betsy and Robbie both stood outside the door pretending to put the keycard in the slot. Kendra opened the door quickly for them. Betsy handed her the car keys and a dark colored sweatshirt as well as the T-shirt she'd borrowed earlier. "You might need this dark sweatshirt."

"We haven't heard from my brother-in-law," Kendra said. "I have to go find him. Can you stay with Melvin?"

"I'm going with you." Lenny sat up on the side of the bed and tried to move but a wave of nausea sent him back against the pillow.

"No, you're not," Kendra helped him back on the pillows. "Sorry, Mel, but you would just slow me down. If Brian's hurt, I can't handle two of you. You'll have to stay here."

"Then keep the gun. You need something for protection." He nodded to the gun on the bedside table.

"You need it here," she said. "I'll be all right."

"Take it," said Robbie. "I've got one, unless you want me to come with you."

"Thanks Robbie, but I can go faster alone. If you have a gun, though, I'll take mine." She picked it up and put it in her pocket. "Mel, I'm sorry, but I have to go."

Kendra ran to Lenny and threw her arms around him. He held her with his good arm. "It's all right, baby. I understand. Be careful. I'll be fine."

"He's right, Mrs. McElroy," said Betsy. "You can trust us."

"Don't worry ma'am," said Robbie. "No one will get past us."

"Thank you." Kendra hoped she wasn't making a mistake, but someone had to find out what happened to Brian. She opened the door and checked for activity. Seeing none, she stepped outside. She was in the car and on her way out of the parking lot when Jonathan Cox's car once more drove into the lot. *I sure hope Betsy and Robbie can convince him they are newlyweds who don't want to be disturbed.*

# Thirty-six

Kendra drove Betsy's car to a back lane near the resort – closer to Wolverine Cabin. From that lane, it was about a half-mile hike through the woods and undergrowth to her cabin. Even though it was dark, she remembered the terrain well enough to get through the woods, but she had a small penlight with her if she needed it. About twenty minutes later, cautiously she drew closer to the cabin, ever thankful for the low-hanging Michigan clouds that blocked any moonlight. Moving slowly, she stayed in the thick woods and brush from which she could see the front room window and the front porch. The lamp on the table in the living room gave her a view that sent chills up her spine.

Brian sat in a kitchen chair, ropes wrapped securely around his feet, arms and waist. His eye looked swollen and it looked as if a trickle of blood oozed from the corner of his mouth. He looked only half-conscious. Paul sat opposite him rocking on a kitchen chair, pointing and clicking his gun like a kid with a new toy. Further down the hall, Angel complained loud enough that Kendra knew she was there – probably locked in a bedroom.

*That means Mark is here somewhere – probably watching Brian's car in case Lenny or I show up. Should I try to take care of Mark and run the chance of Paul killing Brian, or take care of Paul and possibly have Mark capture me? Oh, God, help me make the right decision.*

Not one to dwell unnecessarily long on decisions, Kendra made her choice. With all the stealth she had learned as a child, she made her way to the back of the cabin. Her window was closed but the screen was still open. Someone had closed the door to the room.

Thankfully, the window made no noise as she lifted it. Sounding like a Siamese in heat, angel yelled even louder when she saw Kendra at the window. She tried to shush the cat without making a sound herself. Angel meowed louder.

Kendra wasn't in much better shape physically than she had been the night before. Her arm still hurt and a dull ache pulsated in her head. But, at least she could think clearly and process her thoughts. Ignoring the pain, she climbed through the window and landed on the floor with a muted thump. Paul chose that instant to fire his gun in the front room. The sound covered her landing, but why did he fired the gun? Did he shoot Brian?

Angel flew to her lap. Kendra crouched on the floor beneath the window, heart pounding and gun aimed at the door. She listened for Paul's footsteps. *Surely, he can hear my heart racing like a car engine revving up for a drag race.* Forcing herself to become calm, Kendra realized her heart wasn't making the noise after all. It was Angel. The little cat's purr was so intense and high in volume that if the door were open Paul would surely hear her from the front room. Kendra pulled her closer to her with her free hand, keeping her gun ready in case of need. She listened for activity from either Paul or Mark. Even a groan from Brian would've been welcome.

The back door slammed and Mark called out, "Hey, Paul, what's going on in there? Did he try to get loose?"

"Naw, he ain't going no place. Just got tired of blasted cat's noise and shot at the bedroom." Paul giggled with a wild manic sound. "I don't hear it no more. Maybe I hit him."

Mark's voice became louder, as he moved closer to the living room. "Maybe we better change places, Paul. You're getting too trigger-happy. You kill McNeil and Boss Lady will be upset with both of us. You know she's on her way up here to talk to him. You guard the car. I'll take over in here."

"Think I can't handle an unarmed man all tied up like last week's garbage?" Kendra could hear the sneer in Paul's voice. "I ain't setting out there with all the bugs while you sleep in here. I can handle it just fine. You go back to your own job. I ain't going to kill him – not yet anyway. I want to know where that dame is first. I don't believe for a minute she's at the bottom of the lake. She's too crafty."

"You're crazy, Paul. You know that? You're just plain crazy. I don't know how they ever let you in on this…"

Paul fired another shot toward Mark.

"Hey! Watch where you aim that thing!"

"Don't you ever call *me* crazy again, *Father* Phillips, or they'll be dragging *you* out of the lake. Now leave me alone. I'm having fun." Paul giggled again and the door slammed as Mark apparently went back to his post of guarding the car. Other than the snickering and giggling of Paul, there was no other sound from the room. She still hadn't heard anything from Brian. *I have to know if he's dead or alive. Paul said he didn't kill him, but then Paul isn't all that believable.* Kendra waited a few minutes longer to make sure Paul wasn't going to check on Angel, who had calmed down and was purring with less volume.

Finally, she heard what she had been waiting for – Paul speaking to Brian. "You know, McNeil," he said. Kendra rose to her feet and placed Angel on the bed. "If you would just take me to Kendra, I could let you go and we'd both be happy."

The next sound – Brian's voice – almost brought tears to her eyes. "How would you get me past your friend out there?" Brian spoke with difficulty. *He must be hurt. I hope he's able to walk. I'll never be able to carry him through the woods.*

Paul laughed again. "I can handle him. We might even take him with us. He thinks he had her eating out of his hand until you came along."

"What kind of guarantee would I have that you won't kill me as soon as you have her?" Brian didn't sound all that interested, but probably wanted to keep Paul talking instead of shooting.

Again, Paul's laughter rang through the rafters of the cabin. "You just have to trust me." His manic sort of giggle followed.

"I would rather trust a rattlesnake." Brian spit the words at him.

A loud slap followed, drawing a torturous groan from Brian.

Kendra bit her lip and clenched her fists. She wanted rush out and help, but knew that would only make things worse. She eased the door open a crack. Brian was facing the hallway and Paul stood facing Brian and the front door – presumably guarding it as well as his prisoner. With his back was to the hall, he didn't see Kendra open the door. She waited a few seconds longer. She wouldn't shoot Paul in the back and there was always the chance that Mark would get Brian or her, before she could free him.

She laid out her plan of action in her mind and double-checked her gun to make sure it was completely loaded. She could fire six shots before reloading. *If I can't get Brian and myself out with that, we won't get out.*

Kendra opened the door a little more and slowly inched out of the room, taking aim at Paul as she moved. Brian saw her and probably knew she wouldn't shoot a man in the back, not even Paul Brooks.

"You know, Sheriff," he said, "you really are stupid and crazy to boot." Brian braced himself for either the shot that would end his life, or another slap that would give him more misery. Paul lunged to slap him again, but Angel had slipped out of the bedroom unseen and chose that moment to slash at Paul's ankle.

"Yow!" Paul yelled. "Where did you come from? How did you get out?" He started to kick the cat. "Wait a minute. Cats can't open doors." He whirled around. Kendra took aim.

"She doesn't like you," Kendra said and pulled the trigger. His gun flew out of his hand and he started for her, head down like a charging bull. "You should know better than that, Paul," she said as she dropped her gun and caught him by the shoulders, flipping him over her back the way she had done Vincent earlier. He landed on his back, gasping for air. Kendra picked up her gun and used the butt to put him to sleep for a while.

The back door slammed and Mark rushed through the kitchen. "Paul? Where are you? What's going on?"

Angel once again unsheathed her claws and made contact with a bare ankle. Mark yelled and Kendra whipped around the corner of the hallway, gun pointed in the direction of his voice. Mark kicked at the cat. She leveled her aim, fired and saw his gun fly from his hand. His eyes widened, then he turned to run, but Angel wrapped herself around his ankles and he sprawled across the floor, hitting his head on the floor. He was out cold.

Kendra ran into the kitchen and returned with a sharp knife that she used on the ropes holding Brian in the chair. “Kendra Donovan, you are absolutely nuts. Why are you here? You could have been killed.”

“You’re welcome.” She answered as if he’d said, *Thank you.* “How bad are you hurt?”

“I’ll live,” he said between clenched teeth, “bruised or fractured rib or two. Nothing serious.”

The fillet knife made short work of the rope. Handing Brian half of it, Kendra said, “I’ll get Mark, you take care of Paul. Better put a gag in their mouths in case they feel like yelling before the right people find them.” She kept her voice as low as possible, although, even without the bug, someone was sure to hear the gunshots.

After tying up Paul, Brian started for the kitchen door and the back porch. “Where do you think you’re going? There could be someone else out there.”

“Maybe, but important stuff is in my car – you know, gun, phone, etc. I’ll just have to take a chance. Cover me.”

“Brian, don’t…” He was already out the door, so Kendra rushed to keep watch and cover him, holding her breath while he got what he needed from a hidden compartment under his seat. She exhaled as he held the door open.

“Come on,” he said. “Let’s get out of here.”

“Not that way. They’re watching your car. Meet me around back by my window. I’ll go out the way I came in.” Kendra didn’t wait for him to argue or question her, but turned, raced back into the house and down the hall, scooping up Angel as she ran.

She was at the window with Angel in one hand and the gun in

the other when Brian got there. He was gasping for breath. He was hurting a lot, but she knew he would keep going. She held Angel out the window and said, “Here, take Angel while I climb out.”

“You aren’t going to take…” He didn’t finish. He took Angel in one hand and held the other ready to help her if she should fall on the way out. She dropped to the ground and would have slid to her knees if his arm hadn’t gone around her waist.

“Thanks. I’ll take Angel. Take my hand so we don’t get separated. If either of us needs to stop, squeeze.” Kendra whispered the instructions.

“Let me have Angel,” he returned. “You need to have one hand free to defend us.”

Kendra ignored his sarcasm and handed Angel back to him then pulled her gun from her pocket and kept it ready. They arrived at the corner of the house, where a small clearing stretched to the edge of the woods. Kendra knew she could make it, but wasn’t sure about Brian.

“We’re going to have to run for the woods,” she whispered. “Can you handle it?”

“I can keep up with you anytime, Kendra Donovan,” he whispered between clenched teeth. “But let go of my hand until we get across. You go ahead of me.”

“Nothing doing,” Kendra hissed. “I didn’t risk my neck to get you out of there only to have you get yourself killed while I run away.” she held tighter to his hand and pulled. “Let’s go.”

He had no choice, but to follow. Seconds later and the darkness of the woods surrounded them. Kendra felt Brian dragging and squeezed his hand to stop. They stood quietly for a minute until his pain and nausea receded.

He squeezed her hand to move on. When she felt the drag of him slowing down again, she stopped long enough for him to gain his breath. She listened for signs of anyone following. Someone or some animal was closing in on them. Brian wouldn’t be able to outrun whoever, or whatever. They stood as still as the trees that surrounded them.

The huge buck she'd seen before stopped in front of them. He stared, surprised as the humans were. Then he shook his antlers, turned and ran back the way they had come. Hopefully anyone who might be looking for them would see the buck and assume it had made any noise that they heard.

Finally, they came to the edge of the road. The clouds of another storm system covered the sky making the night so dark that had Kendra not known Betsy's car was there, even she would not have seen it. She squeezed Brian's hand and turned to whisper, "Stay here until I get the car started. I'll open the door so you can see where it is. I'll take Angel."

Kendra took Angel and ran to the car. She opened the door and pitched Angel to the back seat then got in the driver's seat and started the motor that was so quiet she heard only the initial turning of key in the ignition. The drone of the motor was lost in the night sounds of the forest.

***

Brian felt, rather than saw her take Angel. He could see no car. He had no idea where they were. He heard her running and was surprised when a car door suddenly opened. The dome light gave him a glimpse of Kendra tossing Angel into the back seat and jumping into the driver's seat. Then it went black as she started the motor.

Glad for a few seconds to catch his breath, Brian watched the midnight blackness for another tiny light. Had she left him alone out here in the middle of nowhere? He didn't believe she would do that, but he breathed a sigh of relief when the passenger door flew open.

Brian ran for it as best he could. He slid into the seat and pulled the door shut behind him. His breath came in short gasps between clenched teeth until the pain ebbed. By the time he fastened his seatbelt and could breathe more or less normally, they were on the highway heading somewhere known only to Kendra Donovan.

# Thirty-seven

Brian said nothing on the way back to Wintersville. Kendra tried to concentrate on driving, but her mind whirled like a windmill in a tornado. *He's upset with me. Why? Because a woman saved his hide? Because he wanted to do it himself? Maybe he had a plan of escape, but I couldn't see any. Maybe I wounded his male ego, but I could no more ignore him being in trouble than I could Lenny, or my family. Maybe he's right. Maybe I am nuts.*

Kendra glanced at his profile. It was too dark to see him clearly. Brian was hurt and she had no idea how badly. Lenny wasn't in any shape to do much. Her arm and head still throbbed. How long could she handle both of them in that motel room without too much suspicion? How would they get away without a car?

Thankfully, Brian broke the silence as well as the direction of her thoughts. "Kendra…thanks."

She glanced sideways at him again. "I'm sorry if I upset you, but, I couldn't leave with Lenny without knowing what happened to you. I knew you were in trouble. I had to try to help."

"Kendra, you don't follow orders very well, do you? I specifically told you if I didn't return for you to forget about Lenny and me and get yourself out of here." He paused staring out the window at the dark landscapes. "How did you know I was in trouble?" His voice was softer.

She sneaked another sideways glance at him.

"I tried to call you when I got Lenny out of the hospital to let you know where we were. The recording said the phone either was out of the area, or not turned on. I knew you would never willingly leave without us and I knew you wouldn't turn your phone off unless its ringing would put you in more danger."

"I wish I had your natural powers of reasoning. You're right, of course. When I got back to the cabin, I saw Paul in the house and Mark heading toward the car. I knew they weren't there on a friendly visit, so I put the guns, my phone and wallet in a hidden compartment under the seat of my car. I wasn't too concerned about what they did to me, because I knew you and Lenny were safe. If I'd had any inkling that you would pull a stunt like this, I would have been more specific with my instructions."

"Do you really think it would have made any difference?" Kendra couldn't keep the anger from her voice. She was feeling the effects of not having slept for two nights, as well as running for her life and ending up at the cabin in shock. She had been responsible for getting Lenny and herself out of the hospital alive and trying to keep them that way, then doing what she could to help Brian. Now she was exhausted, but needed to stay awake and alert in order to get them all to safety.

"Do you really think I could turn my back and leave you and Lenny to that gang of cutthroats? I came here to find my family. I've tried to be patient while you did what you had to do. If you're going to get this mess cleaned up so I can have my family back, I have to keep you alive. So don't go patting yourself on the back thinking I was doing it for you. Everything I did was for me. And I will continue to do what I have to do until I am reunited with my family." Kendra stopped suddenly, choking back threatening tears.

"Kendra, I'm sorry. We're all under a lot of pressure and tension." He paused giving them both a chance to get emotions under control. Changing the subject, his words were mixed with curiosity and awe. "Did you really get Lenny out safely? No one showed up to stop you?"

Kendra laughed through the sparkle of tears that hung on her eyelashes. As she drove into Wintersville, she told him about their escape from the hospital. "I didn't want to involve Betsy and Robbie, but she involved herself and we really needed her help."

"Kendra, I'm truly speechless. You trusted them enough to

leave Lenny with them? What if...? Never mind. That's another of your uncanny gifts, knowing who to trust and who not to trust." He paused then asked, "By the way, where did you learn to shoot that way? That was perfect marksmanship."

"My dad taught us how to use the guns when he bought them for us. He made us practice with him every day. He said having a gun was useless unless we knew how to use it and use it wisely. 'Never harm when you can disarm' is his motto. I practice with him every week in Akron."

Brian shook his head. "So…eh…do you have any plans for what we do next?"

Kendra chanced another glance at him. The streetlights cast a shadow across him but she could see him grinning. At least he wasn't angry any more. "No. You're the boss. I just took over in an emergency."

"Thanks a lot. Well, you, Lenny and I will look at all the options and go from there. Does that sound reasonable?"

"Maybe."

"Maybe? What's that supposed to mean?"

They pulled into the motel parking lot. Kendra had watched carefully, even driving around the block a couple of times before pulling in. She drove passed their door and parked at the end of the building on the walkway. "It means we might have more trouble. That's our room on the end. Did you notice anything unusual?"

"No. Was I supposed to?"

"Uh-huh. There should have been a big poster on the door that said, *Just Married – Do not Disturb.* It isn't there, which means either Betsy took it down because she was forced to do so, or someone else removed it."

"You have an idea? A suspicion?"

"Jonathan Cox. He was here earlier trying to get in the room. The manager chased him away. I saw him again, as I left, but I thought Betsy and Robbie would be able to convince him we weren't there. Can I use your phone? I didn't bring mine."

"Sure. You going to call Betsy and ask her what's going on?"

"Sort of." Kendra punched in the number for the motel. The manager answered. "Hello, this is Susan Coleman." She used her best Southern accent that caused Brian's eyebrows to shoot up almost to his hairline. "I know my sister left instructions not to be disturbed, but it's very important that I get in touch with her…Oh, I'm so sorry. I'm so upset and worried I don't know what I'm saying. My sister is Marie McElroy. She's there with her new husband, Melvin. They were just married a couple of days ago and…" Kendra stopped and sniffed as if she were crying. Brian looked fascinated.

"Oh, I'm so sorry. Like I said, I'm so worried. Our daddy didn't want her to marry Melvin and threatened to kill him if she did. I just learned that daddy is up there looking for her. I'm so afraid he might have found her…Oh, yes, he's tall, white bushy hair, wears dark rimmed glasses…There was? Oh, please can you call the police. I'm so far away and I'm so scared for Marie. Can I talk to her? No? Please, you've got to help her. He'll kill them both… Oh, yes, please do that. I'll call you back in ten minutes if I don't die from sheer fright before that. Thank you."

Kendra closed the phone and handed it back to Brian. "Stay put," she ordered and got out of the car. "The manager is going to come and check on them. While he's at this outside door, I'll use the inside door."

"Kendra, don't you think you've taken enough chances?"

"Not until we're all out of this mess." Kendra closed the door and ran to the side entrance and into the building. A large crack down the middle of the door to their room along with the hanging doorknob told here someone had broken down the door. She listened she heard the pounding on the outside door and the manager calling to them.

"Mrs. McElroy, this is the motel manager. I need to talk to you. Your phone seems to be out of order."

"What do you want?" called Robbie through the door. "We told you we didn't want to be disturbed."

"It's important. I have an urgent message from Mrs. McElroy's sister. She said it was urgent and private. I can't yell it to the town."

Silently Kendra eased the door open. Across the room by the window, Doc Jones stood with his arm around Betsy's neck, a gun pointed at her head.

"Drop the gun, Doc," Kendra said, not really expecting him to obey her. She hoped she would at least catch him off guard enough for Betsy to move out of her line of fire.

"You drop it Donovan or I'll blow her brains out."

"Sorry, Betsy," said Kendra and started to lower her gun.

Doc laughed and shifted Betsy so he could take better aim at Kendra. Betsy kicked him in the shins. Surprised, he loosened his grip on her and she went limp, falling to the floor. Kendra fired.

She missed his gun, but put a hole through his wrist. He dropped the gun. Lenny grabbed for it while Robbie reached for the outside door. Jonathan Cox stepped from the bathroom behind Kendra and caught her around the neck, holding a gun to her head.

"Drop it, Lenny. You too, missy." He poked the gun in Kendra's temple to emphasize that he meant her.

She dropped her gun and Lenny pulled his hand back from his reach for the other one. Robbie stepped back away from the door. In the noise and confusion, no one had heard the door click. It flew open and Brian aimed his gun at Jonathan Cox. Kendra grinned and dug her fingers in Jonathan's wrist. She twisted, forcing his hand away from her head.

"This one is yours, Brian. Don't miss." Kendra pushed harder and sent the gun away far enough for him to take aim. If he missed, at least she tried. Cox tightened his other arm around her neck. Brian fired and for Kendra everything went black.

# Thirty-eight

From somewhere faraway, Kendra heard voices. She was still alive! She rubbed her neck and tried to understand all the confusion. Betsy slipped an arm under her and helped her to sit up.

"Robbie, the gun." Lenny was giving orders. Kendra opened her eyes to a blur, but could see enough to know that Brian was about to fall.

Robbie dived across the bed to retrieve Cox's gun. Lenny got Doc's. He turned and said to Brian, "Sit down, pal, before you fall down. She's all right, just winded. Betsy's with her."

Brian abruptly dropped to the chair by the desk. Cox and Doc both held their bleeding hands, yelling obscenities until Lenny pointed his gun at them. "Doc, sit here and shut up," he ordered, pointing to the second chair.

Brian got up and Lenny said, "Over here, Cox." He indicated for the man to sit in the vacated chair. "Don't either of you make another sound. I'm not as steady and may not be as accurate with my aim as my friends. I would have to aim for larger areas – like heads and chests." Both men sat holding their wrists and glaring at Lenny.

The manager, who had followed Brian into the room, stood wide-eyed, taking in the scene of confusion. As if it suddenly occurred to him this was his motel and he had a duty to perform, he reached for the phone.

"Who are you calling?" Brian placed his hand over the phone.

"The county sheriff. There's been a shooting. Got to report it. That's the law." The man looked at Brian with an air of superior knowledge about the law of the land.

"Don't call the sheriff," said Brian. "Call the State Police.

Sheriff Brooks is a part of this gang."

The manager's eye widened even more. "It doesn't matter to me where I report the shooting, as long as I report it." He shrugged his shoulders and called the State Police as instructed.

Brian moved over, dropped to the floor beside Kendra and wrapped his arms around her. "Kendra that was absolutely the most harebrained stunt you've pulled yet. I could have killed you! How do you think I could live with myself if I had?"

"Brian," still feeling tightness where Jonathan Cox had his arm around her throat she could only whisper. "I trusted you. I knew you wouldn't let me down."

"Kendra Donovan, you *are* nuts. Do you know that?"

She nodded and tried to grin at him. "You told me that before. Now, help me up. Never mind, you're hurt. I'll make it."

"Just sit here with me for a minute. Please?"

"Oh? Are we in a romantic mood?" she whispered and grinned at him.

"No. I just want to keep you out of trouble for five minutes. You've been going nonstop for almost forty-eight hours. Relax for a minute and let us clean up this mess."

"I can't relax until it's really over. You know that." Her voice was coming back as she exercised her vocal cords. "There are still the Franklin sisters, Mrs. Cox and who knows who else." The old anger and frustration of having obstacles thrown in her path returned.

"It's not your concern, Kendra." Brian held me tighter.

"Until I see my family again, everything about this mess is my concern. Now please let me up so I can determine what *I* need to do next."

"Kendra!" Brian couldn't keep the exasperation from his tone. "Why don't you just go home and wait? It is almost over and…"

"You know I can't do that. I won't return home without my family." Kendra pulled herself away from him and stood extending a hand for him. He ignored it and pushed himself up clenching his teeth against his pain.

"You need to see a doctor. Betsy, take a look at him and tell him to see a doctor." Kendra glared at him, hands on hips.

"I don't need a doctor and no one needs to take a look at me." Brian clipped the words and moved back beside Lenny.

"The State Troopers will be here shortly," said Lenny, "but Kendra's right, Brian. Until we apprehended the entire gang, she's in this up to her neck and we need to get out of here before the State Troopers arrive. We'll just have to trust these folks to keep our secret until we're done."

"Lenny, you've been around Kendra too long. You're beginning to sound like her. We can't leave. And if we do, she can't go with us."

"Sorry pal, but if we go, she goes. She's risked her life in triplicate tonight. I'm not going to throw her to the wolves now." Lenny stared at Brian who glared back at his friend.

"We have our orders. We cannot under any circumstances take her…" Brian glanced over his shoulder at Kendra who was getting more than a little irritated with them. She stood with hands on hips, tapping her foot, waiting for them to work it all out. "…you know where," he finished.

"While you *boys* are trying to determine my fate, might I remind you that you have about three minutes, or less, before the State Troopers arrive? I suggest we borrow Betsy's car again. She and Robbie can tell the Troopers they were enjoying their honeymoon when these two thugs burst in both doors shooting at each other. The manager ran down to see what was happening and called the Troopers because he was tipped off by an anonymous phone call that these men were wanted by the FBI. The Troopers will keep them under wraps until the FBI shows up to claim them."

They all stared at Kendra with open mouths. Sirens wailed in the distance moving closer with each tick of the clock. Kendra pulled the car keys from her pocket and dangled them, urging an answer.

"Go," ordered Betsy, nodding toward the door. Kendra didn't wait for a second command. She ran for the car. Lenny and Brian had no choice but to follow. As they ran around the end of the building, she already had the motor running. Lenny grabbed the back door and slid into the back seat leaving the front for Brian.

"What's this?" Lenny asked as a furry creature leaped to the rear window. Then he laughed as Angel landed in his lap. "Angel. I should have known. That's the real reason you went back to the cabin, wasn't it?"

"Lenny! You know better than that, but I certainly couldn't leave her behind to be killed, or worse, could I?" By the time Kendra had backed the car from the sidewalk, they had the doors closed and their seatbelts buckled. She was barely on the highway when flashing red lights passed them and turned into the motel lot. Kendra leaned back and pressed the gas pedal further to the floor.

"Can I ask where we are going?" Brian glared at her.

"You can ask all you want," she answered staring straight ahead, still feeling angry that as much as they had been through, he still would have left her behind.

"Are you going to tell us?" He tried to be more specific.

"No."

Lenny went into a fit of giggles. "Forget it Brian. When she gets like that, you aren't going to get anything out of her. I don't know what happened between you two tonight, but somehow you got on her wrong side."

"Lenny, I'm not deaf and I'm not invisible." Kendra spit the words out in a short staccato. "Nothing happened between us. He was beaten and tied to a chair. I disarmed Paul and Mark then untied Brian. We tied them. We left. End of story. Go to sleep – both of you. I'll wake you when we get to where we're going. If you need to call any of your backup guys to take care of Paul and Mark, see the troopers and round up the rest, I suggest you do it. I'll pretend I'm deaf, since you seem to think I am anyway."

Brian turned abruptly to face Lenny and winced as pain shot through his side. Through clenched teeth he asked, "How much did you tell her?"

"Me? I didn't tell her anything. I was out of it most of the time. She got me to the motel room and made me take a pill and go to bed. Every time I woke, she was pacing and trying to call you. By nightfall, she called Betsy. They came and she left. I tried to tell you not to underestimate her. She's sharp and full of surprises."

Kendra blessed the darkness that hid her grin. She didn't want them to know she was pleased with Lenny's praise. However, weariness from the last two days was quickly numbing her senses. She wasn't sure she could even keep the car on the road, but they couldn't take her where she wanted to go. It was up to her to get them there. She knew where to go and prayed that she could stay awake long enough to get them all there safely.

# Thirty-nine

Brian made the calls. He had to. It was his job. He finished his calls and started to put the phone back in his pocket when it rang, startling all of them. Brian dropped the phone in his lap, recovered it and held it as if an electric current had suddenly entered that piece of electronic equipment. Lenny, who had been dozing, sat up and leaned forward.

"Brian here. Yes...We did that…I'm not taking her anywhere…No, Lenny isn't either, but I think you ought to know she saved our lives tonight. There would be no wrap-up without her…" Kendra and Lenny heard the anger in Brian's voice. He handed the phone to Lenny.

Lenny didn't need to ask who was calling. "Yeah…We did what we were told to do… that's right…without her help we would be dead and your drug ring would still be going strong…I know what you told us…We did not reveal anything…"

Kendra also knew who was on the other end. She held out her hand for the phone. Grinning Lenny handed it to her. Brian started to protest, but waited. "Mr. Severs," she said her voice dripping with feigned camaraderie. "So good to hear your voice again." Suddenly her voice turned icy. "It's good to know you're working so hard to keep me from finding out what I've known since that day in your office. I told you then I knew my family was alive and where they were. The only thing I didn't know was why. Now I know that. If you're concerned about who told me, you did with your phony photos and idiotic story of murder and suicide. Good-bye, Mr. Severs. Have a good life – if you can live with yourself." She closed the phone and handed it back to Brian, who chuckled as he replaced it in his shirt pocket.

"Kendra, how did you know who that was?"

Lenny laughed until tears rolled down his face. "I told you she knows more than she lets on. You knew who Brian was the first night at the lodge, didn't you?"

"Yes."

"You couldn't have known me," Brian sputtered. "We never met. I never saw you except that day in Severs' office and then I watched from the two-way mirror in his office. You couldn't have seen me." Brian carefully turned to look directly at Kendra, although he could only see her silhouette in the darkness.

"I didn't know your name, but I knew you were with the FBI." Kendra glanced at him from the corner of her eye. "When I walked into Severs' office that day, you were there and hurried into the other office. I didn't see your face, but I saw your build and your hair. I knew you were watching through the two-way mirror. I also knew Severs had a tail on me the minute I left his office. When I pulled into Palisades the tail kept going, so it made sense that someone who could get close enough to keep me out of trouble as he so aptly put it was already here. You were as close a match to the man I saw in his office as I would ever get."

"And you played along making us think…" Anger gave an edge to his voice.

"Brian, I tried to let you know. You wouldn't – or couldn't – trust me. I trusted you because I realized you were here not only to watch me, but also to learn what put my father in danger. I wasn't that important to the FBI, except that I knew where to start looking. They didn't. They were afraid I would do exactly what I did, get someone excited enough to give themselves away. It was all right if I got killed in the process, I wasn't one of them and I was dispensable."

"Kendra, baby, don't sound so cynical," Lenny said laying a hand on her shoulder.

"Sorry, Lenny. My father's been in the FBI too long for me not to pick up innuendos and gossip. I know more than even my father knew that I learned from going to the office with him. If he had realized how much I was picking up, he wouldn't have taken me back with him. I had to keep it to myself, until I needed the information I've garnered to survive and keep my friends alive."

"You still consider us friends, after what you know?" Brian sounded incredulous.

Kendra flashed a quick grin at him then turned her eyes back to the road. "You are both very good. It took everything I could come up with to keep a step ahead of you. Except I didn't know Lenny was playing on both sides of the fence. You had your orders and I don't fault you for that. You would have given me what I wanted if you could. We did have some fun in the midst of it all, but now I'm tired of playing cops and robbers and hide and seek. I just want to go home. And home is where my family is."

"Kendra, baby, you know we can't take you there – or help you find it. I don't understand the order, but it *is* an order. We can lose our jobs if we take you to them." Lenny squeezed her shoulder and looked into her face via the rear view mirror.

"He's right," said Brian. "I wanted to at least reassure you and was told specifically not to lead you on in any way as far as your family was concerned and under no circumstances was I to take you to them." Brian laid a hand over hers.

"Don't worry about it," said Kendra. "You aren't taking me anywhere. You've told me nothing. Like I told Severs, I knew that day in the office where they are and I'm taking us there. You can sit back, relax and take a nap, or I'll stop and let you out somewhere along the way, but I'm going home. I'm tired and bone weary. If I can stay awake and keep this car on the road for approximately another twenty minutes, we'll be at the cabin where they are."

Lenny and Brian looked at each other and started laughing. "I keep telling you not to underestimate her," said Lenny. "I, for one, am ready for a couple days R and R in the forests of Michigan. We can wrap it all up from there without ever giving our cover away."

"I hate to be the bearer of bad news, *boys,* but who doesn't know you're with the FBI? The gang knows who you are Brian, or they wouldn't have captured and held you for *Boss Lady* – whoever she is. And Lenny, you wouldn't have been shot and tracked by Doc and Jonathon Cox to finish the job. You have no cover to blow."

Brian and Lenny looked at each other then at Kendra and broke into laughter again. "She's right," said Brian, "but, we still need to protect your family."

"From me? Never mind, don't answer that." Kendra made a sour face then grinned. "Severs is going to have to be really creative to bring them back from the dead – unless he's hoping the drug gang will find them and blow the place up. Then he won't…"

"Kendra!" Lenny sounded shocked. She smiled at him.

"Sorry," she said, "I know he's your boss, and my father's boss, for that matter, but he's never liked me and I'm afraid the feeling is mutual."

"Probably because you're smarter than he is," said Lenny.

"Maybe."

They all laughed.

"Anyway," said Lenny, "I'll be glad to wrap this case up and get home to my wife and little girl for a while."

"Lenny! You never told me you were married." Kendra's eyes flew open wide in surprise. "Here you keep asking me to marry you and you have a wife! And a little girl! What are you trying to do, become a bigamist?"

"Kendra, sweetheart, I will always love you, but I was never *in* love with you. I hope you knew that. I hope you knew it was all in fun, even when we were kids." Lenny looked so miserable when she glanced in the rear view mirror that she started laughing.

"Lenny, you've always been as much a brother to me as David. That's how I always saw you. I could no more be in love with you than I could with David. What's she like? How old is the little girl? I hope she looks like her mother!"

"Kendra! You sure know how to hurt a guy." Lenny laughed and told them about his wife, Allison, and their two-year old daughter. "Her name is Kendra Allison."

Kendra thought he was teasing and glanced in the mirror. His beaming face brought tears to her eyes. "Lenny, why?"

"Because, Allison is her mother's name and Kendra is the most beautiful sister I ever had."

"Hey, you're going to cause her to wreck the car," Brian laughed as he reached over and wiped tears away so she could see.

"What about you, Brian?" Kendra was afraid to ask, but had to know. "I suppose you have a wife and two or three kids, too."

Brian was startled. He was quiet for a minute. Finally, he said, "No wife, yet, but I have a girl who has waited several years for me. I guess I should..."

"What do you mean waited years? Brian, my boy, if you love her you better do something about it. She won't wait forever." Lenny slapped him on the back. He turned to me. "How about you, baby? I know you're not married. Got any prospects, besides that louse who fired you?" Lenny laughed then realized she was too quiet. "Sorry, baby, I'm not thinking too clearly tonight."

"Don't worry about it. We've all been on the run with trauma after trauma thrown in to boot. I'm all right." Kendra kept her eyes on the road trying to understand her feelings. *Why should I feel so shaken to know Brian has a girl?* Suddenly she braked and made a sharp turn to the left.

"I almost missed the road," she said as she turned onto a dirt road that wound around the forest for about ten miles. About half way was another dirt driveway that looked more like an old logging path that led to a log cabin hidden from view, but Kendra knew it was there. It was well after midnight. The cabin looked dark and deserted. No vehicles in sight. No sign of life. Her heart sank. Had she been wrong? She dropped her head on the steering wheel, too weary to move.

Brian pulled his phone from his pocket and punched in some numbers. "It's me, Brian. Did you hear the car? No, I'm not alone. Yes." He closed the phone and put it back in his pocket. "He wanted to know if I was alone and if Lenny was with me. He didn't ask about anyone else." Brian grinned as a light came on in the cabin and the door opened and Calvin Donovan walked toward the car to meet them.

"Tears are all right now, Kendra." Brian placed his hand on her back and gave her a nudge. She opened the door, turning on the dome light.

"Kendra?" Calvin ran the rest of the way. Kendra was in his arms almost before her feet hit the ground.

"Dad, oh, Dad." She hugged him so tightly her arms ached, especially the one that was hurt.

"Kendra, baby" His tears mingled with hers as they held one another.

David followed him out. "Kendra? Brian what's going on? Did they change their minds?"

"No. We didn't bring her here. She brought us."

"That's right," said Lenny. "She knew all along where you were, but kept quiet for your safety, as well as for ours. My guess is she knows just about everything. She even knew Severs when he called us on the phone tonight on the way up here. She put him in his place."

"Are you men going to stand outside all night and…" Sarah called from the door, but stopped when she saw Calvin and David hugging Kendra. "Kendra? Kendra, baby?" She ran out to grab her daughter with more hugging and weeping.

"Kendra!" Shelly cried as she too ran to meet them. "Oh, Kendra, did you get my message? Did you know what it meant?"

"I sure did, Moppet. Believe me, it made what I had to do a lot easier just knowing for sure you were all alive and well. I think there's someone else in the car looking for you." Kendra grinned at her sister.

"Someone else?" Calvin asked.

"Don't worry, sir, I think this one will keep her mouth shut. Can't say the same for her claws, however. She does a good job of slashing. Right Kendra?" Brian laughed.

Michelle squealed as she felt something soft and furry brush against her ankles. Angel didn't wait for someone to get her. No one had thought to close the car doors and the cat took matters into her own paws. A very loud purr accompanied by a few "meows" sent Shelly to her knees. She scooped the cat into her arms and cried, "Angel? Angel! Oh my little Angel. Did Kendra take good care of you? Have you been a good girl?"

"Folks, I don't want to put a damper on the reunion, but Lenny's been shot, I've been beaten, Kendra was beaten, in a wreck and then chased for a day and a half, to say nothing of rescuing Lenny from Doc Jones and me from Paul and Mark. In other words, we're beat. Can we go in?" Brian looked like he was ready to topple.

"Have you eaten lately with all that going on?" Sarah asked.

"We had some burgers when? About eight?" said Lenny. "How about you, Brian?"

"Nothing, but I'm more tired than hungry. If you can show me a corner where I can stretch out, I'll try not snore too loudly."

"What? You don't want to share my bed tonight?" Kendra grinned at him.

"Kendra!" Five voices spoke at once. Only Shelly thought it was funny and laughed.

"Sorry, I couldn't resist. We'll explain tomorrow. I'm with Brian. I just need a place to crash. I'll eat tomorrow. Can I have the glider on the porch?"

"Sure, honey, but are you sure you'll be warm enough?" Sarah said.

"I'll leave my clothes on and grab a blanket. I'll be fine. If I get cold I'll…" Brian glared at her as if expecting more of her humor. "…snatch Angel," she finished, smiling at Brian. He shook his head and headed for the cot in the corner of David's room. David took the couch and put Lenny in the bed.

Kendra curled up on the glider on the porch. At last, she could sleep. She was home. No more trouble; no more running. *Then why do I have the nagging feeling that another shoe is ready to drop?*

She tried to sort it all out, but her mind shut down as sleep came at last – until a nightmare sent her screaming into wakefulness. Not sure if it was a dream or reality, Kendra couldn't stop the screams or the tears that rolled down her face.

# Forty

"Kendra, baby, it's all right. Come on, sweetie, wake up." Calvin had just walked out to the porch when she sat up on the glider screaming. He dropped down beside her, pulling her into his tight embrace. Holding his daughter close he continued to soothe her the way he used to do when she was ten. "Come on, sweetheart. You're all right. We all are."

"Dad?" Kendra opened her eyes when her father's voice finally penetrated the horrors of her dream. Feeling his arms around her, she slipped hers around him and cried all the tears of fear and frustration that she'd been saving since the phony policeman informed her of the murder/suicide.

When Kendra was finally able to speak between hiccups and sighs, she said, "The car went over the cliff with all of you in it. Then someone pushed Lenny and Brian overboard from a speeding boat. I was all alone and…"

"It was only a dream, sweetie. We're all fine." Calvin continued to hold her. Although Kendra felt embarrassed about being so emotional, she couldn't stop the tears. Finally, she leaned back and swiped at her eyes and face with a tissue that Shelly handed her. They were all there – Lenny, Brian, her family – all wanting to comfort her, looking on with concern. Abashed, she covered her face with her hands. "I'm sorry. I never reacted that way to a dream before."

"That dream was too close to the reality you've lived with the last couple of months. I'm surprised you held up as long as you did." Lenny knelt before her. "We've all been through some harrowing times, but I think the last couple of days, you outdistanced us by far.

Don't be sorry about your feelings."

"Lenny..." Kendra wanted to say so much to him, but words couldn't find their way to her lips. She lifted her shoulders in a helpless motion and settled for, "Thanks."

"Hey Kendra, did you really understand that message I sent you?" Kendra was thankful Shelly sought to change the subject.

She laughed then swiped her hands across her face once more, grabbed another tissue and blew her nose. "I sure did. You told the story of Joseph. His father thought he was dead, but he was alive all the time. I knew deep in my heart that you were all alive, but that message made it more possible."

"You mean that newspaper the kid in Fairplain sold you for a quarter?" Brian asked.

"Yes, David paid him to get it to me. He had his little sister with him and gave the impression he called her Moppet. Brian gave them a couple of dollars for ice cream. That was the day Paul took me off to jail without my purse or any money. I really needed reassurance and your message eased my mind."

Calvin frowned at Shelly and Kendra then glanced at David. "Michelle? Kendra? What are you talking about?"

"I showed you the paper I did with pictures and the Bible story about Joseph," said Michelle.

"But how did Kendra get it?"

"I took it with me when I went for supplies," said David. "Brian and Kendra had just left the sheriff's office and stood on the sidewalk talking. I saw this kid with his sister and pointed her out to him. I gave him five bucks to make sure Kendra got it."

"That could have been dangerous for all of us. We were under orders not to contact her." There was an angry edge to his voice.

"Sorry, Dad. I don't work for Severs. I never believed he was being fair to Kendra – or any of us, for that matter. She needed some reassurance. Brian and Lenny were also under orders and couldn't say anything. She needed to know we were all right." David stared at his father. In twenty-six years, he had never spoken to him like that.

Kendra glanced at her father, who continued to frown. "We'll talk later," he said.

"You saw that message and immediately knew what it was, didn't you?" Brian's eyes were wide with surprise. "You even told me where it was found in the Bible and that it was the story of Joseph, but I didn't make the connection."

"I might not have either, if the kid hadn't said it was a message from Moppet. You asked him what a moppet was and he said, 'little sister called Moppet.' He didn't say *his* little sister, but you assumed it was his sister since she was with him."

"Mr. Donovan, I think I better put in for some retraining when we get out of this. Do you suppose Severs would hire Kendra to teach a course on seeing the impossible?" Brian grinned at her.

"Don't be smart, Brian McNeil," Kendra said. "I knew what to look for. You didn't."

"I suppose you knew Ira Thoburg, too," he said.

Kendra laughed the first time since receiving word that her family had disappeared. It felt good. "Yes. David, it was a wonderful performance."

"Tell me how you knew him?" Brian was serious. "I thought he did a superb job of disguising himself, even adding wrinkles."

"Not as many as the blind beggar," Kendra laughed again. Brian's eyebrows shot up sending Lenny and her into a fit of giggles and chuckles. "Oh, yes, I knew him right away both times, but his name as a beggar clinched it. Melvin McElroy was the name he always used when we played spy games. That's the reason I used it at the hospital. I knew Lenny would understand when he came out of the anesthetic if someone said something to him.

"Ira Thoburg was a masterpiece of a disguise, except you couldn't disguise David's eyes. I would know them anywhere. And…" Kendra grinned at David, "…shall we tell him?"

David laughed, nodded and said, "They all told me I wasn't to let you know who I was. I knew you would recognize me, anyway – both times. At least Paul didn't catch on. I almost blew it when I saw you get out of the car after Paul told me you were dead. If Brian hadn't intervened, I would have caught you in a bear hug."

"I could see that was your intention," said Brian. "We would have been in real trouble if anyone saw you."

"And we weren't in trouble anyway?" Kendra gave him a sarcastic look.

Brian laughed. "Well maybe, but I didn't know how bad it was then."

Turning back to Brian, Kendra said, "I saw the exchange and knew the pressure David had to be under. Remember, I told you on the island that when we were young, we played spy games. David, Lenny and I made up a secret code. It had to do with finger movements. I read in a science fiction book once about someone being able to communicate secretly with his fingers while speaking verbally at the same time. So we developed our own language. It was a combination of sign language for the deaf, Morse code and our own symbols. One hand is all we need, although we can use two if we want to. The fingers speak, either against something, or in the open.

"We can carry on two conversations at once. With our finger language, I learned the family was all right and didn't know for sure who they were hiding from or why. David wanted me to go home. I told him not until we all went together."

"You're kidding." Brian gave her a look that clearly said he thought she was teasing.

"No, watch." Kendra ran her fingers through her hair and said with her fingers, "Lenny, you and David both tell him I said thanks for being there and helping me."

David and Lenny looked at each other and smiled. Then together they said, "She said for us to tell you thanks for being there."

Brian still looked skeptical.

"We never knew when we were kids, how important that language would be," said Kendra.

"Kendra Marie," Sarah broke in, "it's already after noon. I think you need to eat something, whether you want it or not. You can talk later. Lunch will be on the table in about fifteen minutes. Maybe you would like a shower before you eat."

"Do I look that bad?" Kendra smiled at her, remembering her black eye and lump on her forehead. "Never mind, don't answer that. I probably look worse. Do you have some clothes I can wear? Mine got left behind. It's nice we're the same size."

Sarah laughed as she took her daughter's hand and helped her up. With an arm around her, Sarah took Kendra to her room. She found a pair of navy shorts and a light blue T-shirt and headed for the shower humming to herself. *Soon we'll be heading home.*

# Forty-one

The rest were waiting for her at the table when Kendra entered the room fresh from the shower, her hair still glistening wet. David whistled and Lenny started humming the Miss America tune he'd played at the lodge.

"Stop it you two," Kendra laughed. It felt so good to be clean again. It felt even better just to be with family. She sat in the chair they left for her between Lenny and Brian. As they held hands for the blessing of the food, Lenny said, in his finger language, "I'm proud of you, kid."

When Calvin finished the prayer, Kendra excused herself to get a tissue. Sarah started to get up, but Lenny said, "She's all right, Mrs. D. I think I embarrassed her."

"You kids always did enjoy that secret language. You especially enjoyed keeping the adults in the dark about what you said."

Kendra returned in time to pass the food from Lenny to Brian, who looked at her curiously. "Kendra, Lenny keeps telling me that you know more than we think you do. I'm not saying I don't believe him, but I'm curious as to what you know, and how you know it. Do you suppose…?"

"That I can fill you in? Sure, I don't mind, now. I didn't want to say anything before that would get in the way of your investigations. You had your orders, as I'm sure my father did, but Severs couldn't order me – well he could, but I didn't have to listen."

David smiled and nodded. Brian glanced at one and then the other.

"I already told you I saw you in Severs' office. I didn't know your name, but I knew who you were when I saw you at the lodge.

Severs had a tail on me from the time I left his office. He was with me when I left Akron and stayed with me until I turned into Palisades, so I knew someone would be there to take over. It had to be you – or Lenny."

Brian stared, mouth open. Then he shook his head. "Did you know Lenny was with the FBI?"

"Not then. I knew Lenny from the time we were kids. I knew he wasn't a professional pianist – although he's much better than he was when we were kids. Neither was he a professional photographer, so I suspected he was with the FBI." She grinned at Lenny. "You aren't a bad photographer, but you would never make a living at either music or pictures. Those were your pictures Severs showed me that day in his office."

"How did you know that?" Lenny and Brian both asked together.

Kendra laughed. "I didn't. I only suspected it. You both just confirmed it."

Calvin threw back his head with pleasure. "Looks like she psyched you on that one, boys."

"Severs knew that one of my hobbies is photography. He asked me to come up with some photos to convince you of the deaths. I thought it was a stupid idea, but I went through my album and pulled out three photos that I thought would satisfy him and give you a clue as to what was going on. Apparently it worked."

"But how did you know from those pictures all that you said you knew?" Brian asked. "I saw them. They were just random shots he came up with at the last minute."

"What are you talking about?" Shelly asked.

Kendra answered. "Mr. Severs sent a phony policeman to see me the day you left. He told me you were all dead – murder/suicide. He said the car went off the mountain to make me think you went south through West Virginia. They said the entire car – metal and all – disintegrated – which I knew was impossible. It took the FBI almost a week to find enough *human* ashes – presumably from the crash site – to give me anything concrete."

"Severs said he would handle it. I didn't think he would be so... How could he think anyone would believe...?" Calvin was at a loss for words.

"Dad, he always thought Kendra was just a stupid little girl. He never believed her capable of anything important," David said.

"He thought I would just accept his explanation and 'get on with my life' as he put it," Kendra said.

"Didn't he offer you any proof? What was he going to do when we all returned alive and well?"

Kendra laughed again. "He will have a really hard time explaining that to the press," she said.

"He didn't..." Calvin stared at his daughter.

"He sent me a ten inch square metal box that was supposed to hold all of your remains and insisted that I bury the box immediately – complete with an advertised funeral – front page of *The Beacon Journal*. I decided that he didn't want me to have the ashes examined in the first place, and he needed to let *someone* know you were really dead, in the second."

Kendra chuckled then added, "He didn't know I took some of the ashes and sent them to my friend at the forensic lab in Ohio State Medical School. Joe called me just before I left to ask why I wanted him to analyze ashes from pine needles and paper mixed with dirt." She laughed harder at the expressions – especially Calvin, Brian and Lenny.

"Surely he didn't..." Calvin started, but clamped his mouth shut before saying something derogative about his superior.

"Yes, he did. He didn't think I would know the difference between human remains and burned trash."

"But surely Severs... never mind," he said shaking his head. "Go on with your account."

"I refused to have a church funeral. I only allowed the graveside service because I thought it might be important for someone to believe you were dead. The day after the graveside service, I went to see Severs to get some answers. That's when I saw Brian. He was in

Severs' office. Apparently, Severs told him to hide as I burst in on them. He went into the connecting office. I knew he was watching us through the two-way mirror."

"How did you know about…?"

"The mirror? David and I learned about it when we were what – about seven?" David nodded.

"Severs tried to brush me off, but I wouldn't budge. I wanted to clean out your desk. He said he had already done it, but he wouldn't give me any of your personal effects. He was keeping everything on file – even family photos. No one had death certificates. The funeral director said the FBI had them. The FBI said the funeral director had them. All of that together told me you were alive and Severs expected you to return to your office."

Lenny chuckled and Brian smiled. He had seen the interchange.

"Then Alice brought in a file folder, which he wouldn't let me see. He pulled out three photographs – one was the car going up a mountain, one showed the crash site and the third was supposed to be after the crash. It was a nice picture of the car, complete with license plate. Too bad Lenny didn't know you drove the station wagon the day you left."

Lenny, who had just taken a drink of water, sprayed it out and started coughing. Kendra reached over to pat him on the back and continued her story. "The second and third pictures of the crash – one before and one afterward – weren't the same location. The third was an aerial view of this forest area. One year when we were up here for vacation, Lenny, David and I took a helicopter tour of this area. Lenny took pictures. I still have the one he gave me. That's the one Severs showed me – a blown up version of it. That's how I knew where you were. I just didn't know why and didn't want to put you in more danger until I found out."

"So you decided to spend a little time in our old vacation spot and see what you could learn. But, if he indicated we went south, how did you know to come to Michigan?"

"That was simple," Kendra said. "You didn't take clothes for a southern vacation and when the bills came, I checked the gas card. Your last gas purchase was in Toledo. And your computer message to me had vacation in all caps – which always meant Michigan."

Calvin smiled at her. "Maybe I should've encouraged you to become one of us. Sounds like you've outwitted the top people at the office."

Kendra made a sour face. "That's not difficult to do."

Lenny, Brian and David broke into hearty laughter. Calvin frowned and said, "Kendra, that's not very…"

"I know." She grinned. "But, it's the truth. Anyway," she continued, "I knew you must have found out something that put you in danger, or at least someone thought you knew something."

"Actually, Lenny would have been in as much danger as I was. Paul planned to kill us when we arrived, because he was afraid I would catch on to something fishy at the lodge. Lenny was already here as an undercover agent and if I didn't show up, they would assume he told us and they would know he was with us. He would be in danger."

"So if you came you were in trouble and if you didn't Lenny would be?"

"That's about it."

"So Severs *killed you off* to save both of you. Makes sense in a Severs sort of way." Kendra said.

"So, how did you…" Brian started.

Kendra continued, "Severs unknowingly relieved my mind that you hadn't been kidnapped by gangsters of some kind, so I figured it had to have something to do with someone knowing who you were. I just had to wait and play it by ear until Doc Jones tried to kill me and I overheard the whole gang talking – well, almost the whole gang. Lenny wasn't there and they mentioned Brian's name. At that point everyone I knew and had trusted and thought were my friends seemed to be on the wrong side of the fence."

Kendra told them her experience with Paul, wrecking her car, and Brian taking her to the infirmary. Then staring at the ceiling and forcing her words into a cold, matter-of-fact, emotionless sound, she told them about all she heard in the infirmary and of her running with her pursuers searching for her until she made it back to the cabin.

"I had no idea Doc Jones was in on it, or I never would have left you there," Brian said.

"I guess for a while I thought you *did* know and that's *why* you left me there. It sounded like Lenny was with them. I was too scared to trust anyone, but I didn't know where to go. I had no car, so I couldn't come here. I don't really know what I was thinking going back to the cabin, although if I had been thinking I would have known that Brian would be there. Maybe I did know. Some memories are a little foggy. But I remember I heard his voice while I was in the infirmary."

"How could you…? The *bug?*" Brian was surprised.

"Yes. It took me a while to figure that out. As I said, I wasn't thinking too clearly, when I ran. I was cold and drenched to the bone. I guess it's a miracle that I even made it back to the cabin. Or that Brian understood what I needed. Once I was more or less, back to normal," she flashed a smile a Brian, "I realized that when I heard his voice it was scratchy – or full of static. I heard another noise that I finally realized was Angel purring beside the *bug.*"

"You mean the cabin was bugged?" Calvin asked. "Why and by whom?"

"It was put there the afternoon I arrived. I suppose they thought I might try to call you or someone who might know where you were. Mark met me at the cabin and helped to carry my stuff in. Angel, by the way, took an instant dislike to him. She practically chased him out of the cabin. Later she showed me the little butterfly-shaped *bug* on the lamp. I wouldn't have noticed, because there were several similar decorations around the room. I fixed it up in a box with cotton so I could let them know what I wanted them to know and silence it when I didn't want them to hear."

"How did you know how to do that?" Calvin looked more surprised than even Brian and Lenny had been.

David chuckled and Kendra flashed him a smile. "David and I learned that one day at the bureau when we were wandering around the building. Mark took me to a spaghetti place called the *Italian Café*, which supposedly opened a couple of months ago. He said he had only been at the lodge a week himself, but another time mentioned he had been to the spaghetti house a number of times. Toni addressed Mark as *Padre* even though Mark wasn't wearing his collar. Toni had to have known him before. I knew Toni and Giorgio Estrada from college. They were good musicians, but always in trouble of some kind, so I'm sure they must be involved in some way."

Brian and Lenny exchanged glances. Lenny started giggling the way he used to do when they were kids and she said, or did, something that he and David thought she didn't know. She turned to see if he was going to share his joke.

"Go on," Lenny said. "Brian and I thought they were involved, but had nothing on which to base our assumptions."

"By the way, the old men disguises were really good. Mark didn't notice, but I felt a lot better knowing you two were right behind us."

Lenny started laughing again and Brian lifted his eyebrows in understanding. "That's what the fit of coughing was all about. She said something to you in your finger language."

"Yes," laughed Lenny.

"Do I dare ask what she said that sent you into a fit of coughing?"

"I wasn't coughing as much as I trying to hide the laugh. Remember I was drumming on the table. It was after Mark made those *remarks* about us. She said, 'That's not very nice language for a gentleman to use in front of a lady.' I was surprised that she knew who we were, although I shouldn't have been."

Brian laughed. "I won't ask what you were saying. Go on," he said.

"I knew Paul Brooks had to be involved. He was always in trouble and trying to get us in trouble as kids. He tried more than once to get me alone. He hasn't changed much. But beyond that, Paul knew Brian spent the night with me the night Vincent was killed. Mark also knew and was very jealous."

"Brian spent the night with you?" Sarah's eyebrows were almost to her hairline, as she looked first at Brian then at Kendra "What would Robert think about that?"

"That's another long story. But to make it short, when I got back from my *funeral* leave, he had replaced me."

"Replaced you? With another secretary or another girlfriend?" She looked confused.

"Yes. End of that story." Kendra looked down at her plate, took a bite of sandwich then continued her account. "Vincent was just an unfortunate hothead whom they used to try to get rid of me. They were afraid I would be stubborn enough to stumble onto something. I think they killed him because he figured out too much and they were afraid he would say something that would give them away. They couldn't control his drinking. When he made a comment about my dad being an FBI Agent and getting what was coming to him, Mark, Toni and Giorgio all heard him. They had to silence him. If they could pin it on me, they would be rid of both of us."

Kendra's family stared at her. Calvin finally said, "Is this our daughter? After all you endured and suffered, you still had the courage to keep going until you found us?"

Kendra smiled at her father. "You taught me well." Lenny squeezed her hand. David winked at her.

# Forty-two

Kendra took a drink of iced tea, looked around the table and asked, "Is there anything else you want to know? I think I covered everything, except who is the *Boss Lady* that Mark spoke about when I went back for Brian."

"That's pretty evident," said Lenny. "From what you told us, Elizabeth Franklin seemed to be calling the shots while you were in the infirmary. She always was a little bossy."

"There's something else that keeps nagging at my mind, but I can't put my finger on it, yet." She frowned. "Actually a couple of things."

"You mean there's something about this case you don't know?" Lenny smiled and winked at Brian.

"You're the one who said I knew it all. I didn't," she replied. "I'm not sure why the FBI is in on a simple drug ring operating in the state of Michigan. There must be more to it – other states involved, kidnapping, foreign involvement." From the look on Calvin's face and the smile on David's she knew she had hit another nerve.

"You're right, Kendra. The FBI wouldn't be involved in a simple in-state drug problem." Her father looked at her with more respect. "We've been working with the CIA because we know other states are involved and at least one overseas contact. We have a name, but haven't been able to make the connection to anyone in the ring we know."

Kendra stared at her father as if reading his mind. Tears welled up and threatened to overflow. She shook her head and blinked hard to force them back. Not another friend.

"Kendra? What is it? You *can't* know that," Calvin said.

Lenny took her hand. "You do know, don't you?"

"I think so." Tears started down her face as she whispered, "Papa Giovanni."

"Kendra! How do you know someone named Giovanni? We do have a name of Julio Giovanni from Italy. What do you know about him?" Her father looked at her more with suspicion than curiosity. He even sounded angry. They had been working for a couple of years on this case.

"We called him Papa Giovanni. He was a wonderful musician. We played music together. He taught me some Italian ballads and told me stories of Italy. Papa Giovanni was Mama Estrada's father – Toni and Giorgio's grandfather. He used to laugh about his Italian daughter marrying a Spanish farmer."

"That's it! That's the connection to the folks up here that we needed." Calvin was ecstatic as he jumped up to call in the information. He didn't even notice the pain and anguish on his daughter's face. These were more friends whom she had loved and trusted.

Kendra continued with less excitement than her father. "The man we found in the lake was probably Angelo Giovanni, a cousin of Toni and Giorgio. I thought I recognized a ring he was wearing. Toni and Giorgio both have one like it. So did another cousin, Roberto something or other. He was probably the first man they found floating in the lake."

Calvin stared at Kendra as if she were a stranger. Her pain at yet another loss of cherished friends spilled over her eyes and down her face.

"Does anyone mind if I go for a walk to the overlook?" Kendra stood and started for the door not really expecting an answer. Lenny and Brian understood. One more trusted friend could no longer be trusted.

Calvin paused in his dialing and answered her. "Until we hear from the boys that everyone is rounded up, we can't be certain that someone won't show up here. No one is supposed to know where we are, but...well, you found us."

"But, Dad, I knew about this place."

"How did you know? We never came here when we came to Michigan for vacation."

"David, Lenny and I were here lots of times after Lenny got his driver's license."

"Kendra! How much more are you going to tell us that we didn't know about our own daughter?" Sarah looked horrified.

Kendra laughed. "Don't worry Mom. We were good."

David and Lenny both laughed with her as Sarah's face turned scarlet. They all knew what she was thinking.

"Kendra Marie Donovan! Is that anyway to treat your mother?" Calvin hardly ever spoke sharply to her.

"Sorry, Mom, but we *are* all adults now. Even Michelle is almost eighteen. David, Lenny and I did a lot of things that you would never have approved of. We learned a lot about life and death, things that saved our lives the last couple of days. I couldn't have lived through it without that background."

Kendra knew by the look on her mother's face, that she was going to get a lecture so she decided to change the subject. "By the way, did you folks know that Lenny is married and has a little girl?" It worked, as she knew it would. They all began to question Lenny.

"Lenny? Why didn't you tell us? Tell us about them now."

Kendra took the opportunity to move to the porch where she hoped to be alone with her pain and grief. She wanted desperately to go to lookout point, but wouldn't go without her father's permission as long as there was still a chance of danger to her family. She had been through too much to find them. She certainly wouldn't do anything foolish now which would destroy them. Instead, she sat on the glider to think.

Brian's cell phone rang as she left the room. He followed her out, answering it as he moved to the other end of the porch. Kendra got up and moved toward the door to go outside and give him more privacy. He didn't talk long and called to her before she opened the screen door.

"Kendra?"

His voice had a strange sound, almost as if he were choking. Kendra turned abruptly to answer him. Even in the shadow of the porch, she could see he had gone pale as he suddenly sat down on the glider.

"Brian? Are you all right?" she hurried back to sit beside him.

"You didn't want me to get in my car for my gun and phone. Why?"

It was an odd question, but suddenly she knew why he asked it. "Brian, who?"

"You *did* know. I could have been blown to kingdom come."

"No, I didn't know. I suspected. I tried to stop you, but you already had the door open before I could tell you why I didn't think you should get in the car. Then there was no point in saying anything. I thought I must have been wrong. I smelled dynamite powder on Mark's hands when I tied him up. Brian, what happened?"

"Paul managed to get away from them. He killed Mark and took my keys. When he turned the key in the ignition, the car blew up."

"Oh, no. Paul wasn't a nice person, but no one deserves that kind of death. Brian! It was meant for you."

"You really did save my life. I would have taken my car if you hadn't stopped me. I've been such a stubborn, pigheaded fool, that I couldn't even properly say thank you. Kendra, I don't know how you do it, but like Lenny said you're sharp and full of surprises. I can just picture you in Severs' office – as the head of the FBI, that is." He tried to laugh, but was still shaken by the news he'd just received.

Suddenly Kendra felt as if a very large, angry animal had just kicked her in the stomach. She gasped.

"Kendra? What is it?"

"Brian, that's it! That's what's been puzzling me! Myrtle Cox in the infirmary said something to the effect that those pictures must have told me something. Brian, no one knew about the pictures except the people in Severs' office that day."

"Kendra, what are you saying? I'm not sure I like where this is leading. Do you think that I…?"

"No, Brian, not you and certainly not me. Who does that leave?"

"Seymour Severs? Come on Kendra. He's a jerk sometimes, but the leader of an organized crime ring? Personally, I don't think he has the brains for it. Without Alice to run the office he would…Alice?"

"You got it! Boss Lady coming up from somewhere south of here – like Akron? She had access to those files. The intercom light was on the entire time I was in the office, so I know she heard everything we said."

"If that's the case…I hate to say it, but I think you're right. We better tell the rest and get some backup up here."

Before either of them could move, a shot rang out and a bullet whistled above Kendra's head, barely missing her. Brian pulled her to the floor and yelled for the rest to stay in the house.

# Forty-three

"Someone must have figured out the photos." Kendra spoke with difficulty since Brian was on top of her, keeping her *safe,* while he was calling in some backup. They needed to get here before it got too dark to find the place.

"What's going on out there? Was that a gun shot?" Calvin started out the door. Another shot from the woods sent a trickle of blood down his face where the bullet grazed his cheek on the way to the wall.

"Get down in there. Cover the back and sides of the house. Throw me my gun." Brian took charge, firing his orders in rapid succession from the porch floor. Wood covering the bottom third of the porch walls protected them somewhat as long as they stayed down.

"Brian, you're crushing me," Kendra said. "Let me up so I can help."

"Just stay put. You've done enough helping. It's our turn now."

"Don't get chauvinistic on me. We're being shot at and you need all the gun hands you can get." Anger made her voice sharp.

Brian didn't have time to answer her. Calvin called from the edge of the door. "Here you go. Catch." He threw the guns – first Brian's, then Kendra's. Brian had to roll off her to catch his gun. Kendra lifted her arms, caught her gun and rolled away from Brian, as another bullet barely missed her father.

Brian pulled out his cell phone. "Keep them off my back while I try to find out what's going on." His irritation made his words sound like a barked command. If their lives hadn't depended on a clear head and straight aim, Kendra would have balked. Another bullet whizzed past Brian's head. He dropped to his stomach to use his phone. Kendra fired back at the spot where she had seen the flash. A yell and a curse from the woods immediately in front of the cabin followed.

Brian grinned. "Good shot." He turned back to his phone. "Al? What's going on down there? We're surrounded and..." Another shot shattered a lamp on the table beside the glider. "Yeah, that was a shot. Who's up here and how did they find us?"

Brian listened muttering under his breath. "Well get some help up here on the double and patch me through to the Staties...Yes, this is FBI Agent Brian McNeil, AK-573. Why did you turn Doc Jones and Jonathan Cox loose? You were told to hold them for the FBI...What? Yeah, I understand. Do you know where the old hunter's cabin is on Ridge Valley Road?"

Another shot came through the thin wooden wall on the bottom third of the porch, grazing Brian's arm. He almost dropped the phone. Kendra shot back again making a connection. "Yes, that was another shot. There are seven of us here. We can hold them off for a while, but you need to get out here before it gets dark." He closed the phone and Kendra scooted next to him to check his wound.

"I'm fine," he said, "just a graze. We need to get inside. I'll cover you then you cover me and don't argue. We don't have time for that."

"Yes, *sir*," she answered with a good bit of sarcasm.

"Go," he said and started shooting toward the woods. Kendra dived for the kitchen floor, sliding across it as another bullet whizzed over her head. She jumped to her feet and darted to the window. Calvin and Lenny covered the door and the three of them shot into the woods while Brian took his turn at diving for the kitchen floor. Another shot made connection followed by yelling and cursing.

"What's up?" Calvin asked.

Brian got his breath, jumped to his feet and took the other kitchen window.

"Severs office called the State Police and told them there'd been a mistake, that no order was given to hold Cox and Doc Jones. They turned them loose. Mark and Paul are dead. Paul shot Mark and then tried to take off in my car, which exploded when he turned the key – Mark's handiwork from what Kendra says. Our visitors outside must be Doc, Cox – maybe his wife, the Franklin sisters, and possibly *Boss Lady* whom Kendra and I figured out must be Alice Markle. Hard to tell how many more they have with them."

"The Estrada brothers," Kendra said. "I heard someone swear in Spanish when one of my shots connected."

"Alice Markle?" Calvin stared at them as if they were trying to play an April Fool's joke in the middle of June. "Are you sure?"

"As sure as we can be under the circumstances. Kendra can explain later. Right now, we have to stay alive until the State Troopers and the rest of our gang arrive. Just hope they don't get cute and start throwing…" Before he could finish the sentence, something hit the porch door, sending flames licking up the door like a thirsty animal seeking relief from a drought.

David snatched the fire extinguisher from the wall and tore across the kitchen. "Cover me," he said and dived for the porch floor where he sprayed the chemical on the flames. More gunshots from the woods – those folks weren't going to give up very easily. Another flame ball hit the side of the cabin. There was no way to reach it from inside the house. It would be suicide to go out.

Brian whipped out his phone and punched in a number. "Al, we're going to need some firefighter planes up here or the whole forest will be in flames … Thanks, pal."

A window shattered in a back bedroom. "Shelly? Where are you?" Kendra called out and Shelly answered with a scream from that bedroom.

Kendra flew down the hall and kicked the door open before anyone realized what was happening. A man was half in and half out of the window, his gun pointed at Shelly, who stood rooted to the middle of the floor.

Kendra tackled her, throwing her to the floor as the gun fired. She rolled Michelle over, pushed her under the bed, righted herself and fired at the window. The man's gun flew out of his hand and blood started its slow trickle down his arm, as he tried to push himself out. Lenny and David rushed in, grabbed him by the neck and pulled him into the room before he could back up an inch.

Another firebomb shattered the window of the bedroom across the hall. Angel streaked from that room ears back, fur bushy and flew under the bed with Michelle. From the safe arms of her human, Angel voiced her displeasure.

Sarah darted to the bathroom at the end of the hall between the two bedrooms. She grabbed another fire extinguisher from under the sink and soon had the blaze under control, then out. More gunfire from both sides. Another fireball hit the roof. The blaze at the side and on top would soon have them either burned alive or running from the cabin to be picked off one by one as they tried to flee.

*Oh, God, did you bring us this far, to have it end this way? We've done all we can do. We need help.*

Calvin came into the bedroom looking haggard. Blood stained his face where the bullet had grazed him earlier. "Kendra, get Michelle and your mother. We'll cover you while you make a run for the car." He reached for Michelle's arm and pulled her from under the bed. Sarah blocked the door.

"Have we come this far as a family, Calvin Donovan, to be separated in death? I don't think so. You stay – we stay." She folded her arms in a stubborn stance that they had all seen many times.

"Sarah, I can't stand to see my girls destroyed." Tears streaked his face.

"Do you think we can stand it any better to see our men destroyed?" She glared at him, refusing to back down. "We'll not go. If we perish, we perish. If we stand, we stand."

"Sarah…" Calvin and Sarah embraced forgetting their daughters were watching. Tears stung Kendra's eyes. She took Michelle's hand and led her out of the room to where David, Brian and Lenny were with the unknown man from the window.

"Where's Mom?" said David. "We've got to get you girls out of here."

"We *girls* aren't going anywhere you *boys* don't go," said Michelle. "Mom's right. We're in this together. If we die, we die together. Right, Kendra?"

"You got it Moppet." Kendra smiled at her baby sister who had somehow become a woman. A blur of emotion gathered in her eyes. "Whatever the outcome, we're all in this together. I didn't go through hell and back the last few days just to run off and leave half my family in ashes – that's assuming we would get any further than the door anyway. Sorry, guys, but…" She stopped, cocking her head to one side.

"Kendra? You hear something?" Brian moved closer to her.

"Don't you hear it?"

"I hear a plane of some kind going over. They fly over all the time." David looked baffled.

"Not just any plane, David. A firefighter plane. It has a different sound. And helicopters. Help is on the way, if we can just hold on a little longer. Dad…," Kendra called out.

"I called Al to get the planes, but surely he didn't have time yet to…" Brian didn't finish.

"The Lookout probably saw the flames from the ranger's tower," said Kendra. "There's one not far from here – at least there used to be."

Sarah and Calvin came out of the bedroom hand in hand, smiles on their tear-streaked faces. "Kendra, I have to tell you before it's too late how proud I am of you. You've grown into a beautiful young lady. You have…"

"Dad, don't get all mushy. We don't have time for that. Besides, I'm not dead yet. And neither are you. Listen. Firefighter planes and helicopters. We've got to hold on a little longer until they can help."

Brian's phone rang. He whipped it out of his pocket. "McNeil, here. Al! I hope you're calling from one of those air vehicles we hear… Yes, fire on the roof and fire in the front. We took care of the ones inside. Thcy have us surrounded… can't go out…Thanks pal." Brian smiled and closed his phone.

"I hear more gunfire on the other side of our visitors out there. We have ground troops too?" Kendra glanced at Brian.

"We sure do. They'll be getting everyone rounded up within minutes. I think we'll be able to close this case very soon."

The drone of planes became louder as they dropped lower. Sounding as if the planes were only inches above the roof, a spray of water hit the roof and side of the cabin. A hiss of steam shot skyward sounding like music to the weary warriors. Returning a second and third time, the planes continued until the firefighters were sure the fire was out and wouldn't spread to the forest. About the time they finished, Al and his men brought in a dozen men who said Doc Jones hired them "to help him get squatters off his land." Doc Jones, Jonathan Cox and the Estrada brothers were with them.

"Kendra, *novia femenino*, if only you had married me, I wouldn't be in this mess," Toni said trying to look contrite.

"Toni, I'm sorry you chose this way to go. You could have done well in your restaurant and with your music. And you have a beautiful wife. No one could have kept you out of this mess but you. I'm sorry for you."

Toni shrugged. "That's life, *novia femenino*. Maybe in another time – another circumstance." He shrugged again. Kendra shook her head and turned away.

Al grabbed his chirping phone. "Yeah, good show. We're good here. They're tricky, so watch them closely. Send a couple of police vans out here. We got about a dozen or so hired killers as well as several of the leaders." He replaced the phone and turned to Brian. "They have the ladies." He laughed and added, "If you can call them that."

"Myrtle Cox and the Franklin sisters?" asked Lenny.

"And the big Boss Lady, herself," said Al.

"I thought Elizabeth Franklin…" Al shook his head and Lenny looked confused.

Brian and I exchanged glances. "You want to tell them? You figured it out first."

"It's your case," Kendra said. "You tell them."

"Will *someone* please tell us something!" said David and Lenny together.

Brian and Kendra laughed. "Kendra figured the leader had to be someone in our home office. That night in the infirmary, Doc and the others had information that could only have come from there," said Brian. "She and I were ruled out, because…well, we just were. That left Severs and Alice Markle. We decided Severs isn't bright enough to run an operation this big, and they kept calling her the *Boss Lady*."

"Alice Markle? You weren't joking earlier? She really was the top dog in this outfit?" Calvin's look was incredulous. "Maybe it's time for me to retire. I'm not as observant as I used to be."

"Don't feel bad, Mr. D." said Lenny. "The rest of us didn't know either. I've been playing both sides of the field and never had a clue. How did you figure it out, Kendra?"

"While I was in the infirmary someone made a remark about me figuring out something from the pictures. The only people who knew about the pictures were Brian, me, Severs and Alice. It was simply the process of elimination."

Sirens in the distance announced the approaching vehicles to transport the prisoners. A short time later, they were closing the door on the last wagon. Sarah had been in the kitchen making coffee and gathering articles to take care of wounds. When the rest returned to the cabin, she wouldn't take no for an answer. She knew Calvin and Brian had been hit and she wasn't sure about the rest. After all, she was a trained nurse and she would not let her loved ones go unattended.

# Forty-four

Sarah gathered alcohol, gauze, tape, scissors and anything else for taking care of the wounded, and spread them across the table. She pulled a chair close to it and turned first to the ones who were bleeding from gunshot wounds. "Brian, let's have a look at that arm."

"It's just a scratch," said Brian. "I'll have it taken care of when I get back to Wintersville."

"Tomorrow? I don't think so," said Sarah. "You'll have it taken care of immediately. Now you just sit down here and let me have a look at that arm."

Brian chuckled. "You know, for a minute there I almost thought that was Kendra talking. I see where she gets her stubbornness. But, I'm leaving tonight. I'll return Betsy's car and get started on the paper work. Are you coming with me Lenny?"

"What do you mean you're going back tonight?" Kendra asked. "Mom, take a look at his ribs while you're at it. He doesn't have sense enough to take care of himself." Anger and frustration made her words catch in her throat. "And Lenny ought to be in the hospital, not running around chasing crooks, putting out fires and whatever."

"Kendra, they have their work to finish." Her father was no help.

"Fine. Let them go. I guess I…oh, never mind. I'm going for a walk." She started toward the door.

"Kendra, it's ten o'clock. You don't need to be traipsing around in the dark, kicking up animals or falling over cliffs. And I think your mother needs to look at your at arm. It looks swollen. You've been using it too much when it should have been in a sling from what the boys told me." Calvin's stern words reminded her of when she was a child.

"Dad, I'm not ten years old any longer, in case you haven't noticed. My arm is fine. It's just a sprain. I'll be back in time to leave in the morning. Mom can look at it then if she wants to. She has more important things to take care of right now." Kendra grabbed her jacket off the hook by the door and was gone before anyone could stop her.

***

Calvin ran to the door and called after to her. "Kendra Marie Donovan, you come back here this instant." Kendra kept running until she was lost to his sight. He stomped back into the kitchen, grabbed his jacket from the hook and started after her.

"Calvin Donovan." Sarah had never used that tone of voice with him before. He turned abruptly to face her. "Let her go. I think she's had enough tension. She needs time alone. Kendra is your daughter, not one of your men."

"Your wife's right, Mr. D." said Lenny. "Kendra's all right. She knows her way around. I know where she's going. Brian and I will go say goodbye before we leave."

Calvin Donovan glared then dropped into a chair. "Sorry," he said. "She's right. I guess I still think of her as a child, but a child couldn't have survived the way she has," he said shaking his head.

He sat for a minute or so then, rose, hung his jacket back on the hook, and poured a cup of coffee. He went to the porch and sat on the glider in the dark wondering when his little girl had grown up.

***

Kendra stood on the dark path listening, hoping someone would come with her. She wasn't afraid, but she wanted someone – anyone to comfort her. Well, maybe not *just anyone*. She waited a while longer – listening, hoping.

Sarah apparently had finished caring for Brian's wound, checked his ribs then told Lenny to sit down.

"I'd better change that bandage," she said. "You'll need to see a doctor, when you get back to wherever you're going. It looks good, but you don't want to lose the use of your arm. You were lucky."

"I had a good nurse before I went to the hospital," he said. There was a slight pause and Kendra could almost see her mother lift her eyebrows in question. Lenny laughed. "Kendra took care of it, cleaned it, stopped the bleeding and bandaged it. Then she and Brian took me to the hospital, where the doctor took the bullet out."

"Kendra? I didn't know she knew anything about nursing. I've been a nurse since before I was married, but I never knew she was even interested. Our daughter is always a surprise. I suppose next, she'll tell us she's joining the FBI."

Brian and Lenny both laughed. "Don't think we haven't tried to influence her in that direction, Mrs. D.," said Lenny. "She says she's had enough of cops and robbers, but she would sure make a good undercover agent. Don't you agree, Brian?"

"She would be excellent. But then, Kendra is smart enough and caring enough to be good at anything that she sets her mind to. She won't let anyone hold her back." There was another pause then Brian said, "You ready to take off, Lenny. We have a lot to do yet before we can fly out of here tomorrow."

"I hear you, buddy. Let's go find Kendra and say goodbye and then I'm ready. So long folks. Shelly, take care of Angel. She did her share in cleaning up this mess."

Kendra had heard enough. She ran up the hill to the boulder where they used to sit. She didn't want them to find her hiding in the brush beside the path. For some reason, her eyes kept spilling out tears. She was more exhausted than she thought.

***

Brian and Lenny left the cabin, gravel crunching as they moved toward the car. "You go, I'll wait here," said Brian. "You're the one she cares about."

"Brian, that almost sounded like jealously. I know you better than that, so I'll accept it as fatigue. She's known me longer. She's like a sister to me. She cares a lot about you too. She couldn't be that closely involved with our lives, and possible deaths, and not be affected. She'll be hurt if you don't at least say goodbye."

"Then why did she run off and make us go after her? If she's so danged concerned, why didn't she wait to take her walk after we left?" Brian kicked the dirt with the toe of his shoe.

Lenny said, "Suit yourself, pal. I don't know what's happened between you two, but you've been flip-flopping from best friends to arch enemies ever since we left Wintersville. Maybe you're right. I'll tell her goodbye for you."

"Do you know where she is?"

"I'm sure she went to a place we used to call *Top of the World,*" Lenny said as he started up the path. The full moon and stars seemed close enough to the earth to reach up and pluck them from the sky. Brian followed Lenny. They got to the top of the path and stopped as if waiting for something.

***

"Are you two going to stand there gawking at me all night, or do you want to come and sit for a while?" Kendra spoke without raising her voice, or turning around.

Lenny laughed. "I should have known you heard us. We tried to be quiet, but you always did have sensitive hearing. We just want to say goodbye." They moved to the boulder and sat on either side of her. Kendra didn't turn, but focused on the twinkling in the distance – probably from fishermen's cabins. Lenny sensed she had been crying. He took her chin in his hand and turned her to face him.

"Kendra, baby it'll be all right. We've said goodbye before." He wiped her face with his fingers and drew his good arm around her. Sarah had insisted on putting his left arm in a sling again. "You never did like to say goodbye. I always had to chase you down." He laughed and Kendra gulped back the tears and smiled at him.

"It was different then. But, we always knew we would be back the next summer and pick up where we left off. This time it's been years and it will be years again – if ever. You never write. You didn't even let us know you were married!"

“Kendra, you’re right. I’m sorry, but I guess I just never thought anyone was that interested in what I did after I grew up. I saw your dad from time to time. I thought he would keep you informed about me.”

“You should know he never talked about anything at the bureau. I was always his little girl, who needed to be protected.” Kendra tried not to sound bitter, but didn’t succeed. “I’m sorry, Lenny. Please don’t pay any attention to anything I say tonight. I don’t know what’s wrong with me. I can’t think.”

“It might have something to do with trauma,” said Brian from the other side. “Most women would have been in hysterics when the first shot was fired tonight, but you reminded me we needed you – and we did. You’ve been shot at, had your house set on fire, to say nothing of all you went through before we even got here. Kendra, you’re not God. Accept your limitations.”

“Lenny, take him back to wherever you found him, will you?” Kendra glowered at Lenny and nodded toward Brian. Lenny threw back his head and laughed. He stood and kissed her on the cheek. “I’ll keep in touch, Kendra. I promise.”

“I’ve heard that before. Lenny, please be careful and take care of yourself. And if you get yourself killed, give your wife instructions to call me so I can at least come to your funeral.”

Lenny laughed again. “I promise,” he said. “You take care of yourself, Kendra. You’ll get over this and get on with your life. I promise that too.”

“I hope you’re right, Lenny.”

“Want to walk back with us?”

“No.”

“You can’t climb a moonbeam and get away from it all, you know.” Lenny laughed again and turned toward the path. “Coming Brian? I’ve got the keys. I just slipped them from her jacket.” He stopped to wait for Brian.

“Lenny Richardson, you thief!” Kendra jumped down to run after him, but Brian slid off the boulder and caught her as she landed.

"Kendra, I'm sorry about all that's happened," he said holding her at arm's length.

She tried to pull away from him, but he gripped her more tightly. "Please don't flip me over your shoulder," he said. "My ribs hurt and I really don't want to fall off that cliff."

"Brian, I'm sorry. I don't want to hurt you, but I don't want to be hurt either."

"I know." He took a deep breath and continued, "Kendra, I've been an undercover agent for a number of years and I've had similar assignments working with beautiful young women. Sometimes they thought they were in love with me." Kendra jerked to pull away, but he held her tighter. "Please, let me finish. I always reminded them it was the romance and excitement of the adventure and they would forget me in time. I always knew I was safe because Susan was waiting for me.

"This time was different. I forgot Susan existed until you asked in the car about my marital status. I'm the one who fell in love this time. I think you did too, but I can only speak for me. Now, I'm torn between what I want and what I believe is right. Susan has waited so long for me, how can I turn my back on her? You have shown me what I've always hoped for in a woman, how can I send you away? Kendra, I love you, but I have to go – at least until I can sort out my own feelings. Please forgive me." He let go of her and turned to follow Lenny who waited by the path.

"Brian." Without moving, Kendra spoke hardly above a whisper, but he heard her and turned to face her. "Thank you. I can handle it better knowing you didn't just use me and you're struggling to do what's right and fair for Susan, as well as for you and me. I can't help it that I fell in love with you, but I can help holding on when I need to let go. Please take care of yourself, Brian."

Brian took a step toward her.

"No," Kendra said waving him away. "It'll only make it harder. Someday…"

"Someday," he said.

Kendra heard the crunching the stones and twigs as they made their way back down the path. Leaning against the stone, she slid to the ground, sitting with her back against it. The car started up and she heard the sound of tires on dirt and gravel fade away. Drawing her knees up to her chin, Kendra dropped her head on her folded arms.

Once again, footsteps crunched on the trail. Kendra knew it was either her father or David. Either would be welcome. A few minutes later, Calvin eased his six-foot frame down beside her and took her in his arms.

"Brian said you would be here. Honey, I'm sorry about all of this. I tried to tell Severs it was a bad idea, but he was the boss and…time was short…"

"It's all right Dad. It's not your fault. Every action I took was my own choice – except I didn't know I was falling in love until it was too late to stop. It'll all work out somehow."

"Kendra baby, what can I say? You've grown into a beautiful young woman and somehow I missed that. What happened to the awkward teenager that used to follow me around the office? Maybe Brian and Lenny are right. Maybe you ought to consider the FBI as a career."

Kendra pulled back and looked into his eyes. "Dad, you aren't the only one who still thought I was a little girl. I don't think Seymour Severs or the FBI, are ready for the likes of me – nor am I ready for them. I couldn't live by their rules."

Calvin laughed a hearty chuckle. "Kendra, my girl, I think truer words were never spoken. What do you say we go home? The ground is cold and damp and we have a lot of packing to do. We'll stop by Wolverine Cabin tomorrow and pick up your belongings and say goodbye to this place forever."

"Somehow that makes me even sadder. It's such a beautiful place and we had so many wonderful years here. Surely someone could make a go of a decent vacation spot."

"Maybe, but I've had it for now. I just want to get back to my own home and some kind of normal routine. What will you do, Kendra? Do you have anything in mind?"

"No. Maybe I'll just work for a temporary service until I can recover from…everything. I'm not ready to face the daily world of nine to five again. I guess I've outgrown office work – at least Robert's kind of office work. I need something more challenging. Besides…" she grinned at her father, "I'm sure Brian will work things out and find a way to contact me when he knows what is happening between him and Susan and where his next assignment will be. I'll make myself available. We'll work it out. But, Dad…"

Calvin stood and pulled me to her feet. "Yes?"

"Next time you plan a mystery vacation, make sure Seymour Severs – or anyone else at the Bureau – doesn't know where you're going. That game of hide and seek was a little longer and more painful than I care to repeat."

# ABOUT THE AUTHOR

Mary Lu (Pennock) Warstler was born in Oak Hill, West Virginia. She is a 1956 graduate of Collins High School.

In September 1957, Mary Lu married Rodney J. Warstler and became a full time Minister's wife. They have four children, nine grandchildren, and six great-grandchildren.

In 1980, Mary Lu received her B. S. in Education with a minor in music from the University of Akron. After teaching learning disabled children for two years, she enrolled at Methodist Theological School in Ohio and received a Master of Divinity in Theology in 1985.

Mary Lu and her husband, Rodney, are both ordained United Methodist Ministers. On July 1, 2000, she joined her husband in retirement where she pursues other areas of ministry – primarily writing. They live in Copeland Oaks Retirement Community at Sebring, Ohio.

Mary Lu loves animals, especially cats, of which she has two – Katy (a four-year-old part Siamese) and Charlie (a one-year old female gray cat) – rescued from the Humane Shelter. She has cared for cats, dogs, goldfish, hamsters, guinea pig and mice while raising four children.

Mary Lu has written numerous worship resources, plays, sermons and ten novels. In her *spare* time, she enjoys reading, writing, painting, music and needlework of all kinds,

Made in the USA
Charleston, SC
11 September 2013